PRAISE FOR TAWNA FENSKE

LET IT BREATHE

"This charming romp from Fenske evokes the best of romantic comedy, with its witty characters and wacky but realistic situations."
—*Publishers Weekly*, Starred Review

ABOUT THAT FLING

"Fenske's take on what happens when a one-night stand goes horribly, painfully awry is hilariously heartwarming and overflowing with genuine emotion . . . There's something wonderfully relaxing about being immersed in a story filled with over-the-top characters in undeniably relatable situations. Heartache and humor go hand in hand in this laugh-out-loud story with an ending that requires a few tissues."

—*Publishers Weekly*, Starred Review

THE FIX UP

"Extremely charming and undeniably sexy . . . I loved every minute."
—#1 *New York Times* and *USA Today*
Bestselling Author Rachel Van Dyken

"Sexy banter in the boardroom, romantic movies with a sexy alpha geek, and humor that will leave a smile on your face until the very last page."

—*New York Times* and *USA Today*
Bestselling Author Kelly Elliott

MAKING WAVES

Nominated for Contemporary Romance of the Year, 2011 Reviewers' Choice Awards, *RT Book Reviews*

"Fenske's wildly inventive plot and wonderfully quirky characters provide the perfect literary antidote to any romance reader's summer reading doldrums."

—*Chicago Tribune*

"A zany caper . . . Fenske's off-the-wall plotting is reminiscent of a tame Carl Hiaasen on Cupid juice."

—*Booklist*

"This delightfully witty debut will have readers laughing out loud."

—4½ Stars, *RT Book Reviews*

"[An] uproarious romantic caper. Great fun from an inventive new writer; highly recommended."

—*Library Journal*, Starred Review

"This book was the equivalent of eating whipped cream—sure it was light and airy, but it is also surprisingly rich."

—Smart Bitches Trashy Books

BELIEVE IT OR NOT

"Fenske hits all the right humor notes without teetering into the pit of slapstick in her lighthearted book of strippers, psychics, free spirits, and an accountant."

—*RT Book Reviews*

"Snappy, endearing dialogue and often hilarious situations unite the couple, and Fenske proves to be a romance author worthy of a loyal following."

—*Booklist*, Starred Review

"Fenske's sophomore effort is another riotous trip down funny bone lane, with a detour to slightly askew goings on and a quick u-ey to out-of-this-world romance. Readers will be enchanted by this bewitching fable from a wickedly wise author."

—*Library Journal*

"Sexually charged dialogue and steamy make-out scenes will keep readers turning the pages."

—*Publishers Weekly*

FRISKY BUSINESS

"Up-and-coming romance author Fenske sets up impeccable internal and external conflict and sizzling sexual tension for a poignant love story between two engaging characters, then infuses it with witty dialogue and lively humor. An appealing blend of lighthearted fun and emotional tenderness."

—*Kirkus Reviews*

"Fenske's fluffy, frothy novel is a confection made of colorful characters, compromising situations and cute dogs. This one's for readers who prefer a tickled funny bone rather than a tale of woe."

—*RT Book Reviews*

"Loaded with outrageous euphemisms for the sex act between any type of couple and repeated near-intimate misses, Fenske's latest is a clever tour de force on finding love despite being your own worst emotional enemy. Sweet and slightly oddball, this title belongs in most romance collections."

—*Library Journal*

"*Frisky Business* has all the ingredients of a sparkling romantic comedy—wickedly clever humor, a quirky cast of characters and, most of all, the crazy sexy chemistry between the leads.

—*New York Times* and *USA Today*
Bestselling Author Lauren Blakely

ALSO BY
TAWNA FENSKE

Standalone Romantic Comedies

Let It Breathe
About That Fling
Eat, Play, Lust (novella)
Frisky Business
Believe It or Not
Making Waves

The Front and Center Series

Marine for Hire
Fiancée for Hire
Best Man for Hire
Protector for Hire

The First Impressions Series

The Fix Up
The Hang Up
The Hook Up (Coming January 2017)

Schultz Sisters Mysteries

The Great Panty Caper (novella)
Getting Dumped

Now That It's You

TAWNA FENSKE

Montlake
Romance

Text copyright © 2016 Tawna Fenske
All rights reserved.

Published by Montlake Romance, Seattle

www.apub.com

Amazon, the Amazon logo, and Montlake Romance are trademarks of Amazon.com, Inc., or its affiliates.

ISBN-13: 9781503937772
ISBN-10: 1503937771

Cover design by Shasti O'Leary Soudant

Printed in the United States of America

To Michelle Wolfson of Wolfson Literary Agency.
For selling this book based on the letters TBD.
And for never batting an eyelash when I say things like,
"I think I'll write romantic comedies about death,
grief, infidelity, alcoholism, forgiveness, and
divorce. Only with penis jokes." But most of all, thank you
for being my tireless champion, advocate,
support system, business partner, and friend.

CHAPTER ONE

Meg Delaney kept one hand clenched on the steering wheel as she slammed her fist into the smiley-face balloon hovering over her right shoulder.

"Get!" she growled. The balloon bopped between the headrests, leering at her in metallic yellow and black.

"Come on, relax." Meg's best friend, Jess, caught a fistful of ribbons trailing from the balloon bouquet and dragged the whole mess out of Meg's line of sight. "You're going to crash and kill us both and then how will you explain that to the cops?"

"Not very well if I'm dead," Meg pointed out, keeping a wary eye on the red and blue balloon that slipped from Jess's grasp. It bounced bright and cheerful against the backseat roof of her Subaru, broadcasting its *get well soon* message in a loopy script. The weird cursive font made the last word look more like *soup* and Meg wondered if she should have opted for an edible gift instead of balloons. Maybe a bouquet of cake pops or a tin of yogurt-covered pretzels.

What did etiquette dictate when visiting your ex-fiancé in the hospital after two years of not speaking?

Meg put both hands on the steering wheel at ten and two, trying to ignore the damn balloon lurching in her rearview mirror. There was nothing she needed to see behind her anyway.

"Just keep your eyes on the road," Jess warned. "Any karma points you're earning by visiting Sir Cheats-a-Lot in the hospital would be wiped out if you caused a car wreck."

"It's not about the karma points, it's about closure." Still, Meg loosened her grip on the steering wheel and reminded herself to breathe. The tension in her shoulders had nothing to do with wayward balloons and everything to do with the fact that she hadn't seen Matt Midland since she'd stood trembling at the front of the wedding chapel and responded "I can't," instead of "I do."

But that was two years ago. Water under the bridge, or something like that. Thanks to the passage of time and the words of a really nice therapist, Meg knew it was time to bury the hatchet, let bygones be bygones, close one door so another one could open and—

"You're muttering to yourself in shrink-speak again," Jess said.

"Sorry." A rainbow-striped Mylar balloon caught a current from the car's heater vent and lurched into Meg's peripheral vision. She fought the urge to swat it out of the way as she hit her turn signal and merged into the next lane. Her tires made a *shh-shh* sound as they cut through a puddle of standing water, and Meg stole a glance at the sky. The clouds looked like pregnant gray bunnies, which meant more rain on the way for Portland.

"What sort of surgery did you say Matt's having?" Jess asked.

"I'm not sure. His ex-golf partner's girlfriend's hairdresser told my mom it's just some routine procedure. It seemed like a sign."

"A sign that in a city of two-point-three million people, you still can't escape weird chains of connection to an ex?"

"A sign that this would be the perfect way to extend an olive branch. He always loved it when people fussed over him when he got sick or had his tonsils out or whatever."

"Good old Matt," Jess muttered. "Always the center of attention."

"Be nice. I'm mending fences, remember?"

"Absolutely. You won't mind if I wait in the car while you run in there with your fence-repair kit and balloon bouquet?"

"That's fine." Meg steered the car toward the off-ramp that led to Belmont Health System. "Probably best, anyway. I'd like to keep this as simple as possible. Just apologize, wish him well, and move on with my day."

And with my life, Meg thought, wondering why she'd spent this long stewing and agonizing and thinking bitter thoughts before she'd taken the initiative to reach out to the man she'd been ready to tie her life to. She'd once imagined them sitting toothless in matching armchairs, holding hands while grandchildren frolicked on the floor of their shared nursing home suite. She'd gone from loving him fiercely to hating him with equal ferocity before settling into the murk between those two emotions.

The least she could do was take him some damn balloons.

The *get well soon* balloon bumped the side of her head, and Meg slapped it out of the way as she pulled into a parking space near the back of the visitor lot. Her heart was pounding in her ears, and she wished for the hundredth time she didn't sweat like a pitcher of ice water when she got nervous. She switched off the car and plucked her blue *Where the Wild Things Are* T-shirt away from her breasts, trying to get some air flowing.

"You can do this," Jess said. "And if you do it quickly enough, we can still make happy hour at Sip."

"Right." Meg nodded and glanced at her watch. It was five minutes earlier than she'd aimed for, but that was a good excuse to walk slowly, maybe compose herself a bit.

She took another shaky breath and pushed open the door. With the balloon ribbons in a tight grip, she stepped out onto the asphalt. Glancing down at her jeans and leopard-print Dansko clogs, she wondered if she should have dressed better to visit her ex in the hospital. Maybe high heels and a dress as a concession to how Matt had always wished she'd dressed during their ten years as a couple.

Just be yourself, Meg commanded as she nudged the car door shut with her hip and moved toward the hospital. She'd done a contract job here a few years ago when the hospital hired her to overhaul their food services department, so she knew right where the post-surgical recovery wing was. Gripping her balloons, Meg turned down the corridor and put one foot in front of the other as she breathed in the scent of iodine and cleaning fluid. An auburn curl slipped over her eye and she tucked it back behind her ear, wishing she'd had the foresight to braid her hair back off her face or put it up in a smart chignon.

But at least she was here. That counted for something.

If she'd timed this right, Matt would be sitting up in bed by now, eating a bowl of lime Jell-O and flipping through television channels. His ink-black hair would be perfectly styled already, and he'd be laughing at something on TV, pointing at the ESPN announcer's tie or the news anchor's too-bright blouse and making wisecracks to the nurse or the janitor or anyone else who'd listen.

Matt always knew how to draw an audience.

Meg found the room number easily enough and hesitated outside the door. She straightened the balloons, making sure they all faced forward and looked cheery and conciliatory.

What did a conciliatory balloon look like? Meg couldn't recall standing in line at Hallmark and seeing any balloons that said, "Sorry I left you at the altar, but maybe you shouldn't have fucked your acupuncturist."

She was stalling.

Meg took a deep breath, then another and another until she started to feel dizzy and wondered what would happen if she passed out on the floor.

At least you're already at the hospital, she reassured herself as she reached out for the door. It was slightly ajar, and her fingers had just grazed the knob when the door flew open.

A tall, familiar figure barreled through, his face pale and his sandy hair disheveled. Meg jumped back, partly from surprise, and partly to avoid being trampled by Matt's younger brother, Kyle. His jaw was clenched and dusted with stubble, and as his green-gray gaze locked with hers, he stared like he had no idea who she was.

Meg took another step back. "I—um—Kyle, hi. It's me, Meg."

Okay, that was stupid. For crying out loud, she'd dated Matt for ten years before the wedding that never happened. She and Kyle used to play Boggle and thumb wrestle over the last piece of pumpkin pie at Thanksgiving. She hardly needed to introduce herself.

But the way Kyle was staring at her now suggested otherwise, or maybe it was just the shock of seeing her here. He looked like a man who'd just seen a ghost, or maybe a squirrel humping an aardvark.

He still hadn't said a word.

Meg swallowed hard and gripped her balloons, forcing herself to greet her former-almost-brother-in-law with the warmest smile she could muster. "Kyle," she said. "It's so good to see you. I just wanted to come wish Matt a speedy recovery and take a shot at making peace. Is he feeling up to a quick visit?"

Kyle continued to stare at her, eyes glinting oddly under the fluorescent light in the hallway. For a moment, Meg thought he might not answer at all. When he finally did speak, his voice was so low she almost didn't hear him.

"That's going to be a problem," he said.

Meg bit her lip. "Because of how things ended? Look, I know I handled that badly and your whole family hates me, but I just wanted a chance to apologize and maybe chat for a minute or two about how life's going now."

A tiny muscle twitched in Kyle's temple, and he studied her, unblinking. "At the moment, Meg, life's not going all that great for Matt." His words were clipped and brittle, and Meg fought the urge to take another step back. "And I really doubt he's going to be chatting with you anytime soon."

"Because he's still angry?"

"Because he's dead."

♦ ♦ ♦

Kyle watched Meg's face go from flushed and earnest to a shade two hues lighter than the white T-shirt he'd dug out of the hamper this morning. The silver-flecked brown eyes he'd always thought seemed warm were frozen in the same expression she'd wear if he slammed her hand in the door. He knew he'd been too blunt, but it was too late to take the words back.

It was too late for a lot of things.

He'd found out twenty minutes ago that the brother he'd spent his whole life butting heads with over bubble gum and girls and careers and finances—his *only* goddamn brother—had suffered a massive heart attack and died.

It wasn't even a heroic death, which would have pissed Matt off more than anything. Hair transplant surgery? For crying out loud.

Kyle shook his head and stared at his brother's pale-faced fiancée.

Ex-fiancée, he reminded himself. The current fiancée was in the next room having a screaming match with Matt's surgeon.

"I didn't even know he was taking Viagra!" Chloe shrieked from the adjacent room. "And anyway, how was he supposed to know not to take a big dose the night before a hair transplant?"

"Ma'am, I'm very sorry, but the pre-surgical literature explains the risks of nitric oxide and the anesthesia we use for this procedure. We went over those with him at the consultation. Your fiancé may have chosen not to inform us he was taking medication for erectile dysfunction, but he was presented with the information when we—"

Kyle leaned over and pulled the door shut, hoping like hell Meg hadn't heard the conversation.

He couldn't tell anything from her expression, except that she looked like she might be on the brink of losing her lunch. Her fingers were twisted up tight in the ribbons attached to a ridiculously cheerful mess of helium balloons, and she was biting her lip the way she always used to when she felt uncomfortable.

Why the hell was she here?

Why the hell was *he* here, for that matter? It's not like he and Matt had been close. They'd fought like ill-tempered badgers more often than not, caught in a weird web of competition and jealousy with a dash of reluctant fondness thrown in for variety. It was just a fluke that he'd come to see Matt in the hospital today, just in time to learn they'd never spend another Thanksgiving bickering over football and sweet potatoes.

"Dead," Meg repeated, and Kyle realized it was the first word either of them had spoken in three minutes. She sounded like she was testing it out to see how it sounded. Not good, apparently. Her eyes filled with tears and he watched her throat working to swallow the lump he could guess was just like the one that had been lodged in his throat for the last twenty minutes.

"Dead," Kyle confirmed. "So now's really not a good time."

"My God, Kyle—I'm so sorry. I had no idea. I heard it was just a simple procedure and I thought—"

She stopped there, not vocalizing what she'd thought, but giving Kyle a pretty good idea just the same. Tears were spilling down her cheeks in earnest now, and part of him wanted to pull her into his arms, to offer her some small measure of comfort or to claim some for himself.

But this was Meg, for God's sake.

Meg.

She was still beautiful, even with red-rimmed eyes and her nose running like a faucet. He should offer her a tissue or show her the door but he just stood there like a moron noticing the way her auburn curls still fell in chaotic ringlets around her shoulders and her pale-blue T-shirt clung and dipped and curved around breasts he'd always done his damnedest not to look at.

Dammit, what kind of jerk was he? Was he seriously ogling her while his brother was being wheeled to the hospital morgue by an orderly who looked like Napoleon Dynamite?

It's not like this is the first time you've had inappropriate thoughts about Meg.

Which was true, but now was hardly the time to do it again.

"Look, I don't know what to say," he said.

"I'm so sorry for your loss," Meg choked out. "If I'd known—"

A door burst open at the end of the hall, and Kyle swung his gaze away from her and toward the stampede of relatives descending upon them like a pack of bison. Aunt Judy, Uncle Arthur, a cousin whose name escaped him at the moment but he felt pretty sure rhymed with *snot*. Scott? Lamott?

Jesus Christ, what's wrong with you?

He spotted his mom at the head of the pack with puffy eyes and a crookedly buttoned blouse. She wore one navy shoe and one black one, and the sight of his sophisticated mother looking so undone made Kyle's heart ball up like the wad of Kleenex she clenched in one fist.

Meg gave a muffled cry beside him, and Kyle turned to see her gripping the balloon ribbons hard enough to carve deep grooves in her fingers. Her mouth fell open and she took a step back as the mob drew . closer.

Kyle looked back at his mother, not sure whether to hug her or get out of her way. He was saved from doing either as his mom's gaze landed on Meg and she thrust one manicured finger toward her former-future-daughter-in-law.

"You!" she barked, her eyes glittering with fury and tears as she swung her gaze from Meg to Kyle. "What is *she* doing here?"

♦ ♦ ♦

Ten minutes later, Meg sat sobbing in the driver's seat, her hair glued to Jess's lip gloss as she tried not to get snot on her best friend's cashmere sweater.

"Oh, sweetie," Jess soothed. "You couldn't have known. I'm so sorry."

"I just—*dead*," she repeated, not able to come up with any word more suitable than that.

Then again, that one pretty much summed it up.

"I've spent the last two years hating him for sleeping with Annabelle," she choked out. "Just when I was ready to *stop* hating him—"

"I know," Jess soothed, petting Meg's hair. "I know. Two years of hating him and a few days of trying *not* to hate him is still no match for nearly ten years of loving him."

Which was true, Meg knew, though it was hard to categorize exactly what she felt now. Grief? Loss? How could she feel those things for someone she hadn't seen in two years? Someone she'd actively despised, then gradually forgotten, or at least tried to forget. They could have even become friends again, in a perfect world.

"I never got to say I was sorry," Meg said. "For leaving him at the altar like that. I never apologized."

"So you're even," Jess said, "for the fact that he cheated on you and didn't think to tell you about it until the night before the wedding. And the fact that you've spent the last two years working your ass off to pay for the wedding that never happened."

"It was my choice." Meg drew back from the hug and mopped her nose with a stiff Burger King napkin. "No one else should have been stuck with the debt when I was the one who called off the wedding."

Jess shook her head, and Meg could see she was biting back the urge to argue, or to call Matt a cheating, spineless dickhead. Now was hardly the time for that, so Jess settled for handing her another napkin.

"Between the cheating and the debt, don't you think that cancels out the runaway-bride thing?" Jess asked.

"I have no idea. Where's the manual on the checks and balances of adultery and aborted weddings?"

Jess gave a small smile and tucked a curl behind Meg's ear. "I keep it on a bookshelf in my living room. It's right next to the wine cabinet. Come on, I'll show you. But first, get out of the car."

"What?"

"You're in no shape to drive. Give me the keys."

Meg looked down at her hand and realized she was holding the keys in a death grip, along with the strings to the damn balloon bouquet. She dropped the keys into Jess's palm, then unraveled the ribbons from around her hand.

"Holy cow," Jess said, poking the deep rivets furrowed into the flesh of Meg's fingers. "What were you doing with these?"

"Practicing my skills with a garrote, apparently." Meg winced and felt a fresh surge of guilt rising in her throat. Making a wisecrack about strangulation mere minutes after her ex-fiancé's death had to be up there on the list of things that would get her a one-way ticket to hell.

Meg let go of the ribbons, releasing the balloon bouquet into the backseat before turning and pushing open the driver's side door. Her legs were still shaking as she made her way around the car while Jess scooted over the gearshift and got into the driver's seat. Meg slipped into the passenger seat and buckled her seatbelt, numb to the motions of it all as Jess cranked over the engine.

"It'll be okay, honey," Jess said as she backed out of the parking spot. "Is there anyone you need to call? Mutual friends or his college roommates or something?"

Meg thought about it, then shook her head. "It's not really my place, is it? I'm not part of the family."

Not anymore, she thought, recalling the coldness in Sylvia Midland's eyes when she'd spotted Meg outside her son's room. Even the aunts and uncles she'd met only a handful of times had looked like they wanted to drag her down the hospital hallway by her hair. She could hardly blame them. The last time she'd seen them, they'd been dressed in suits and summer dresses, watching slack-jawed as she turned and bolted from the church, knocking down pew bows as she ran.

They looked like they hated me, she thought. *Then and now.* The idea was hardly surprising. Wasn't that why she'd kept her distance all this time?

On her own side, Meg's family and friends had few kind words to say about Matt. When she was still reeling from his confession and desperate to explain why she'd fled her own wedding, she'd told them about Matt's affair. It was the sort of thing she'd normally keep private, not wanting to air their dirty laundry or add fuel to her own fear that she'd done something to drive him to cheat in the first place. But she'd told her whole family in a moment of weakness, and the story spread as quickly as their new disdain for Matt.

So they'd drawn the battle lines cleanly between her family and his, unfriending each other's colleagues and cousins on Facebook and cutting each other's faces out of family pictures.

The thought gave her a momentary pang of sadness. Part of her had missed the Midland family Christmas cards and his mother's coq au vin and the quilt rack she'd felt obligated to return.

But she'd never told anyone what she'd missed the most about being cut off from the Midland family.

Meg's brain filled with the stricken look on Kyle's face as he'd stood there outside his brother's hospital room. She closed her eyes for a moment. It was enough to flush a fresh wave of tears from her eyes, and Meg opened them again to let the tears flow.

Jess reached over and squeezed her hand. "I'll take a shortcut. We'll be there in ten minutes."

"Thank you," Meg whispered.

A purple and black polka-dotted balloon bopped her on the side of the head, and Meg shoved it away, crowding it into the backseat with the rest. The motion pushed more balloons forward, creating a burst of brightly colored Mylar shapes bumbling their way toward the front of the car.

"Stop!" Meg shouted.

"It's okay," Jess said, ignoring a shark-shaped balloon that bumped the side of her head as she turned down the side street leading away from the hospital. "It's not bothering me."

"No, stop the car," Meg said, frantic now to get rid of the cheery orbs pushing and bobbing and reminding her that nothing would ever be the same again. She grabbed the ribbons as Jess slowed the car.

"What are you doing, Meg? You can't just let them go. They're hazardous to wildlife,"

"I know," she said, pushing open the car door before Jess brought the car to a full stop in the bike lane. "I just need to get rid of them."

She staggered onto the sidewalk with her fistful of balloons, thinking this was how people went crazy. One minute you're making friendly overtures to your ex and the next minute you're stumbling teary-eyed down the road with a balloon shaped like a banana beating you in the back of the head.

Meg looked around while Jess sat silent in the driver's seat, waiting. She couldn't pop them. All that racket seemed inappropriate when they were idling here less than a mile from where Matt took his last breath.

Off to the side, a metal bench sat waiting for bus passengers. Meg hurried over, kneeling on the asphalt to cinch the ribbons around one of the legs. Her fingers felt numb and useless, but she managed to tie the knot and stand up again, her knees still wobbly.

There. She surveyed her work, then nodded. Someone else would find them and claim them. Someone else would take them to a sick relative who'd smile and laugh and reach up to touch the plump, colorful shapes.

She turned back to the car and moved around to the passenger side, winded and spent as she dropped into the passenger seat again.

"Feel better now?" Jess asked.

"A little."

"Probably better than that dead pigeon you almost stepped on."

Meg turned in her seat to look behind them as Jess pulled away from the curb. *Get well soon!* the balloon commanded the corpse of a gray and green bird.

Meg closed her eyes and slid down in her seat, wondering if pigeons mated for life the way doves did, wondering if she had any right at all to feel this undone.

CHAPTER TWO

Kyle's hands barely touched the steering wheel, his whole body looser than he actually felt. He'd had twenty-four hours to digest the news of his brother's passing, which mostly left him feeling like a complete fuckup at this whole grief thing.

Shouldn't he be tense? Or teary-eyed or ripped in two? He felt all those things, to some degree, but mostly he felt numb.

He'd left his mother's house right after breakfast, determined to escape the crying and arguing and muffins that left greasy puddles in their cardboard box. He didn't fault his family for their grief. It just didn't look anything like *his* grief.

Turning the car down a narrow side street, Kyle realized he had no actual destination in mind. Instinct had taken him back toward the hospital, which made no sense at all. Matt was long gone from there, probably in a crematorium at the funeral home or something. He tried to picture it in his mind, hoping the image might tap into the fountain of grief he knew should be bubbling inside him.

Instead, he found himself wondering what a crematorium looked like.

You're losing it, man.

He blinked to clear his head, turning to look toward the hospital even though Matt wasn't there anymore. His eyes landed on a droopy balloon bouquet tied to a bus stop bench on the side of the road.

Get well soon! a shiny balloon declared over the body of a dead pigeon. Kyle stared at the balloons. They looked like the ones Meg had brought yesterday, but that was silly. They couldn't be hers. His mind just wanted an excuse to latch on to an image of her.

He didn't realize he was smiling until he caught sight of his own reflection in the rearview mirror. Then he felt like a dick. What the hell kind of guy smiles the day after his brother dies?

He tried focusing on the dead pigeon instead, hoping to conjure some tears even if they were for the wrong reason. Dammit, he owed Matt some show of emotion.

But the memory of that bird just led him to another one of Meg. Thanksgiving Day, more than three years ago. The weather had been dreary and the whole family had gone out for a post-meal walk. She'd spotted a dead dove on the ground, then looked up to see a second bird on the power line above. Her eyes had filled with tears, and Kyle stopped walking to make sure she was okay.

"They mate for life," she'd said.

Matt had caught her hand in his, tugging her along. "Come on, you'll get bird mites."

But Meg had pulled her hand free. "Doves mate for life," she'd repeated, looking from the dead bird to the live one cooing overhead. "That one must be the partner."

Kyle remembered feeling something heavy and hot pressing against his chest. He'd looked at her face clouded with sentiment, and he'd ached to take her in his arms.

But he hadn't, obviously. For crying out loud, she'd been on the brink of becoming his brother's wife. The most he could offer was a squeeze of her hand as he moved ahead and fell into step beside his parents.

But he'd seen tears glinting in her eyes over pumpkin pie that evening and knew she was thinking of the bird.

He shook his head now to clear the rest of the memory. The part he'd wondered about ever since. He turned the car down another narrow street. He hadn't realized where he was driving until that moment, but now it all made sense. Pathway Park. It was one of Matt's favorite spots. He used to boast it was the best place in Portland to ogle joggers in skimpy sports bras and short shorts.

As Kyle pulled into the parking lot, he had to admit his brother had a point. A buxom brunette trotted past wearing something that looked more like an eye patch than a sports bra, and Kyle tried not to stare as he got out of the car.

Remembering the ducks that paddled the river looking for handouts, he rummaged in his backseat looking for a pack of crackers or something to throw for them. He found a Ziploc bag of marshmallows and tried to remember how they'd gotten there. A camping trip with Cara; that was it. They'd made s'mores and snuggled under a green wool blanket just a few months before they split in August. The memory seemed hollow, like it belonged to someone else. Kyle clenched the baggie in his fist and wondered if ducks ate marshmallows.

He shoved the car door shut and turned toward the park. The air was somewhere between crisp and comfortably tepid, and he smelled crumbled leaves and river water on the light breeze. His boots sank into soggy grass and the squish of it beneath his soles gave him an odd sort of comfort. He took a few steps forward, glancing at the blonde in a pink sports bra who bounced past on his right.

"Hey, there," she called grinning at him over her shoulder. "Love that shirt."

"Thanks." Kyle looked down to see he was wearing the same plain white T-shirt he'd dug out of the hamper the day before. He looked back up to see the blonde jogging in place a few feet away.

"Let me amend that," she said, brushing a perfect sheen of sweat from between her breasts. "I love the way you fill out that shirt."

"Uh, thanks?"

The blonde laughed. "My name's Stacey, and if you'd like to go out sometime—"

"Actually, Stacey, now's not a great time."

"I didn't mean *now*, silly. Obviously I'd want to shower first." She shot him a suggestive look, probably waiting for him to say something flirtatious about the shower.

But Kyle just stood there, biting back the urge to tell her he wasn't in the mood for a soapy grope-fest with a stranger the day after his brother died. Then again, his brother would have been the first person to hit on a woman no matter who died. Maybe this was a sign from Matt.

"Maybe later," Kyle said, shuffling past her and making a beeline for the north end of the park. There was a bench he remembered on a ledge overlooking the river and a path fringed with evergreens. Matt always liked sitting there, claiming it had the best view of the joggers. The *female* joggers. Kyle wasn't in the mood for ogling, but he did feel like finding a connection to his brother.

What he didn't expect to find was Meg.

He spotted her instantly, her rust-colored ringlets blowing behind her as she sat silhouetted against the river, shoulders hunched in a choc-olate-colored poncho he knew would match her eyes. He stood there for a few beats, staring at the back of her head, wondering what drew her here to this same bench he'd been aiming for.

The river twinkled like broken glass in the faint haze of sunlight seeping through the clouds. A pair of swans chugged past near the riv-erbank and Kyle remembered the doves again.

Meg turned then like she knew he'd been watching her. He was right, the poncho did match her eyes, and though they were a little puffy, he was relieved to see they looked dry. At the moment, anyway.

She blinked at him, then gave a small wave. He was walking toward her before he'd made up his mind to do that.

"How did you know?" she asked, her voice soft as the underside of a maple leaf.

"Know what?"

"That this was our spot." She shoved her hands between her knees and gave him a sheepish sort of smile. "Matt and I used to come here all the time. He said he found the ducks soothing."

Kyle nodded, not willing to taint her memory of Matt. "Matt always liked this place."

He stood there with his hands dangling at his sides, not sure what to say. She made it easier for him by sliding to one end of the bench and gesturing toward the empty space beside her. "There's plenty of room," she said. "If you wanted to sit here, too."

Kyle hesitated, then took a few steps forward until he found himself settling onto the cool wood beside her. Something smelled like lilacs, but it was October in Portland and lilacs were long gone, so it must be Meg's hair. She'd always smelled sweet and flowery, like a mix of lilacs and honeysuckle or peonies or some other flower he couldn't name. Matt used to complain that everything he owned ended up smelling like he'd spent the day in a greenhouse, though Kyle never saw the problem with that.

"What's with the marshmallows?" she asked.

He'd forgotten he was holding them. "They're for the ducks."

"I didn't realize ducks had a sweet tooth." She frowned. "Or would it be a sweet beak?"

"That sounds like the name of an eighties band. 'Coming up next, we have "Quack in Black" by Sweet Beak.'"

She laughed, her smile reaching all the way to her eyes. Then she froze like she'd been caught cursing in church. Her face folded back into a neutral frown, and Kyle considered telling her it was okay to smile, even now.

But hell, he wasn't exactly the authority on grief. Maybe he had it all wrong.

"So how are you doing?" she asked.

"Okay, under the circumstances."

She shivered, even though it wasn't particularly cold out, and pulled the hood of the poncho up over her head. It should have looked ridiculous, like a Jedi costume, but on Meg the hood made a frame for her lovely face.

Kyle gripped the bag of marshmallows tighter. "Sorry you didn't get to say goodbye."

"Thanks." She bit her lip. "Did you get to?"

"Not in so many words, but we did talk a little before the surgery."

What had they even discussed? Stupid shit about baseball and an argument about their first babysitter's name. Christ. If he'd known it was the last conversation they'd ever have, he would have just agreed her name was Sunny, even though he knew damn well it was Valerie.

Meg nodded and looked out at the river. She was quiet a moment and, knowing Meg, she was probably perfectly content to sit in silence. She'd never been one for blurting out her thoughts, tending instead to muzzle herself around his outspoken family. But something about *this* silence made Kyle edgy.

"How's work?" he asked.

"Good," she said automatically. "Still catering. Business is good."

"Good," he said, then wanted to kick himself for repeating the same meaningless word she'd already used twice. Surely he could do better. A "great" or a "peachy keen" at least. He cleared his throat. "So how's your mom?"

She reached up and fiddled with her earring, making it jingle like a wind chime. "She's fine. Still living in northeast Portland."

"I'm not surprised. How about your—" He stopped himself, not sure if her father was still a touchy subject.

But Meg didn't need him to finish the question. "My dad's fine. Mom took him back *again* after his latest girlfriend kicked him to the curb for sleeping with the neighbor."

"Sorry."

"It is what it is."

"True," Kyle agreed, not sure what that expression was supposed to mean, but figuring it was time for a subject change.

It was Meg who offered it. "Does it make it harder or easier, you think, you and Matt not being very close?"

He was surprised by the bluntness of the question, and even more surprised to find himself answering without hesitation. "I don't know. Easier, maybe, because we didn't spend much time together. Harder, maybe, because I feel like we should have."

She nodded again, her eyes still fixed on the river. The sun glinted in the curls that fluttered beneath the edges of her hood, and a faint breeze carried the lilac scent to him again.

It might have been a nice moment if it weren't for the approaching ogre.

Kyle blinked twice to clear his vision, but he wasn't seeing things. There was definitely an ogre lurching toward them, clad in a burlap cape and carrying something that looked like a medieval ax. The weapon was made of foam or rubber, as was the dagger on his belt.

The ogre was followed by a man in chainmail wearing a helmet adorned with horns and walking beside a woman strumming a small harp and wearing a purple gossamer gown. Kyle sat back on the bench, relieved to know he'd finally gone crazy. It seemed like a sign the grief was kicking in.

"Good morrow, fair maiden," the ogre said to Meg as he dropped to one knee in front of her. "I see you wear the cloak of Verdanen."

Meg looked down at her poncho, her hands balled up under the fringed hem. "I, uh—"

"Hark!" The woman with the harp pointed at Meg's chest, and Kyle stared dumbly as well. The swell of her breasts was evident even under the bulky brown garment, and he wondered what it would be like to get lost in all that softness.

"The stone of Plutarnius!" the woman reached out to touch the acorn-sized gem on a chain around Meg's neck. "His majesty will be greatly pleased to learn we have rescued the empress who wears it."

The man with the horned helmet knelt before Meg, presenting his foam sword like a gift. "My lady," he said, bowing his head. "My sword is at your service, and I offer my fellowship and protection as your most devoted servant."

The ogre and the woman in gossamer followed suit, kneeling and bowing before Meg like she was a member of a royal family that governed lunatics. Kyle expected her to jump up from the bench and run like hell. She seemed tense beside him, too quiet for too long.

Instead, she reached out and placed her hand on the first man's helmet. "Thank you, Sir—uh—"

"Reginald."

"Sir Reginald."

"Milady."

The woman played a few notes on her harp, keeping her head bowed. Kyle could see the tops of oddly pointed elf ears sticking through her hair, and he leaned close to Meg and lowered his voice. "Uh, what's going on here?"

Meg turned to face him, her curls tickling his chin. "They're LARPers," she whispered back.

"Lepers?"

"No, LARPers. Live Action Role Play. It's sort of like make-believe for grownups."

"What for?" he whispered.

She shrugged. "To check out of real life for a while, I guess."

Kyle looked down at the three bowed heads. Checking out of real life didn't seem like such a dumb idea.

He looked back at Meg, then pointed at her chest. Not at her breasts, at the necklace. "Stone of Plutarnius?" he murmured.

Meg fingered the necklace. "I got it at a garage sale," she whispered. "It cost two dollars and Jess said it looked good with my gray coat."

The man in the helmet looked up then and gave them both a formal nod. "Sir Knight," he said to Kyle. "We must form our parties. The quest awaits."

Kyle swallowed. "Quest?"

The woman in purple looked up. "For the chalice, of course."

"Of course," Kyle agreed.

"Let us make haste," the ogre said, pointing at the baggie in Kyle's lap. "I see you bear weapons?"

He looked down at the baggie of marshmallows. "Uh—"

"Poison gas," Meg said. "Or arrows or lightning bolts. I saw it on TV once."

"What?"

"That's how LARPers simulate throwable weapons," she said. "They toss little beanbags or foam pellets or—"

"Marshmallows," Kyle finished, regarding the baggie with renewed interest. He looked back at Meg to see her assessing him.

"So, which are they?" she asked.

He hesitated. Playing make-believe with a bunch of crazy lepers the day after his brother died would probably earn him a ticket straight to hell. He'd probably end up on a talk show featuring the world's most insensitive bastards. Or worse, his mother would find out and he'd feel like hell for doing something silly and irreverent while she sat home flipping through pages of Matt's baby book, her thumb stroking the tiny lock of baby hair taped to the first page.

Kyle swallowed and gripped the bag of marshmallows. "They're lightning bolts."

"I thought so." Meg nodded and rubbed her palms down her denim-clad thighs. "Shall we play?"

◆ ◆ ◆

Meg wasn't sure what had gotten into her.

One minute she was sitting stoic and respectful, behaving as appropriately as any not-quite-widow should.

The next minute she was asking her ex-future-brother-in-law to join her in a role-playing game.

"Not that kind of role-playing."

"What?"

Meg blinked, startled to realize she'd spoken aloud. "Role-playing. Um, not the kind where one person dresses in a naughty schoolgirl costume and the other pretends to be the stern headmaster with—"

She stopped talking, wishing she could yank her tongue out of her mouth with a pair of pliers. What the hell was wrong with her?

But if Kyle was wondering the same thing, he didn't say it. He lowered his voice again, even though the LARPers kneeling at their feet were close enough to hear every word. "You want to play."

Meg couldn't tell if it was a question or a statement, so she hesitated, then nodded. "If you do. I mean, if you don't think it's too—"

Too what? Disrespectful? Nuts?

It was both of those things, but Kyle put his hand over hers and Meg decided disrespectful and nuts might not be the worst things in the world.

"Let's go," he said.

For a second, Meg thought he wanted to leave, and she got up and turned toward her car. But Kyle rose beside her and cleared his throat. "Behold!" he announced, hoisting his marshmallows overhead. "I am honored to join forces with our new allies in a quest to seek the chalice.

I am trained in various forms of combat, while my lady is a respected healer with great skill in treating battle wounds."

"Indeed," Meg heard herself saying as she rose to stand beside Kyle. "I also know many spells and am joined by my invisible dragon, uh . . . Fallopian."

Kyle raised an eyebrow at her, and she could tell he was trying not to laugh. None of their new teammates broke character, and the woman in the purple gown extended her hand. "I am Trinity Leaftree of the western stone elf tribe."

"And I am Ufnar Gnarlug," the ogre volunteered, resting a hand over his heart. "My clan and I giveth thanks for your alliance."

Sir Reginald doffed his horned helmet and gave a dramatic bow. "Sir Reginald Ironroot Roundbear, at your service."

"Very pleased to make your acquaintance," Kyle said. "I am Sir Tonsillectomy Xanthan Gum."

Meg snorted, then coughed to cover her laughter. She extended her hand to Sir Reginald, who promptly planted a kiss across her knuckles. She tried to think of a name that didn't sound like a disease or a moniker for a fat poodle. "I am Empress Cattywampus Dipthong."

"And her fierce dragon, Fallopian," Kyle added, pretending to stroke the beast's neck.

Trinity grabbed Meg's arm and gestured toward the woods. "My lady, I suggest we move south to lay an ambush to thwart invaders from the east."

"I concur," Ufnar agreed, scratching his chin with a hand coated in green makeup.

Meg glanced at Sir Reginald, pretty sure he was a teller at her bank, or maybe a clerk in the men's department at Macy's.

But for now he was Sir Reginald, and Meg was Empress Cattywampus and Kyle was whoever the hell he'd said he was, and none of them were regular people dealing with mortgages or jobs or grief that threatened to grab them by the ankles and pull them right through the ground and into the soft, damp dirt. The thought of being someone different made Meg a little dizzy with excitement and maybe a twinge of guilt.

"Lady Cattywampus, did you bring Fallopian's leash?" Kyle asked.

"Indeed," she said, holding up the invisible tether for her invisible dragon. "It is one made of rainbows and cobwebs."

"Then we shall see if our last round of dragon obedience training hath paid off?"

Beside her, Sir Reginald thrust his foam sword into the air. "Long live the king!"

"Long live the king!" Meg repeated, throwing her fist in the air.

"All hail his majesty!" Ufnar hoisted his rubber ax in the air and Meg wished she had time to round up a weapon of her own. She settled for patting her invisible dragon on the head.

"Have a lightning bolt," Kyle said, handing her a marshmallow.

"Thank you." Her fingers grazed his as she took it from him, and she reminded herself this was wrong on so many levels.

But something about it felt right, too. Matt would have laughed at them for sure, which made the whole thing seem okay in a way.

"Let us journey forth," announced Trinity, her purple gown fluttering in the breeze as she turned and ran toward the woods.

Ufnar and Sir Reginald followed, weapons raised in the air as they jogged into the trees. Reginald's horned helmet fell off and he chased after it for a few steps, stumbling as he ran.

Meg looked at Kyle. "You sure you're okay with this? It's a little weird."

"Isn't that the point?"

"I suppose so."

"Matt would die, wouldn't he?" Kyle grimaced. "God, that just slipped out."

"It's okay. You're right though. He'd think this was nuts."

"So we owe it to his memory to sally forth and join the quest."

Meg nodded. "Agreed."

They jogged after the others, catching up to them easily since Trinity had stopped to strum her harp and sing a few lines about a porcupine and a golden spoon. Sir Reginald was whacking at some dense shrubbery with his foam sword, while Ufnar plodded along growling.

"Hark!" Sir Reginald yelled, throwing his arm to the side. "Someone approaches."

Meg stopped, but not quickly enough. She ran smack dab into the back of Kyle, her cheek colliding with the solid plane of his shoulder blade. He turned and caught her by the shoulders, his palms curving around them. "Is my lady harmed?"

"Nay," she said, feeling herself blush. "Your lady is just clumsy."

"I remember that about you," Kyle murmured. He hadn't dropped his hands from her shoulders yet, and something about it felt comforting. "I'll never forget the time you fell off that stand-up paddleboard, conked your head with the paddle and lost your bikini top."

Meg laughed and felt her blush deepen. "God, I'd almost forgotten that. It got caught under that Jet Ski and Matt had to chase the guy down to get it back. Then he put his swim trunks on his head and did the chicken dance so I'd stop being embarrassed about flashing a bunch of strangers."

"He always knew how to get someone laughing again."

A wave of nostalgia nearly knocked her backward, and she didn't know whether to laugh or cry. She was spared from doing either when Sir Reginald shouted again.

"Who goes there? I command thee to name thyself."

Meg looked up to see six strangers emerging from the trees in medieval armor made of cardboard. They stepped forward shoulder-to-shoulder, raising weapons that looked like foam pool noodles painted silver.

Ufnar raised his ax. Sir Reginald lifted his sword. Kyle reached into his bag of marshmallows.

"Prepare to do battle!" Trinity screamed, pulling a plastic dagger from a sheath on her thigh.

Kyle looked at Meg. "Does Fallopian attack on command?"

"Of course." Meg loosened her grip on the imaginary leash. "Sic 'em, boy!"

Kyle plucked a marshmallow from his bag and drew it back like the world's tiniest baseball.

"Charge!" shouted Sir Reginald, lurching forward with his foam sword flying. A man carrying a giant sledgehammer made of foam bopped him on the side of the head, but Reginald kept fighting while Ufnar lunged at another man with his axe.

"Lightning bolt," Kyle said, tossing the marshmallow at a man in a gray cape. The man screamed and fell to the ground, clutching his chest. He began to writhe and gasp, putting on an impressive display of fake death while Trinity ran circles around him chanting a spell in some language Meg thought sounded vaguely like Pig Latin.

"Poison gas!" Kyle shouted as he tossed another marshmallow, clocking a tall man in the forehead before pivoting to chuck one at another attacker. "Really sharp arrow."

Meg grabbed the reins on her imaginary dragon. "Commence fire-breathing," she shouted, aiming the dragon's snout at a man charging Reginald.

Kyle made a sound like a cappuccino maker, and it took Meg a moment to realize that was his interpretation of a dragon breathing fire. Meg palmed the marshmallow he'd given her and chucked it at a woman locked in fierce combat with Trinity.

"Lightning bolt!" Meg shouted.

"I already used the lightning bolt," Kyle reminded her.

"You don't have more than one?"

"Lightning bolts are a limited commodity."

"Uh—rotten egg."

"Really? That's the best you've got?"

The woman she'd tossed the marshmallow at jumped to the side, then took another swipe at Trinity with a dagger made of tinfoil.

Kyle handed Meg another marshmallow. "Try again."

"Heat-seeking missile!" Meg shouted, hurling her marshmallow at a man charging her from the left. The man raised a foam shield and the marshmallow bounced off. Kyle leapt forward, stretching with his palm out.

"Got it!" He caught the marshmallow in one hand, throwing his body in front of Meg as he took aim and hurled the weapon again. "Tell your dragon to cover me!"

"Fallopian—sic balls."

"Aaaargh!" Their newest attacker fell to the ground in front of them, pantomiming a hideous and painful death.

To Meg's right, Ufnar screamed and clutched his shoulder. "My arm! I've lost my arm! Do something!"

Meg and Trinity rushed toward him, then dropped to their knees in the dirt as Ufnar fell to the ground. "Can you reattach limbs, Empress Cattywampus?"

Meg nodded, trying to remember what she'd learned watching the TV special about LARPing. Trinity pulled a ribbon from a small silk pouch around her neck and handed it to Meg. "Take mine."

"Thank you." Meg laid the ribbon on Ufnar's shoulder, hoping this was more or less how things were supposed to go. "By the power granted to me by The Great Spatula and Lord Kumquat, I command thee to heal thine limb and be made whole again."

Ufnar blinked, then looked from Meg to Trinity and back to Meg again. "My lady, you have saved me. I owe you my very life."

"'Tis nothing," Meg assured him. "You would do the same for me."

"That's it, run away!" Sir Reginald shouted, and Meg looked up to see the last of their attackers fleeing the way they'd come.

Behind her, a shrill chime echoed through the trees. At first, Meg thought it was somehow connected to the game, but she turned to see

Kyle pulling his phone from a pocket. He scowled at the screen and muttered something under his breath.

Ufnar sat up and frowned. "Sir Tonsillectomy Xanthan Gum—you have broken the cardinal rule of technology."

Kyle turned away, putting a hand over his left ear as he raised the phone to his right and said, "Hi, Mom."

Ufnar began to protest, but Meg shushed him. "His brother just died," Meg whispered as Kyle walked into the trees murmuring into the phone. "It probably has to do with funeral arrangements or a memorial service or—"

"You're reviewing the will *now*?" Kyle growled, and Meg looked up to see him scowling with the phone to his ear.

"Or a will," Trinity whispered.

"Or that," Meg whispered back.

"Mom, I don't really think now's the best time to get into—right. I know. I get it." Kyle fell silent again, his scowl deepening as he listened to whatever his mother was shouting. Meg could hear Sylvia's voice from fifteen feet away, though she couldn't make out the words.

Kyle shook his head, then looked up from the tree branch he'd been stripping of its needles. His gaze locked with Meg's, and she started to look away, but something stopped her. Something in the intensity of his expression, or maybe the fact that she was almost sure she heard the word *Meg* from the other end of the line.

"I'm with her right now, actually," Kyle said, his eyes never leaving Meg's. "We'll be there in ten minutes."

CHAPTER THREE

Meg twisted a damp tissue in her hands and thought about prison interrogation and Chinese water torture. Anything, really, would be more pleasurable than this conversation with Matt and Kyle's mother.

"So what do you have to say for yourself, young lady?"

Sylvia peered at her over the top of her glasses, a look that had not failed to discombobulate Meg since the first moment she met Sylvia after her fourth date with Matt. Back then, Sylvia had called Meg "cute" for ordering a margarita with dinner, and Meg had promptly knocked the beverage into her own lap. The fumble made her look incontinent as well as classless, and things hadn't changed much in ten years.

Meg forced herself to meet Sylvia's gaze across the spotless Midland family living room. She ordered herself not to cry, not to slouch, not do any of the things her body desperately wanted to do.

Like flee.

Meg cleared her throat. "I'm aware of the debt," she said. "Matt took the photographs for my cookbook a few months after we got engaged. He offered it as a favor at the time."

"At the time, you were planning to actually *marry* my son instead of leaving him brokenhearted at the altar."

"Right." Meg bit her lip, resisting the urge to fire back that the marriage might have happened if Matt hadn't felt the need to play hide-the-salami with his acupuncturist. This wasn't the time to start dragging skeletons out of the closet and throwing their bones around, especially not with Kyle sitting five feet away with his arms folded over his chest. He hadn't said much of anything, and Meg wondered why he was here at all. She didn't dare let her gaze stray to his corner of the room as Sylvia continued her lecture.

"So it seems perfectly reasonable that my son—a sought-after commercial photographer—would bill you for those photos after you failed to uphold your end of the wedding plans," Sylvia said. "Can you explain to me why you haven't paid your debt?"

Meg swallowed and clenched the tissue tighter. "Because he decided to charge me ten thousand dollars. And between that and paying off all the debt from the wedding, I didn't find that many nickels between the cushions of my sofa."

The words came out snarkier than she meant them to, and from the corner of her eye, she saw Kyle shift in his chair. She desperately wanted to look over at him—for strength or reassurance or just the sight of those ash-flecked green eyes.

But she couldn't get distracted right now. She couldn't afford to let Sylvia see a chink in her armor. A trickle of sweat slid between her shoulder blades, and Meg wished she'd thought to smear her whole body with antiperspirant before setting foot in Matt's childhood home again.

"I see." Her former-future-mother-in-law looked back at the paperwork. "Well, you haven't made very good progress paying off your debt."

"I have, though. It's completely paid off. The wedding planner was paid in full last July, and I made my final payment for the reception hall back in—"

"Not for the wedding," Sylvia interrupted. "For my son's photographs. For his time, talent, and hard work on your little cookbook project. According to these records, you still owe more than three thousand dollars."

Meg wiped her palms on the legs of her jeans. "With all due respect, I think you're mistaken. I'm pretty sure it's less than half that. Maybe fifteen hundred dollars? I can have my bank pull up the canceled checks if you want proof."

"Please do. In the meantime, the fact remains that regardless of the amount, you still owe money to Matt's estate."

Meg gritted her teeth, biting back the urge to argue. It wasn't worth it, not now, not when she'd already paid off most of the ten thousand dollars she probably shouldn't have agreed to pay in the first place.

"I'm working on it," she said. "If I get this new catering contract with—"

"I don't care how you get the money, Meg. We need this debt paid in full by the end of the month so we can settle up Matt's affairs."

Matt's affairs are what started all this, Meg thought, but bit her tongue. Speaking ill of the dead wouldn't do anyone any good right now, and besides, it wasn't fair to lay the blame at his feet. If she hadn't cut and run, maybe he wouldn't have lashed out by billing her for photos he'd taken as a favor to help her achieve her dream of publishing that damn cookbook.

For all the good that did.

Meg cleared her throat. "I'm sorry," she said, not entirely sure how she meant it. "I'm sorry for everything, Sylvia. For your loss and for the way I handled things two years ago, but most of all for—"

"We're done here," Sylvia said, looking away as her eyes turned dark and glittery. "You can mail the check to our attorney. His name is on the card I gave you."

Meg nodded and stood up, grateful her legs seemed capable of carrying her all the way across the room and to the door. Feeling eyes on her back, she turned to see Kyle watching her. His expression was unreadable, but he didn't look away.

"Meg?"

She tore her gaze from Kyle's and looked back at Sylvia. "Yes?"

"Thank you." Her voice was tight and she kept her gaze fixed on a far corner of the room, but Meg could see the tears she'd been holding back had started to spill down her cheeks. "For making him happy during the early years."

Meg swallowed hard, fighting the urge to read it as an insult. As an implication she'd failed to keep making him happy for all ten years of the union.

Is that why he cheated?

"You're welcome," Meg said softly, pushing the words up past the lump in her throat. "I was lucky to be with him for such a long time."

She turned and walked out of the room, determined not to look back at Kyle.

◆　◆　◆

Kyle stood on Meg's doorstep the next evening with a clay pot of daisies in one hand and the unsettling feeling he was picking her up for a date instead of showing up to apologize for his mom or his silliness in the park or his gruffness at the hospital or—

Hell. He had a lot to be sorry for.

Before he could figure out where to start, the door flew open and Meg stood there barefoot and wide-eyed. "Kyle! What are you doing here?" Her gaze shifted to the daisies. "You brought me flowers?"

He shrugged and shifted the pot from one hand to another. "People have been sending flowers nonstop for the last few days. My mom suggested I bring you some."

"Daisies." She reached out to touch one of the feathery white petals. He pushed the pot toward her, and she seemed to hesitate before wrapping her hands around it. She stared down at the sunny yellow centers like they were foreign and befuddling instead of something that grew in half the yards on her quiet suburban street on the outskirts of Portland.

She raised her gaze to his, and Kyle felt his guts do a somersault. "These were supposed to be our wedding flowers," she said. "Matt brought me daisies on our first date. He used to buy them for me every year for my birthday, sometimes in these wild colors like fuchsia or neon orange."

Kyle swallowed down the lump in his throat and nodded. "Maybe Mom remembered that. It's as close as she'll get to an apology."

Meg pulled the flowers to her chest and shook her head. "She doesn't need to apologize. She lost her son, for heaven's sake. She's hurting."

"She still could have handled things a little better. It's not like they need the money. She's just really focused on getting Matt's estate in order because it gives her something to do. Something to help her feel useful. Otherwise, I'm not sure she'd even get out of bed right now."

He thought about the look on his mom's face when he'd found her going through a box of old photos at Matt and Chloe's place that morning. "I just can't believe he'll never sit across from you at another Christmas dinner," she'd said, holding up a faded snapshot of her two sons wearing hideous matching reindeer sweaters the year they were both in middle school.

Kyle had put his hand on his mother's shoulder, wishing like hell there was something he could say to make her feel better. To make Matt come bursting through the door again with his trademark grin and a story about a client who hired him to photograph a collection of famous sports legends' old jockstraps.

No one was better than Matt at cheering people up.

Now, Kyle looked at Meg and saw some of his mom's sadness in her eyes. Her fingers were clenched tight around the flowerpot and a familiar bracket of lines carved the space between her eyebrows. "Your mother's grieving," she said softly. "Grief makes people do odd things."

"Like running around a forest throwing marshmallows and pretending to be a medieval warrior?"

One corner of her mouth tugged up. It wasn't quite a smile, but Kyle felt something shift warm and soft between them. "Something like that," she murmured.

She let go of the flowerpot with one hand and wiped her brow, leaving a smudge of flour on her forehead. He wondered what she'd been baking, and felt a sudden ache to invite himself into her kitchen and pull out a barstool the way he used to. Back then he'd drop by sometimes on Wednesday nights, making some excuse to talk with Matt about football or art or trends in men's tube socks. Anything, really, for a chance to spend a few hours helping Meg roll dough or fold napkins while he sipped beer at their familiar granite island.

But this wasn't the same house she'd shared with Matt. Everything had changed, and not just her address.

"I'm sorry, where are my manners?" Meg's voice jarred him from his thoughts, and Kyle blinked as she stepped aside and gestured behind her. "Would you like to come in?"

He hesitated, not sure what the right answer was. The truthful one was yes, but he wasn't sure it felt appropriate to be alone with his dead brother's ex-fiancée in her living room so soon after Matt's death. Where the hell was the etiquette manual on all this?

He cleared his throat. "You don't look like you're dressed for company."

Meg laughed, and it occurred to Kyle that most women would have taken offense. But Meg just pushed the door open wider and stepped aside, her Marvin the Martian T-shirt slipping off one shoulder as she moved. Her bare feet made a shuffling sound on the blonde-wood floor, and Kyle breathed in the scent of cinnamon and flowers.

"Please," she said, tucking a red-gold curl behind one ear. "You've seen me in my pajamas on Christmas morning with no makeup. You held my hair back when I threw up at the family picnic after eating

Aunt Judy's potato salad. I'm pretty sure we're past the point of dressing up for each other."

Kyle nodded, still reeling a little from the idiocy of his own remarks and the onslaught of all those memories. Meg and Matt had been together ten years, long enough for their names to become a single word. *Meganmatt.* She was practically a member of his family.

But there was nothing family-like about the way Kyle felt his blood heat up as he stepped past her into the entryway. He shoved his hands into his pockets, wondering what kind of asshole he was for trying to figure out if she was wearing a bra under that T-shirt. Her shoulder was bare where the fabric slipped over it, and he saw no trace of straps as she tugged the collar back where it belonged.

"So this is your place," he said, surveying the high-beamed ceilings and the overstuffed beige sofa lined with silky-looking pillows in bright floral patterns. It was simple, but very Meg. He spotted a vintage kidney-shaped coffee table he remembered from the house she shared with Matt, and he wondered how they'd decided who got what furniture when they split.

Something moved in the center of a paisley armchair, and Kyle looked over to see a massive orange tabby curled in a tight half-circle. The cat twitched its tail and opened one eye.

"Hi, kitty," Kyle said. "What's your name?"

The cat opened both eyes and stared at him. Its fur was thick and long, and Kyle thought about walking over there and scratching it under the chin. Apparently the cat was imagining it, too, and wasn't keen on the idea. The beast stood up, arched his back, and gave a ferocious hiss. It jumped off the chair and headed toward the back of the house.

"That's Floyd," Meg said. "He doesn't like men. Or women. Or—well, anyone."

"Friendly guy."

"He has his moments. I got him two years ago. Figured the law says single women must have at least one cat, so—" she shrugged, trailing off. "Anyway, this is my place."

"It's nice."

"Thank you."

A long, tense silence followed, and Kyle watched Meg turn to set the flowerpot on a little entry table. She fussed with the leaves for a bit, then adjusted the knickknacks beside it, fiddling with a purple stone frog and a small copper tree Kyle remembered making for her twenty-fifth birthday. It was one of his first forays into metalwork, and he remembered Matt giving him a nod of genuine approval.

"Great work, bro," he'd said. "It could almost work as one of those earring holder thingies. She can use it to show off the diamond hoops I got her."

Meg finished fiddling with her decor and turned to face him. She shifted her weight from one foot to the other, then tugged her left earlobe.

"You've always done that."

The words left Kyle's lips before he had a chance to consider them, and he wished at once he could grab them out of the air and stuff them back down his throat.

But Meg cocked her head to the side and gave him a curious look. "Done what?"

Kyle swallowed. "Tugged your earlobe when you think of something you're not sure you want to say aloud."

She quirked one eyebrow at him. "How do you know that, if I don't actually say it out loud?" she asked. "Are you psychic?"

"Nope. I noticed it years ago when you and Matt started dating. You'd tug at your ear and then blurt out something risqué or funny or maybe a little embarrassing. After a while, it seemed like you started censoring yourself."

"But I still tugged my ear," she said, her expression utterly bewildered.

"Yep."

She stared at him a moment, and Kyle wondered if he'd gone too far. He remembered watching his gregarious brother tease Meg about some goofy thought she'd voiced over dinner, calling her "Mouthy Meg" and ruffling her hair every time she blurted something unexpected.

Eventually, Meg stopped.

It hadn't occurred to Kyle until just now that maybe she'd never noticed.

"Tell you what," he said, feeling like he owed her something for peeling back a blanket she might have preferred to keep tucked tight around her. "If I catch you tugging your ear, I'll confess three embarrassing things about myself."

She cocked her head to the side, studying him. "What for?"

"Just showing you the world won't end if I say something that's a little uncomfortable. That sharing an embarrassing thought isn't so bad. If I can do it three times, you can manage once. Deal?"

She eyed him warily, and Kyle held his breath, hoping he hadn't crossed some line. Hoping he wasn't being too presumptuous by implying they'd have any contact beyond this, especially after two years of radio silence. She kept her gaze locked on his for a few seconds, then nodded once. "Give me an example."

"Okay," Kyle said, fumbling around in his memory to find something appropriately mortifying. It wasn't tough. "Embarrassing item number one: I spent two hours in my gallery last week helping customers before I noticed my fly was undone."

Meg laughed, and he watched her shoulders relax a little. She leaned back against the wall, her posture more casual now. "And here I thought you'd gotten all classy and refined now that you're no longer a starving artist."

"How do you know I'm not starving?"

She shrugged. "I can't vouch for your eating habits, but your career seems to be going well. You've been on the cover of every arts publication in the galaxy this past year."

"In several other galaxies, too. Those Martians can't get enough of mixed metal."

He hesitated, then leaned against the wall beside Meg, his shoulders at the same level as hers. There were still at least eighteen inches between them, but there was something intimate about it. Something that left him feeling much more connected to her than if she had invited him inside to sit with her on the sofa. If he lifted his hand, his fingers might graze hers, but he stayed still and let the old familiarity flow between them, washing away some of the awkwardness.

Kyle cleared his throat. "Confession number two: Last month I tried to email a photo to a client to show the progress of a sculpture they commissioned," he said. "Instead, I accidentally attached an image of a tortoise penis."

Meg laughed. "At least it wasn't *your* penis."

"Good point, though maybe I could have passed that off as art."

"Doubtful. Let's hear your third confession."

Her smile hadn't faded yet, and Kyle fished for one more gem to keep it from disappearing. "I accidentally clogged the toilet at a fancy gallery party last year and was so embarrassed I slipped out the back door and never told anyone I was leaving."

She snorted. "God, Kyle." She shook her head, her eyes still bright with laughter. "Those were good, I'll give you that. Color me impressed."

"The fact that you're impressed by my ineptitude seems like a sign one of us has a screw loose."

"It's probably you."

"I won't disagree." Kyle cleared his throat. "So is it your turn?"

"I guess." Meg bit her lip. "You were right that I was thinking something I didn't want to say out loud, but it wasn't really like the stuff you just shared."

"Do you want to tell me?"

She sighed and closed her eyes, the back of her head still resting against the wall. "I was just thinking how weird this feels. There's a part of me that's still really, really angry with Matt for the affair," she said, her words coming out in a frenzied rush now. "Like so angry I want to kill him, and then I feel guilty for even *thinking* that, and then I also feel really, really angry with myself for walking out the way I did instead of making a clean break or having the respect to talk things over with you or with your family, and then in the middle of all that anger I think about how Matt's gone forever and now you're standing here in my living room and I can't decide if the sick ache in my gut is because I feel guilty or because I feel sad or because I missed our friendship so much these last two years."

She was breathless by the time she got all the words out, and her eyes were still closed. Kyle noticed her lower lashes were damp and he watched a single tear slip down her left cheek. He ached to reach out and swipe it away, but he stayed rooted in place.

Meg opened her eyes and took a deep breath. She rubbed the back of her hand over her cheek and gave a sheepish shrug. "And now I feel like a total dumbass."

"You're not a dumbass."

"I kinda wrecked the jovial vibe you had going."

"Under the circumstances, I think it's okay not to be jovial."

Meg gave a tiny little half smile and blew a curl out of her eye. "I should have made up a story about having toilet paper stuck to my shoe."

"I missed you, too." Kyle swallowed, still not daring to move closer. "As a friend, I mean."

"Friends." Meg nodded. "We *were* good friends, weren't we? I mean before everything—" She waved a hand, encompassing *everything* with one small gesture.

As if that could be enough.

"Yeah." Kyle's throat felt tight, but he cleared it and kept going. "Matt and I always had a hard time relating unless it was over some bullshit testosterone-fueled competition. Then you came along and—" he swallowed again, sidetracked by the memory his first glimpse of Meg, with the sunlight in her hair and bare feet in the grass and her hand linked with his brother's. "You connected us," he said at last. "Matt and me."

Meg nodded. "I'm glad." She blinked hard. "I just wish . . . never mind."

He watched her left hand start to lift, but she dropped it back to her side. He wondered if it had been en route to her earlobe, and felt bad for making her self-conscious.

"I wish things hadn't ended the way they did," she said at last.

"With you and Matt?"

"That, too. I shouldn't have cut and run. But I also regret losing friendships. I know that's how breakups go, but it was still hard. Having your family punish me by cutting me out like a bruise on a pear. I guess my family did the same, punishing Matt for cheating in the first place—"

"You took it as punishment?"

"Of course. How did you see it?"

Kyle shoved his hands in his pockets, not sure how they'd gone from lighthearted banter about tortoise penises to adultery and forgiveness and death.

But maybe this conversation was long overdue. Two years overdue, to be exact.

"I guess I saw it as making a choice to have my brother's back." He swallowed, remembering the dark spiral of depression that gripped Matt after the breakup. Kyle had promised he'd never breathe a word about it to anyone, and he hadn't. He still wouldn't, not even now.

He cleared his throat and met Meg's gaze again. "Being there for your family is important, even if that comes at the expense of another friendship."

The words hung there between them for a moment, and Meg studied him so intently he had to fight the urge to look away. He watched her digest the words, and he braced for an argument or a flash of defensiveness.

But that wasn't Meg's style. It never had been. When she finally spoke, it was a single word. "Interesting."

"That's it?"

"I'm not sure what else to say." She wiped her hands down the legs of gray yoga pants that hugged her thighs, and Kyle tried not to imagine that softness against his own palms. "How about a peace offering?"

He nodded at the flowers. "You mean besides secondhand daisies?"

Meg smiled. "Did your mother really ask you to bring them?"

"Not in so many words. But she asked where I was taking them, and when I told her, she said it was a good idea. And she did tell me to take these ones, instead of the ones in a tacky plastic pot. Does that count?"

"Close enough," Meg said and turned away. "Follow me."

Kyle would have followed her off the end of a dock with his pockets full of rocks, but he guessed that wasn't her plan. He wasn't surprised when she trudged toward the kitchen, her bare feet making a soft slap against the wood floors.

He was surprised when she spun around with a red flowered apron and began tying it around his waist. He looked down, conscious of Meg's hands fluttering near his belt buckle.

"Your idea of a peace offering involves dressing me in ruffles?"

"Doesn't yours?"

Kyle smiled. "What are we making?"

"A coconut lime tart. It was Matt's favorite."

Kyle nodded, annoyed with himself for feeling jealous of a dead guy who still had the power to dictate dessert from beyond the grave. "What can I do?"

"Wash your hands first," she said, moving past him toward the kitchen sink. "Then I'm going to have you grind up those graham crackers for the crust."

He watched her flip the water on, then grab a plastic bottle of dish soap to lather her hands. "Why don't you use that little built-in soap dispenser thing next to the faucet?"

"It's broken," she said. "Hasn't worked since I moved in."

"Let me see."

He put a hand on her waist and nudged her aside, then dropped to his knees and crawled under the kitchen sink. "Do you have a screwdriver?"

"Flathead or Phillips?"

"Phillips."

"No."

"Flathead?"

"No."

Kyle rolled his eyes. "How about a butter knife?"

She handed one under the sink while Kyle fiddled with the soap dispenser.

"Sorry," she called from above. "I left all the tools with Matt when we split, and I never got around to buying my own."

"It's fine." Kyle twisted the knife into the screw head, careful not to bust the tip. He pried off the dispenser, checking for air leaks and clogs. He adjusted one of the valves, then used his shirt-sleeve to wipe some goopy green residue from the mouth of the bottle. He screwed the whole thing back into place and crawled out from under the sink, wiping his hands on his pants before giving the dispenser a good pump.

"Holy cow, it works!" Meg turned to him, beaming. "Thank you."

"No sweat."

She bit her lip. "That's one thing I always liked about you."

"That I fix soap dispensers with a butter knife?"

She laughed. "No, that you don't give me a chance to argue that I don't need help or I can do it myself. You don't shout at me from the couch asking 'Need help?' in that way most guys do when they're hoping the answer is no. You just jump right in and make yourself useful."

"Wow." Kyle ran his hands under the water and worked up a good lather. "That's a whole lot of psychoanalysis for a soap dispenser."

"It's a compliment, jackass. Take it like one."

"I will. Thank you."

"Sure." She handed him a dish towel. "Really, thanks. To be honest, I forgot that thing didn't work."

"Glad to help."

Kyle turned his attention to the graham crackers while Meg began digging through the fridge. They worked in companionable silence for a while, with Kyle grinding graham crackers in the food processor and Meg moving close beside him to splash in some melted butter.

"So tell me about this cookbook," Kyle said. "The one Matt took pictures for?"

"What do you want to know?"

"I remember hearing something about it that year before the wedding, but that's when I was living part-time in Montana."

He kept his voice even, hoping she didn't ask about his year out of state. About the reason he'd looked for the first excuse to get out of town the moment she and Matt announced their engagement.

"Right." Meg blew the curl off her face again and sighed. "You weren't around to witness the whole fiasco."

"What do you mean?"

Meg shrugged and began squeezing lime halves in a funny contraption. She was doing it with more force than the job seemed to require, but what the hell did he know?

"It was stupid, really. I had this big dream to put out an aphrodisiac cookbook with all these cool recipes I created and a lot of fun stories about ingredients that boost libido."

Kyle felt himself getting a little dizzy, but he focused on pressing his graham cracker crust into the tart pan she'd handed him. "So what happened?"

"Zilch. None of the agents or editors I queried had any interest in the project."

"Fools."

"Thank you." Meg sighed. "Anyway, I decided to self-publish it."

"Ah. So that's why Matt took the photos?"

"Yeah. A friend of mine who's a graphic designer laid the whole thing out in exchange for me doing the catering at her wedding, and Matt volunteered to take all the food pictures."

"Volunteered?" He thought about his mother's accusations and wondered how Matt might tell the story differently.

"We were a few months from getting married," Meg said. "It wasn't a big deal for my photographer husband to take photos for my cookbook any more than it was a big deal for me to volunteer to cater his office Christmas party. It's just the sort of thing couples do, you know?"

"But then the wedding didn't happen."

"Right. And the book sold a whopping twelve copies, three of which were to my mother."

"I'm sorry."

"It's okay. It was a dumb idea anyway."

The sadness in her voice made Kyle turn to look at her, but she kept her eyes averted, focusing now on beating an egg with enough force to set her whole body in motion, which wasn't unpleasant to watch. But the rigid set of her jaw gave him a stronger urge to hug her than ogle her.

Neither seemed like the right thing to do, so he settled for pressing the butter-damp graham cracker crumbs into the edges of the tart plate.

"I remember that feeling," he said. "Back when I was starting out as an artist. I'd have this awesome, spectacular idea for a sculpture and I'd stay up all night for weeks on end getting it just right, only to have one gallery owner after another tell me it wasn't what they were looking for."

"Probably didn't help having a brother who was this super-famous sports photographer making it all look so easy."

"You're right," he agreed. "Though commercial photography was always a lot different from the sort of art I wanted to create."

Meg nodded. "I remember you talking about that. Everyone kept telling you to give it up and go get a desk job."

Kyle laughed. "Yeah, I probably should have listened. Would have spent a lot less time eating Ramen noodles and sleeping on friends' couches."

"But look at you now." She looked up and smiled, curls falling around her face. "You have your own gallery and sculptures in rich people's houses all over the world."

"You've been reading too many art magazines." He felt oddly self-conscious, so he slid the tart plate in front of her. "Does this look okay?"

Meg nodded. "Could you stick it in the oven and set the timer for ten minutes?"

"Yep." Kyle turned to the stainless-steel monstrosity on the other side of the kitchen and opened the door to slide the crust into the pre-heated depths. Something caught his eye on the bookshelf overhead, and he pushed the oven door shut so he could take a closer look.

"Is this your aphrodisiac cookbook?"

Meg turned and glanced at the glossy book he'd pulled off the shelf lined with all her other cookbooks. Her cheeks went a little pinker as she nodded. "Yeah, that's it."

She sounded a little shy about it, but Kyle flipped the cover open anyway and began to skim. Food descriptions and photos lined each glossy page, with a beaming picture of Meg chopping parsley catching Kyle's attention more than it ought to. "This is amazing."

"Yeah. I know sports photography was his thing, but Matt used to take pretty great food photos."

"I meant all these recipes. 'Blood orange-roasted asparagus with blackened Anaheim peppers and pine nuts?' That sounds incredible."

Meg smiled. "The capsaicin in the peppers gets the blood flowing and stimulates nerve endings, and the vitamin E in asparagus can help boost testosterone, while—"

"You came up with all of these recipes?"

She nodded, using a spatula to point to a page he'd just flipped to. "That section with the lavender is my favorite."

"Can we make some of these?"

Meg raised an eyebrow. "Right now?"

"Sure, why not?"

There were a million reasons why not, and Kyle damn well knew it. But he waited anyway, hoping maybe she didn't see it the same way he did. Or maybe that she did.

"You want to make dinner together from my aphrodisiac cookbook?"

"Sure." He closed the book, and set it on the counter. "Whenever you have time, I mean."

"Now's good."

"Really?"

"Sure. It can be like our own memorial to Matt or something."

"Absolutely," Kyle said, though that wasn't at all what he'd had in mind. He picked up the book again, turning more slowly past the photos. They really were beautiful. His brother had been a damn fine photographer, though it was Meg's words that grabbed him. Her descriptions of succulent lamb and avocado drizzled with honey were making his mouth water, or maybe that wasn't the food at all.

He looked up at Meg and knew damn sure it wasn't the food. "Let's do it."

CHAPTER FOUR

Meg couldn't believe she was standing shoulder to shoulder with her former-future-brother-in-law in her kitchen, the two of them making dinner together like it was the most natural thing in the world.

It used to be. How the hell had two years gone by?

"Does this look right for the mango?"

Meg turned to see Kyle with a smear of something orange on his sleeve. She peered around his shoulder, flummoxed by the size of him. It had been a long time since a man—any man—stood at her counter chopping tropical fruit.

"Maybe a little smaller," she said. "We want to be able to tell it apart from the papaya."

She dumped a few chopped sprigs of fresh mint and lavender into the bowl, grateful the little herb garden on her back patio was still giving up the goods even though October had spit frost on her windshield two mornings this week. She checked the timer on the pork loin in the oven and thought about how nice it felt to have an excuse to make a meal like this.

She ran her finger over a photo in her aphrodisiac cookbook and tried to remember the night she'd come up with the recipe. *New Year's Eve day.* She could picture it clearly, even though it was nearly four years ago. She remembered drizzling the blood-orange olive oil over the basil-wrapped scallops and carrying the whole thing into the living room on a bright blue plate.

"I'm thinking of writing a cookbook," she'd told Matt as she set the tray on the coffee table and curled up beside him on the sofa.

"What's that?" he'd asked absently, plucking a scallop off the platter as he flipped to the next page in his favorite photography magazine.

"A cookbook," she told him. "I think I might like to write one. Something with recipes using aphrodisiac ingredients."

"You're pretty damn delicious." He'd squeezed her knee, and Meg had felt herself glowing with the compliment, even if it wasn't precisely what she'd wanted him to praise right then.

"Thank you," she said. "I thought I'd include something about the history of aphrodisiacs. Maybe a few sidebars with interesting science stuff behind the ingredients. I think there's a market for it."

"Could be," he'd said, flipping a page again as he chewed the end of a toothpick he'd removed from one of the scallops. "You've gotta have a platform to write nonfiction."

"I'm a chef," she said, a little hurt he didn't seem more enthusiastic about the idea. "And I have a degree in biology, so I know a few things about pheromones and human nature and—"

"Damn, can you grab me a napkin, honey? This sauce is getting everywhere."

A hand on her shoulder jolted Meg from the memory and back to the present—to her kitchen and Kyle holding out a bowl of tropical fruit salsa with a curious expression on his face. "Sorry, I didn't mean to startle you."

"You didn't."

Kyle cocked his head to the side and gave her a knowing look. "You just did it again."

Meg felt a flush creeping into her cheeks and she dropped her hand from her ear. "I did not."

"You did, you tugged your earlobe." He grinned. "Come on, let's go eat this in the living room while the rest of dinner cooks. Grab us some wine and I'll come up with three embarrassing things to tell you."

Meg rolled her eyes and tried to muster up some indignation. The man was bossing her around in her own kitchen and acting like he knew her every thought and feeling when she hadn't even seen him for two years. Who the hell did he think he was?

The guy who knows your every thought and feeling when you haven't seen him for two years.

Hell. Meg grabbed the bowl of warm cinnamon tortilla crisps and a chilled bottle of Viognier and headed into the living room. She set both on the coffee table and started to head back to the kitchen for glasses, but realized Kyle had beaten her to the punch.

"How'd you know I'd bring white wine?" She picked up one of the thin, mouth-blown glasses with its narrow stem, a little startled to remember it had been an engagement gift from one of her aunts. She set the glass down and looked at Kyle. "I've got a whole cabinet full of red wine glasses, but you grabbed the ones for white wine."

"Educated guess," he said, popping a chip in his mouth. "White wine pairs better with tropical fruit. I might play with welding tools for a living, but I'm not a total Neanderthal."

Meg snorted and dropped onto the sofa beside him. She grabbed a corkscrew off the table and opened the wine. "Pretty sure no one would ever mistake you for a Neanderthal."

"You did."

"What?"

"I think it was nine years ago. No, eight. It was during my 'primitive period.' You and Matt stopped by to check out the new sculpture I'd been working on and you said it looked prehistoric."

"That's hardly calling you a Neanderthal." She poured the wine, careful not to fill the glasses too high. She hadn't eaten much these last two days, and the last thing she needed was to have the alcohol go to her head. She set the bottle down and took a sip, enjoying the bright crispness of the wine and the warmth of Kyle's body beside her on the couch. She leaned back against the couch, feeling her shoulders relax for the first time in days.

"I'm sorry, though," she said, "if I discouraged you as an artist."

"You didn't."

"I'm sorry if Matt did, then." She winced as she heard her own words on instant replay in her head. She'd apologized for Matt plenty of times in their years together, but never to his brother.

And never when there was no chance of Matt doing it himself.

But Kyle didn't seem to react so she took a small sip of wine and continued. "I know he said some kind of lousy things about your work over the years," she said. "Creative differences, I guess."

"I guess," Kyle said. "Brotherly rivalry can be fierce enough without both guys working in artistic professions."

"Right," Meg said, plucking a cinnamon-dusted chip from the bowl. "Anyway, I hope I wasn't insulting. About the prehistoric piece or any other."

"You weren't. And that piece did kinda look like a drunk caveman chiseled it out of melted crayons."

"Well—"

"But it sold for twenty thou last summer, so I can't complain."

Meg dropped her chip. "Twenty thousand dollars?"

Kyle laughed and shoved a chip in his mouth. "Sorry. I don't usually throw dollar figures into conversation. That's me being an insecure prick who urgently wants his big brother's girl to know he's made it as an artist. No more couch surfing or begging my parents for loans."

"I'm happy for you." Meg set her wineglass down, her gut twisting a little on the big-brother's-girl comment, but she let it go. She caught a glimpse of movement from the corner of her eye and looked up to see Floyd sauntering back into the room. Her cat cast a wary glance at Kyle, then moseyed into the dining room where he leapt onto a barstool to keep a watchful eye over them.

"That's my first embarrassing confession, by the way," Kyle said.

"What? Oh." Meg bit her lip. "Are we really going to do this? I've already forgotten what I was thinking about in the kitchen."

"No, you haven't." Kyle stretched his arm out, and for a moment, Meg thought he was going to rest his hand on her thigh. Instead, he grabbed the chip she'd dropped and handed it back to her. "Let's see, confession number two. I didn't cry when Cara left me this past August or when I found out Matt died two days ago, but I did cry when I had to put Karma to sleep last fall, and I'm pretty sure that makes me the worst human being on the planet."

"Jesus." Meg swallowed hard, fighting the urge to reach out and touch his arm. "You're not the worst human on the planet. Not by a long shot."

"Thanks. You're wrong, but that's kind of you to say."

"She was a good dog," Meg said. "Karma, I mean. Not that Matt wasn't a good brother or Cara wasn't a good girlfriend, but—"

"I know."

Meg picked up her wineglass again, twisting the stem in her hand as she stared down into the pale liquid. "This won't make you feel any better, but I think I've cried enough for the both of us since yesterday. And then I think maybe *I'm* the worst human on the planet, because what the hell entitles me to react like some sort of grieving widow? For God's sake, I hadn't seen Matt for two years, and I'd barely stopped hating him, so I hardly—" she stopped as her brain caught up with the words coming out of her mouth. She looked up at Kyle. "I'm sorry. I shouldn't talk about hating him. Not now. Not with you sitting here in my living room."

Kyle reached out and caught her free hand in his, offering a quick squeeze before drawing his hand back. It was an innocent gesture, something comforting and friendly, but it sent an arc of heat up her arm just the same.

"It's okay."

Meg took a shaky breath, but said nothing. On the barstool just over her shoulder, Floyd gave a disdainful look and closed his eyes.

"You're entitled to feel sad," Kyle said. "Hell, you and Matt lived together almost ten years before you got married. Er, almost got married."

"Almost," Meg repeated.

"You earned whatever it is you're feeling, Meg. It's not like the rest of the family cornered the market on emotions."

She nodded. "On the same note, I think you need to go easy on yourself. Feeling sad doesn't always require tears."

"How about we both agree there's no right or wrong way to grieve and we cut ourselves some slack."

"Deal."

"Okay." Kyle took another sip of wine. "Third confession: I kept tabs on you the last couple years. Nothing really creepy—I mean, I didn't stalk you in public bathrooms or anything. But I wanted to make sure you were okay after the split."

"I was," Meg said softly. "Better than I expected to be."

"I know."

"It's how I knew I made the right choice. I was sad, obviously, and heartbroken. But I also felt like this huge weight had been lifted from my shoulders."

Kyle looked at her for a moment, and she waited for him to tell her Matt felt the same way. She braced herself for the sting of hearing the man she'd loved for ten years had walked away from the church that day feeling grateful to escape being shackled to her for life.

But Kyle said nothing, probably because he had more tact than she did.

"I'm glad you landed on your feet," he said finally. "You always were resilient."

"Thanks." Meg folded her legs under her, conscious of her knee brushing his on the sofa before she settled. "Wow, we've kind of moved on a bit from tortoise penises and clogged toilets."

"Maybe we're evolving."

"Is that what it is?"

"Or maybe I'm just nosy. Want to tell me what you were thinking in the kitchen, or do you want me to butt out?"

Meg bit her lip. "It's okay. Honestly, I didn't realize how often I censored myself until you brought it up."

Kyle rubbed the back of his hand over his chin, and the soft *scritch-scritch* sound was oddly soothing. "You don't have to tell me if you don't want to," he said. "I'm not trying to pry. Just thought you might like to get something off your chest."

"Maybe I would." Meg took a shaky breath. She couldn't tell him everything she'd been thinking about the cookbook and her bitterness over Matt's disinterest. She couldn't tell him about the silly argument they'd had later that night over how often bath towels should be washed, and she *really* couldn't tell him about the make-up sex that left her feeling cold and disconnected from the man she'd intended to marry.

She couldn't say any of that, but she settled for something close.

"I guess I was thinking about the cookbook. How I wish things had gone differently with that, and that people would have gotten to read all my delicious recipes or see Matt's beautiful photos. It would have been nice to have it out there in the world for more than just my mom and Jess to enjoy." She took a sip of wine and shrugged. "I know that's unrealistic. You're an artist. Obviously you're a lot more acquainted than I am with the fact that disappointment comes with the territory."

"It's a beautiful cookbook," Kyle said. "Truly."

"Thanks. You want to know a secret?"

He quirked an eyebrow at her. "How did I earn another confession?"

"By being a good listener."

"Yes," he said, smiling a little. "I want to know another secret."

Meg sighed. "I always kinda hoped that cookbook would be my big break. Like it might lead to more cookbooks and maybe even my own cooking show on television and maybe—" She stopped, not wanting to get carried away. "Well, it doesn't matter now. I'm happy being a caterer. And I'm glad I at least took a stab at chasing my dream, even if it didn't work out."

"Sometimes dreams run off in different directions when you chase them," he said. "Like herding cats."

They both looked at Floyd. Floyd gave a low growl and closed his eyes.

"Anyway," Kyle said. "I think you should be proud of the cookbook, even if it didn't sell like hotcakes."

"I never understood that expression. I've worked in retail and in a lot of restaurants, and hotcakes aren't really all that popular."

"What sells better?"

Meg shrugged. "Bacon. Chewing gum. Romance novels."

He laughed. "How about stuff like toothbrushes and toilet paper?"

"Sure. Or porn."

"Aren't they pretty much giving porn away on the internet these days?"

"True. Same's true for the cookbook. Help yourself if you want one. Take a couple. Maybe your parents would like one."

"I'll do that."

He didn't say anything again for a moment, and Meg wondered if they'd run out of things to discuss. When he finally did speak, his voice was low and soft. "I'm sorry."

"For what?"

"For what Matt did. With Annabelle, I mean."

"It's not your fault."

"Still." He cleared his throat. "I wish things had ended differently."

It struck her that he didn't say he wished things hadn't ended at all, but she let it pass. It wasn't like either of them were choosing their words very carefully right now.

She was suddenly very conscious of the fact that he sat close enough on the couch for their knees to touch. So close she could feel the warmth radiating from his forearm where it rested behind her on the sofa. So close she could hear his heartbeat if she leaned forward and rested her ear against his chest.

Stop thinking about that.

She should go check the pork. She set her wineglass down and stood up. Too fast. Swaying a little, she reached out and grabbed Kyle's shoulder.

His arms went around her waist to steady her, or maybe it was something else. Instinct? Maybe that's what she felt pulling her down onto his lap, or maybe it was gravity. She'd always been clumsy, and surely that's how she ended up sprawled across his thighs, his hands warm and solid on her back.

They sat there frozen for an instant, faces nearly touching. She was close enough to feel his breath. Close enough to lose herself in the ash-flecked green depths of his eyes. Close enough to lick his nose.

The giggle slipped out before she had a chance to catch it. Kyle pushed her hair off her face and studied her with a bemused look. "You okay?"

She shook her head. "Embarrassed. Clumsy. But okay otherwise."

"What's so funny?"

She reached for her ear, then stopped herself. Dammit anyway. "I was thinking about licking your nose."

Kyle raised an eyebrow. "Is that what you meant about grief making people do weird things?"

"Something like that."

He nodded. "You know what I did last night?"

"What?"

"Spent an hour on eBay looking for a record player so I could listen to a Kenny Rogers album I found in some of Matt's stuff."

"That's not so weird."

"I fucking hate Kenny Rogers."

Meg smiled. "You're right. That's weird. Know what I did?"

"What?"

"Spent ten minutes combing Floyd last night before I realized I was using my own toothbrush."

"Also weird. And a little unsanitary."

"I threw it away afterward."

"Good call." He blew out a breath that ruffled Meg's hair, his brow creasing a little the way it did when he was pondering something. "Okay then, I went to the store to get groceries this morning and got halfway through shopping before I realized I wasn't wearing shoes."

"No one stopped you?"

"Nope. Not even the produce guy I stopped to ask where I could find cantaloupe."

"I thought you hated cantaloupe."

"I do." He shifted a little, and Meg was suddenly very aware she was still sitting on his lap. "But Matt always liked it, and I wanted to give it another shot."

Meg smiled. "Definitely weird. But in a nice way."

"Thank you," he said. "You know what else might count as weird grief?"

"What?"

"Kissing you."

"Oh." She blinked, not totally sure she'd heard him right.

But the way he was watching her mouth told her she'd definitely heard right, and the way her body fizzed with desire told her she wanted the same damn thing.

She swallowed hard, not daring to breathe. Every molecule in her body screamed for him to do it. To make the tiny space disappear between their lips so she could know after all these years whether Kyle's were as soft as they looked. She took a breath, imagining she could already taste him. She watched as his gaze lifted to hers and his expression shifted to the one he got sometimes when she set a plate of her chocolate rum cake in front of him.

"That would definitely be weird," she murmured. "Kissing each other, I mean."

"Weird good or weird bad?"

"Yes?"

She didn't move. He was probably waiting for her to get off his lap or put her mouth on his or say something helpful like "kiss me" or "stop" or—

Beeeeeeeeeeeeeeeeeeeep!

Meg scrambled off his lap in a tangle of limbs and cinnamon chips and guilt, hurrying to put as much distance as possible between them as she ran for the kitchen. "The oven!" she shouted, though it was probably unnecessary. The man had surely heard an oven beep before.

But he'd never come that close to kissing her before.

And she'd never come that close to wanting him to.

♦　　♦　　♦

"That was amazing."

Kyle grimaced, wishing every other word out of his mouth didn't sound like he was thanking her for a blowjob. "Dinner, I mean," he clarified, which earned him a befuddled look from Meg.

He stood up from the table, bumping the fork off his plate and dropping his napkin on the floor while Meg watched from across the table. She stared at him like she was trying to figure out when he'd gone insane.

It was right about the time I almost kissed you.

He thought about the other time that same urge had seized him, though circumstances had been much different. What if he'd acted on it back then, kissing her senseless the way he'd desperately wanted to?

"I'm glad you enjoyed it."

"What?" It was Kyle's turn to stare.

"Dinner." She dabbed the corner of her mouth with a napkin and Kyle grabbed his plate to keep himself from grabbing her.

"Let me get the dishes." He reached for her plate before he realized it was still loaded with piping hot food. She gave him a funny look and took the plate back, then set it down and speared a piece of asparagus.

God, he was losing it.

He sat back down, ordering himself to breathe deeply. He had to stop looking at her. He glanced to the side and saw Floyd staring at him from the barstool. Floyd narrowed his eyes and gave a low growl.

"Kyle, it's okay," she said.

"No, it's not."

"I'm not talking about the dishes. Or the cat."

"Neither was I."

She stared at him a moment, then nodded. "Do you want to pretend it never happened? The kiss, I mean."

"Technically, it didn't happen."

Meg rolled her eyes. "Do you want to pretend it didn't *almost* happen? Blame it on grief or Viognier or the aphrodisiac qualities of cinnamon."

"Let's do that." Kyle folded his hands on the table, then unfolded them. He wanted to stand up and run out the door and he wanted to jump across the table to take Meg in his arms.

None of those seemed like a good idea at the moment.

He clenched his jaw, biting back the question he'd thought about asking her all evening. For three years, actually.

Do you remember that Thanksgiving when—

No. Now wasn't the time.

Meg took a sip of wine, then pushed back her chair and walked to the kitchen. She pulled two copies of her aphrodisiac cookbook off the shelf, then turned and walked back to the dining room. As Kyle stood up, she handed them to him.

"Here you go. I can tell you're ready to bolt from the house like it's on fire, and I don't want you to forget these."

He shook his head. "Sorry, Meg."

"I'm not. I got daisies and a great tip about a nervous habit I never knew I had."

"Then we'll go ahead and call it a win." He tucked the cookbooks under one arm and stuck out his hand to shake hers. "I think I'd better say goodnight."

She grabbed the hand and pulled him close, wrapping her arms around his middle. The squeeze she gave him was tight and warm and felt too damn good. "Don't be an idiot," she said. "We always hug goodbye, you big jerk."

The hug was so soft and familiar that Kyle dissolved into it, resting his chin on top of her head the way he used to. He breathed in the scent of her and tried to remember the last time he'd hugged her.

The day before the wedding. The day you ruined for everyone.

When Meg pulled away, he didn't know whether he felt more relieved or disappointed.

"Don't be a stranger," she said.

"Don't be an idiot, don't be a stranger—anything else you'd like to command me not to be?"

"Sorry. Stop being sorry." Meg smiled, then gave him a nudge toward the door. "Go on, get out of here. You said you're going to Bend tomorrow?"

"Yeah. Some Hollywood producer commissioned a piece for his vacation home there. I'm driving it over in the morning, making sure it gets set up right in the media room."

"Drive safely."

"I will." He turned and walked away, then hesitated at the door. "Thanks again for everything, Meg."

"Maybe we should keep in touch?"

Kyle nodded. "Maybe we should." He twisted the doorknob, not sure if that was the best idea in the world or the worst.

CHAPTER FIVE

"Nice work, son!" The famous TV producer whose name Kyle kept forgetting pumped his hand with surprising ferocity as they gazed up at the metal sculpture of a walrus holding an umbrella. It wasn't the weirdest piece Kyle had ever been commissioned for, but it was damn close.

"I'm glad you like it." Kyle stared at the sculpture, since that seemed more tactful than staring at the mole on the guy's temple that looked vaguely like an avocado.

"It's perfect there next to the window, don't you think?" The producer gazed up at it with such a reverent expression, Kyle couldn't help but feel proud.

"Absolutely. I designed it with all this natural light in mind."

"You know, I'd love to have something for my place in Pacific Palisades."

"I'd be happy to work with you again," Kyle said. "I'm a little booked up at the moment, but why don't we chat next week? Maybe look at some photos of the space, talk about what you're envisioning."

"I don't suppose you've got anything that's already finished?"

Kyle wiped a dust rag over one of the walrus's tusks, then tucked the rag in the back pocket of his jeans. "Sure, there are plenty of things in my gallery. I think I have my portfolio out in the truck. Got a few finished pieces in there you could take a look at. Want me to go to grab it?"

"I'll follow you out there. I could use some fresh air."

They trudged together through several long hallways that were the approximate size of Kyle's entire house. Kyle followed close behind, trying to remember the guy's name. Emeril? Edmond?

Emmett, that was it. Emmett Ashton. He'd have to remember that when he told Meg about this later. She'd always been thrilled by celebrity gossip.

The thought of seeing Meg again filled him with something warm and liquid, like sipping Scotch in a hot tub. He'd spent the whole drive out here thinking about kissing her, about what might've happened if the damn oven hadn't beeped. The fantasy had been a welcome distraction from thoughts about his brother. What would Matt think if he knew Kyle was having illicit thoughts about Meg?

At least she's not his fiancée anymore. It would have been worse if he'd known it when she was.

But now Matt was dead, and Kyle would never have to worry again that his brother would peer into his ear and see all those shameful thoughts huddled in his brain. Thinking of Matt made his throat feel achy and he closed his eyes for a moment to make them stop stinging.

He opened them again as Emmett led them through the slate entryway and out into the bright sage-scented sunshine. Kyle breathed deeply, amazed by the difference the 170 miles made between Portland and Bend. The air was drier here in the desert, and the towering basalt cliffs of Smith Rock jutted like orange-red claws on the horizon.

Kyle popped the door on his truck, wishing he'd had the foresight to get rid of all the McDonald's wrappers and vacuum the dog fur off the seat. He shoved a Coke can onto the floor and grabbed a leather-bound book from under an old flannel shirt. He flipped it open and held it out so Emmett could see.

"These are photos of some of my finished pieces." He pointed to one on the first page. "This one's currently in a gallery in Portland, but the show is up next month. It's called Shadow Dance."

"Nice. Great lines. I really love the copper running through there. How big is it?"

"About thirty-six inches from pedestal to the tip of the wing."

"I'm looking for something a little bigger."

Kyle nodded and thumbed through the pages until he reached the middle of the book. He turned it back around and held it out, pointing to a piece he'd finished a few months ago. "This one in the bottom right corner is nearly eight feet tall. There's a collector in New Mexico who's been asking about it, but it's not sold yet."

"Very nice. I'm not sure my wife would go for it. That's a little too big." He frowned, then pointed to a photo in the top right corner. "How about this one?"

Kyle felt the air leave his lungs. He swallowed hard, resisting the urge to shove the guy's finger off the page.

"I don't think so."

"No? It looks like it's about the right size, and it's a gorgeous interpretation of the female form. All those curves and flowing lines and—"

"That one's not for sale."

Emmett gave him a look. "Everything's for sale for the right price."

"Not that one."

He stared at Kyle a moment, then cocked his head to the side and gave him an appraising look. "I'd pay double your asking price, whatever it is."

Kyle closed the book and set it back on the seat. "Why don't I just email you a few images of some of my other pieces? That might be easier. I'll make sure to include all the measurements so you know how the piece might fit into your space."

Emmett seemed to pause for a moment, then nodded. "Fair enough."

Kyle stuck his hand out. "Thank you, sir, for the work."

"Don't mention it. Thank *you*, for driving all the way out here. Especially so soon after your brother passed."

"I needed the distraction," he said. "The alone time."

"I remember that," he said, leaning back against Kyle's truck. "I lost my brother ten years ago. Did I tell you that?"

"No, sir."

"Killed by a drunk driver."

"I'm sorry."

"The hell of it was that we hadn't talked for almost a year." Emmett raked a hand through his hair. "He'd gotten pissed at me about something I don't even remember now. Anyway, took me a long time to stop beating myself up for that."

"I think I'm a long way from that," Kyle said, not sure why he felt compelled to share with a stranger. "From getting over the regret, I mean."

His thoughts drifted back to that dark time after the canceled wedding. He remembered the acrid taste of fear when Matt wouldn't get out of bed for a week. When he wouldn't eat or shower or even talk about what happened. If Kyle hadn't dragged him to the doctor, if the doctor hadn't understood the gravity of clinical depression—

"You never really get over it," Emmett said, jarring Kyle back to the present. "You just figure out how to live with all the little regrets poking at your guts like needles and leaving you all sore on the inside."

Kyle nodded, not able to formulate a response with his own collection of needles stabbing into his spleen.

"Anyway," Emmett said, "You'll get there eventually. I can promise you that."

"Thank you, sir."

The producer looked at him. "The name's Emmett. You can call me that, you know. You don't have to call me sir."

"Thank you, Emmett."

He grinned. "You know, I have a lot of friends who are really into art. Why don't you give me a few more business cards so I can hand them out?"

"I appreciate that."

Kyle shoved the portfolio back in his truck and started digging for the box of cards he kept somewhere in here. Maybe under the tool belt or beneath the old shopping bag or—

He bumped something off the seat, sending a book tumbling out the door. Emmett reached out and caught the spine in one hand.

"Got it!" He turned the book over, flipping it face up so he could see the cover. *The Food You Love: An Aphrodisiac Cookbook*. Meg's cookbook. Kyle started to reach for it, but Emmett had already opened to the first page.

"An aphrodisiac cookbook? Hoo, boy—my wife would go nuts for this. She's always researching libido-boosting food and checking out new recipes." He flipped to the next page, whistling under his breath as he traced a finger over one of Matt's pictures. "You order this on Amazon? I should get one for her."

"Actually, a friend of mine wrote it," he said. "And my brother took the photos."

"No kidding? Kiki would love this. Our anniversary's coming up."

Kyle hesitated. "Why don't you go ahead and keep it?"

"You sure?"

"Yeah." He nodded. "I know where I can get more. It's the least I can do after all the business you're giving me."

The producer laughed and flipped the book closed. "Is this my consolation prize for that piece you won't sell me?"

"Yep."

"Kiki's gonna freak out over this." He tucked the book under one arm and clapped Kyle on the shoulder. "You sure you won't take me up on a couple nights in the guesthouse? It's awfully nice out here."

"I'd love to, but I've gotta get home to my family. You know how it is."

"I do. Which is why I can imagine it might feel good to get away for a little bit right now."

Kyle nodded and pulled out his keys. "Thanks, but I should pass."

He might have felt okay taking off for a day, but overnight? No way should he leave his parents alone to deal with all the sorting and planning and going through Matt's things. When he'd stopped by this morning to check on his mom, she'd been staring at her coffee mug with a blank expression. He'd reached out to top it off for her before realizing it was filled to the brim.

"Matt gave it to me for my birthday three years ago," she'd murmured, turning it around so he could see the lettering on the front.

Coffee makes me poop.

The thought of Matt choosing it for her made him smile almost as much as the realization that she'd kept it. He'd bent down and kissed her on the cheek, breathing in the familiar scent of expensive cosmetics. His dad had walked in then, looking ten years older than he had a month ago. He'd given Kyle a weak smile and rested a hand on Sylvia's shoulder.

"You'd better get going, son. It's a long drive."

Still. Maybe he should have postponed. What kind of jerk was he for driving out here today and leaving them to tend to that stuff on their own?

The kind of jerk who almost kisses his brother's fiancée.

"Ex-fiancée."

"What?"

"Nothing," Kyle said, reaching out to shake the man's hand. "I'll be in touch. Enjoy the sculpture."

♦ ♦ ♦

Meg handed Jess a blue and white flowered bowl filled with popcorn, then dropped onto the sofa beside her. She tucked her legs up under her butt and reached behind her to scratch Floyd under the chin. The cat gave a soft purr from his perch on the back of the sofa and stretched his paws out in front of him.

"This is what I love about coming here," Jess said, shoving a fistful of popcorn in her mouth.

"The pleasure of my company?"

"That, too, obviously. But also that you don't just shove a bag of chemical-laden crap in the microwave and call it popcorn. What is this, anyway?"

"That one's drizzled with rosemary-infused olive oil and dusted with truffle salt," Meg said. "The one we had earlier was popped in bacon grease and laced with chives and bacon crumbles."

Jess grinned and shoved another handful of popcorn in her mouth. "If there's anything better than having a caterer for a best friend, I don't know what it is."

"How about a really wealthy best friend who likes to shower all her pals with cash?"

Jess snorted and chewed her popcorn. "Can't help you there. I take it you're still stressed about getting the money for Matt's parents?"

Meg shrugged. "I'm working on it. I'm pretty close. I have a job in three days for a charity event that should have about three hundred guests. If I take the check from that and call the lender for my student loan to ask for just a few extra weeks—"

"This is bullshit."

Meg sighed. "Don't start."

"Come on, I was sitting right there in your living room when Matt offered to take those stupid cookbook photos. He said, and I quote, 'You can pay me in blowjobs, babe.' Didn't he even write it on a napkin?"

"Ew." Meg made a face. "We were all tipsy that night. How do you remember that?"

"I was scarred for life by the visual. I just remember he was a royal prick about it. Very condescending."

"It was a long time ago," Meg said for lack of anything better to offer.

"Not really. You guys were only a few months from the wedding at that point, weren't you?"

"We both had a lot on our minds."

"You mean like how to bone someone else before walking down the aisle?" Jess shoved another handful of popcorn in her mouth. "Sorry, I didn't mean to sound harsh," she puffed around the kernels. "But seriously, what in the world would possess him to stick his dick in another woman when he had a beautiful, willing partner at home?"

"I have no idea." Meg poked a finger into the popcorn bowl, not willing to admit how often she'd wondered the same damn thing. Not willing to admit how often she'd wondered if she'd done something to drive him to want to sleep with someone else.

Deep down, didn't that cross the mind of every woman whose man found himself in another woman's bed?

Floyd stood up and stretched, then dropped down onto the couch beside Meg. He cast a disdainful look at Jess, then bumped the bottom of the popcorn bowl with his head.

"Cut it out, asshole cat," Jess muttered.

Floyd responded by purring and rubbing his mouth on Jess's arm, leaving a streak of drool across her wrist.

"I swear you have the weirdest cat on the planet," Jess muttered. "He only likes people who insult him."

"Which explains why he loves you," Meg said, scooping up her indignant feline and rubbing behind his ears. Floyd growled and struggled to get down, so Meg set him on the ground at her feet. He gave a plaintive meow and twined himself around Jess's ankles a few times before jumping back on the couch. He stomped across their laps and headed for the far end of the sofa where he curled up and fell asleep.

Jess picked up the remote and aimed it at Meg's television. "You want to watch another episode?"

Meg shrugged and stroked a hand down Floyd's back. "I'm kinda burned out on all the kissing. Let's watch something else."

"You? Burned out on kissing? This is a first."

Meg reached up and touched her earlobe, then thought of Kyle. She felt her face flush with heat and she dropped her hand to her lap feeling a weird mix of guilt and desire.

"What?" Jess said, watching her face. "What is it?"

Meg bit her lip. "I almost kissed Kyle last night."

Jess blinked at her. "You did?"

"Or he almost kissed me. I'm not really sure. It all happened so fast."

"Why did you stop?"

"I'd like to say it was because we both realized it was a stupid idea and we were channeling our grief in an unhealthy way." Meg frowned. "In reality, the oven beeped."

Jess looked thoughtful as she scooped up another handful of popcorn and chewed. "Why is it stupid?"

Meg rolled her eyes. "Um, because I spent ten years in a relationship with his brother?"

"At least you already know the family."

"The family hates me. Besides, nothing really happened. Thank God." She hesitated, rolling an unpopped kernel between her fingers. "There was this other time about three years ago, actually."

"What?" Jess gaped. "You kissed Kyle three years ago?"

"No! Absolutely not. Not even close."

"Then what?"

"It's nothing," Meg said, wondering why she'd even brought it up. "We were out for a walk and I saw this dead dove on the ground and a living one on a wire overhead, and I know they mate for life and—" she stopped, surprised to feel her eyes welling after all this time. "Anyway,

I kept thinking about it all evening and getting choked up, so I ducked into the den so no one would notice."

"Kyle noticed."

Meg nodded. *Kyle, not Matt.* She didn't need to ask how Jess had guessed, and knew her friend understood it was about more than just a dead bird.

"Yes," she said, clearing her throat. "Kyle noticed, and he came back to check on me."

"Did something happen?"

"No. Not exactly."

Meg shook her head, remembering the way he'd stepped into the room smelling like cloves and firewood, his gray-green eyes glinting in the amber light from the desk lamp.

"I googled it," he'd told her, his voice soft and urgent. *"You're right about the doves. They mate for life."*

Meg had nodded, not wanting to say anything for fear of bawling like a stupid baby.

"But the thing is," Kyle had continued, *"if something happens to one of them, they almost always re-partner."*

A lump had risen in Meg's throat, and the tears inched closer to the corners of her eyes. She'd glanced toward the door, but the clatter of dishes in the kitchen and the blare of football-fueled shouting in the family room told her the rest of Matt's family was nowhere near.

She'd turned back to Kyle, startled to realize how close he was. *"Thank you,"* she'd whispered, not needing to say anything else.

He looked at her then—really *looked* at her. The first time anyone had done that for a long time. Neither of them said a single word, but their gazes seemed frozen together like a tongue on a metal flagpole. They were still at least a foot apart, but it was the closest she'd felt to anyone for years.

Maybe ever.

"Nothing happened," she told Jess now, her voice firm enough to jar her back to the present. "There was this—connection, I guess. But we didn't even hug. He did touch my elbow."

"Your elbow?" Jess gave a mock gasp, pretending to be scandalized.

Meg smiled and looked down at her lap. How could she explain that with that single, half-second touch, he'd left her feeling more unraveled than she'd ever felt before?

She looked up again to see Jess studying her. "You think he wanted to kiss you? Or you wanted to kiss him?"

Meg dropped the popcorn kernel back in the bowl, not willing to answer either question. "I never would have let that happen. Seeing how infidelity shaped my parents' relationship—it's not a line I'd ever cross."

"Not like Matt did."

"Not like Matt did," Meg repeated, feeling hollow. "Anyway, it's possible the connection with Kyle was all in my head. He moved to Montana a week later, and I was so busy with wedding planning that I put it out of my head. I really hadn't thought about it until last night."

Jess nodded, looking thoughtful as she grabbed more popcorn. "I always liked Kyle. I wish he *had* kissed you. Last night, I mean."

"Not a good idea." Meg shook her head. "Can you even imagine?"

Jess shrugged. "I'm not sure it would be the weirdest thing in the world."

"No? Look at the underside of the popcorn bowl."

"What?"

"The bowl you're holding. Look at the bottom of it."

Jess frowned, then raised the bowl overhead and peered at it. "*M* plus *M* equals butt cheeks?"

"It's supposed to be a heart," Meg said. "My grandmother painted it before she died, which is why I can't get rid of it despite the fact that it's really damn creepy to eat popcorn out of a bowl with my dead ex's initial on it."

"Your initial is there, too," Jess pointed out as she lowered the bowl.

"I'm just saying. There's too much baggage there with me and Kyle. No matter what, we'd never escape all the ghosts of that other relationship."

Jess shrugged and drained her wineglass. "I disagree."

"No, it's true. There's no way around the fact that I was engaged to his brother."

"Of course. I'm just saying that it's not insurmountable."

"It is," Meg insisted.

"It's *not*," Jess replied. "But I'd rather watch that cupcake show than argue with you. What channel is it on?"

"Not a clue." Meg stood up and grabbed the empty wine bottle as she headed toward the kitchen. "You want to stick with Pinot Grigio, or do you want something else?"

"You don't have any red open, do you?"

"Half a bottle of Chianti from when I made lasagna a few days ago." She picked the bottle up off the kitchen counter and studied it. "It's probably still good. That was the night before Matt died, actually."

Meg thought about the lasagna, remembering how she'd carefully layered the cheese and sausage and noodles and sauce while rehearsing in her mind what she'd say to Matt at the hospital the next day.

Look, I know we both did some things we regret, but I wanted to tell you I'm sorry and that I'd like to put it all behind us and maybe even work toward renewing our friendship if—

"Meg!" Jess shouted. "Get in here now!"

"What?"

"Hurry!"

Meg felt her pulse speed up and she started back toward the living room with the Chianti bottle still clutched in her hand. "Did you spill the popcorn? It's okay, just—"

"No, right now, come here!"

The volume on the television slid to a deafening level and Meg sprinted out to see Jess aiming the remote at the screen with a wide-eyed look on her face.

". . . So, yeah," the blonde actress was saying as she crossed her legs saucily. She leaned into Jimmy Fallon's desk, making her sequined gown twinkle. "I've already made three recipes from this book and I have to tell you, I've never felt so—"

"Horny?" Jimmy Fallon flashed a salacious grin at the audience, who responded with applause and loud whoops of encouragement.

"Oh, stop!" The actress gave Jimmy a playful swat, flashing a wedding ring that could have doubled as a paperweight. "I'm not kidding, I can't believe this aphrodisiac stuff works, but if you read the little sidebars—"

"That's my book," Meg said, dumbfounded.

"No shit, Sherlock," Jess said.

"My book is on *The Tonight Show*." She gripped the back of the sofa, not believing her own eyes.

"It would appear that way."

"How did Kiki-Fucking-Corso get my book?"

"I have no idea. Can't anyone order it on Amazon?"

"Well, yeah, but no one has. I've had the link up there for almost three years and I've sold less than a dozen of them. None in the last year. How did the most famous actress in the universe get my—"

"So, Kiki," Jimmy said, and Meg stopped talking. "Are you the new pitchwoman for this book or something?"

"Of course not," she said, tossing her trademark blond tresses. "I'm just enjoying the benefits of it, and also really loving the little details. You know, the character I play in my new movie is a chef, so I've been reading everything I can get my hands on and—"

Kiki continued prattling on about her new movie, but Meg stood staring at the cover of her cookbook perched on the edge of the host's desk.

"I don't understand," Meg said.

Jess picked up her phone and hit a button. "Siri, how many viewers does *The Tonight Show* have?"

Meg swallowed hard as Jess stared at the screen of her iPhone. She held it up, though Meg couldn't possibly see anything from this distance. "Four-point-five million. Four-point-five million people just saw Kiki Corso recommend your cookbook."

"I have to sit down."

Meg felt her knees start to buckle, but she gripped the edge of the couch tighter to keep herself upright. Somewhere in her hazy peripheral vision, she saw Jess stand up and set the popcorn bowl on the coffee table and walk around the sofa to Meg's side, but Meg's eyes were still glued to the screen.

"Are you okay?" Jess grabbed the wine bottle from her hand, and Meg looked down to see she'd spilled some on the floor.

"I'll get that," Jess said, hustling into the kitchen to grab a rag as *The Tonight Show* faded to a commercial. "Why don't you go sit on the sofa and let me wait on you?"

"What?" Meg blinked and looked away from the television, her gaze shifting to her best friend. "What the hell for?"

"You're about to be famous, hon." Jess grinned. "I want to be the one who poured you your first glass of champagne."

CHAPTER SIX

Kyle glanced at his watch, wondering if it was too late to drop by Meg's house on a Monday night. He'd tried to call at least a dozen times over the last week, but her phone went straight to voicemail. At first he'd figured she was screening his calls, maybe avoiding him after the disastrous kiss-that-wasn't-actually-a-kiss incident.

He didn't blame her.

But when her phone started giving him the *mailbox is full* message, he'd started to worry. Dropping by her house unannounced was probably a dumb idea, but so were a lot of things he'd done when it came to Meg.

He pressed the doorbell and glanced at his watch again, realizing this was the third time he'd looked at it in the last five minutes and he still had no idea what time it was. Nine p.m. What if she was out on a date? What if she was already in bed? What if she—

"Kyle."

Her voice washed over him like a warm wave, and he looked up to see her standing in the open doorway.

He swallowed, taken aback by the sight of her. Something had changed in the ten days since he stood here last. Her hair was even wilder than usual, piled in a frizzy ball on top of her head and anchored by something that looked like a chewed-up pen. Her feet were bare as usual, but her eyes looked oddly frantic, and was her T-shirt on inside out?

"I'm sorry, were you on the phone?" He gestured at the iPhone in her hand, and Meg looked down at it like she'd never seen it before.

"God, the phone hasn't stopped ringing all week. All day, all night—then there's the email and the Facebook messages and the hits to that silly blog I haven't updated for three years and—"

"What are you talking about?"

Meg cocked her head to one side. "Haven't you heard?" She gave a wry little laugh and shook her head. "Sorry, why would you? Just because I've been bombarded by this stuff for a week straight doesn't mean the rest of the world has."

He stared at her, trying to figure out what the hell she was talking about. "Does this have something to do with Matt?"

Her throat moved as she swallowed, and he watched her fingers clench tighter around the iPhone. "I guess it does." She pushed the door open wider with her knee. "Why don't you come in. Unless you're on your way somewhere?"

He shook his head and stepped into the entry, his shoulder brushing hers as he moved past. She turned and trudged toward the kitchen, leaving him to shut the door behind him and make his way into the living room as Meg banged and clattered in the kitchen.

Kyle looked at the paisley armchair where Floyd was curled up napping. As though sensing Kyle's gaze on him, Floyd opened one eye and gave him a disdainful look.

"Hey, pretty kitty." Kyle walked around the chair and reached out to scratch behind the cat's ear.

Floyd hissed.

Kyle drew his hand back. "Sorry, man."

Floyd growled and closed his eyes again, while Kyle stood watching him. "You're kind of a jerk, aren't you?"

The cat opened both eyes and looked at him a moment, then began to purr. It was a low, soothing sound that made Kyle feel warm all over, so he reached out again and stroked a hand down the cat's back.

Floyd stopped purring and growled.

Kyle drew his hand back. "Asshole cat."

Floyd resumed purring.

Kyle shook his head and glanced toward the kitchen. "Your cat is insane," he called.

Meg emerged carrying two bottles of beer and a tray loaded with fancy-looking meats and cheeses. "I like to think of him as special."

"I guess you could say that." Kyle shook his head and turned his attention from the cat to the piles of cheese and salami and prosciutto and crackers Meg set on the coffee table. "How do you do that?"

"Do what?"

"Whip up the perfect hors d'oeuvres plate no matter what time an unexpected guest drops by?"

She smiled in answer and dropped onto the couch. Kyle took it as his cue to do the same, though he kept a safe distance between them this time. No more near-miss kisses. No more touching or fantasizing or thinking illicit thoughts about his brother's girl.

Meg lifted her beer bottle to her mouth and he watched her throat move as she swallowed, then followed her hand as she rested the bottle on her knee. Kyle set his own bottle on the coffee table, waiting. The air felt prickly with tension, and he stared at Meg hoping she'd volunteer the reason for it.

"So you haven't heard about the book?" she asked.

"What book?"

"My cookbook. The aphrodisiac cookbook was on *The Tonight Show*, and everything's gone crazy since then."

"*The Tonight Show*?"

"Yeah, Kiki Corso got a copy somehow and started talking about it during her appearance, and the next thing I know, I've sold a gazillion copies. The print-on-demand place I was using can't print them fast enough, so this publisher offered some ridiculous amount for exclusive distribution rights, and all these literary agents started calling me about—"

"Wait—who's Kiki Corso?"

"She's an actress." She looked at him like he'd just admitted to eating dog kibble for lunch, and it occurred to him that he probably ought to be more aware of pop culture.

"Only the hottest actress in Hollywood right now," Meg continued. "I'm pretty sure you're the only man in America who doesn't have her in the starting lineup of his spank-bank."

"I don't watch TV. Or movies. Or—" he stopped himself as it dawned on him he was probably missing the point. "Who's Kiki Corso married to?"

Meg's brow furrowed, and she took another sip of beer. "I'm not sure. I think she divorced the drummer for that rock band a couple years ago, but then she married a director or a producer or—"

"A TV producer? One with a mole that looks like an avocado?"

Meg looked at him like he had aardvarks crawling out of his ears. "I have no idea."

Kyle stared, trying to make sense of it all. "He bought one of my sculptures. I gave him that cookbook."

"You—oh my God, Kyle!" She threw her arms around his neck so fast he lost his breath, or maybe that wasn't the reason. She was practically in his lap, and it reminded him of the last time they'd been situated like that on this same couch. He knew he shouldn't get carried away, but her hair smelled flowery and fragrant and her body was lush and warm against him and he wasn't entirely sure he remembered his own phone number, let alone the reasons he shouldn't give in to temptation and kiss her while her mouth was this close to his.

Your brother's wife. Ex-wife. Ex-fian—whatever.

Meg drew back while he was still puzzling it out. "You're the reason," she said. "I've been trying all week to figure out how my cookbook suddenly went from being a little no-name, print-on-demand project to being an international bestseller."

"Are you kidding me?"

"No, that's what I've been trying to tell you. I'm famous, Kyle. That cookbook is the hottest thing since *Fifty Shades of Grey*."

"That's a book or a movie or something, right?"

"Yes." She rolled her eyes and gave him a punch in the shoulder. "Jeez, you really do live under a rock."

He shook his head, still trying to digest her news about the book. "So your book is famous?"

"Can you believe it?"

"Congratulations, Meg. You deserve it." He wanted to hug her again, but he shoved his hands under his ass to resist temptation. Then he remembered that made it damn hard to drink his beer, so he slid one hand out and reached for it. He took a few big gulps, hoping to cool his libido in the process.

"Thanks," she said. "I'm still sort of in shock. I guess now I know the meaning of the phrase *overnight success*."

"That's a funny way to describe a book that's been out in the world for three years."

She laughed and reached for a piece of salami. "Good point."

"So what happens next?"

"I'm not sure. It's all happening so fast. I talked to a lawyer and I got a literary agent and she's already got some sort of bidding war going on over the rights for this book and another one I've been thinking about doing. Everything's been crazy the last few days and I haven't had a chance to eat or sleep or—" she stopped, sniffing under her arm. "God, I stink. I need a shower."

Kyle felt a little dizzy at the thought of Meg wet and naked with water sluicing down her bare arms and soap between her—

"I'm happy for you, Meg." He took a deep breath and another swig of beer. "I really am."

"Thank you." She sipped her beer, then set the bottle on the table and looked at him oddly. He watched her left hand rise, and he reached out and caught her wrist before she made it all the way to her ear.

"Confession number one," he said, not letting go of her hand. "I felt bad giving your cookbook away to my client, but I knew I'd never give that second copy to my parents because they'd just get pissed. I wasn't planning to tell you about it."

"You're forgiven."

Kyle smiled, glad to see she didn't seem hurt. "Confession number two: In addition to being completely ignorant about TV and movies, I don't understand anything about publishing. Doesn't it usually take a long time for a book to become a bestseller?"

"Usually, yes. But this is a fluke thing. I guess it happens sometimes with celebrity endorsements. Pippa Middleton wears a new scarf or J. Lo buys a certain brand of quinoa and suddenly everyone has to have it."

"I have no idea who Pippa Middleton, J. Lo, and Quinoa are, but the rest of that sounds good."

Meg laughed and Kyle ached to lean closer and capture those beautiful lips with his. "Confession number three," he said. "I know we agreed to forget the kiss didn't happen—"

"Almost happen."

"And I know we agreed it would have been a bad idea—"

"A terrible idea."

"But I drove three hours to Bend and three hours home last Friday and I'm pretty sure I spent the entire time imagining what that kiss would have been like."

Meg stopped laughing, and he watched her fingers tighten around the beer bottle. "How was it?"

"Pretty amazing."

She licked her lips. "I'm happy our imaginary kiss was everything you hoped it would be."

"All the more reason it can never happen," he said. "It's been built up too much."

"Probably true. Kind of a shame we'll never get to find out."

"Agreed," Kyle said, wishing that weren't true. "But if kissing your brother's fiancée—ex or otherwise—is off-limits, kissing your dead brother's fiancée ranks somewhere between pedophilia and eating the last donut on the list of moral crimes."

"Sounds like a pretty broad range." Meg sighed. "You're right, though. Obviously, it can never happen."

"Right," Kyle said, working like hell to project indifference instead of the grim disappointment that threatened to grab him by the throat. "So what was your thing? What were you thinking when you tugged your ear?"

She looked down at her lap and he watched her pick at the edge of the label on her beer bottle. "I was thinking I wish Matt had gotten to see the cookbook take off."

Kyle nodded, wishing he'd never brought up the kissing thing in the first place. For crying out loud, the primary link between him and Meg was his own brother. The least he could do was refrain from ogling her.

"That's nothing to be ashamed of," Kyle said. "Why wouldn't you want to say it out loud that you wish he'd gotten to see it?"

Meg shrugged, still looking at the bottle. "Because I didn't think it for the right reasons. I wanted him to see it so he'd know I could be a success and that I was right and he was wrong. And it's pretty shitty to want to one-up a dead guy."

Kyle shook his head. "He would have been happy for you."

"I doubt that."

"It's true. We didn't talk about you much. Not after—" he cleared his throat. "Not after the wedding. And yeah, he had a rough go of it at first."

"He was pretty pissed?"

"Yes," Kyle said cautiously, not willing to break his brother's trust and admit Matt's emotional state had gone well beyond *pissed*. "He got over it, though," Kyle added. "I think he'd moved on."

"You think he'd forgiven me?"

"I like to think so."

"Me, too." She looked up, and he felt relieved to see there were no tears in her eyes. Unfortunately, what he was about to say might change that.

Kyle cleared his throat. "Speaking of Matt, that's part of the reason I stopped by tonight."

Meg blinked. "Oh. I never thought to ask. I just started blathering about my cookbook and never gave you the chance to get a word in edgewise. I'm sorry."

"It's okay. I wanted to tell you about Matt's memorial service."

He watched the color drain from her face, and he hurried to fill the silence that followed. "You don't have to go. No one's expecting you to, and under the circumstances—"

"Do your parents know you're inviting me?"

"Yes."

"Are they okay with it?"

He nodded, and watched a flicker of relief in her eyes. "We were going through old photos last weekend and my mom pointed out how many of the shots had you in them. 'She was part of his life for a long time.' That's what she said."

"That's sweet."

"When I told her yesterday I'd like to invite you to the service, she said, 'I think that's a nice gesture. I have some things for her.' Probably some of the pictures. Anyway, she'd like to see you there. We all would."

"Thank you." She swallowed, and he noticed her eyes had gone glittery. "I figured I'd already missed the funeral. It's been almost two weeks, so I just assumed it already happened."

Kyle shook his head. "My mom wanted to wait. Give more family members a chance to fly in. It's more of a memorial service than a funeral."

"Oh." She nodded and plucked at a loose thread on one of the throw pillows. "When is it?"

"Saturday afternoon. It's at the Presbyterian church in Tigard at two p.m. We'll have a short service and then walk across the street to Salvador's Brewhouse where we've reserved this huge reception area—" he stopped himself, shaking his head. "God, I'm describing it like it's a social event."

"That's how he would have wanted it." Meg offered a small smile, and Kyle realized it was true.

"You're right. Matt would have wanted it to be the event of the season."

"Thank you for inviting me."

"Will you come?"

"Do you think I should?"

"Yes. So do you think you will?"

She seemed to hesitate, then nodded. Her eyes locked with his and then she said the two words Kyle had spent her whole engagement guiltily hoping she wouldn't utter.

"I do."

CHAPTER SEVEN

Jess squeezed Meg's hand so hard she thought she heard the bones crack. The pain was oddly comforting, and Meg squeezed back as the final notes of "Somewhere Over the Rainbow" echoed through the church.

Meg looked around, wondering if the song was from the CD Matt bought when they vacationed in Hawaii seven years ago. She remembered him buying a ukulele in a gift shop and pretending to serenade her on the balcony of their hotel. He'd hammed it up wearing boxer shorts and a lei made of plastic flowers, making Meg laugh until she snorted mai tai out her nose.

"It's almost over, hon," Jess whispered, handing Meg another tissue. "You've got this."

Meg nodded and wiped her nose, her gaze drifting to the front row of seats. Kyle sat holding his mother's hand, his head bowed low. She couldn't see his face, and she wondered if he'd mustered up the tears he'd been so worried about.

Next to Kyle sat his father. Robert's shoulders were rigid and his navy suit jacket looked like the same one she remembered him wearing at his fortieth anniversary party with Sylvia. A fresh wave of memories hit her, and Meg tore her gaze off the family.

"Thank you for coming with me," she whispered to Jess.

"No problem," Jess whispered back as their fellow mourners began to rise. "You came with me for my first Brazilian wax. It's a similar level of discomfort, with the bonus of not getting stuck to the seat afterward."

"Ew," Meg whispered back, trying not to smile. The last thing she needed was to be caught grinning like an idiot at her ex's funeral.

The other mourners were shuffling toward the door now, so Meg stood up. Her legs were shaky like she'd just done a barre class, and she stuffed her crumpled tissue in her purse. Kyle and his family were making their way up the aisle, shaking hands and thanking people for attending. Meg watched, heart frozen in her chest, as he drew closer.

"Meg," he said softly, his hand enveloping hers as his gaze settled on her face. His eyes were clear and bright, but not tear-filled. "Thank you for coming."

"Thank you for inviting me," she murmured as he released her hand. She turned to Sylvia, who gave her a stiff nod of acknowledgement.

"I'm so very sorry for your loss," Meg whispered.

Sylvia nodded again and grabbed Robert's arm. "Thank you."

They moved past her, Sylvia's platinum-blond hair glowing orange and blue in the sunlight that streamed through the stained-glass window. A pretty brunette with shoulder-length curls hustled forward and fell into step beside Sylvia, touching her arm, and Meg tried to remember if she was a cousin or one of Matt's college friends. Maybe she was someone Matt dated after her, the woman whose voice Meg had heard at the hospital that day.

More people drifted past, their faces blending into a blurry sea. Jess grabbed Meg's elbow. "You still up for the reception?"

Meg nodded. "Yes. At least it's in a bar. Matt would have liked that."

"Somewhere out there he's already lifting a pint."

They slipped into the ocean of bodies and Meg bobbed along murmuring words she hoped sounded comforting to family members she barely remembered meeting. When they finally reached the door, Meg stepped outside and gulped a huge lungful of air, grateful to be free from the press of bodies and the threat of contagious tears.

The afternoon light was thick and eerie, filtered through clouds that couldn't decide whether to be yellow or gray. It had been drizzling when they first arrived, but the rain had stopped and now puddles lurked everywhere like muddy landmines. She started across the street, tiptoeing around one puddle, then the next. She dodged sideways and felt herself starting to topple, but Jess grabbed her.

"Damn high heels," Meg muttered.

"Hon, you'd trip barefoot on a gymnasium floor."

"Been there, done that."

"Seventh grade gymnastics?"

"And the sock hop dance our freshman year. And that basketball game in college when we all rushed the floor and I lost my flip-flops under the bleachers."

"You're hopeless," Jess said as she pushed open the door to the reception hall. "Please, dear God, let there be readily available alcohol."

"It's a bar. I'm guessing there's alcohol."

"Right, but I need to be able to obtain some in under five minutes."

They both surveyed the room, Jess looking for the bar and Meg looking for—*not Kyle*. She ordered herself not to think of him as she let her gaze travel from face to face, giving nods of acknowledgment to people she wasn't certain she'd met before.

"Bingo," Jess said, and Meg turned to see her pointing toward a bar in the far corner.

"I don't need anything," Meg said, but Jess was already trotting off in that direction, probably with vodka cranberry on the brain. Just as well. Meg needed something to do with her hands, and holding a glass seemed marginally better than shredding snotty tissues.

She smoothed her palms down the gray and black pinstriped dress she'd chosen that morning after staring into her closet for an hour wondering what the hell Matt would have liked her to wear to his funeral.

Then she'd felt idiotic for dressing to impress a guy she hadn't seen for two years, whom she'd never see again ever, and the thought had made her want to say "to hell with it all" and dress in the orange tie-dyed sundress he'd always hated. Luckily, Jess had talked her down. And accompanied her to the event. And driven her here like she was some kind of helpless, elderly aunt.

"Pardon me," someone murmured as he brushed past en route to the bar, and Meg realized she was standing in the way. She turned left and headed into another room, one that seemed blessedly less packed with people. As she approached a card table lined with framed photos of Matt, she realized she recognized most of the shots.

Matt on the edge of the Grand Canyon, a photo Meg had taken five years ago on a two-week road trip. They'd munched Doritos and laughed themselves silly at the goofy names of brothels lining remote stretches of Nevada highway.

Matt on a mountain bike in a grove of trees. She hadn't taken that photo, but the shirt he wore was one she'd bought him for his thirtieth birthday.

Matt and Kyle with their arms looped around each other's shoulders, looking a little drunk at a family barbecue four years ago.

Meg picked up the frame and stared down at the faces. Her heart twisted a little as she saw how happy they looked, so vivacious and healthy. Those matching gray-green eyes, Matt's square, chiseled jaw and Kyle's stubbled one. She thought about the soft *scritch-scritch* sound as he'd rubbed his hand over it the other night, his face close to hers, his lips *right there* as she shifted on his lap and—

"What a great-looking man."

Meg whirled to see the brunette who'd been walking next to Sylvia at the church. She had curly hair and bright green eyes that made Meg think of a lime Popsicle.

"Y—yes," Meg stammered, setting the picture frame back on the table. "Very handsome."

"I just can't believe he's gone."

"Gone?" *She's talking about Matt, not Kyle.* "Right." Meg swallowed, wondering who sucked all the air from the room. "Much too soon. And so unexpected."

"I'm Chloe," the woman said, shifting an etched water goblet from one hand to the other. Something about the glass looked familiar, but Meg forced herself to pay attention to Chloe's words. "I'm Matt's fiancée."

Meg blinked, pretty sure she hadn't heard right. "Matt's fiancée?"

"We were planning our wedding for June. Now?" She shrugged and looked sadly at the photo, and Meg wished she knew what to say.

"I don't know if I'll be able to get my deposit back from Sunridge Vineyards," Chloe said. "That's where the wedding was going to be held. At their new event pavilion?"

Meg nodded, really unsure what to say this time. She settled for offering her hand. "I'm M—"

"Meg, I know. Come on. You should probably meet the others."

"Others?"

Chloe turned, and Meg followed numbly, allowing Chloe to lead her to the next room, which was smaller and more airless than this one. She let her gaze drop to the water goblet in Chloe's hand again, and she realized why it looked familiar. The etched initials *MM* twinkled back at her from the rim, and Meg stumbled with the recognition.

Our wedding glasses, she thought, regaining her balance as she hurried to catch up with Chloe. *The ones we ordered with our monogram. Meg and Matt, MM.*

Chloe turned and caught her staring at the glass. She halted midstride and held it up to give Meg a better view. "It's a nice touch, isn't it? All the glasses have his initials. Matt Midland. We found them in the garage, and it seemed like he was sending us a message."

"Right," Meg breathed, not sure what that message might be. "They're nice."

Satisfied, Chloe turned away again and marched up to a trio of women chatting in the corner. None of them looked familiar, but they all had curly hair and wore dark sheath dresses that accentuated curvy figures.

A brunette turned and gave Meg a once-over with silver-flecked brown eyes that nearly matched the pair Meg saw looking back at her each morning in the bathroom mirror.

Beside her was a blonde with longer, looser curls pinned on top of her head. She turned, too, studying Meg with an interest that seemed oddly familiar.

The brunette shifted her monogrammed glass to her left hand and extended her right to Meg. "Cathy with a *C*. I was after you, but before Chloe."

"Oh," Meg said, wishing she could come up with another syllable or two to utter. "It's lovely to meet you." She shook hands with Cathy-with-a-C, admiring the silver bracelet that looked like something Matt tried to give her one Christmas before she told him she had an allergy to nickel.

"Kathy with a *K*," the blonde offered, not extending a handshake. "I was before you, but after Brittney. Is Brit here?"

Chloe shook her head and took a sip from her glass. "She was invited, but she couldn't make it. Opening night at her new restaurant."

"I can't wait to try it," said a second brunette with curls tumbling to the middle of her back. She nodded at Meg. "I'm Marti. Matt and I had a short little thing right before you, but I worked with him for a few years after that, so I knew all about you."

Meg swallowed, trying to process what was happening. She'd known Matt had other girlfriends before her, of course, and she'd assumed there were others after. He'd been five years older, so his life and love experiences had dwarfed hers when they'd met at her twenty-second birthday party.

Studying Kathy-with-a-K, Meg realized why she looked familiar. The girl Matt dated for three years before her, the one whose smiling face taunted Meg from Sylvia's collection of family photos on the mantle, the one Matt had once described as "not that interested in sex" in a misguided effort to soothe Meg's jealousy.

At the time, it made Meg feel smug and superior. Now, she just felt sad.

"Brittney sent her regards," Chloe said to Cathy-with-a-C. "She wanted to meet you."

"Brittney Fox?" Meg asked, trying to place the name.

"Before both of us," supplied Kathy-with-a-K. "Though I found out later he was still hooking up with her the whole first year we were together."

"There's a shocker," muttered Cathy-with-a-C, shaking her head. "A leopard doesn't change its stripes."

"Spots," Marti corrected. "A leopard doesn't change its spots."

Cathy-with-a-C rolled her eyes. "A zebra, then—"

"And anyway, he *had* changed," Chloe insisted. "He was faithful to me from day one, and he'd made all kinds of changes in his life like trying yoga and giving up red meat and working with a therapist and—"

"I used to hate you."

Meg looked at Kathy-with-a-K, alarmed to realize the woman was speaking to her. Maybe she hadn't heard right. "I'm sorry?"

"I hated you. For years, actually."

"But we've never met."

Kathy shrugged and took a sip of her drink. "I hated that you moved in together so soon, when it took him three years to move in with me. And then when you two got engaged—"

"After almost nine years," Chloe pointed out, folding her arms over her chest. "He proposed to me after only three months."

Meg opened her mouth to reply, but stopped herself. What did she even say to that? And why did Chloe's words sting so much? She'd known all along that Matt had been a bit of a player in the years before they met. He'd even confessed once that he hadn't always been faithful to others, but he insisted to the end he'd been true to her. He swore it, even when he'd come clean about his dalliance with Annabelle.

"It was just the one time, Meg, I swear to you—"

But it hadn't mattered. One time or a hundred times; it was all the same to Meg.

"So what do you do, Meg?"

Cathy-with-a-C was looking at her, and Meg cleared her throat and wondered where the hell Jess had gone. She might want that drink after all. "I'm—"

"She's a chef, like all of us," interrupted Kathy-with-a-K. "Or a caterer or a baker or something like that. Matt only dates women who work with food."

"Or beverages," Chloe said. "Matt was very supportive of my dream of starting my own kombucha company. He even arranged it so I could quit my job at the bakery to spend all my time developing the business plan and brewing new flavors and—"

"Wait, you're not Meg Delaney, are you?" Cathy-with-a-C stared at her. "You are! You're the one who wrote that cookbook! The aphrodisiac cookbook everyone's been talking about?"

Kathy-with-a-K sniffed. "Can't say I ever needed any help in that department."

Marti rolled her eyes. "That's not what I heard."

Meg took a step back, then another, wondering if she'd walked into some sort of alternate universe populated by women who looked vaguely similar and had loved Matt or maybe still loved Matt. She had to get out of here. She had to escape the press of bodies and the echo of memories and the clamor of voices—

"I'm sorry, would you excuse me?" Meg stepped back again. "I need to find the restroom."

Chloe pressed her lips together, clearly disappointed in Meg's bladder. "Down the stairs, take a left, it's at the end of that hall," Chloe said. "Hurry back, though. You should definitely meet Sarah."

"Is that Sarah with an *h* or with no *h*?" asked Kathy or Cathy or Marti—hell, Meg couldn't be sure.

She was practically running now, making a beeline for the door as she dodged two women she recognized as photography colleagues Matt worked with five years ago. Were they exes, too?

Meg shook her head and skirted a cluster of uncles. *It doesn't matter now*, she told herself. *What difference does it make if you held a special place in his life or if you were just one of many?*

She was moving so fast when she hit the stairs that she had to catch herself on the railing. The stupid high heels wobbled as she took the steps two at a time and wished she'd picked a dress that wasn't so snug around her thighs.

Panting by the time she reached the bottom of the stairs, Meg glanced left. Three or four women were lined up outside the restroom, each of them representing some conversation Meg didn't want to have. She looked the opposite direction where the hallway veered sharply down a dimly lit corridor. She hesitated, then turned that way, marching like she had a purpose to forestall any questions about where she was headed.

Her lungs filled with air as the voices faded behind her and her footsteps slowed with her pulse. She just needed a few minutes alone, someplace quiet to collect her thoughts. She spotted a door up ahead and reached for the knob, praying it led to a quiet conference room or an unoccupied office.

She pushed it open and breathed in the scent of Pine-Sol and bleach. The space was dim and spacious, and she could see rows of paper towels and tissue lining a shelf overhead.

"Cleaning closet," she murmured. "Close enough."

Meg stepped inside, letting her eyes adjust to the darkness as she pulled the door closed behind her before anyone could notice the crazy redhead ducking into a supply closet. As soon as the door was closed, her breathing slowed to normal, and she unclenched the fists she hadn't realized she'd been gripping.

Blinking a few times to clear her vision, she squinted around the little room. Something that looked like a mop lurked in one corner, the wheeled yellow bucket beside it glowing oddly in the light seeping around the edges of the door. The high heels were killing her, so she toed them off and said a silent prayer the floor wasn't too filthy. The concrete felt cool and soothing under her bare feet, so it seemed worth the risk for that small slice of comfort.

She thought about fumbling for a light switch, but decided against it. It would be just her luck to have one of Matt's relatives amble past and decide to switch the light off, and then how would she explain the fact that she was standing barefoot in the broom closet at her ex's funeral reception?

She should probably text Jess to say she'd gone to the bathroom, but she just needed a minute to herself. With a sigh, she took a step deeper into the closet. It was bigger than it looked from outside, and the shelves seemed tidy and well-stocked. She did a slow turn, then closed her eyes and leaned back against the wall.

At least, that's what she tried to do. The wall moved. It was warm and bumpy and had hands that reached up to cup her elbows.

She gave a startled cry and started to struggle, but the hands were gentle and the voice in her ear was as familiar as the cedar scent now tickling her nose.

"Hello, Meg."

◆　◆　◆

Kyle felt pretty sure groping his brother's ex-fiancée in a closet at Matt's funeral reception was a new low even for him.

But hell, it's not like he tried to grope her. And it's not like he stalked her here, either. He'd just wanted a few quiet moments alone to collect his thoughts and escape the throng of relatives eager to tell him what a great guy Matt was and how Kyle looked just like him and did he think Matt would have liked the service?

Of course Matt would have liked the service. It was all about Matt.

But that was a shitty thing to think, so he'd come down here to give himself a time-out, maybe take a stab at being less of a jerk.

Only now he was here holding Meg from behind, her body pressed lush and round against him, and he remembered the upside of being a jerk.

Kyle cleared his throat. "It's just me, Meg," he whispered against her ear.

She turned to face him, and he dropped his hands from her elbows, breathing in the lilac scent of her in the dim little closet. Her hair brushed his arm, and Kyle had to fight the urge to reach for her again.

"Kyle? What are you doing here?"

"Oh, you know—taking inventory of the toilet paper, making sure the fire extinguisher is up to code, checking to see if the mop needs to be replaced."

"So, escaping?"

"Pretty much. You?"

"Same thing."

They both went quiet, and Kyle used the opportunity to study her face in the dim interior of the closet. He'd been in here ten minutes, so his eyes had adjusted to the darkness and the ghost beams of light seeping around the door gave him enough to see the glint of silver in her eyes, the subtle curve of her cheek. Her expression was uncertain, but she hadn't made a move to leave yet.

"So this is awkward," she said.

"Being at your ex-fiancé's funeral, or being in the closet with his brother at said funeral?"

"Both." She seemed to hesitate. "Wait, I thought it was a memorial service."

"It was. *Funeral's* just shorter to say."

"Right." Meg bit her lip. "I take back what I said earlier. This is actually the *least* awkward moment of the last hour for me."

"That's depressing."

"It's a memorial service. Isn't it supposed to be depressing?"

"Not if you ask Aunt Judy. She insists it's supposed to be a celebration of life. If she had her way, we'd all be wearing jingle bells and dancing on the bar."

"I can think of worse ideas," Meg said, her eyes meeting his in the dim half-light of the closet. "So how are you holding up?"

"Okay." He hesitated, not sure how much information to volunteer. But hell, she'd asked, and there was something about being in the closet that gave this whole thing the air of a Catholic confessional. At least, he imagined this might be what the confessional was like, minus the push broom and the jumbo pack of Hefty bags.

"I guess—" he swallowed. "I guess I thought the service would give me some closure."

"Did it?"

"No. I just keep replaying conversations in my head. Arguments I used to have with Matt about my career choices or my eating habits or whose turn it was to take mom out to lunch."

"I've been doing the same thing. Rehashing old arguments, I mean. I'll catch myself doing it and I'll realize I'm even making the facial expression that goes with the point I'm trying to make."

Kyle nodded, though she probably couldn't see him in the darkness. "I know what you mean. I caught myself grinning like an idiot in Costco yesterday after I made a particularly valid argument during my replay of a fight we had in high school."

"I take it things didn't unfold that way in real life?"

"In real life Matt gave me a wedgie and threw my car keys in the toilet, so I'd say no. Of course, I retaliated by putting Doritos in his bed. I'd like to think our methods for solving disagreements improved once we reached adulthood."

"I saw Matt pour a beer on your head once, so probably not."

"How about you?" he asked. "Do your imaginary arguments go differently this time around?"

"Yes," Meg murmured. "It's stupid. I've been sticking up for myself a lot more, making these clever, well-thought out arguments in my own defense, and then I just feel like a dumbass for fighting with a dead guy."

"A dead guy you hadn't seen for two years."

"Exactly. Who does that?"

"Both of us, apparently. It must be another one of those stages of grieving."

"I suppose." She didn't say anything thing for a moment. When he felt her fingers brush his, he gave a little jump.

"Sorry," she said. "I didn't mean to scare you."

"You didn't. I just wasn't expecting you to touch me."

"I wasn't trying to touch you. Not like that, I mean. Just checking to see if the door locks."

"It doesn't. I already checked."

She went quiet again, and Kyle thought it might be time to leave. Their closet conversation had run its course, and he'd probably be wise to get out of here before someone found them like this.

But then he heard her voice again, soft and hesitant. "Tell me about Cara."

The words caught him by surprise, but he kept his expression flat even though she probably couldn't see it. "What do you want to know?"

"You were together a long time. Why did you split up?"

He laughed. "We're at my brother's funeral and you want to talk about why my girlfriend dumped me?"

"Sorry. We don't have to—"

"It's okay," Kyle said, not really minding the question. "Like I told you the other night, I wasn't that broken up about it. Not sad enough to even muster a few tears."

"What happened?"

"The short version? She wanted to get married and have babies."

"What's the long version?"

"She wanted to get married and have babies and I didn't."

"Thanks for elaborating."

Kyle shrugged, wondering why she was asking. "It was nice while it lasted, but ultimately we just wanted different things."

It was the truth, though maybe not the whole story. Guilt twisted his gut as he remembered Cara's tears, the hurled accusations. *You'll never look at me the way I've seen you look at—*

"Did you know Matt didn't want to marry me?"

"What?" He blinked in the darkness, trying to read Meg's expression instead of just her tone, which was soft and cautious.

"Matt. He never wanted to get married. Not to me, anyway."

"That's not true," he insisted, even as a tiny voice in the back of his brain asked, *Isn't it?*

Meg sighed and leaned against the door. "It's okay, I knew. I mean, we dated for more than eight years without him ever once bringing up the subject of marriage."

"You didn't talk about it at all?"

"I said *he* didn't bring it up. Once a year, I'd broach the subject. I tried to play it cool, to act like I didn't care that much, but all I had to do was say the word *marriage* and he'd act like I just shoved his testicles in a vise and started cranking.

"Ouch," Kyle said, trying not to picture it. "He obviously changed his mind at some point. I never thought he had it in him to make such a romantic gesture with a proposal."

"He didn't."

"What?"

"He didn't make a romantic gesture with the proposal. That whole story we told the family was completely made up."

Kyle stared at her, remembering the glow in her cheeks, the beautiful wildness in her eyes that autumn when Matt had stood up at the dinner table and said they had an announcement. Meg had sat there beaming, regaling them all with the story of Matt getting down on one knee at a candlelit restaurant with a solitaire in a champagne flute and a cello quartet playing their favorite song—

"I don't understand," Kyle said.

"We made it up," she said. "Well, I made it up. I was embarrassed about how it really happened, so I just sort of blurted out this imaginary version of events. When Matt saw how everyone ate up that version of the story, he just sort of went with it."

"What really happened?"

Meg sighed. "Like I said, I made a big effort to only bring up marriage once a year. We were watching a football game on TV and one of the players started talking about his wife in an interview—about how she was always there for him and was his rock through all the ups and downs. Anyway, I made a comment about how sweet that was. How the word *wife* sounded so much steadier than *girlfriend* or *partner*.

"What did Matt say?"

"I believe his exact words were 'Jesus Christ, Meg—enough with the nagging already.'"

"God." Kyle felt his hands clenching at his sides, and he cursed the part of himself that wanted to go back in time and punch his brother. Admittedly he hadn't been on the same page as Cara when it came to marriage, but he liked to think he hadn't been a dick about it.

"Normally, I would have just let it drop," Meg continued. "I never wanted to be a nag, you know? But I guess I was thinking it had been eight years and I wasn't getting any younger and—well, anyway, I asked why he was so opposed to marriage."

"Why was he?"

"I don't know. He never said. He picked up a bowl of potato chips and walked into the guest room to watch the rest of the game. We didn't say another word about it until two nights later when he came home from work and slammed this little velvet box on the counter while I was in the kitchen making crab cakes."

"The ring?" he guessed, hating this story the more he heard.

"The ring," she confirmed. "I looked up and he said, 'Here. We might as well do it.'"

"'We might as well do it,'" Kyle repeated. "It has a certain romantic flair to it."

"Matt never claimed to be a romantic," she said, sounding a little defensive. "I knew that from the beginning, and I was fine with it."

The prickly note in her voice made Kyle bite back the criticism flaring up at the back of his brain. "Okay."

"Anyway, he tried to put the ring on my finger, but my hands were covered in crab meat and egg, so I tried to rinse them off really fast, but the ring slipped off and went into the garbage disposal, and I spent the next twenty minutes trying to fish it out."

"I guess that's more unique than fishing it out of a champagne flute."

"I don't really like champagne anyway."

"So you said yes?"

She hesitated, and he watched her brow furrow a little in the muted half-light. "You know, he never actually asked. And come to think of it, I never said yes. I just started wearing the ring and planning the wedding and trying really hard to believe he'd love being married once it actually happened."

"I guess you never got to find out."

"No," she said, her voice soft in the darkness. "I guess not."

Kyle hesitated, knowing he was treading on thin ice. No way in hell would his brother want her to know about those dark, somber months after the split. But Kyle could throw her a bone, couldn't he?

"Even if you're right that he didn't want to get married, I know he loved his life with you," he said softly. "He didn't want that to end."

"Neither did I," she said. "Not then, anyway."

She paused, and he wondered if she was thinking of a way to leave or a way to stay here for a little while longer.

"I met Chloe," she said at last. "She seems nice."

"She does? You're sure you met Chloe?"

Meg snorted. "I was being polite."

"Why? Chloe usually isn't."

"She's probably just grieving," Meg said, but didn't sound convinced. "I didn't even know Matt had a fiancée."

"I think we were all sort of hoping she'd take a cue from you and call it quits before the wedding, but it wasn't looking likely."

"Sounds like they got engaged pretty quickly?"

Her tone was even, but there was something else in her voice. Something beyond casual curiosity. Kyle waited a few beats, wondering if she'd take back the question. Tell him she'd rather not know.

She didn't though, and Kyle found himself reaching out to touch her hand. "Don't do this, Meg."

"Don't do what?"

"Torture yourself. Compare the proposal you got with the one Chloe got and make it some failing on your part."

"I want to know," she said.

"Morbid curiosity?"

"We're at a funeral. Can you think of a better time to be morbidly curious?"

Kyle sighed. "They got engaged on a beach in Barbados at sunset."

"Oh," she said. "I mean, I guess they could have had a fake engagement story, too—"

"I saw photos," Kyle said. "He had his camera set up on a tripod in some bushes nearby. There might have also been a skywriter—"

"Okay, stop," she said, shaking her head. "You're right, I don't need to torture myself. It's not a damn competition, anyway."

Kyle swallowed hard, hating the sadness in her voice. Hating the question he was about to ask her. "Did you still love him? When he died, I mean—were you still in love with Matt?"

"God, no!"

Was it wrong to love the vehemence in her words? Kyle cleared his throat. "You're sure?"

"Positive." She shook her head in the darkness, and he watched the glint of light in her curls as they slid over her shoulders. "I know it doesn't seem possible that I could have stopped loving him that quickly, but the second he told me about the affair, it was like someone flipped off a light switch. I don't know how else to explain it."

"Then why do you care how he proposed to someone else?"

"Because I'm a woman," she said. "Even if I'm glad I didn't marry him, and relieved that I dodged that bullet, it doesn't mean I wouldn't have wanted to be deemed worthy."

"You're worthy."

She laughed and Kyle realized he sounded like a fucking inspirational poster. He could think of a million adjectives to describe Meg—funny, warm, clever, beautiful, creative—but *worthy* had never crossed his mind.

"What the hell does *worthy* even mean?" he muttered. "Like it's someone else's job to validate your worth?"

"It's not, I know. But I'm female. I'm human. Deep down, don't most of us want someone to lay claim to us? To have someone love you so much they grab on tightly and say 'Mine!' and never let go?"

"That sounds like a motive for a restraining order."

Meg reached out and squeezed his hand. "I can always count on you to make me smile, Kyle."

A dull pang of longing rattled through his gut. His fingers were still linked with hers, so he squeezed her hand back in lieu of any other sort of gesture he might want to make. "He did love you, Meg. In his own way. How could he not?"

"Thanks. I don't know if that matters now, but it's nice to hear."

Kyle cleared his throat. "So are things still going well with your book?" It was an abrupt subject change, but he wasn't ready to end the conversation yet and he worried she might leave if the silence stretched out. Her hand was warm in his, and he wondered if she'd forgotten they were still touching.

"It's crazy," she said. "It's the number one book on *The New York Times* Best Sellers list. Well, number one on the Advice and Miscellaneous list. But can you imagine?"

"That's great," he said, meaning it, even if he didn't have much of a notion what any of that meant. "I tried to make one of the recipes the other night."

"Really? Which one?"

"The risotto. Only I didn't have risotto, so I tried to use Rice-A-Roni. I also didn't have white wine, so I used beer instead, and I had to use romaine lettuce instead of basil and margarine instead of sesame oil and—"

Meg laughed. "So basically, you made a totally different recipe?"

"Pretty much. It was just as well. I was home alone with Bindi, so revving my libido with an aphrodisiac dinner probably wasn't the best idea."

"Bindi?"

"My dog. Australian kelpie. I got her at the pound a few months after Karma died."

"What's an Australian kelpie?"

"Picture a normal herding dog like a border collie or a heeler."

"High energy, you mean?"

"Now picture it on crack. That's a kelpie."

"I'd love to meet her."

"She'd love to meet you. She loves women. Doesn't see enough of them, so she goes bananas when anyone with boobs and no Y chromosome comes to visit."

"My double-X chromosomes and double-*D* boobs will have to drop by sometime. Maybe we'll bring you a few groceries, while we're at it."

"I'd like that," he said, his brain perking up at the boob comment. He remembered her telling him once that she'd learned to make fun of her own boobs as a self-conscious teen who got tired of being teased and decided to beat her tormentors to the punch. *"I looked like two olives on a toothpick,"* she'd said, and he and Matt had both laughed.

The quiet between them stretched out in the darkness, and Kyle cleared his throat again. He could hear her breathing in and out, could smell the lilacs in her hair and feel the warmth of her flesh where her fingers joined with his. She hadn't let go yet, and he wasn't sure if he should be the one to break the contact between them. Had anyone noticed they were both missing? He should probably get back out there, lose himself in sea of aunts and uncles and co-workers and—

"Kyle?"

"Yes?"

"You know the other night when we said kissing would be a dumb idea?"

His brain started to spin, and Kyle held on to her hand, keeping himself rooted in place. "Yes."

"It would be. But I still want to do it. Just once, to know what it's like."

He tried to think of what to say. Something flippant to make her laugh or something profound to make her feel.

He was still thinking about it when he felt her hand on his cheek. He reached for her then, forgetting all his hesitation as her lips met his in the darkness. Her mouth was as soft as he'd always imagined and she tasted like sunshine and white wine, even though he didn't think she'd had anything to drink. He drew his free hand up to cup her face, marveling at the silkiness of her skin, the soft whimper in the back of her throat, the fact that he was really here kissing Meg—*Meg*, for crying out loud.

When she drew back, he had to bite back a scream of frustration. Her breath sounded faster in the darkness, and her grip on his fingers was so tight he wondered if she remembered she was touching him.

"So that's what it's like," she whispered.

He laughed, his voice echoing off the walls, and he hoped no one walked by right then and heard them.

"That's what it's like," he said.

"It was different than I thought," she said. "Sweeter."

"You thought I might be the type to shove you up against the wall and have my way with you?"

"Jesus." Her sharp intake of breath told him he'd just shocked her, but before he could apologize, she was whispering again.

"Yes. I'll admit it, that's always how I imagined you."

"You imagined me?" The thought intrigued him.

"I don't mean when I was with Matt," she said, her words soft and rushed. "I just meant since the night on the sofa."

"Right," he said, not wanting to admit he had a different definition of *always*.

From the first moment I met you . . .

He considered asking her about that Thanksgiving night three years ago. Had she felt something, too, or was it all in his head?

"We should probably get out of here," he murmured, wishing he could do anything but that. Wishing he could stay here forever.

"You're right. Jess has probably sent out a search party by now. How long have I been in here?"

Not long enough, his brain telegraphed, but instead he answered, "Ten or fifteen minutes."

"Wow. You move pretty fast."

He laughed. "Me? You're the one who kissed me."

"I did, didn't I?"

"Damn straight."

"Well, in that case, this was the best kiss in a cleaning closet at a funeral that I've ever experienced."

"Likewise."

"I'm going to slip out now. Maybe give it a few minutes before you leave?"

"You don't think it would be a good idea for someone to spot us ducking out of a closet together at my brother's memorial service?"

"Probably not. Especially with my lipstick smeared all over your mouth. Here, I think I have a tissue somewhere—ew, wait, that one's used."

"It's fine," he said, wiping his mouth with the back of his hand. His lips were still tingling, and it seemed like a damn shame to remove any traces of the best kiss of his whole life.

She took a deep breath and let go of his hand. "Okay then," she said, stuffing her feet back into her shoes and gaining a few inches of height. "Thank you, Kyle. I feel better now."

"Don't mention it."

There was a sliver of light creeping through the edge of the door, and he watched her press her ear against it, listening for voices. "Sounds like the coast is clear," she murmured.

"Good luck."

She pushed the door open, and Kyle heard the clamor of voices coming from upstairs. Light washed over the inside of the closet, and he stepped back a little, not wanting anyone to spot him if they did happen to walk by.

But the hall must have been empty, because Meg stepped out into the light. She turned and gave him the barest hint of a wave, then pushed the door shut behind her. He listened to her footsteps echoing down the hall as she walked away, and he felt a pang of sadness that had nothing to do with the fact that he'd just attended a memorial service.

Your brother's *memorial service, you disloyal ass.*

Kyle closed his eyes and leaned back against the wall, listening to the thud of his own heartbeat. He waited until it slowed down a bit, listening at the door as a pair of voices trickled past talking about a memory of a time Matt shared his glove with another player at a Little League game.

That was me, thought Kyle, not sure if it mattered. *Me who shared the glove, not Matt.*

But it had been Matt who made the kid laugh. The boy had a drunk dad and a dead mom and a lower lip that would quiver when he looked up into the stands and saw his father hadn't come. Matt took him under his wing, telling him filthy jokes and glowering at anyone who mocked the kid's hand-me-down uniform.

That's the Matt I want to remember, Kyle thought, his throat swelling tight with the memory. *The Matt who gave wedgies to defend a poor kid's honor.*

He wasn't sure if five minutes had passed, but the coast seemed clear and he was sure he'd heard Meg's footsteps fading up the stairs several minutes ago. He pushed the door open, squinting as the light hit him in the face.

A woman was walking down the other end of the hall toward the bathroom, but she had her back to him, so Kyle slipped out the door. He shut it softly behind him, hoping he didn't smell too much like cleaning products. He lifted his shirtsleeve and sniffed, but didn't notice anything especially fragrant. Maybe a trace of Meg's perfume, but that was probably all in his head.

He took the stairs slowly, not eager to get back to the crowd upstairs. He hadn't hit the bar yet, so maybe he'd grab a beer or a plate of food and—

He froze at the top of the stairs. Ten feet away, Meg was standing at the edge of the railing, her fingers clenched so hard around it her knuckles had gone white. Beside her, Kyle's mother was talking fast, her cheeks flushed as she thrust an envelope at Meg.

Kyle stepped forward, a cold prickle moving up his arms as he heard his mother's words.

"This is your official notice of legal action," Sylvia said. "You can contact our attorney if you have any questions."

Meg's face was ashen, and she looked at the envelope like Sylvia had just blown her nose on it. She reached out and took it, and Kyle could see her hands were shaking.

"What's going on here?" he asked. He took in his mother's red-rimmed eyes with dark circles beneath them, and his heart twisted. He looked at Meg, feeling his chest clench tighter at the sight of her pale, bewildered expression.

His mother was first to speak. "I'm protecting your brother's legacy," she said as tears glinted in her eyes. "I'm making sure his work wasn't all in vain."

"How are you doing that?" he asked, not sure he wanted to hear the answer.

"By claiming his half of the cookbook."

CHAPTER EIGHT

"So what did your agent say?"

Jess grabbed one of Meg's cucumber and salmon crudités and took a bite, propping her feet on the edge of Meg's coffee table.

"She said it's after ten p.m. on a Saturday on the East Coast, so she needed a little more time to track down the legal team."

"But does she think you ought to fight it?"

"Of course," Meg said, glum at the thought of fighting anything. She just wanted to curl up in a ball and savor the notion that someone besides her mom and her best friend had read her cookbook.

"Good," Jess said, taking another vicious bite of the crudités. "You did all the work on that damn book. You deserve to reap the benefit."

"Not *all* the work—"

"Honey, you paid off your debt to anyone else who had a hand in it. That graphic designer you bartered with to lay the whole thing out—she's not showing up on your doorstep demanding a cut, is she?"

"Of course not. I catered her wedding for free." She shrugged. "I did send her flowers the other day though, and thanked her for doing such a beautiful job making the book pretty."

"See? Debt settled. Just like it was with Matt. He took those photos as a favor to his fiancée. Just because you didn't walk down the aisle doesn't negate the fact that he's the one who *volunteered* to do the pictures. How many of his office parties did you cater without ever expecting a dime from him?"

"Too many to count," Meg admitted. "And you're right, it's not like I ever demanded a share of the business deals he closed over my bruschetta."

"Exactly. It'd be like the guy who fixed your laptop showing up to demand a share of the book sales because you couldn't have written it without him."

"Not exactly like that," Meg pointed out, feeling a pinprick of guilt between her ribs. "I paid the laptop guy with cash. It's the barter system that keeps this from being a clear-cut case, according to my agent."

"Tit for tat," Jess muttered. "Or in this case, tit for pic."

"Ew."

"Well, it's true. You two were sleeping together. You were engaged to be married. In a way, you were both swapping sexual favors for each other's work on a regular basis."

"Thank you. Bringing prostitution into the equation is exactly what we need to make this less complicated." Meg sighed. "If I'd finished paying off that damn bill right away, this might not be an issue."

"You were paying off the *wedding*," Jess pointed out. "Some arbitrary photography fee he imposed just to get back at you was hardly your top priority."

"Yes, but it's the backbone of their lawsuit now. The fact that he hadn't been fully paid when he passed away."

Jess chomped another appetizer. "It's too bad you never had any sort of contract."

"I never thought we needed to. We were getting married, and we'd had a joint checking account for years by then. Any proceeds would

have just gone into that account, and then the book didn't sell any copies anyway and—"

A knock sounded at the door, cutting off the defense that was starting to sound weak even to Meg's ears. She and Jess both turned toward
the foyer, gazes fixed on the large figure standing on the other side of
the frosted-glass panel in her door.

"Ten bucks says it's your closet kissing companion," Jess murmured.

"No bet."

"I still can't believe you ditched me for thirty minutes this afternoon to lock lips among the cleaning supplies."

"I told you, I was only in the closet ten minutes. The rest of the
time I was being cornered by Chloe and the clones."

"Yeah, after meeting her, I can't blame you for wanting to run off
and gargle bleach."

The knock sounded again, and Meg pushed herself up off the sofa
and headed for the door. Part of her hoped Jess was right and Kyle
would be standing on the other side. She'd wanted to flee the funeral
right after Sylvia's confrontation, but it had taken her a while to find
Jess. Then she'd had another run-in with Chloe, and in all the confusion, she'd never said a proper goodbye to Kyle.

She heard Jess on her heels, and turned to see her best friend sling-
ing her purse over her shoulder. "You're leaving?" Meg asked.

"Assuming that's Kyle, you're going to need some time alone
together. And I need some time alone with my vibrator. Call me later
with the details."

"Ew," Meg said, swinging open her front door.

"Bye-bye," Jess said to Kyle, patting him on the shoulder as she
breezed past. "Go easy on her, bud. She's had a rough day."

"Unlike the guy who just buried his brother?" Meg muttered, looking up at Kyle. "Sorry about that. She doesn't think sometimes."

"It's okay. He wasn't buried, anyway."

"Cremated. You know what I mean." She bit her lip. "Are you okay?"

"Fine. All things considered, anyway. I wanted to talk about what happened today."

Meg snorted. "You might have to narrow that down a little. You mean the part where Chloe got drunk and called me a filthy whore before your dad dragged her out to the car?"

"Technically, she called you a filthy hoo-er," Kyle pointed out. "Thanks to the aforementioned drunkenness, there was an extra syllable in the word."

"Which let me enjoy it twice as much." She cleared her throat. "Then there's the fact that you kissed me in a closet."

"Technically, *you* kissed *me*. But I'm not here to talk about that, either."

"So that leaves your mom." Meg gripped the door a little tighter, not sure she wanted to be having this conversation right now. But there was no avoiding it, was there? She sighed. "Or I guess I should say, your mom's decision to hit me with both a bouquet of daisies and a lawsuit in the middle of a funeral reception."

"Her timing and presentation could have used some work," he admitted, peering over the top of her head toward her living room. "Are those the smoked salmon appetizer things you used to make?"

"Yes. Would you like one?"

"Please."

"Come on, then."

She turned back toward the living room and headed for the sofa, conscious of Kyle right behind her. Having him close was giving her flashbacks to the kiss, which was a lot more pleasant than the flashbacks she'd been having all evening. Her ears were still ringing with the sound of Sylvia lecturing her on artists' rights and the importance of honoring commitments, her voice so high and shrill that everyone had turned to stare.

Meg sat down on the couch and waited for Kyle to join her. He seemed to hesitate, then sat on the loveseat instead.

"Keeping your distance?"

"Look, Meg—"

"No good conversation has ever started, 'Look, Meg . . .'"

He sighed and picked up one of the crudités, but he didn't bite into it. "I know my mom caught you off guard, but she has a valid point."

"What point would that be?" she asked, feeling her temper flare. "You mean the one where she said I'd be nothing—I repeat, *nothing*—without Matt? Or the one where she called me an ungrateful bitch? Or the one where she said she always hated my cooking?"

"You have to admit, all that name-calling kept the funeral from being too dreary."

Meg folded her arms over her chest, annoyed he didn't seem more upset by his mother's insults. "Forgive me if I'm not feeling honored by the opportunity to provide some levity."

Kyle sighed and set the snack back on the platter. "I know my mom can be a jerk. God knows that's her default setting most of the time. But as an artist, I think she has a valid point."

"Come again?"

"Matt did take those photos. His artwork is a big part of what makes that book so amazing."

Meg swallowed hard, ordering herself to breathe. "I'm not disputing that. I'm only saying the debt's been paid already. Like I told your mom, I put the last check in the mail two days ago."

"Right," Kyle said, his voice equally strained. "And according to my mother, it hasn't shown up yet."

"Well, I sent it. It's for eighteen hundred dollars."

Kyle frowned. "According to the records, you still owed close to three thousand dollars."

"That's not true," Meg said, hating the panicky note in her own voice. "I tried to get electronic records of the canceled checks from my bank, but apparently there was some sort of technical glitch when they got bought out by a bigger bank last month."

"So you don't have any proof."

She glared at him. "It's not like Matt was sending me a receipt every month. Look, I'm sure that's what was left. I've been scrimping and saving and mailing those damn checks to Matt every month for two years."

"I don't want to quibble about dollar figures, but Matt's accountant disagrees about what you still owed."

Meg gritted her teeth and stared at him. "The bill was bullshit in the first place, Kyle. Ten thousand dollars for something he offered to do for free?"

"What did you do with your engagement ring?"

The question startled her so much it took her a moment to remember. Before she could answer, Kyle had picked up the appetizer again and shoved it in his mouth. "In a lot of cases of a broken engagement, the bride-to-be keeps the ring with the idea that it was given as a gift, and legally, the gift can't be revoked."

"Exactly," Meg said warily, not sure if Kyle was taking her side or luring her into some sort of complacency.

"But did you know there have been plenty of court cases where the bride has to give back the ring? The legal argument is that it was a conditional gift, contingent upon the marriage taking place, and the acceptance of the proposal is an agreement to those terms. If the wedding doesn't happen, the conditions haven't been met and the ring goes back to the giver."

Meg folded her arms over her chest. "Not that it's any of your business, but I researched this when we called off the wedding. There's something called a fault-based approach where the courts determine who caused the broken engagement and the other person keeps the ring."

"So you're saying it was Matt's fault?"

Meg took another shaky breath, wishing she didn't feel the thick bubble of temper flaring at the base of her neck. "I'm saying a guy who tells his bride the night before the wedding that he's been sticking his dick in his acupuncturist might be considered at fault for the fact that the wedding didn't happen."

She saw Kyle flinch and felt a twinge of guilt for bringing up his dead brother's dick, but he seemed to recover. "No one's disputing that a portion of the fault was Matt's. But he was the one who chose to come clean instead of keeping the secret from you. He made a mistake, and then he tried to atone for it. It was your choice not to forgive him."

Meg glared. "So you're saying the whole thing was *my* fault because I'm the one who didn't forgive and forget?"

"That's not what I said. But I do think you earned at least a little blame for dumping him in the most public fashion imaginable. You could have just postponed the wedding, maybe tried joint counseling or something."

Meg stood up, blazing now. "You think I did it to humiliate him? You honestly think I didn't stand there at the front of that church praying to God to give me the strength to just forgive him and go through with it? You think I didn't have every intention of saying 'I do' until the last possible second when every fiber of my being screamed 'I can't!' and I had no choice but to run?"

"I don't—"

"You want the goddamn ring back? You can have it. It's in my jewelry box."

"Meg, wait—"

She whirled again to face him, too angry to tamp down her temper now. "Do you know why I still have it?" she snapped, fists clenched at her side. "After we got engaged, I took it to a jeweler to see if I could have the white gold replaced with something that didn't have nickel in it. Stainless steel or something affordable. I kept having allergic reactions to the gold, but I didn't tell Matt because I didn't want him to feel bad."

"Meg—"

"You know what the jeweler told me? It's not real."

"What?" He stared at her, his face registering the same shock she'd felt that afternoon in the jewelry store.

"The diamond. The 'big ol' rock' Matt was always bragging about giving me? It's something else, not even a real diamond."

"Cubic zirconia?"

"No, something else. I think it's called moissanite. The thing is, I didn't care. I never wanted a big huge diamond. I didn't want a diamond at all."

"What did you want?"

"I didn't care!" She threw her hands in the air, annoyed with herself for the torrent of words spilling from her mouth, but she felt powerless to stop them. "I would have been happy with a beach agate or a piece of glass. Or I would have really enjoyed having something special, like my grandmother's birthstone. Something to show he paid attention to my life and to the things that really mattered to me."

"What was your grandma's birthstone?"

"A sapphire." Meg shook her head, afraid they were getting lost now in the insignificant details. "That's not the point, though. To have him lie to me about it. To have him pretending the ring or his feelings or our relationship was something it *wasn't*—"

She broke off there and clasped her hands together, letting the words hang between them for a moment. A stupid, silly part of her felt like crying, but she ordered herself to hold it together. "I never told anyone that. About the ring, I mean."

"That you knew the stone wasn't real?"

She nodded, blinking hard until the threat of tears had faded. "Not even Matt."

"Not Jess?"

She shook her head. "I didn't want anyone to know. I didn't want them to think my own fiancé thought so little of me that he'd lie about something that never mattered to me in the first place." She shrugged. "Anyway, you can have the ring back. I'll go get it."

She started to move that direction, but Kyle stood up and grabbed her hand. "Meg, I don't want the ring. That's not why I brought it up."

She looked down at her hand in his, staring at their interlaced fingers as though they might hold a clue to how she should feel about all this. When she looked back at Kyle, he was watching her with an intensity that made heat rise in her cheeks.

"So why did you bring it up?" she asked. "What's it to you where the engagement ring ended up?"

"I was making a point about broken engagements and gifts and the law. To show you the courts have a lot of different ways of looking at this, and it's not as black and white as you seem to think."

Meg nodded, conscious of his fingers still twined with hers. "So you're saying this thing with the book is going to play out in the courts."

"It looks that way, doesn't it? I mean assuming you're not just going to roll over and cut my mother a check."

"Is that what you think I should do?"

He seemed to hesitate, then turned around, not letting go of her hand. "Come on," he said, pulling her toward the door.

"What? Where are we going?"

"I want to show you something."

"What if I don't feel like going anywhere with you?"

"You do."

Damn straight, her heart telegraphed, while her brain pointed out she was wearing dirty sweatpants and a Scooby-Doo T-shirt. Meg dug her bare heels into the floor, which left her feeling like a reluctant cocker spaniel trying to avoid a walk.

"Wait," she said. "We're not leaving the house, are we?"

"Yes."

"Can I at least put away the food or put on some pants or blow my nose or—"

"You have five minutes," he said, letting go of her hand. He folded his arms over his chest and held her gaze for a few beats. Then he nodded. "And bring the ring."

♦　　♦　　♦

"I thought you didn't want the ring back," Meg said behind him as Kyle fumbled the key into the lock and then rolled back the barn doors that led to the studio behind his gallery.

He turned to look at her and his heart cinched up into a tight ball when he saw those speckled brown eyes studying him. "I don't want the ring," he said. "But if you don't want it, either, there's something I'd like to do with it."

"It's all yours," she said. "Make a doorstop out of it if you like."

"Not a bad idea, but not my plan."

He turned around again and led the way into the studio, flipping on the overhead lights as he went. He heard Meg rolling the barn doors closed and he thought about telling her not to bother, that he liked the night air blowing through the open space.

But he didn't want anyone strolling in off the street. It wasn't quite eight o'clock, but it was already dark outside and the raccoons that frequented the alley behind the gallery had a fondness for wandering through to look for sparkly objects.

There were plenty of those here.

"So this is where you work." He turned to see Meg walking the perimeter of the room, her gaze traveling from one sculpture to another. She held her hands twined behind her back like a kid afraid of breaking something in a glass shop.

"You can touch anything you want," he said.

"What?" She looked at him, and Kyle's pulse quickened at the flush in her cheeks.

"The—uh—the art. You can touch any of the pieces if you like. One of the advantages of working with large-scale mixed metal is that most of it's pretty sturdy."

Meg laughed. "Have we met? In case you've forgotten, I'm the girl who broke Karma's 'unbreakable' dog toy."

"She told me on her deathbed she forgave you."

"That's a relief."

Meg moved slowly around the room, and Kyle moved with her, trying to imagine what things might look like from her eyes. His studio space wasn't particularly tidy, since gallery visitors didn't get to wander back here. There were scraps of bent steel in one corner and a pile of copper shavings on the floor by his workbench. Big windows along one wall gave him plenty of natural light to work by, but right now they showcased an inky black sky pinpricked with stars. The air in the studio smelled like sawdust and metal, and next to Meg's perfume, it was the sweetest scent he knew.

"You've never been in the gallery, right?" he asked.

"Right." Meg turned and bit her lip. "After—well, I just thought I might not be welcome."

"It's okay," he said. "How about I give you a tour?"

"I'd love that."

She sounded like she meant it, which made Kyle's heart swell. He watched her tuck a curl behind one ear, and he noticed the earrings she wore were a pair he'd made for her one Christmas long ago.

He swept an arm out to the side. "As you've probably guessed, you're standing in my work space now. This is where I do all my planning and sketching and welding and sawing and tearing things apart so I can start again."

"Do you only work with metal now?"

"Mostly, but I integrate wood sometimes or even glass."

"Usually big sculptures?"

"A lot of those, but I still play with jewelry sometimes. I've even tried my hand at a couple of swords using Damascus steel."

She smiled. "Those are probably a little sharper than the ones used for LARPing?"

Kyle grinned back. "Sure, but they're no match for marshmallows."

Something about the shared memory seemed to shift the tension between them, which was odd. They had plenty of shared memories from a decade of family connection.

But they didn't have many that were theirs alone.

Meg tore her gaze from his and let it travel around the hodgepodge of art that lined the edges of his workspace—an unfinished sculpture of a tractor, a big sheet of punched tin, a box of old railroad ties he'd been meaning to sort through.

"Does everything you make here go into your gallery when it's done?" she asked.

Kyle shook his head. "Nope. Some of it's commissioned by private collectors and some of it's going into galleries in other cities. And some of it's yet to be determined." He toed a spare piece of steel on the floor at his feet, wondering what it would be by this time next year. "That's the beauty of doing this kind of work," he added. "Sometimes you don't know how something's going to turn out."

She looked at him for a moment, then nodded. "That is the beauty." She turned and took a step forward, then reached out to stroke a tentative hand over a half-finished T. rex sculpture made from pieces of an old chain-link fence. "You know, that's true of you," she said, her hand moving over the dinosaur's neck while her gaze didn't quite reach his.

"What's true of me?"

"The fact that you don't know how something's going to turn out." She shrugged, eyes still on the sculpture. "I remember getting to know you that first year Matt and I dated. I was fascinated by the notion of having two artistic brothers in one family when I can't draw a stick figure to save my life."

He laughed. "I'm kinda hoping there's never an occasion where you'll need to draw a stick figure as a lifesaving measure."

She glanced at him and smiled, but he could tell her mind was still drifting down that path of memories. Back to those early days when Matt had been this big-shot photographer showing off his star-studded portfolio and his photo credit in *Sports Illustrated* and his hot new girlfriend, while Kyle had still been trying to figure out how to pay for a box of Cap'n Crunch.

"I remember meeting you that first time," she said. "You were this grungy guy in ripped-up jeans playing guitar on the street corner to earn money for art supplies."

"Considering how badly I played guitar, I think I made enough to buy a box of pipe cleaners at the Dollar Store."

She took her hand off the dinosaur and moved on, stepping closer to a copper piece he'd started two days ago. He still didn't know what it might turn into, but at the moment it bore an uncanny resemblance to a toboggan.

"I remember you asking Matt for twenty bucks to get your power turned back on," Meg said, stroking a hand over the giraffe. "Matt was worried about you freezing to death in that crappy little apartment, but all you cared about was getting your electric band saw running again."

"First piece I sold, I went out and bought a cordless saw. Problem solved."

Meg laughed and drew her hand back from the toboggan. She looked at him, and Kyle had the unnerving sense she was staring straight through his eyes and into his brain. "Did you ever think you'd end up here?"

"Yes."

She looked at him. "Really?"

He raised an eyebrow at her. "You sound surprised."

"I am, I guess. I didn't realize you were so—"

"Cocky?"

"Confident," she said. "I guess I didn't realize back then that you had this sort of direction. That you'd set goals and had a plan to reach them."

"I wouldn't go that far. I just knew what I wanted and I went after it."

She nodded, and he watched her bite her lip. "I can see that."

A familiar pang hit him in the chest, but he ushered her forward and pointed to another sculpture. "This one's going in a gallery in Connecticut. I have a show out there in the spring, so I'll be flying out to get things set up there."

Meg reached out and ran a finger over the hammered bronze surface, and he noticed how small her hand looked. Had he ever noticed that before?

You always noticed. You noticed everything about her.

"Did I read somewhere that you work mostly with reclaimed materials?" she asked.

"When I can get them, yes. All the copper in that piece over there came from the roof of an old office building that got torn down near the Pearl District last winter. See all the punched tin on that piece over there?"

"This one?"

"It's an old barn roof. And that steel right there came out of the old mental institution in Salem."

"Is it finished?"

"Not quite."

"The mental institution, huh? Is the piece called *Looney Bin*?"

He laughed. "Believe it or not, I considered that. Also *Bughouse*, *Funny Farm*, and *Coocoo Shack*."

"So what's it called?"

"Fluidity Number Nine."

"I was close." She reached out to touch it. "It's beautiful. Very rough and raw, but it still manages to be fluid and graceful."

"Yes," he said, thinking he'd had art critics describe his work that way before, but it had never meant as much as hearing those words from Meg. "Come on," he said. "I want to show you the gallery. That's where all the finished pieces are."

He led her through a narrow hallway, maneuvering around piles of stainless steel and a pile of old car parts he'd been meaning to tear apart. "Careful of that stack right there. It's a little tippy."

"I know the feeling."

"Tippy, not tipsy."

"I know. I'm permanently poised to fall over, remember? I hope you have good insurance."

"I think I'm covered." He stopped at the end of the hallway, making Meg crash into his back. "Sorry," he said.

"You did that on purpose."

She was probably teasing, but it was a little bit true. He'd wanted to feel her pressed up close against him, to have her body up against his in the darkness. Feeling guilty, he hit the light switch.

A bright wash of light filled the gallery, spotlighting the twinkling array of copper and steel, tin and bronze. The pieces in here were mostly large, with a few smaller ones filling in space along the walls and shelves. He even had a small case of jewelry near the front, though he didn't make a lot of it.

The space was airy and open with knotty maple floors and walls painted the color of vanilla bean ice cream. There were lights scattered all over the space, positioned to illuminate the artwork. A faint hint of sage hung in the air, and Kyle ran a hand over the pedestal that held a metal bowl he'd filled with small pinecones and bits of high desert foliage.

Meg stepped forward and Kyle watched her face to gauge her reaction. Her gaze skittered from one piece to the next, and she pivoted to take in the whole space. "Holy cow," she breathed. "You made all this?"

"Yep," he said, trying not to beam like a smug bastard.

"This piece is beautiful." She reached out as though to touch it, then drew her hand back and shoved it in the pocket of her jeans. "I love the branches and the trunk and the way it all flows together."

"Thank you. Trees are one of my favorite subjects."

"Is this copper?"

"Nope, steel. But I used a salt and vinegar solution on it and then set it out in the sunlight to oxidize. It gives me the strength of steel but the patina of copper."

"Very nice." She squinted at the label on the pedestal of a smaller brass and pewter piece on the shelf. "Karma?" She stroked a hand down the figure's back, then laughed. "You sculpted your dog?"

"I made that right after she died."

"How sweet." She turned and looked at him. "Do you have a favorite?"

"Yes."

"Which one?"

He hesitated. "It's not here. It's back at my house."

"Can I see it sometime?"

"Maybe sometime," he agreed, deliberately vague.

"Did Matt have a favorite?"

Kyle shrugged, fighting the urge to feel annoyed that all conversations seemed to loop back to Matt. Was that the only connection between them? He hoped not, but maybe he was fooling himself.

"I'm not really sure Matt had a favorite," he said. "He liked that one in the front window, but I always thought it was because it's the most expensive."

"Probably a good guess." Meg wandered over to it, and Kyle watched her as she took in the shape of it, the curves and angles and edges. She gave an almost infinitesimal shrug and moved on, strolling the perimeter of the gallery.

He stood rooted in place, watching as she touched and admired and bent down to peer more closely at a grouping of smaller figurines on a low shelf. He watched where she lingered, wondering if there were certain pieces that spoke to her more than others. He'd had thousands of people study his art over the years, and couldn't think of a time he cared this much what someone thought of it.

She stepped into the center of the gallery, seeming to notice the giant calla lily for the first time. "Whoa," she said, standing on tiptoe to peer inside. "This one's cool."

"Thanks."

"It's huge." Her voice echoed a little as her chin brushed the edge of the petal, and she stood on tiptoe to peer deeper into the flower. "What's the story behind this one?"

He grinned. "You want the story I tell my mother, or the real story?"

She pulled her head out of the lily. "Which one's true?"

"There's a little truth to both stories, I guess."

"Then let's hear them both."

Kyle nodded, and rubbed a palm down the leg of his jeans. "If you ask my mother, I was inspired by the calla lilies my father brought her for Easter brunch last year. It's a representation of family harmony and tradition and the love my parents have shared for forty-three years."

Meg folded her arms over her chest. "And the real story?"

"The real story is that it's a stylized representation of Cara's . . ." he stopped, clearing his throat in hopes that Meg could fill in the blank herself.

It took her a few beats, but he knew she'd gotten it the instant her eyes widened. She took a step back. "Oh," she said, glancing at the lily again. "Ew?"

"Not *ew*. Not at all. The female body is beautiful."

"I didn't mean it like that. Just thinking I might not have stuck my head so far inside it if I'd known." She walked around to the other side of it, her discomfort seeming to give way to curiosity. "It is beautiful, you're right."

"Thank you," he said. "I'll tell Cara you thought so."

She laughed and trailed a hand over the stem. "You're still in touch?"

"Not like that."

"I didn't mean it like *that*," she said, rolling her eyes at him. "So she knows her lady-business is on display in your gallery for everyone to see?"

"Well, it's not like there's a label on it that says, 'Here's my ex-girlfriend's bikini biscuit.'"

"Bikini biscuit?" She snorted. "That's a new one."

"You prefer hush puppy? Coochie? Honey pot? Panty hamster? Cave of wonders?"

"God," she said, laughing. "You haven't changed a bit, have you?"

Kyle grinned, not sure whether to take that as a compliment or an insult. He decided it might be a little of both. "Besides trees, the female form is one of my favorite subjects, though I don't usually focus on a single part of the anatomy."

"I'll be watching for your display of kneecaps in the future." She walked around to the other side of the sculpture, and Kyle felt an unexpected surge of pride at how intrigued she seemed. "It's really intricate. The sculpture, I mean. I can't comment on Cara's bajingo."

"Thanks. It's sturdy enough it could be displayed outside if someone wanted that. The sculpture, not Cara's lady garden."

Meg snorted. "Please don't feel the need to elaborate on its ability to withstand weather conditions like intense moisture or pounding heat."

"You said it, not me."

Meg took another step to the side, coming full circle now to stand beside him. "Does it ever weird you out a little? Having your ex-girlfriend's vajayjay right there in the middle of your gallery?"

He shrugged. "Not really, though it sometimes makes me laugh to have people stroking it or asking how much it costs."

"How much does it cost?"

He nodded to the price tag near the corner of the base, and watched her eyes go wide again. "Holy cow. That's one expensive cha-cha."

"Literally and metaphorically."

"What do you mean?"

Kyle shrugged. "Cara got the house when we split."

"I didn't know you bought a house." Meg frowned. "Wait, you bought a house together, but you didn't want to get married?"

"I thought it was a good compromise."

Meg rolled her eyes, then ran her palm over the stem again. "I think it would weird me out, having this constant reminder of a failed relationship."

Kyle shrugged. "I don't really see it like that. Whether there's tangible evidence or not, aren't exes always sort of hovering around the periphery of our day-to-day lives?"

"I suppose that's true." He watched as she tugged at her earlobe, then flushed a bright crimson.

He grinned. "Confession number one—"

"No!" She shook her head, backing away from the calla lily. "Sorry, I'm pleading the fifth on this one."

Kyle raised an eyebrow. "Really? I'm intrigued."

"Don't be. It's just—some things are okay to stay secret, don't you think?"

"If you say so."

Meg wandered away from the sculpture, ending up back in the corner where they'd started. "This is amazing, Kyle. You should be very proud of what you've built for yourself."

"Thank you. I am."

She folded her arms over her chest and regarded him with a look he knew signaled a shift in conversation. "So," she said, leaning back against the wall with her eyes locked on his. "Ready to tell me why you wanted me to come here?"

CHAPTER NINE

Kyle cleared his throat, not sure he was ready yet to transition to the lecture part of the evening, but knowing she was onto him. "You don't think I brought you here just to see my gallery?"

She smiled and shook her head. "Nope. It's very nice, but that's not what this is about."

"Thank you." Kyle sighed and shoved his hands in his back pockets. "All right, Meg. I brought you here because I wanted you to see for yourself how much heart and soul and sweat and tears and dedication and love and personal experience goes into an artist's work."

"I can see that," she said, her voice wary now.

"And I wanted you to consider my mother's case from that point of view. From Matt's point of view."

She stared at him for a moment, then looked up at the ceiling. When she turned back to him, her expression was guarded.

"Can I ask you a question?"

"Sure."

"Why are you taking her side? You and your mom have never gotten along that well. Or is it about taking Matt's side?" She frowned at that notion, seeming to consider it. "But the two of you were always at each other's throats. *Literally*, at least once that I remember."

She didn't need to say anything else. Kyle remembered the fight like it was yesterday, even though it had happened nearly six years ago. They'd been drinking beer and bullshitting about a gallery opening they'd attended the week before. When Kyle made the mistake of telling Matt his new metallic print of a race car looked a little over-processed, Matt had responded by shoving Kyle.

He'd tried to pretend it was playful, but Matt's words had been anything but.

At least I'm earning a living off my art, baby brother. Just last week, I had a photo on the cover of Men's Health, *and here you are three months behind on your power bill.*

Meg had been the one to pull them apart, ordering them to separate corners of the room like a pair of squabbling children. In hindsight, Matt's bouts of temper were probably a sign of the depression lurking deep in his big brother's psyche, but that hadn't occurred to Kyle until years later.

Kyle cleared his throat. "I remember the fight, Meg." He felt his chest growing tight and he folded his arms over it to keep his heart in. "Obviously, that wasn't the proudest moment for either of us. Matt or me."

"Obviously."

"He was still my brother."

They let those words hang between them a moment, neither of them willing to concede. Clearly, this battle wasn't going to be won tonight. The lawsuit or any of the rest of it. Maybe it was best to just drop the subject and let things shake out in the court system.

But didn't he owe it to Matt to at least take a stab at defending his legacy? Didn't Matt deserve his loyalty, after all?

Meg dropped her hands to her sides. "That cookbook was my baby, Kyle."

"I know that. But it takes more than one person to make a baby."

She looked at him, then shook her head slowly. "You know, that's actually a good analogy. You seem to be looking at this whole cookbook thing like Matt and I rolled around naked together and produced it."

Kyle winced, wondering if she knew that the idea of his brother rolling around naked with Meg was the last thing he wanted to imagine.

"But the thing is," Meg continued, "it wasn't like that. I know you weren't privy to our conversations, so it's my word against your brother's. But the way it happened was more like a sperm donation."

"You're equating Matt's photos to *that*?"

"In a way, yes. I went to the sperm bank, paid my fee, went home with the turkey baster and—"

"Okay, I get it," he said, not sure whether he was more annoyed or turned on by the picture she was painting.

Meg sighed. "I know we didn't have legal contracts in place, and believe me, I regret that. But this is like the sperm donor's family coming after the baby. Or not even the baby—more like the income the baby makes when it suddenly becomes a stockbroker and makes millions in spite of the fact that the sperm donor and his family scoffed at the baby and never believed he'd amount to anything and—"

"Okay, Meg," he said. "You've made your point." Her words had touched a nerve, though he didn't want to admit it. He felt something tearing him in two. Half of him wanted to prove loyalty to his brother, to make up for some of the shitty things between them over the years. But part of him knew what it felt like to be that damn baby. Or to produce a baby no one believed in or—

Hell, he was getting lost in the damn metaphors, and maybe this whole conversation was pointless anyway. He raked his fingers through his hair, not sure where to go from here.

It was Meg who extended the olive branch first. "I'm sorry," she said. "I wish things were different."

"Me, too."

"I want us to be friends again."

Kyle felt his heart twist. "So do I."

"How about we agree not to talk about this stuff? About the lawsuit or the cookbook or anything having to do with your family."

"That seems like a tall order."

She shrugged and shoved her hands in her back pockets, which gave her a softer, more approachable look. Not that Kyle should be approaching her. Not that way, at least.

"I'm willing to try," she said.

"I'll give it a shot."

"Friends?"

"Friends," he confirmed.

The silence between them stretched out for a good long while, making it clear the friendship thing was easier said than done. A clock jittered loudly in the corner, and Kyle wondered if he should just take Meg home. It was getting late, and it had been a helluva long day for both of them.

"Why did you ask me to bring the ring?"

Her voice startled him, and it took him a moment to figure out what the hell she was talking about. He'd almost forgotten, but it seemed like the perfect chance to move on to something more constructive. "I'll show you," he said, moving past her and into the hallway. He flipped the lights off in the gallery and heard her hustling behind him to catch up. She was only a foot or two behind, but he still gave a start when she touched his arm.

"Oops," she murmured, latching on to his shirtsleeve. "I have terrible night vision."

"My fault—I should get lights in this hall." He stopped walking and fished in his pocket. "Dammit, I left my phone in the studio."

She laughed. "You're going to call an electrician?"

"No, I was going to use a flashlight app."

"It's okay, I can just hold on to you."

She was still clutching his sleeve, and Kyle looked down at the dark outline of her hand on his arm, conscious of how very close she was. It was too dark to see her face, but he could feel the heat from her body and it made his blood begin to simmer. A wisp of her hair floated on a current from the heat duct overhead, and Kyle fought the urge to tuck it behind her ear. What was it about being alone in the darkness with her that brought out the urge to do foolish things?

He heard her breathing beside him and felt the warmth of her fingers through the thin cotton of his sleeve. It seemed unusually hot in the hallway, and the scent of flowers in her hair was making him dizzy enough to do something dumb.

Meg must have read his mind. "You're thinking about that kiss in the closet, aren't you?"

"How did you know?"

"Because so am I." Her grip tightened on his arm.

"I haven't stopped thinking about it all day."

"Me neither."

His heart was pounding in his throat, and he tried to remind himself of the million and one reasons this was a terrible, horrible idea.

But all the reasons were clouded together and jumbled with the singular thought of how very, very badly he wanted to kiss her again. To twine his fingers in her curls and angle her mouth toward his, to run his hand up her side and feel her hot and alive beneath his palm.

Meg's hand slid up his arm, moving slowly, giving him plenty of time to pull back, to remind them both why they shouldn't do this.

But it was all over the instant her fingertips grazed the back of his neck. Something primal took over, and Kyle backed her up against the wall, not sure if she pulled his face to hers or he boosted her up to meet his kiss. He didn't care whose idea it was. He didn't care who started it.

All he cared about was kissing Meg again.

◆　◆　◆

Meg felt the moan deep in Kyle's throat as he pressed her up against the wall and claimed her mouth with his.

I'm kissing Kyle again, she thought and wondered how she'd ended up here twice in one day after a decade of not allowing herself to even consider it.

There was less hesitation now than there'd been a few hours ago, though she wasn't sure if that was his doing or hers. This wasn't her ex's funeral, and this wasn't her ex's brother. Not now, anyway. This was just Kyle—*Kyle*—kissing her in his space, on his terms, and not because he felt sorry for her, either. He wanted her, if his hands on her ass were any indication.

He cupped both cheeks and boosted her up against the wall, and Meg started to protest. "You'll hurt your—"

The word *back* got smothered as their mouths collided, and he was kissing her too hard for the protest to make a difference. She felt her legs twine around his waist by instinct. She was no hundred-pound waif. Years in the kitchen sampling her own creations had seen to that, and her boobs alone probably weighed more than half the girls he'd dated over the years.

But he didn't seem to be struggling and hadn't dropped dead from exertion, so Meg let herself relax as Kyle's fingers found the hem of her T-shirt. She thought about sucking her stomach in, but who was she kidding? He'd seen her in a two-piece at least a dozen times, and he didn't seem repulsed. Actually, he seemed to revel in her skin, his fingers skimming her curves, taking their time to memorize all her flesh before moving upward to get to the good stuff.

The instant his palm closed over her breast, Meg groaned against his lips. He felt so good, and it had been so long since anyone touched her like this.

Had anyone touched her like this?

She tried to remember what Matt's hands had been like, then felt disgusted with herself for not remembering, or for trying to remember right now, in this moment, with the heels of Kyle's big hands grazing her nipples. She shoved Matt from her mind and ground herself against the hardness that pressed against Kyle's fly, wanting to feel all of him at once.

His fingers slid behind her and found her bra clasp. He seemed to hesitate there, and she wondered if he was waiting for her to tell him no, to demand he show her some respect or take his damn hands off her and treat her like a lady.

Meg broke the kiss and locked her eyes on his in the darkness. "Do it," she said with a fierceness that surprised her. "Tear the fucking thing off if you have to."

"Yes, ma'am."

He fumbled a little with the clasp, and she cursed her boobs for requiring bras with a billion little hooks and a veritable fortress of underwire. "Welcome to the world of industrial-strength bras," she said, trying to be glib about it. "Do you need me to—*oh*."

The clasp popped open and she saw the flash of his teeth as he grinned in the darkness. "Got it. I might be a slow learner, but I get there eventually."

"Thank God," she said as his hand closed over her bare breast.

He went back to kissing her, one hand sliding over her breasts while the other cupped her ass. Her legs and arms were shaky, and she wasn't sure if it was from nerves or the effort of keeping herself wrapped around him this way. It was hot in this hallway, but she couldn't tell if it was them or the space. The sharp tang of copper drifted from his studio, blunted by the scent of leather and something she thought might be wood smoke or maybe just Kyle. Part of her wished she could see him, that she could know the blaze of heat in his eyes as she ground herself against him and pressed her breasts into his palm.

But part of her feared the light. Would they be doing this if they could see each other? Would they turn shy and hesitant? She wasn't willing to find out.

She dug her nails into the back of his scalp and arched against him, loving the feel of those work-roughened hands on her skin. She did remember Matt's hands, after all. They'd been smooth and long-fingered, but Kyle's hands were big all over. A man's hands with calluses and ridges. How many times over the years had she let her gaze drop to those hands, wondering what they'd feel like as a contrast to Matt's more refined touch?

Stop thinking about Matt, dammit.

She felt Kyle tense between her legs, and worried for a second that he'd read her mind. She broke the kiss.

"What are you thinking about?" she asked.

"No," he said, and kissed her again. "What did you say earlier? 'Some things are okay to stay secret.'"

"Fair enough," she said, licking her lips. "How about I tell you what I'm thinking?"

"Does it involve my hands on your body?"

She laughed. "Definitely. I think you should take my shirt off."

"Okay."

"And your shirt."

"Right."

"And your pants. And—I don't suppose there's a bed anyplace nearby?"

He nodded, or at least that's what it looked like in the darkness. "Actually, yes. There's a cot in the studio," he said. "It's not much, but—"

"As long as it's horizontal, I'm good." Meg unclasped her fingers from around his neck and lowered herself to the ground. She tugged down the hem of her T-shirt, then folded her arms over her chest to form a makeshift bra in place of the one he'd left unhooked. "Lead the way," she said. "Slowly, though. In addition to having terrible night vision, I'm also without my underwire now. Thank you for that."

"My pleasure," he said, and slipped a hand around her waist.

They were both speaking in whispers, and Meg wondered why that was. Were they afraid of disturbing old ghosts, or afraid of scaring each other away?

Kyle steered her down the hall and paused at the entrance to the studio. She saw him start to reach for the light switch, then hesitate. He must be thinking the same thing she was about the lights, wondering if they'd chicken out without the cover of darkness.

She took a step forward, then felt her foot catch on something. "Ooof," she said. Kyle's hands shot out to catch her around the waist, and she felt a flush heating her cheeks. "Sorry. I tripped on something."

"My fault. There are a lot of somethings to trip over in here." He flipped the lights on, and Meg stood blinking in the brilliant white wash of it.

She looked up at him and smiled. "Hi, there."

He smiled back, almost shyly. "Hello."

"Fancy seeing you here." Meg tucked a curl behind one ear and scuffed her clog across the floor.

"You're beautiful."

She laughed and returned her arm to its folded position, trying to look casual and cool instead of like a girl trying desperately to support her own boobs. "Thank you." She glanced around the studio, wondering if he'd been kidding about the cot or if she was kidding herself about this being a good idea. "Where's that bed?"

"Right this way." He put his hand in the small of her back again and steered her toward the far corner of the studio, while Meg did her best not to trip over her own feet. "I brought it in a couple years ago when I was working crazy hours on a sculpture and I found myself sleeping on the floor just to catch a quick nap."

"You mean it's not where you bring all your floozy art groupies for threesomes?"

"No, I use my penthouse in Paris for that."

She giggled as he ushered her around a tall, tri-panel wood screen she guessed was there to offer some sort of privacy during his catnaps. There were a lot of windows in this place, though she supposed he could just put the blinds down. The cot was small, tinier than a twin bed, and the Batman sheets erased any suspicion that this was Kyle's regular seduction spot.

Meg walked to the edge of the cot and turned to face him. She hesitated, then uncrossed her arms. A flash of self-consciousness moved through her, and she wondered for the briefest moment what he'd say if she told him she'd changed her mind.

But she hadn't. Not even close.

He stood frozen before her, seemingly waiting for her to make the next move. So she did.

She caught the hem of her T-shirt in both hands and tugged it over her head, wishing she'd perfected one of those supermodel disrobing maneuvers she'd seen on TV.

But the look on Kyle's face told him he wasn't concerned with her moves.

"Holy Christ," he said as Meg dropped her T-shirt on the floor. Her bra was tangled up in one of the arms, so she stood there topless and exposed in the bright wash of light from the studio.

His reaction made her bold, so she straightened her back and opened her arms to the side to give him the full view. A cruel puberty had left her occasionally self-conscious about her breasts, but this wasn't one of those times. In moments like this, she knew they were her nicest asset.

Meg licked her lips. "In case you were wondering, they're real."

"I know," he said, taking a step forward and sliding a hand up the curve of her waist. "Believe me, I know."

She wanted to ask if Matt had told him or if he'd figured it out for himself in the closet, but bringing up Matt right now didn't seem wise.

"I get a lot of speculation," she said as he bent to kiss the side of her neck. She gave a small hiss of pleasure and closed her eyes. "You know, 'big boobs, small body,' it doesn't add up in people's minds, and—"

"They're definitely real," he said as his hands moved over them, steady and sure. "So are you. So is this."

She was too dizzy to know exactly what he meant, so she slid her arms around his waist and gave herself over to the pleasure of his mouth moving up her throat and behind her ear. She gasped as he kissed her shoulder, taking his time, getting to know her body.

She wanted to know his body, too.

Her fingers found the hem of his shirt and tugged up. She wasn't quite tall enough to execute the move seamlessly, and ended up stuck just below his chin. He stopped kissing her shoulder long enough to help her tug it over his head, and they both laughed when his arms got tangled up in the sleeves.

"You'd think we'd never done this before," Meg murmured.

"We haven't."

"You know what I mean," she said, kissing his shoulder. "With each other."

Kyle dropped his shirt on the ground and smiled, bare-chested and beautiful before her. She started to reach out and touch him, but he grabbed her by the waist and turned them both around so they faced each other in the opposite direction. Then he sat down on the cot, putting himself eye-level with her breasts.

Or mouth-level.

"Oh," Meg gasped as his mouth found her nipple and began to work magic. She twined her fingers in his hair and closed her eyes again, giving over to the sensation. Dropping her head back, she felt him taste and suck and stroke until her knees began to quiver.

"Please say you have a condom," she whispered.

"I have a condom."

"Thank God." She sank down onto the cot beside him and planted a kiss on his right shoulder.

He pulled her down onto the cot with him, lying back with her whole body pressed against his. It was a tight fit with two of them, barely enough room for them to lie on their sides facing each other. Somehow, Meg managed to get his pants down over his hips, and he grabbed them from her before she could toss them aside. "Wallet," he murmured as he kissed her breasts.

"Now's not the time to go shopping."

"Smartass," he said, delivering a light nip to the underside of her breast. "Here, take this."

He slid the condom into her hands and reached for the button on her jeans. Meg tore the wrapper open while he made quick work of getting her out of the rest of her clothes.

With the condom out of its packet, she reached for him with her free hand. The instant her fingers closed around him, she sucked in a breath. "Oh, my God."

She stopped herself there, afraid of what might come out of her mouth next. None of her thoughts were appropriate.

I haven't slept with anyone since him.

You're bigger than he was.

I hope this doesn't change things.

She pushed the thoughts from her head and focused on feeling instead. She slid the condom on, rewarded by his gasp of pleasure.

"I can't believe we're doing this," she murmured against his shoulder.

"Don't think," he said, rolling onto his back and pulling her on top of him. "This isn't about using our brains."

She couldn't help giggling then as she straddled him with her knees pressed against his hips. "What body parts should I focus on then?"

"Let me show you."

He reached between their bodies and positioned himself at her opening. She didn't need any further invitation. Meg slid down over him, gasping as he moved hard and slippery into her. A soft cry slipped from her throat, and she hoped like hell he didn't have any close neighbors.

Kyle smiled and moved his hands to her hips. She began to rock, slowly at first, letting their bodies adjust to each other. His hands moved to her breasts and stroked them, spurring Meg to quicken her pace.

"That's it," he whispered, moving with her. "Just like that."

She twined her fingers with his, palms brushing nipples, fingertips sinking into flesh. He drew his hips up and slid deeper, and Meg cried out again.

She closed her eyes and let her head fall back as she rode him faster now. She could feel the tension building inside her, which seemed much too soon. Usually it took forever, or at least longer than this. She opened her eyes and looked down at him, and she could tell by the tense cords in his throat he was close, too.

"Do it," she whispered.

"You first."

The wave hit her, then another and another until she felt something burst open inside her. A white, hot heat flashed through her, and Kyle's gaze locked with hers.

"*Yes!*"

His eyes widened, and she felt him pulse inside her. She couldn't tell where his spasms started and hers ended, but she knew the odds of it happening like this were slim. That some strange, otherworldly force was at play here, making them explode together like magnets lit on fire.

When it was over, she closed her eyes and sank down onto his chest. He stroked her back until their breathing slowed, then rolled her to her side. She curled against him as his hand stroked her waist, smoothing her skin like he was trying to memorize the curve of her hip.

"Holy wow," Meg said.

"My thoughts exactly."

She took a few gulps of air, then moved back so she could look up at him. "That was unbelievable."

"I'm surprised we didn't break the bed."

She laughed and snuggled closer to his chest, soothed by the sound of his heartbeat under her ear. Her own pulse began to slow, and she stroked her fingers over the fine hairs on his forearm. Kyle was so still, so quiet, that for a moment Meg thought he'd fallen asleep.

"What are you thinking?" he murmured.

She lifted her head from his chest and smiled. "That I'm really happy right now."

"Me, too. Deliriously happy. Stupidly happy. Insanely happy." He smiled, but Meg noticed it didn't quite reach his eyes.

She slid her hand to his chest, resting her palm over his heart. "Is everything okay?"

He seemed to hesitate, then nodded. "I feel amazing. Like—top five moments of my entire life right now."

"I'm sensing a 'but' here."

He grinned and reached down to squeeze her backside, and Meg gave a squeak of mock indignation. "I'm sensing a butt, too," he said, cupping her cheek in his palm. "And it's the best butt I've ever had my hands on."

She giggled and squirmed against him, rolling to rest her chin on his chest. "You're changing the subject."

"Yeah," he murmured. "I guess I am."

She waited, not wanting to push him. His heart was steady beneath her palm, a deep, comforting thud she could feel all the way up her arm. "Want me to confess a few things to make it easier?"

Kyle smiled and pulled her closer. "You don't have to, but I'm always eager to hear your secrets."

"Okay," Meg said, thinking about it. "Since we're naked, maybe they should be sex secrets."

"I like the sound of this."

She smiled. "Confession number one: I've never had a one-night stand."

"Really?"

"Yep. I guess you could say I'm sort of a serial monogamist."

"How do you mean?"

"I dated the same guy for two years in high school, then another guy for almost three years in college. There was one more relationship that lasted about a year, and then I met your brother."

She let those last words hang there in the air between them for a moment, and she watched his face for a reaction. His gaze held hers, sure and steady, and he didn't seem uncomfortable. Still, Meg wondered if it was taboo to bring up Matt right now, while they lay tangled naked together in sweat-damp sheets.

Kyle reached up and brushed a damp curl off her face. "What about since then?"

"Nope." She shook her head, and the curl slipped back over her eye. "I haven't dated anyone since—since—"

"The split," Kyle supplied, saving her the trouble of saying *the wedding* or *your brother* or something equally awkward.

"Right," she said, smoothing her hand over his chest.

"Wow. I guess I'm surprised. Does that mean you've been with only four men in your whole life?"

She smiled and planted a kiss over one of his ribs. "Five," she said. "There's you."

He laughed. "Right. Can't forget me."

"Definitely not. Not after that. Not after—" She hesitated, wondering if it would be going too far to say what she'd been about to tell him.

"What?"

Meg bit her lip. "Not after the best sex of my life."

He stared at her in stunned silence. "You don't have to say that, you know."

"I know. And I wouldn't say it if it weren't true."

Was it her imagination, or did his heartbeat seem faster beneath her palm? His gaze was steady, even, watching her with an intentness that nearly made her blush.

Still, he didn't say anything, and Meg felt an uncomfortable urge to fill the silence. "I guess that's a lousy thing to say, isn't it?" she said. "To imply I'm comparing. Especially given the obvious fact of who I'm comparing you *to,* especially today of all days just a few hours after—"

She couldn't finish the sentence. Saying *Matt's funeral* right here, right now, seemed like the worst thing she could possibly utter. The worst thing to even *think* after sex. Worse than "I have syphilis" or "Why does your penis bend to the left," neither of which was true, but her brain was starting to spiral down a dark path now as her own heart began to race.

But Kyle pulled her back from the edge. "Hey," he whispered. "It's okay. We've just been as intimate as two people can possibly be. I think it's okay to say what we're thinking, even if it's not the textbook dialogue people normally have after sex."

She gave him a small smile, relieved he didn't seem upset. "I didn't mean to disparage him," she said, cautious not to say Matt's name. "Things were fine a lot of the time. It was rocky there at the end, but I know a lot of that was my fault."

"How do you mean?"

She hesitated, wondering if he really wanted to know. His interest seemed genuine, but still. She was so out of practice with dating and intimacy, and she didn't have a clue what was okay to say here.

She chose her words carefully. "I was pretty upset when the cookbook didn't take off the way I'd hoped it might," she said slowly. "Between that and all the stress of planning a wedding, I guess I just— I didn't feel like it. Sex, I mean." She closed her eyes, feeling the words start to flow now that she'd tugged out the cork. "I always wondered if that's why he did it. Annabelle, I mean. It's not like our love life completely dried up those last few months, but I know it only happened a handful of times and I'm sure even then he knew I wasn't really in the mood and—"

She stopped herself again, pretty sure she'd gone too far. But Kyle slid a hand down her body and pulled her closer. "Hey," he murmured. "Open your eyes."

Meg obeyed, and the force of Kyle's green-gray gaze sent her heart thudding again.

"It wasn't your fault, Meg," he said softly. "Please believe me when I say that. You could have sewn your legs together and had your breasts replaced with toasters and it still wouldn't have given him the right to cheat on you. Do you understand?"

She nodded, wanting to believe him, wanting even more to move on to another topic of conversation. "Okay," she said. "I think we've covered my three confessions."

He watched her for a few more heartbeats, then lifted his hand and smoothed her hair back again. Then he drew his hand back and began to count fingers. "Serial monogamy, best sex of your life, and—well, I guess you get credit for that last one. Or maybe you get double credit for the best-sex-of-your-life comment."

Meg smiled, glad to see he was back to joking. She waited, wondering if he still planned to voice his own confession. It was okay if he didn't. She'd shared enough for the both of them, opening up in a way she really hadn't planned on.

Still, she caught herself listening for his voice.

"My confession," he said at last, "is that while the last hour with you has been one of the finest in my entire life, it seems wrong to have that happen on the day that's been one of the worst in my life."

Meg nodded, understanding completely. "That makes sense." She bit her lip. "Do you believe in God or cosmic forces or some other kind of puppet master out there controlling the universe?"

"I think so."

"Me, too." She stroked a hand over his chest, feeling his heartbeat strong and steady beneath her palm. "And I like to think that he or she or it or whatever's out there moving the chess pieces around has a way of making sure we never get more than we can handle. That if you're going to be handed something really lousy, you also get something pretty great to balance it out."

He looked at her for a moment, the intensity of his gaze nearly taking her breath away. Then he reached up and trailed his fingers over the back of her neck, stroking her softly until she lowered her head to rest on his chest again.

"I like that," he said softly. "I like that a lot."

Neither of them said anything for a long time after that. Meg felt herself drifting, not to sleep exactly. But off into another realm where there wasn't any room for regrets or sadness or anger or any of the rest of that.

Right now, it was just the two of them. Kyle and Meg, a pairing of names that sounded both familiar and foreign.

Kyle and Meg, she thought to herself, testing it out. *Meg and Kyle.* There was something thrilling about those syllables, something so different from the "Meganmatt" she'd grown used to over the years. Something that made her heart rate slow again, her breathing drop to a peaceful rhythm that matched his.

It's just us for now. The only two people in the world.

"Hello?" called a familiar voice. "Kyle, are you here?"

And his mother.

CHAPTER TEN

Meg would have known the sound of her former-future-mother-in-law's voice anywhere, even without the walls of Kyle's studio amplifying it to a disturbing series of echoes.

She wasn't used to hearing the voice while naked.

Kyle's face went white. He fumbled on the ground for their clothes and came up with a tangled pile that included his jeans and Meg's bra and T-shirt. He dropped the mess into her lap and stood up, while Meg tried to remember if they'd latched the sliding wooden door. She'd definitely closed it, but was it locked?

"Hang on a sec, mom!" Kyle yelled as he yanked his jeans on. "I'll be right there."

Meg struggled into her own jeans, not quite sure where her panties had ended up. Unencumbered by the need to don a bra, Kyle had already pulled his T-shirt over his head and was padding barefoot around the privacy shade. Meg clasped her bra in front and wriggled it around so she could get her arms through the straps, wondering if she should just crawl topless under the cot and hide. She heard the barn door move on its rails, but it sounded like he'd only opened it a few inches, just enough to peer outside. Meg flipped her T-shirt right-side out.

"Mom," she heard Kyle saying on the other side of the studio, his voice tinged with concern. "Are you all right?"

"I just needed to talk to you, sweetie."

"I'm kind of in the middle of something," he said. "Are you okay?"

Meg yanked her T-shirt over her head and tried not to think of what Kyle had been in the middle of moments before. God, had they really done that?

Damn straight, her body telegraphed with glee as every nerve ending in her did a little shiver of pleasure.

"It'll only take a second, sweetie."

"Mom, wait—"

The sound of the barn door rolling all the way open bounced through the studio, and Meg pictured Sylvia shoving her way past Kyle. He was a good foot taller than his mother, but Sylvia had speed and a mother's instincts on her side.

"For heaven's sake, I drove all the way here, Kyle. The least you can do is give me five minutes."

"Of course. It's just that if you'd called, maybe I—"

"You weren't answering your phone."

"Right." He cleared his throat, and Meg pictured him running fingers through his hair. "Like I said, I'm kind of in the middle of something."

"This won't take long."

Meg heard the shuffling of footsteps and stood up, looking for a place to hide. She spotted a bathroom right behind her, and thought about ducking into it. She should give them some privacy, not to mention putting an extra barrier between herself and her former-future-mother-in-law.

"I wanted to talk to you about Meg."

Or she could stay put. Meg bit her lip. Then she sat down on the cot.

"This can't wait?" Kyle asked.

"You seemed upset this afternoon when I brought up the subject of your brother's book. I hope you know—"

"It's not *just* Matt's book. His name's not even on the cover."

"That's another thing," Sylvia said. "Why didn't she give him proper credit?"

Meg balled her fists up and ordered herself to breathe. *They weren't there*, she reminded herself. *They don't know how it happened.*

But Meg did. She remembered every detail, every word out of Matt's mouth the night she'd brought up photo credits.

"I'm an established photographer with a respected brand," he'd told her. *"I've had my work on the cover of* Sports Illustrated*, for crying out loud. I don't want my name on some little self-published cookbook."*

She remembered cringing at his words, but trying to hold it together and be a professional about it. He was a commercial artist, after all. He knew that side of things better than she did. *"So how do you want me to credit you?"* she'd asked. *"Should I have Daphne put your byline under each photo, or—"*

"Just leave me out of it, babe. It's not like it's my best work or anything. I didn't even use my new Nikon for those shots."

She hadn't rated his best lens or his name on the cover of her book. It had stung at the time, but not as much as the next words out of Kyle's mouth.

"You're right," he said to his mother. "I'm sure Matt would have wanted his name on the cover of a bestselling book."

Meg swallowed hard and balled her fists in the blanket on the cot.

"Of course he would," Sylvia said. "I'm glad you see it my way."

"But you're forgetting it didn't start out as a bestselling book."

"That's not the point here, Kyle. That woman robbed him of—"

"That woman," Kyle interrupted, "may have a good explanation for why Matt's name isn't on the cover. Have you asked her about it?"

"I don't need to. I know my son. He would have wanted credit. Come on, Kyle, you know your brother was a stickler for that sort of thing."

"Artists make strategic choices all the time when it comes to artistic credit."

Meg dug her bare toes into the floor and wondered if Kyle would be defending her to his mother if she weren't sitting thirty feet away. He had to know she was listening, right?

Across the room, Sylvia huffed. "You're not suggesting Matt doesn't deserve credit?"

"Of course not," Kyle said. "But I have a friend who does computer animated design. Really artsy stuff, it's big in Japan. But she picks up side jobs for magazines, and she uses a pseudonym so no one gets it mixed up with her real work. Or what about ghostwriters? Plenty of writers pick up side work and never have their name on anything."

"Hmph," Sylvia said, her heels tapping across the floor. "Well, I suppose the photo credit doesn't matter as much as making sure Matt's estate is fairly compensated."

"Agreed."

Those two syllables sent a tiny dagger into Meg's heart, but it wasn't like he was saying anything she hadn't already heard him say. She certainly didn't expect a roll in the hay would change his point of view.

"Mom, I know you're hurting right now," he said, and the sympathy in his voice made Meg's chest squeeze. "Maybe the best thing to do would be to wait a little bit. Give things a chance to settle down a bit before moving ahead with this lawsuit."

"I just miss him so much."

"I know you do. So do I." Meg pictured him putting his arm around her, maybe tucking her head against his shoulder the way he and Matt used to do when she cried over sad movies or squabbles with their father.

"I feel like this is what Matt would want me to do," she said. "I feel like I owe him something."

"I know," Kyle said softly. "So do I." There was a dark note in his voice, something low and hollow that made Meg shiver.

"It's our job now to protect your brother's legacy."

Sylvia's heels tapped across the floor, louder this time, and Meg sat up straight on the cot.

"Mom, where are you going?"

"I need to use the restroom."

Oh, hell.

Meg bolted up. She leapt over the cot, her bare feet hitting the concrete floor on the other side. The door gaped open, so Meg scrambled into the bathroom and yanked at the doorknob, trying to pull it closed behind her.

The damn thing wouldn't budge.

She jerked again, frantic now. Sylvia's footsteps were getting closer and a fine sweat broke out on her arms and legs and pretty much everywhere she had pores. Desperate, she spun around and pushed the toilet handle down.

Then she turned and pasted on her friendliest smile.

♦   ♦   ♦

Kyle felt his heart stop when he rounded the corner to see Meg standing in the doorway of the restroom. He could hear the toilet tank refilling behind her, and he watched her tug down the hem of her T-shirt and smile.

She wiped her hands on her jeans and took a step forward. "You're out of paper towels, Kyle," she said, then cut her gaze to his mother. "Sylvia, hello. How are you holding up?"

"I'm fine," Sylvia said tightly.

"What brings you down here at this hour?"

His mother stared at Meg like she'd just piddled on the floor. "I could ask you the same thing."

Meg shrugged like it was no big deal and reached into her pocket. Kyle was busy glancing around for the damn condom wrapper—where the hell had it gone?—so he almost missed Meg's next move. He caught a flash of something in his periphery and looked back to see her pulling the engagement ring out of her pocket. His heart stopped, but Meg held out the ring like it was the most normal thing in the world.

"Kyle asked me to bring this by," she said, holding it out to him.

He took it without a word, still too dumbfounded to participate in the conversation.

His mom stared at the ring, then looked at Kyle. "What on earth for?"

Kyle swallowed, finding his tongue at last. "A lot of people use old jewelry to create something new. It offers a sense of closure."

Meg looked at him, startled, then nodded. "That's right. Now seemed like the right time to do that. As a tribute to Matt."

"And obviously, it makes sense for me to be the artist to handle the transformation," Kyle said. "It would give me closure, too."

"Of course." Meg nodded. "I have a great deal of respect for Kyle's work."

"And this way the ring won't just be sitting in a jewelry box or getting shuttled off to a pawn shop." He tucked it in his pocket, wondering if his mom noticed the tension between them. He sure as hell did. "Something Matt had a hand in choosing will live on."

His mother looked from him to Meg and back again, her expression not unlike the one she'd worn when she caught him his senior year with a bong he'd convinced her was a perfume bottle. Kyle wasn't sure if she was buying the story, but she didn't seem inclined to argue.

Looking surprisingly unruffled, Meg stepped aside and gestured toward the restroom. "I'm sorry, you needed to use the powder room?"

His mom gave Meg a deeply suspicious look, then stepped past her into the room.

"Careful," Kyle called after her. "The door sticks a little."

He gave it a good shove, nearly knocking his mother backward as she pulled it toward her. The instant he heard the lock click, he grabbed Meg by the arm and yanked her away from the door. He glanced back at the restroom, wondering if his mother was holding a glass up to the wall.

"I'm so sorry," he whispered in Meg's ear. "I had no idea she'd drop by."

"It could have been worse," she whispered back. "If she'd shown up thirty minutes earlier—"

"God, I'm going to have nightmares about that until I'm sixty."

"I'm already wondering whether she'd have let you finish before she clubbed me in the head with your claw hammer."

"Relax, I keep the claw hammer at home. She'd have used my sledgehammer."

The toilet flushed and Meg jumped away from him like he'd caught on fire. That's when he noticed the pink thong sticking out of the leg of her pants. He bent down to grab it right as his mother pushed the bathroom door open and came clicking out.

Kyle bolted upright and balled the panties in one hand, but there was no hiding them. His mother's gaze dropped to his fist and she frowned. Kyle swallowed hard, then reached into his pocket and pulled out the ring.

"It seems to be in good condition," he said, stroking the satiny pink fabric over the edge of the metal. "I'll just get it polished up and then I can start working with it."

His mom stared for a moment, then made another *hmph* sound and turned away. "I have to get back to your father," she said.

"Tell him I said hello," Kyle called, hoping his mother hadn't noticed Meg's face turning the approximate shade of a cherry tomato.

He shoved the panties in his back pocket and followed his mom to the front of the shop, wanting to make damn sure the door locked behind her. "Are we still on for lunch Monday?"

"Cristos at one." She turned and gave him a perfunctory hug, pulling back before he could even get his arms around her. She pinched his cheek. "Don't be late."

"Take care of yourself," Kyle said as she pulled the barn door closed behind her. He flipped the lock and waited until he heard her car door slam before he turned back to Meg.

"Holy shit."

Meg nodded. Her face had gone from flushed to pasty white, and she looked like she might throw up. If he'd thought there was any chance they'd get naked again as soon as his mom retreated, Meg's expression assured him it was more likely she'd sprout wings and fly around his studio.

"I suppose that could have been worse," he said cautiously.

Meg nodded, looking at the ground. "Not much worse."

"She never stops by the studio like that. She's probably lonely or something."

"Isn't your dad with her?"

"A little more these last few weeks, but you know how he is."

She nodded again, not saying anything. It was something they'd always had in common, the absentee father who wasn't really there even when he was.

But right now, Meg didn't seem inclined to bond over family similarities. She bit her lip. "I think I should go."

The energy between them had changed, he could feel that. What he didn't know is whether his mom's appearance had done it, or if Meg would have rolled off the cot with regrets no matter what.

Kyle swallowed. Hell, he didn't regret it. He'd do it again right now if he could, which probably made him the biggest asshole on the planet.

He spotted his keys on the workbench and put his hand over them. "You sure you don't want to talk for a minute? Maybe grab a cup of coffee or something?"

She hesitated, and her eyes dropped to the floor. They both seemed to notice the condom wrapper at the same time, fluttering like an injured butterfly in the heater vent beside the cot. He wondered if his mom had seen it, but decided he had bigger things to worry about.

"Come on," he said, and Meg looked up at him. He held out his hand and Meg took it, bridging the gap he could already feel widening between them. "I'll drive you home."

CHAPTER ELEVEN

Meg was elbow-deep in five dozen cream puffs when her phone rang Monday afternoon. She felt it vibrating in her back pocket, and hustled to wipe the lemon cream filling from her fingers onto the edge of the bowl.

The phone buzzed again as she ran one hand under warm water, and Meg jerked her hand out of the water to wipe it on her apron. She fumbled the phone out of her pocket and swiped at the screen with a greasy finger.

Straight Shot Literary Agency.

A fleck of pastry cream made it look more like *snot* than *shot* and Meg wiped it off with her sleeve and tried again, her butter-slick finger slipping ineffectively off the iPhone screen.

She had to admit she felt a twinge of disappointment knowing it was her agent and not Kyle, or maybe that was relief. She'd dodged two calls from him yesterday, unsure what to say now that they'd taken things to such an intimate level.

She was spared from figuring it out as she swiped at the screen a third time, finally connecting the call for real.

"Hello?"

"Meg! How's my favorite new client?"

She smiled and wondered if Nancy Neel said that to all the authors she represented, or just the ones who'd spent the last two weeks on *The New York Times* Best Sellers list.

"Assuming you mean me, I'm good." Meg lifted the hem of her apron and wiped her forehead, belatedly remembering she'd cleaned her pastry bag on the hem of the garment earlier. She glanced in the mirror over her sink, admiring the giant blob of lemon cream in the center of her forehead, speared by a big strip of lemon peel that made her look like a pitiful unicorn. She used her sleeve to wipe it away, grateful this wasn't a video call. "I'm busy, but good," she added.

"Excellent. Did you get those documents I sent over about German translation rights?"

"Yes. I haven't had time to look at them yet, but as soon as I finish up this catering job, I'll—"

"That's right, I forget you still have a job." Nancy sounded almost amused by that. "Well, as soon as I start sending you royalty checks, it'll be up to you whether you want to keep that up."

Meg picked up a cream puff and pried the top off, thinking about whether she'd ever want to give up catering entirely. "I love cooking," she said. "And baking. And coming up with new recipes."

"Of course you do. But now's the time to dream big. More book deals, maybe a regular magazine column or even your own television show."

Those last words echoed in Meg's ears, and she set down the cream puff to grip the edge of the counter. "Sure. That sounds good. All of it."

God, she sounded like an idiot. Nancy had to know Meg was in way over her head when it came to dreams of fame and fortune, but at least she was polite enough to treat her like a real professional instead of a clueless kid.

"The sky's the limit, Meg." Nancy cleared her throat. "We just have one tiny issue to deal with."

"Right," Meg said, and felt herself crash back down to reality. "You mean the lawsuit?"

"I mean the lawsuit. You've spoken with the attorney I asked you to meet with?"

Meg nodded, which was dumb, since Nancy couldn't see her. "Yes. Franklin. He seemed very nice."

"We don't want him to be nice. We want him to be an animal in the courtroom." She seemed to pause then, probably recognizing a court battle was the last thing Meg wanted. "If it comes to that, of course."

"Right," Meg said. "I talked with him quite a bit about verbal agreements and collaborative work and what might hold up in court and—"

The words got hung up in her throat, and Meg felt her hands start to shake at the thought of this whole thing blowing up in such a dramatically legal fashion. Maybe it wouldn't need to escalate that far.

"The Midland family's not backing down, Meg."

She closed her eyes and nodded. "I know."

"You know I signed you as a client with the understanding that this work was yours alone," Nancy said, and Meg braced herself for a lecture on how she'd misrepresented herself.

But instead, Nancy just laughed. "And as far as I'm concerned, *The Food You Love* cookbook *is* yours alone. We just need to find a way to prove that."

"Okay," Meg said, opening her eyes and feeling like she'd dodged a bullet somehow.

"Look, it would be helpful if you could dig through your records from that period when your ex-fiancé agreed to take those photos," she said. "Anything that shows his state of mind at the time or the kinds of things you discussed before he started clicking away."

"I'll see what I can do."

"The more detail, the better. Old emails, maybe love notes he might have left you—anything that talks about his intention to take those photos as a favor to you as your fiancé and not as a collaborator who expected a portion of the proceeds."

"Right." Meg heard a glum note in her own voice. There were no love notes. There never had been, which hadn't bothered her before. Meg cleared her throat. "I'll see what I can do."

"It'll all work out," Nancy said. "Try not to lose too much sleep over it."

"All right," Meg said, wanting desperately to believe her.

"In the meantime, you keep thinking about what your next book proposal might look like."

"I've been giving it some thought," Meg said. "I have a few ideas, and I can email you some things I'm kicking around."

"Perfect!" A blare of car horns sounded in the background, and Meg pictured her agent walking down some New York City street, maybe catching a subway or staring at a billboard in Times Square or doing something equally exotic instead of standing in her kitchen with a smear of pastry filling on her forehead.

"Okay, I have to run," Nancy said. "We can talk about this more when I'm in town later this week."

"This week?" Meg frowned. "Wait, you mean you're coming to Portland?"

"Didn't I tell you? I'm flying to LA for a conference, and I changed my flights so I can stop off and meet you. I'll be there Thursday. Here, I'll send you the flight information now."

"Oh," Meg said, dazzled by the idea of meeting her literary agent in person. Hell, she was still dazzled that she even *had* a literary agent.

"All right, I sent it. Check your inbox and tell me when you're free to meet. Oh, and Meg?"

"Yes?"

"Try not to worry too much about the lawsuit."

"Okay," Meg said, then clicked off the phone, wishing like hell it were that easy.

♦　♦　♦

Kyle had half expected his mother to be annoyed that he'd chosen to bring his dog as his lunch date.

But as he watched his mom slip a piece of bacon under the table, it occurred to him he might not have given his mother enough credit.

"Is that good?" Sylvia murmured, patting the little black and brown dog on the head as Bindi took a gentle bite of the proffered treat.

A bespectacled waiter strolled out to their table and refilled their water glasses from a tall pitcher, then stooped down to replenish Bindi's water dish. With a quick adjustment to the umbrella shielding them from the unseasonable burst of fall sunshine, the waiter turned and retreated back inside.

"The service here is always so nice," Kyle's mother said as she broke off another piece of bacon from her BLT and slipped it under the table. Bindi perked up her ears and cocked her head to one side, then licked Sylvia's fingers.

"Good girl, Bin," his mother cooed while Kyle took a bite of his club sandwich. He was still chewing when Sylvia looked back up at him. "So how are you holding up?" she asked.

Kyle finished chewing and swallowed, the bread making a thick lump in his throat. "Okay, I guess. How about you?"

He watched his mother's eyes grow misty, and she looked away, wiping her hands on a napkin. "I'm still just in shock." Sylvia pulled a bottle of hand sanitizer from her purse and dumped some into her hand, while Kyle took a gulp of his water and tried to force the bread lump down. "It'll be three weeks tomorrow. Did you know that?"

He nodded and took another sip of water. "It doesn't seem real. Friends keep sending me sympathy emails and Facebook messages and I keep thinking there has to be some mistake. He can't really be gone."

His mother nodded and wiped one eye with the edge of her wrist. "I know. I find myself getting irrationally angry at people who've sent sympathy cards or called to express their condolences. Like maybe if they didn't do those things, he might still be here."

Kyle set down his water glass and reached for his mother's hand. It felt small and bony and he wondered how he'd missed the fact that his mom was old enough to be a grandmother.

"Kyle?"

He looked up at the sound of a familiar voice and saw Cara walking toward their table. She wore a pale blue dress and an expression of mild shock. As she approached the table, she laid one hand over her heart and the other on Kyle's shoulder.

"I'm so sorry," she said. "I heard about Matt. I honestly don't know what to say." She turned and looked at Kyle's mom. "Sylvia. I can't even imagine what you're going through."

"Thank you, dear." Sylvia attempted a smile, but the gesture fell flat. She lifted her hand out from under Kyle's and dabbed at her mouth with a napkin even though she hadn't eaten anything at all.

Cara took her hand off his shoulder and glanced from mother to son, probably at a loss for what to say next. Kyle could relate. He had no earthly idea what to say to people anymore, especially the well-wishers with tears in their eyes and carefully rehearsed words of condolence.

That's what he loved about being with Meg. He could just be himself without worrying he'd say the wrong thing or deviate from the script on how the brother of the deceased was supposed to behave.

Looking up at his ex-girlfriend now, he tried to think of something to say. Bindi thumped her tail against his shoe, but didn't come out from under the table. It wasn't like her to be shy with new people—especially of the female variety—but it seemed everyone was a little out of sorts.

"I was actually thinking of you the other day, Kyle," Cara said.

"Oh?"

"I was cleaning out the office and found a box of your things. Nothing important—mostly junk—but I didn't want to throw it away without you seeing it first."

"That's nice of you," he said. He felt his mother nudge him under the table, and he looked over to see her giving him a meaningful look.

He knew she was trying to telegraph some message of instruction, but he had no idea what it might be. Maybe he was supposed to offer to pick up the box, or perhaps she wanted him to invite Cara to join them.

But Kyle didn't feel like doing either. His heart wasn't in it. Truth be told, his heart was in a commercial kitchen over on Oak Street.

He looked up at Cara again and she gave him a small smile. Her eyes were kind, and her dark hair was shorter, just a little below her ears now. She was still beautiful, but nothing about her made his heart roll over in his chest the way Meg did.

Kyle cleared his throat. "It's great to see you again, Cara. You're looking good."

"So are you. Really good." She smiled again and took a step back from the table. "Well, I won't keep you. It was nice running into you."

"Nice to see you, too, dear," Sylvia said. "Say hello to your mother."

"I will," she answered. "Please let me know if there's anything I can do."

"We will," Kyle said, wondering why that was one of the things people said to grieving family members. He'd heard it at least a dozen times these last three weeks, along with "My heart aches for you," and "He's in a better place." Phrases Kyle knew were well intentioned, but which had started to grate on him lately.

Cara gave him one last long look, then turned and walked away. Kyle's mother watched her go, twisting her hands in her napkin. When Cara turned the corner at the end of the sidewalk, Sylvia turned back to Kyle.

"I always liked her," she said, setting the napkin down.

"She's a nice girl."

"But not the girl for you?"

There was a note of hope in her voice, and Kyle hated to be the one to dash it. But he couldn't lie to his mom, either.

"I'm afraid not."

Sylvia nodded, resigned. "You know, with every woman you brought home, I always wondered, 'Could that be my future daughter-in-law?' Cara was the only one that made me think 'Maybe.'"

"What about Meg?"

The question seemed to startle them both, and he watched his mother's eyes widen, then narrow.

"I meant when Matt first brought her home," Kyle added, not wanting her to get the wrong idea. Or the right one. "Didn't you say you thought from the very beginning that she was like the daughter you always wished for?"

His mother's mouth tightened, but then she gave an almost imperceptible nod. "Yes. I did say that. She was like part of the family for a long time."

"That's true," Kyle said carefully, not wanting to say too much, but also not wanting to drop the subject of Meg. Just saying her name made something glow warm inside his chest. "I always thought it was odd how quickly we erased her from our lives after everything fell apart."

Sylvia pressed her lips together. "Meg Delaney made her choices. When she did what she did two years ago, and when she did what she did with the cookbook—those choices made it clear how little regard she had for Matt. For this family."

Kyle opened his mouth to argue, to say Meg's choices might have had nothing to do with the family and everything to do with Meg's need for self-preservation. "Matt wasn't completely innocent in that, you know," Kyle said softly. "In the fact that Meg called off the wedding."

"I know that," his mother said, closing her eyes for an instant. "Matt was no saint. But he tried to do the right thing. He tried to come clean so they could start their new life together."

"That's true." Kyle looked down at his water glass, not wanting to say too much.

"I'll never forget the look on Matt's face when she stood up there at the front of that church and said those words. 'I can't.' He looked like she'd reached into his chest and pulled his heart out. He loved her so much, and for her to humiliate him like that in front of all his friends and family—"

She broke off there, her eyes filling with tears. Kyle said nothing, not sure what he *could* say. His mother didn't know the half of it. She had no idea how awful it really had been. Kyle's chest ached with regret, and his limbs felt liquid and useless. He reached for his mother's hand again and gave it a small squeeze. "Let's talk about something else."

His mother dabbed at her eyes with the napkin, then gave a tight nod. "Yes. Let's. Something a little more uplifting than that woman."

Kyle nodded, biting back the words he could never say. *That woman* had been the most uplifting part of these last three weeks.

Or maybe the last ten years.

CHAPTER TWELVE

"Tell me again why we're doing this?" Jess asked as she huffed along beside Meg on Wednesday afternoon, her neon-pink running shorts hitching up on one leg as Jess reached down to scratch a bug bite.

Meg wiped her brow and kept going, wishing her stride was half as long and elegant as her best friend's. She pressed on anyway. "I just feel like I need to get in better shape," she said. "I've been feeling a little squishy lately."

"This wouldn't have anything to do with bumping uglies with Kyle on Saturday night, would it?"

Meg felt the heat creep into her cheeks, but she chalked it up to the exertion of the run. "Not at all."

"Liar."

"Fine. Maybe a little. You try having a man hoist you up and grope you against a wall and not feel—"

"Hell, yes! Where do I sign up for that?"

"My point is that having a guy try to lift me up off the ground is a good wakeup call that I could stand to lose a pound or two."

"Please," Jess scoffed. "It doesn't sound like he was exactly repulsed by your figure. Men like a little squish."

"They like squish in some places. Not all places."

"So you're doing this for Kyle?"

"No way," Meg panted. "I'm doing this for me. I'm not seeing Kyle again. Not like that, anyway."

"Liar!"

Jess's declaration was louder this time, but Meg just shook her head. "Nope. Come on, Jess. I told you it was a stupid idea for me to sleep with him. His family's spent the last two years hating me, and now they're suing me. Can you think of a worse person for me to be fraternizing with right now?"

"Fraternizing, huh? Is that what the kids call it these days?"

"Can we talk about something else?" *Or nothing at all.* Meg was feeling short of breath, and they hadn't even gone a mile yet.

"Fine." Jess turned off on a narrow path leading toward the river, and Meg's mind flashed to the last time she'd been here, running through the woods with an imaginary dragon and Kyle with a bag of marshmallows. Had only three weeks passed since then? It felt like a lifetime ago.

"Did I tell you I'm having coffee with my literary agent tomorrow?"

Jess laughed. "You don't know how much I love hearing you say 'my literary agent.'"

"You don't know how many times I had to practice saying it before it rolled off my tongue."

"So is she going to tell you how much money you've made?"

Meg shook her head. "I don't think publishing works like that," she panted, wiping a sweaty curl off her forehead. "You don't start seeing checks roll in right away, not even for a bestselling book. Hell, maybe I won't make much money at all."

"Please. You've been in the number-one slot on *The New York Times* Best Sellers list for two weeks. Pretty sure that'll earn you more than a cup of coffee and a donut."

Meg frowned. That's precisely what Matt's parents were assuming, too. She knew her attorney had been talking with their attorney, and the thought that she had an attorney at all was as mind-boggling as the idea of having a literary agent. So far, she'd avoided talking further with Kyle about it.

Hell, she'd avoided talking to Kyle at all. It had been four days since they'd slept together, and though he'd phoned several times, Meg kept dodging the calls. She didn't know how she felt about the unexpected shift in their relationship, and she wasn't ready to talk until she'd sorted it all out.

"Everything's just moving so fast," Meg said, not sure if she was talking about the cookbook or what happened with Kyle.

"You know what's not moving fast?"

"Hm?"

"Us." Jess reached over and patted her butt. "Come on, let's kick it up a notch."

Meg groaned. Why hadn't she remembered how much she hated running? It had seemed like a good idea at the time, but now, with sweat pooling between her boobs and her lungs feeling like someone had taken a blowtorch to them, she was reconsidering. How many calories did yoga burn? Or maybe gardening. Anything without so much jostling.

She reached into her sports bra to adjust the girls, nudging her iPhone out of the way and saying a silent prayer her waterproof phone case was sweatproof, too. She should have left the damn phone at home, but her agent had ordered her to stay available. Apparently her lawyer was brainstorming new ideas to defend Meg's cookbook royalties, and they needed to be able to reach her at all times.

Meg jammed the phone deeper into her bra and thought about investing in one of those cool armband phone holders. Maybe if she had something like that, or maybe a dog to go running with every day—

"So anyway," Jess said. "I was thinking about changing my—"

"Starting FaceTime with Kyle Midland."

The voice echoed from the depths of Meg's cleavage and it took her a moment to realize what was happening.

"What?!" Her shriek ricocheted through the park as she skidded to a stop on the trail. Meg stuck a hand in her bra, fumbling to retrieve the sweat-slick iPhone. She felt it vibrate, then heard the distinct buzz of a video-call going through.

"Holy shit, end call!" Meg panted. "Stop FaceTime! Abort!" Meg yanked the phone out of her bra and stabbed at the screen with sweaty fingers. Her thumb skidded off the plastic screen protector, having zero impact on any of the controls. Panicked, she shoved the phone at Jess.

"Do something!"

"What am I supposed to do?"

Jess grabbed the phone and looked around, then down at her own clothing. Her shirt was drenched with sweat, but her shorts looked dry. Before Meg could stop her, Jess was wiping the phone on her rear end.

"Hello?" Kyle's voice echoed off Jess's butt. "Meg? Is that you?"

Jess drew the phone back and held it up so Meg could see. Kyle's face was framed in the center, looking bemused and a little sleepy. Jess angled the phone so Meg's face was in the frame, too, which was a mistake. God, she looked horrible. Red-faced and sweaty and—

"Meg?" he asked again.

Meg stared open-mouthed, trying to think of what to say. Jess started to hand her the phone, then stopped and pointed at Meg's top.

"Fix your boob," she whispered.

Meg looked down to see her right boob making a valiant escape attempt from the sports bra. She reached down and adjusted herself, using her arm to shield the view as she shoved everything back into place.

"Kyle," she said, trying to sound as casual as she could. "Um, good morning. How are you?"

"I'm fine. Looks like you're exercising?"

"Right." Meg wiped a hand over her brow, then took the phone from Jess. "You know me, I live to get fit."

"Since when?"

"Since—shut up, Kyle."

He laughed. "Why did Jess tell you to fix your boob? Is it broken?"

She shot a look at Jess, who was laughing so hard she had to hold on to a flagpole to keep her balance. "Look, Kyle. Sorry, but I didn't mean to call you."

"It was an accident?"

"Exactly."

"How do you accidentally FaceTime someone?"

Meg blew a sticky curl off her cheek and sighed. "If you must know, my boobs called you."

He stared at her. "Your boobs," he repeated. "What did they want to say to me?"

"Nothing. They acted on their own without consulting me."

"They do that sometimes."

She hadn't thought her face could get any redder, but she'd been wrong.

Kyle wasn't done. "So, was that Jess's butt on the screen just a second ago?"

"Hi, Kyle!" Jess crowded in behind Meg and waved at the screen. "Meg's boobs might've called you, but my ass wanted in on the conversation."

"The more the merrier when it comes to video calls."

Jess laughed and pulled her foot up behind her, stretching her quad. "It's good to see you," she said.

"Good to see you, too. You're looking—sweaty."

"We're out for a run. Good for the heart, you know."

"Absolutely," Meg agreed, thinking she might not mind dying of a heart attack on the spot. "So listen, Kyle—"

"I heard you on the radio the other night," he said. "You sounded great."

"Thank you," she said as something inside her softened a little. "NPR did a special on the cookbook."

A dumb thing to say, since he'd obviously heard it. But if he saw the opportunity to tease her, he didn't seize it. "Sounds like things are going great with the book."

She nodded, resisting the urge to bristle. He was just making conversation, not fishing for information to relay to his mother. "That's true."

Kyle cleared his throat. "So, Meg. I'd still like to talk. It's been four days."

"I know," she said, closing her eyes. She'd avoided him like a big, fat chicken, and he had every right to call her on it. It's just that she had no idea what to say now that she'd gone and mucked everything up by sleeping with him.

But standing here with her eyes shut tight and his voice low in her ear, it was impossible not to remember the feather-light kiss he'd skimmed across her cheek when she'd gotten out of the car that night.

Meg swallowed hard and opened her eyes to see Jess eyeing her curiously. "I've just been busy."

"Running?"

"Running. And dealing with cookbook stuff and catering jobs and—"

"So how about Friday evening?"

"Friday?"

"Sure. The day after tomorrow. Are you doing anything?"

"Actually, yes. I'm catering a bachelorette party Saturday and I have to prep a buttload of food for it. I'll probably be at it all night since my assistant called this morning with the flu."

"So I'll be your assistant."

"What?"

"Let me assist you. I'm not the world's greatest chef, but I can chop things."

Meg bit her lip, considering. She could always ask her mom for help, or get it done by herself with a few extra hours of work.

But there was a small, traitorous part of her that desperately wanted to see Kyle again. To work side by side in the kitchen while he hummed tunelessly and chopped carrots and told her about his day. Wasn't that the thing she'd missed most in the past two years of silence?

He must've sensed an opening in her hesitation. "Come on, Meg. Let me help. Besides, I have something for you."

Jess bounced with glee, then pantomimed a few hip-thrusts. Swatting at her friend, Meg tried to steer the phone away so Kyle wouldn't see. "What do you have?"

"I'm not going to give it away on the phone. You have to see me in person. Besides, I need to see Floyd again. I'm determined to make him like me."

"By forcing yourself on him?"

"Nah, I have a new strategy," he said. "What time do you want me?"

Her libido got hung up on the last part of his question, and it took her a moment to answer. "How about five?"

"I can do five."

"Okay, but you have to let me pay you. And we won't be at my place, we'll be at my commercial kitchen."

"You can pay me with dessert."

"That hardly seems fair, but I did just make a flourless chocolate cake."

"Excellent. Are you still working in that culinary space off Oak Street?"

"Yes."

"Perfect. We'll get the prep work done, and then you can take me back to your place."

"What?"

Kyle laughed. "To eat cake and pet your cat. Get your mind out of the gutter, Meg."

"I—"

He was still laughing when he hung up.

◆　◆　◆

"It's good to finally meet you in person, Meg."

Nancy Neel picked up her cocktail glass and took a sip of her dirty martini. The drink made Meg wish she'd ordered something more exotic, and Nancy's manicure gave her the urge to hide her own battered hands under the table.

"I still can't believe you're here in Portland," Meg said. "I didn't think I'd get to meet my agent in person so soon."

Hearing the phrase *my agent* trip off her own tongue gave Meg a tiny thrill, and she picked up her mug of herbal tea and took a sip to hide her giddy smile.

"Yes, well, it wasn't really any trouble to reroute my trip. Besides, you're not just any client. *The Food You Love* is the hottest thing since— well, I was going to say sliced bread, but that's hardly sexy enough to describe an aphrodisiac cookbook, is it?"

Meg laughed and set her tea down. "I'm drinking chamomile tea and wearing clogs. I can assure you being sexy isn't a regular part of my repertoire."

"Hm, actually, I think you've got some good raw material to work with." Nancy eyed her up and down, and Meg wondered if she was supposed to stand up and twirl. "You've got great hair and nice curves. The camera tends to add a few pounds, but you can get away with that when you're a celebrity chef."

"Camera?"

"Yes, I've had a lot of inquiries about television interviews and the like." Nancy twirled her martini glass in one hand. "Of course, we do need to get things settled first with the photography rights and Mr. Midland's estate."

Meg bit her lip and tried not to let the nervousness show on her face. "I'm working on it," Meg said.

"You're sure you don't have any sort of signed contract that can clear this mess up once and for all?"

Meg shook her head. "Like I told you, we didn't think we needed one."

"You *always* need one," Nancy told her. "Even when you're collaborating with a loved one." She gave a brittle laugh and waved her hand. "*Especially* when you're collaborating with a loved one. God, if I had a nickel for every ruined romance that screwed up a perfectly good publishing deal, I'd buy a condo in Bali tomorrow."

Meg gripped her mug a little tighter and stared into it, not wanting to meet Nancy's eyes. "I wish I'd known. I wish like hell I could go back in time and do everything differently . . ." She trailed off, not sure she was still talking about the book.

"Well, lesson learned." Nancy reached out and patted her hand, then took a big swig of her drink. "We'll have you making smarter business decisions in no time. No more sentimental muck for you! In the meantime, let's just hope we can get your ex's family to back down."

"Let's hope," Meg said softly, wishing she felt more confident.

◆　◆　◆

Kyle rapped on the door of Meg's commercial kitchen space right at five, hoping she hadn't changed her mind about letting him help. He tried to remember the last time he'd been here, then realized he knew exactly when it was. The morning before her wedding.

Back then, she'd agreed to let someone else handle the catering for her reception, but Meg had insisted on doing dessert herself. She'd planned a huge display teeming with beautifully decorated cupcakes in exotic flavors like passion fruit and crème brulée, and she'd spent the whole morning decorating hundreds of little paper-wrapped delicacies.

Kyle was still thinking about the cupcakes when Meg threw the door open. "Kyle," she said. "Thank you for coming."

"Happy to help."

Her expression was somewhere between shy and guarded. He'd expected bristly, so this seemed like an improvement. She wore jeans that looked like they'd been washed enough times to give them the texture of velvet, and he ached to run his hand over her thigh. Her hair was loose around her shoulders, and she wore a pink T-shirt that said *eff cancer*.

"I like the shirt," he said, stepping over the threshold of the door. No sense giving her a chance to turn him away and insist she didn't need help. "Lost an aunt to breast cancer a few years back."

"I know," Meg said, shutting the door behind him. "I was at the funeral, remember?"

"That's right, I forgot."

He hadn't, actually, though he'd tucked the memory in the back of his mind with so many other recollections of Meg over the years. Had the tiny webs of laugh lines been there at the edges of her eyes back then, or were those new? He wasn't sure, though he knew his own face had changed in the last decade.

"Thanks again for offering to help," she said, handing him a long, white apron. "I wasn't looking forward to working alone all night to get the prep work done."

"Not a problem." Kyle looped the apron around his neck and began to tie it in back. Meg was doing the same with hers, and he thought about offering to help her tie it, but held off. Putting his hands on her again seemed like the wrong thing to do, at least right now.

She smoothed her hands down the front of her apron and gave him a slightly sheepish look. "So, uh—I probably should have told you a bit more about what we're making."

"You said it's a bachelorette party?"

Meg nodded and bit her lip. "Yes. And the bride has a rather risqué sense of humor."

"How do you mean?"

She cleared her throat and looked down at the counter. "How do you feel about decorating cock pops?"

"Uh—"

"They're kind of like cake pops, only they're shaped like penises."

She turned and bent down to retrieve something out of the cooler, and Kyle tried not to stare at her ass. When she stood up, she was holding a dick on a stick. She thrust it toward him, and Kyle took a step back without thinking about it.

"Holy shit," he said, peering more closely at the cock pop. "What's the stuff around the nutsack that looks like pubic hair?"

"Toasted coconut. I was worried I hadn't gotten the flesh tone right with the royal icing," she said, running a finger around the terrifyingly lifelike head. "But I think it's pretty close, don't you?"

"If it looked any more real, you could be arrested for holding it in public."

"Thank you." Meg beamed and set the cock pop down on the counter. "I just did this one to test out the icing, but I have to do fifty more of them. The cake inside is passion fruit."

"Of course it is." Kyle stared at the cock pop and shook his head. "It shames me to realize I kind of want to bite into it."

Meg laughed. "I made extras so I could practice decorating them. I'll let you take some of those home at the end of the night."

"Defective cock pops? Can't wait to devour one of those."

Meg grinned and put her hands on the stainless-steel counter. "Actually, I'm thinking I might just have you chop veggies for the penis pasta salad."

"Of course there's a penis pasta salad."

"I made all the little penises by hand, which took forever."

"I feel like I should be able to come up with a good hand job joke right now, but I'm honestly at a loss."

"You should have seen me trying to talk the bride out of an alfredo sauce," she said. "Not the best choice with penis pasta."

"Good Lord."

She laughed and brushed a curl off her forehead. "It's fine now, we're going with a basil pesto instead."

"Green dicks? This sounds more appetizing by the minute."

"You can wash up over there," Meg said, pointing him toward the sink. "All those veggies in the bowl can be chopped, and there's a big tray of roasted red peppers cooling over there when you get done with those."

"What are you going to be working on?"

Meg tugged her hair back with an elastic band, then stepped up to the sink to give her hands a quick scrub. "I need to get started on the dickerdoodles."

"Of course you do."

She finished washing her hands, then wiped them off on a big white dish towel. Then she stepped aside to give him a turn at the sink, moving toward the large commercial refrigerator in the corner.

Kyle watched her pull out a massive hunk of Saran-wrapped dough, and he felt his mouth water at the memory of Meg's favorite cinnamon-laced cookies. She set the dough on the counter and pulled open a drawer, drawing out not one, not two, but *three* cookie cutters in phallic shapes. Something about seeing her hands on those odd metal penises made his mouth water in a different way, and he had to order himself not to stare.

"Really, Kyle," she said. "I can't thank you enough for your help."

"It's not a problem. I wanted to see you."

He turned and began scrubbing his hands at the big commercial sink, remembering the time she showed him the trick about rubbing his hands on the stainless steel to get rid of the smell of onions. How long ago was that? Three years? Four?

"I wanted to see you, too." Her voice was so soft behind him that he had to turn to make sure she'd spoken at all. She gave a sheepish shrug and picked up a little paring knife. "I know I've kinda been MIA this past week. I just—had some stuff to process."

"Stuff," Kyle said, drying his hands on the white dish towel as he turned so he could see the side of her face. "You mean like the fact that we slept together?"

Meg jumped like he'd just poked her in the ribs. "Well," she said, turning to face him as her cheeks turned a fetching shade of pink. She didn't say anything else after that, and there was something utterly charming about seeing her at such a loss for words.

That, and seeing her clutching a tin penis in one hand.

Kyle smiled and leaned back against the sink. "I'm ripping the Band-Aid off, Meg. Might as well put it out there so we can stop letting it be awkward."

"Because this isn't awkward?"

"It's less awkward. Or it will be in a few minutes. I hope."

Meg set the cookie cutter aside and bent to pull a knife off the magnetic strip under the counter. Kyle made a valiant effort not to look down her shirt. Or at her ass. Or at her—

"We slept together," Meg confirmed, straightening up. "Or I guess if we're going for the blunt approach, we had sex."

"That we did."

She sighed and set the knife on the counter. "Kyle, I don't know what got into me that night."

"Well, for starters, I did," Kyle said. "I was in you for at least ten or fifteen minutes."

Meg's cheeks went from pink to bright red, and she picked the knife up again. "That's true."

"And I don't regret it."

He let the words hang between them a moment, watching her face for a reaction. She seemed to be considering his words, or maybe her own. When she spoke, her voice was barely a whisper.

"I don't regret it, either," she murmured.

"You don't?"

She shook her head and unwrapped the cookie dough. She sliced off a big hunk, then pulled off a small bit and began rolling it into a ball. "But then I feel bad for not regretting it, because I totally *should* regret it, and—"

"Who says you should?"

"What?"

"Did you consult a rule book that told you how you're supposed to feel after sleeping with someone for the first time?"

"You're not just *someone*, Kyle. You're one of my oldest friends, and you're also my fiancé's brother."

"Ex-fiancé," he reminded her.

"My *late* ex-fiancé." Meg shook her head and smashed the ball of cookie dough with the heel of her hand. "Christ, we did it on the day of his funeral. It just seems so—so—"

"Jerry Springer?"

"I was going to say disrespectful, but it's that, too."

Kyle nodded and stepped into the space beside her. He picked up one of the small zucchinis and turned it over in his hand. Was it just him, or did everything in this kitchen look phallic?

That was probably the point. He put it on the cutting board and picked up a paring knife. "How do you want this cut for the penis pasta salad?"

She turned and looked at him. "Cut it in half lengthwise, then half again so you've got quarters. One-inch slices would be perfect."

"Coming right up."

Kyle was quiet a moment as he began to chop, appreciating the steady comfort of working side by side with her in the kitchen. He'd spent the whole week wondering if sleeping with Meg would dissolve this easy rhythm they'd always found between them, and he was relieved to realize it hadn't.

The conversation might be awkward, but being with her never was.

"So do you want to just write the whole sex thing off as another one of the weird parts of the grieving process?" he asked. "Like going grocery shopping barefoot or combing the cat with your toothbrush?"

He glanced over in time to catch the faintest hint of a smile on her face. "I'd say it's a step beyond those things," she murmured.

"Probably. Still, grief makes people do crazy things. We've already established that."

He was giving her an out, he knew. An excuse and a chance to explain away a one-time dalliance they should probably both agree shouldn't happen again. Part of him wanted her to take it.

Part of him wanted her to turn around and look him right in the eye and insist it was something more. That what happened between them had been brewing for a long time, years, maybe. Since long before that Thanksgiving with the doves.

"Grief," she repeated slowly. "I guess. Everything happened so fast."

He laughed. "We've known each other more than a decade, Meg. I don't think that's fast."

"You know what I mean."

He nodded. "I'll admit our timing was a little—odd."

"To say the least."

"But stranger things have happened."

She nodded and began dumping cinnamon and sugar into a bowl. She used a fork to blend the two together, then she turned and looked at him. "So, your mother called me."

"Holy subject change, Batman."

"You're the one who said it was important to have the awkward conversation."

"Yes, but the sex one was more fun."

Meg picked up one of the dickerdoodle balls and began rolling it in the cinnamon sugar. He suspected it was less about making the cookies and more about avoiding eye contact, but he couldn't really blame her.

"So, my mom called?" he prompted.

"It was actually her lawyer who called. He insists they still haven't received the check I sent last week. The one for eighteen hundred dollars?"

"Right," he said. "The final payment toward the ten-thousand-dollar bill Matt gave you after the wedding."

"Yes. That's one of the arguments they're making to prove I hadn't made sufficient progress on paying off the debt. And if the debt wasn't settled—"

"Then they're entitled to a portion of your royalties."

"So they say."

Kyle frowned and sliced into the zucchini. "So the check hasn't shown up."

"That's what they claim."

He ignored the implication of the word *claim,* resisting the urge to defend his mother. "Did you send the check through certified mail?"

Meg shook her head and frowned. "It was a Saturday when I got paid, and the post office wasn't open. I just wanted to get the check in the mail fast and I didn't realize it would be an issue and—anyway, no. Chalk up one more financial mistake for Meg Delaney."

The bitterness in her voice left him struggling to remember whose side he was supposed to be on here. "What about a copy of the check?" he offered.

She shrugged. "I scanned the carbon copy of it and emailed that to the lawyer, which he insists doesn't prove anything. 'You could have written this today and backdated it.' That's what he told me."

"I suppose that's true," he said cautiously. "If not, I'm sure it'll turn up."

Meg sighed. "It's almost beside the point. They're still gunning for my royalties. They don't care about a measly check for less than two thousand dollars. They want a bigger piece of the pie."

Kyle felt his jaw clenching as he sliced the zucchini in half with more force than necessary, barely missing the tip of his finger. "Dammit." He set the two halves on the cutting board and turned to face Meg. "So, back to the sex."

Meg stopped rolling balls and looked at him. "Wait, what?"

He turned back to his zucchini. "You're clearly uncomfortable talking about us sleeping together."

"Right."

"I'm not so wild about discussing the lawsuit."

"So what does that leave us with?"

"Politics? Euthanasia? Our parents? Stop me when I get to a less awkward subject here."

Meg bit her lip and looked down. He saw her left hand start to lift, and he knew she was going for her ear. She seemed to realize it too, and she stopped herself before he could say a word. He was about to start rattling off confessions when she beat him to it.

"Do you remember the last time we worked together in this kitchen?"

He nodded. "Yes. The wedding cupcakes."

"The wedding cupcakes. You thought I was an idiot for spending the morning before my wedding frosting a gazillion cupcakes."

"I didn't say *idiot*," he pointed out. "I may have called you crazy, but not idiotic."

"You know why I did it?"

"You told me baking helped relax you. That you'd feel less stressed about the wedding if you were doing something productive."

"That was part of it, yes."

"There was another reason?"

She nodded, turning her back to the cookies and leaning against the counter. She looked up at the ceiling, another excuse to avoid looking him in the eye. "I always knew Matt was a little unsure about the whole idea of getting married. Since dessert was one of his favorite things, I thought maybe if I made the world's most amazing, most decadent cupcakes, it would start things off on the right foot with the marriage."

"You thought you'd seal the eternal bond with buttercream?"

She smiled a little at that, but the smile didn't quite reach her eyes. "I didn't want him to have any doubts. I wanted him to start the marriage out thinking, 'Damn, I'm getting a pretty sweet deal here.'"

"Obviously he thought that," Kyle said, pretty sure it was true.

Meg dropped her eyes from the ceiling and looked at him. "That night before the wedding when he sat me down and said he had something important to tell me, I knew it was going to be bad. My brain didn't go straight to an affair, but I knew he was going to drop a bomb on me. I sat there thinking, 'Just wait, please just wait until tomorrow. When you try the cupcakes and everything will be okay.'"

"Meg—"

"But it wasn't okay." She shook her head. "It wasn't enough. *I* wasn't enough."

"You have to know that's not what Matt's cheating was about."

"So what was it about?" She turned and blinked a few times, and he couldn't tell if she was fighting back tears or just reacting to the hint of onions drifting from the Greek restaurant next door. "If it wasn't about me, then what?"

Kyle shook his head. "Not you. You were perfect."

She gave a snort of disbelief. "I was far from perfect."

"Meg, you have to believe no amount of frosting could have made a difference. Matt was going to do what Matt was going to do, and even the best cupcakes in the galaxy couldn't have changed that."

She looked down at her hands and gave a rueful little laugh. "You must think I'm ridiculous."

"Not at all."

She sighed and wiped her hands on her apron. "Tell me something honestly, Kyle."

"Okay." His heart was pounding hard, and his palms were starting to feel sweaty. Did she know something about what happened? About Kyle's role in the affair, or Matt's depression spiral afterward?

Meg cleared her throat. "Do you think I should have gone through with it?"

Kyle let out a breath he didn't know he'd been holding. "Marrying Matt?"

She nodded. "I'm not saying I wish I had. I'm glad I didn't, I swear."

"I believe you."

"It's just that sometimes I've wondered how things would have unfolded if I'd just forgiven him and walked down the aisle like I was supposed to."

Kyle shook his head. "No. No way."

"You're not just saying that to make me feel better?"

"Or to make it less weird in light of the fact that we slept together?" She grimaced, but Kyle kept talking. "Sorry, but no. It would have been better if you'd called it off the night before instead of having that big spectacle at the church, but I understand why you didn't go through with it. And for what it's worth, I'm glad you didn't."

She nodded. "So am I."

The tension in the air was so heavy that Kyle could have taken his paring knife and sliced right through it. He wanted to move on to safer territory, to a conversation that wouldn't leave him feeling hollowed out and empty or like the world's biggest asshole.

God, was there anything left at this point?

"Come on," he said, turning back to his zucchini. "Let's get chopping and you can tell me some of your funniest catering stories. You've surely racked up some new ones in the last two years?"

She smiled, and her relief was almost palpable. He'd just thrown her a lifeline, and she grabbed for it with both hands. "Being the only sober person at the party does have its advantages," she said, turning back to her cookie dough. "Did I tell you the one about the father of the bride who did a striptease to the theme from *Top Gun*?"

Kyle shook his head and she launched into the story, moving them into more comfortable territory. The scent of cinnamon and sugar hovered around them, forming a warm, soothing blanket of kitchen steam. Meg's iPod was playing an old Doobie Brothers song through the speakers above the cabinet, and something bubbled in a copper pot on the stovetop.

Meg laughed at part of her story, and Kyle ordered himself to focus on her, on the soft lilt of her voice and the amusing details of her story.

But there was no ignoring the pressure in his chest, or the niggling in the back of his brain. He knew that feeling well.

He was falling in love with his brother's girl.

Again, or maybe he'd never stopped.

A shitty thing to do, his subconscious chided, *since you're the one who ruined their lives.*

CHAPTER THIRTEEN

It was nearly ten o'clock by the time Meg led Kyle through the front door of her house, flipping the lights on as she moved through the foyer. It occurred to her that she probably shouldn't be doing this. After almost a week of avoiding him so they wouldn't accidentally tumble into bed again and muck things up, here she was inviting him back to her house well after dark.

But hell, he'd been a huge help to her. She couldn't have done all that food prep without him. The least she could do was offer him a piece of cake.

"Watch your step," she called, making a wide arc around the cactus that separated the entry from the living room. "If I'm gone more than a couple hours, Floyd likes to punish me by hiding behind the pot and attacking my ankles when I come through the door."

Sure enough, a fuzzy orange rocket came flying toward her, and Meg dodged to the side to avoid the flurry of teeth and claws.

Kyle wasn't as lucky.

"Whoa," he said, jumping back as Floyd slashed at him with one paw. "You weren't kidding."

Meg tried to muffle a laugh as Kyle continued his kitty dodge dance. "Sorry, did he get you?"

"He missed."

"Don't worry, he'll settle down in a second. Make yourself at home while I grab the cake."

She gestured to the barstools and Kyle took a seat. Meg saw him cast a wary eye at Floyd, who was twining his lanky body around the leg of the barstool.

"Hey, buddy," Kyle said, reaching down to scratch the cat behind the ear.

Floyd hissed and took a swipe at him. Kyle drew his hand back and looked at the cat for a moment.

"You're an asshole."

Floyd cocked his head to the side, then meowed and jumped up on the adjacent barstool. He sat down and eyed Kyle with apparent interest. Kyle eyed him back, probably bracing for another sneak attack.

Meg laughed and turned to pull a massive cake plate from the fridge. She set it on the counter and whisked the lid off to show him. "I haven't cut into it yet. How about I just send you home with the whole thing? This lid snaps on and off easily, so it travels well."

Kyle raised an eyebrow at her. "You're not going to share a piece with me?"

She shook her head. "You earned the whole thing with all the work you did."

"Then did I also earn the right to ask you to slice it up right now and join me for a piece?"

She hesitated, not wanting to be rude. She did kind of like his plan, though.

"All right," she said, pulling a knife from her butcher block. She glanced over at Kyle, who was making another attempt to pet Floyd.

Floyd growled and flattened his ears.

Kyle pulled his hand back and stared at the cat. "You're a real jerk, you know that?"

Floyd closed his eyes and started to purr.

"So that's your deal, huh, cat?" Kyle said. "You like it when I'm not nice to you?"

Still purring, Floyd bumped his head on Kyle's arm.

Meg laughed and flopped a second piece of cake on a plate. "You've finally figured out Floyd's psychological oddity?"

"So that's really it? He hates people who are nice to him, but he loves it when you're mean."

"I suppose so."

"Huh," Kyle said, folding his hands on the counter. "Maybe I should have tried that with you. I was reaching that point until you FaceTimed me the other day."

"You were planning to call and leave insults on my voicemail?"

"Figured it was worth a shot."

Meg handed him a fork. "Eat your cake, goofball."

She shoved a plate at him, along with a cloth napkin printed with pink and brown polka dots. Putting the lid back on the cake plate, she stuffed it back into the fridge and reminded herself to not let him leave without it. Then she grabbed her own plate and walked around the bar to claim the vacant barstool on the other side of Floyd.

"So, speaking of pets, tell me about your dog," Meg said as she forked up a bite of cake.

"Bindi," he said. "I've had her about six months. Got her from a rescue group in eastern Oregon."

"You said she's an Australian kelpie?"

"Yes. A herding dog on crack. Have you ever seen one?"

She shook her head and swallowed her cake. "No, but I googled after you told me. I watched a YouTube video of a kelpie herding a bunch of sheep together and then running across their backs to get to the other side of the flock."

Kyle laughed. "I'm weirdly flattered to know you googled my dog."

"I might have also Facebook stalked you. Speaking of which, I didn't realize you'd unfriended me."

"Sorry about that." Kyle speared his own piece of cake. "Matt gave everyone a guilt trip about it that first Thanksgiving after you split. It just seemed easier to cut ties."

"It's okay, I'm not mad." Meg gave a dismissive wave of her fork before spearing her cake again. "I suppose, under the circumstances, we probably shouldn't be friends now."

"Real friends or Facebook friends?"

"I meant Facebook. Seems like the sort of thing your parents would have a problem with."

"Maybe," he agreed, and Meg tried not to let it sting.

"So, back to the dog," she said brightly, and Kyle looked relieved.

"When I told an Australian friend I'd adopted one, he gave me the most incredulous look and said, 'You got a kelpie, mate? As a *pet*? Isn't that a bit like buying a tractor?'"

Meg laughed. "So they're more like farm equipment?"

"I guess so. A tractor you can snuggle with."

"That sounds—different."

"A switch from Karma, anyway. No more lazy Lab napping in front of the fireplace. It's always go, go, go, go with Bindi."

"I'd love to meet her sometime."

Kyle shrugged. "If you want, you can go out to the truck and say hello."

"What?" Meg set her fork down midbite. "Why didn't you bring her in?"

He laughed. "The way you avoided me the past week I figured I was lucky just to get myself through the door. Didn't want to jinx things by inviting my dog in."

"Ah, see, that's where you misjudged." Meg grinned and dabbed up a cake crumb with her fingertip. "I'd have let you in no problem if you had a dog with you. Besides, you just helped me chop a billion pounds of vegetables. You can invite a whole pack of dogs in if you want."

"What about Floyd?"

They both looked at Floyd, who twitched one ear and gave a low growl. "Floyd loves dogs," Meg said.

"I'm sure he does."

"Go get Bindi," she insisted.

"All right." Kyle polished off his last bite of cake and hopped off the barstool. Meg followed him to the door, more eager than she had any right to be about meeting a dog.

"I have to warn you, she might be a little nutty at first," Kyle said. "I stopped at the park and let her run around for a couple minutes on the way here, but she might get excited and piddle when I first let her out."

"I'll try to keep my toes out of the way."

Meg stepped out onto her lawn and waited while Kyle moved down the path leading to his truck at the curb. He'd parked beneath the streetlight, and Meg could see smudges of dog snot on the windows. Bindi must've heard his footsteps because she popped her head up and looked out the truck window. Her big, black ears swiveled like furry beacons as her black eyes stared out at him from the mask of brown over her long, black snout.

"She's adorable!" Meg called as Bindi stood on her hind legs with her paws on the truck door, poking her nose out through the open window.

"She loves going for rides," Kyle said as he popped the door open. "She hates summertime when it's too hot for her to be stuck in the truck, so she goes everywhere now that the weather's cooled off a little. Come on, girl!"

As Kyle swung the truck door open, Bindi leapt out onto the grassy patch beneath the door, her tail swishing frantically back and forth. Meg dropped to her knees on the lawn and patted the ground in front of her.

"Come on, girl! Come see me!"

Bindi pricked her ears, then scampered toward her on muscular brown legs that moved with uncanny speed. Meg opened her arms wide and Bindi scurried into them, a quivering bundle of tail wags and sloppy licks.

"Hi, there!" Meg said, rubbing her hands down the short, black fur. "Welcome! I love doggies and you're such a pretty one."

Bindi thumped her tail in agreement and collapsed onto her back, an invitation for Meg to rub her belly. Meg complied, looking up to see Kyle coming up the walkway toward them.

"Oh, my goodness!" Meg said, tickling little circles on the dog's belly. "Aren't you the sweetest thing? Who's the sweetest thing? It's you, that's right!"

Kyle stood over them, looking down with a smile. "I'd like the record to reflect that my pet was much more accepting of you than yours has been toward me."

She grinned and planted a kiss on Bindi's forehead. Bindi lolled her tongue to the side in ecstasy. "We're already best friends."

"Such a hussy," Kyle chided. "You, too, Bindi."

Meg laughed. "You're just jealous I didn't greet you like this."

"Guilty as charged. I do love a good belly rub."

Meg stood up and called the little dog to her. "Come on, sweetie. I just made a batch of homemade dog biscuits for the Humane Society. Let's get you some."

"That sounds delicious," Kyle said. "I hope you have something for Bindi."

Meg headed into the kitchen and grabbed the large Tupperware container where she'd stashed the biscuits. She pried it open and turned to watch as Floyd stood up on his barstool and arched his back. Glaring at Bindi, he gave a halfhearted hiss, then jumped down and bumped her with his nose.

"See?" Meg said, watching as Floyd twined himself between Bindi's legs, while Bindi made a desperate attempt to sniff Floyd's butt. "Told you they'd be fast friends."

Floyd took a swipe at Bindi's tail, then head-butted the dog's rib-cage. Meg could hear Floyd purring from five feet away, and it was clear Bindi was too mystified to do any chasing.

"I'll be damned," Kyle said. "So Floyd likes dogs and insults. Good to know."

Meg handed Bindi a biscuit, which she took a bite of before dropping the rest on the floor in front of Floyd. Floyd sniffed it, then nibbled the corner. "Here," Meg said, handing another biscuit to the dog. "You keep this one for yourself."

As Bindi crunched into it, Meg looked back at Kyle. "Sorry, did you want one?"

"Nope, but I'll take another piece of cake."

"I can do that. You want a glass of wine with it?"

"Wine and cake? Don't mind if I do."

"Go make yourself comfy on the couch. I'll bring it out in a sec."

Meg headed back to the kitchen and sliced off another piece of cake. Still aching from her run, she skipped the cake for herself and poured an extra glass of wine from the Sangiovese she'd opened the other night. She set the plate and wineglasses on a tray and carried the whole thing into the living room where Kyle had parked himself in the middle of the sofa. He scooted over to make room for her, so Meg sat down beside him.

Her knee bumped his, and she drew it back, feeling the heat creep into her cheeks. Then she felt ridiculous.

You've slept with the guy, she reminded herself. *It's probably okay if your knees touch.*

God, that was always going to be there, wasn't it? They'd been chatting all evening like old friends, swapping work stories and knife tips while they worked together in her kitchen. But the whole time, Meg's brain kept wandering back to that same old thought.

You were naked together. You had him inside you, hot and hard and—

"Okay, what are you smiling about?"

"What?" Meg asked, taking a sip of wine. "I didn't go near my ear."

"Just because you're not tugging your ear doesn't mean I can't tell you're thinking something you don't want to say out loud."

Meg rolled her eyes. "And what part of me not wanting to say it out loud isn't registering for you?"

"Confession number one," Kyle said, forking up a bite of cake.

"Wait, this isn't how the game goes. There was no ear tugging."

"My game, my rules, which means I can change them anytime I want." He swallowed a bite of cake and forked up another. "Confession number one—I lied to my mother this morning when she asked what I was doing tonight."

His tone was light, but Meg felt her fingers tighten around the stem of the wineglass. "So you're ashamed to have her know you're spending time with me?"

"Confession number two: yes."

"Yes?" She'd expected the answer, but still, it smarted a bit.

"*Ashamed* might not be the right word. I just don't want to have to explain things."

"How *would* you explain it?"

Kyle quirked an eyebrow at her. "Did you miss the part about me not wanting to have to explain it?"

"Yep, just like you missed the part about me not wanting to tell you what I was thinking."

"Which you still haven't done." He grinned and took another bite.

"You haven't given me your third confession yet."

"I'm getting there."

"You can count this as one of your confessions," she said, taking another sip of wine. "I really want to know how you'd explain it. Not to your mom, necessarily, but someone else."

"How would I explain what I'm doing here tonight?"

"Yes. To a friend or an acquaintance or—or *Cara*. How would you explain to your former live-in girlfriend how you ended up here at my house this evening?"

He sighed and set his fork down. "Well, I guess Cara isn't going to buy that I'm just here because I really like your cake. Not that it isn't amazing cake."

"Thank you," she said, hoping he didn't stop there.

"I guess I'd say that my whole life, you've been off-limits. Either because I was dating someone or you were dating—well, more than just *someone*."

"Of course." The grip on her wineglass became a little tighter.

"And even though those two things have changed, the fact that you're locked in a major financial dispute with my family is a pretty big obstacle." Kyle glanced at his cake, then back at her. "Which doesn't mean I don't want to tear your clothes off right now and make love to you on this sofa."

"The sofa?" Meg's voice was high and tight, and she felt a little dizzy.

"Or your bed."

"The bed's nice," Meg agreed weakly, her pulse thudding in her ears.

"Or the kitchen counter. Really, I'm not picky."

Meg took a shaky breath. "We can't do this, Kyle."

"I know." He set his cake plate on the coffee table and folded his hands in his lap. "Believe me, I get it."

"So we're just going to make ourselves crazy talking about it."

"Let's talk about something else." Kyle took a sip from his wineglass. "I have something I want to give you."

"Isn't that what we just agreed not to talk about?"

He laughed and set his glass down, then stood up and headed for the door. Meg wasn't sure if she was supposed to follow him, so she sat tight on the couch and waited. Bindi looked up from the rug in front of the fireplace where she'd curled up with Floyd. She gave Meg a questioning look, but Meg just shrugged.

"I'm sure he'll be right back."

Bindi put her head down and began licking Floyd's ear. Floyd growled and rolled over. The door opened again and Meg looked up to see Kyle walking through the front door with a small box in one hand. It was maybe eight inches long and less than two inches wide, and Meg tried to figure out what was inside.

Kyle moved around the couch and sat down beside her again. "I probably should have given this to you earlier, but I didn't want you to feel like you had to make a big production of using it tonight."

Meg eyed the box with renewed interest. "You're not doing anything to dispel my theory that there's something sex-related in there."

"Open it."

She set her wine down on the coffee table and held out her hand, and Kyle placed the box in her palm. She pulled off the top, more nervous than she expected to be. For a few beats, she stared down at it, trying to figure out what she was seeing. It was gorgeous and shiny and very, very sharp.

"You got me a knife?"

"I didn't get it for you. I made it. Out of your engagement ring. Well, your engagement ring and a few other hunks of metal."

Meg's breath caught in her throat. Her eyes filled with tears, and she picked up the small paring knife and turned it over in her palm. It was the most beautiful kitchen tool she'd ever seen, with swirls of metal on the blade and a sleek, polished wooden handle. A small, clear stone winked at her from the hilt of it, and it took her a few beats to recognize the stone from her ring. Holy crap, he'd really made this for her?

Kyle leaned back against the sofa and watched her. "I probably wouldn't have messed with it if it had been a real diamond or if the metal was gold or platinum, but once you told me that story about having the band redone in steel, I knew I could forge it into something different."

"It's beautiful, Kyle," she said, tears slipping down her cheeks for real now. "How did you do this swirly thing with the metal on the blade?"

"It's called Damascus steel," he said. "I've only done it a few times before, but this seemed like a good project to try it on."

"Damascus steel," she repeated, touching the swirls of metal along the blade.

"Yeah. You use two types of steel with different carbon levels— that darker one there is ten eighty-five. Most people choose something blended with nickel for the second one, since that adds brightness, but I didn't do that with yours."

"You remembered my allergy."

"Of course. So that's why yours has a subtler pattern. The blade should be nice and sharp."

Meg turned the knife over in her hand again, amazed that he'd managed to create something so beautiful from something she'd dreaded seeing in the back of her jewelry box for the last two years.

"Most of the materials came from steel bars I already had in the shop," he said. "It's a little tougher to forge with steel that's already been turned into a ring, but you can see this vein of it running right through here," he said, trailing a finger along the edge.

"My God, Kyle . . . I can't believe you made this. It's incredible. Thank you."

She sat there staring at it, completely undone by the thoughtfulness of the gift and the talent that had gone into creating it. He'd taken an object of hers and turned it into something new and special and entirely different.

That's what Matt did with your cookbook. But you knew that already.

Meg pushed aside the twinge of guilt and looked up at Kyle. "It's amazing," she said. "Thank you."

"Don't mention it."

She put the knife back in the box and set it on the coffee table, then turned back to face him. She hesitated, then put her arms around him. It was supposed to be a platonic hug, a thank you for the gift he'd made her.

But something happened when her body touched his. Something sparked inside her, flaring her whole body to light. The warmth spread through her like a rush of mercury, and Meg felt herself getting dizzy as she molded her body against his.

It could have stopped there with a hug that felt a little too tight, her breasts pressed to his chest in the heat of her living room. But she drew back then, and looked up at him.

Kyle's eyes were wild and a little unfocused, and she could tell from the flush in his cheeks that he felt it, too.

"We can't," she murmured, her mouth already too close to his.

Then she did it anyway, craving the sparks that arced between them the instant her lips touched his. He kissed her hard, his hands already tunneling under the back of her T-shirt to stroke her bare skin.

Her heart was hammering so hard in her head that she thought it might explode—her heart, her brain, whatever.

The pounding was so fierce that it took her a moment to realize it wasn't coming from inside her body.

"Honey? It's your mom. Open up right now, it's an emergency!"

CHAPTER FOURTEEN

"For the love of all things holy," Kyle growled as he sat back, pulling his hands off Meg's bare back like he'd been burned. "What the fuck are the odds? Seriously, are all the mothers in the world conspiring?"

Meg jumped like a kid caught making spitballs in church, and Kyle wondered if all these maternal interruptions would give her some sort of complex.

"Hang on, Mom," Meg called as she tumbled off Kyle's lap and landed with a thud on the floor. She scrambled up before Kyle could offer her a hand, and he felt weirdly relieved she seemed more undone by the appearance of her own mother than his. He watched her sprint for the door, tugging down the hem of her T-shirt in a way that made her look guilty as hell.

But Meg's guilt was the least of Patti Delaney's problems. That was clear the instant Meg threw open the front door.

"Oh, sweetie—I knew you'd be home," Meg's mom sobbed. "Something awful happened."

Kyle stood up, trying to gauge from this distance whether "something awful" was a hangnail or a death in the family. In his limited experience with Patti, he'd learned it could be either or nothing at all. He moved toward the front door with Bindi falling into step beside him, Floyd on her heels. He felt like the leader of some sort of bizarre inter-species parade.

"Hi, Patti," he said, stepping beside Meg. "What's wrong? Do you need help?"

"Kyle," she said, startled enough to take a step back. She regrouped quickly though. "I didn't realize you'd be here. I'm so sorry about your brother, honey."

"Thank you."

He stole a glance at Meg. She wore a guarded expression, which, come to think of it, was exactly how it was anytime he'd seen her around her mother.

"Come on in, Mom," she said. "What's wrong? Tell me what's going on."

"I'll tell you all about it in the living room. Could I maybe get a glass of white wine?"

Okay, so whatever was going on wasn't life threatening. Kyle turned and led Patti toward the living room even though she clearly knew the way. The bulky charm bracelet on her left wrist clattered and tinkled, prompting Bindi to prick her ears and prance behind them with her nose angled up toward the bracelet.

"Honestly," Patti sniffed. "I just don't know what I'm going to do."

"I'm sure we'll figure something out," Kyle said as Meg hurried off toward the kitchen.

Leaving Patti in the living room, Kyle ran to the bathroom and grabbed a box of tissues. He set them on the coffee table, wondering if he should make a quick exit. Meg probably needed time alone with her mother right now. It was getting late anyway, and—

"Kyle, can I get you another glass of red wine, or would you like white?" Meg called from the kitchen.

He looked at Patti, who was busy trying to pet a snarling Floyd. "Here, kitty, kitty . . ."

Floyd growled and skittered under an end table. Kyle turned back to the kitchen to see Meg looking at him with a pleading expression, but he wasn't sure if she wanted him to stay or go.

"Actually," he said, "I was thinking I should probably get ho—"

"Red!" she shouted, grabbing the bottle off the counter with a maniacal look in her eye. "Coming right up."

"Uh, red would be great." Okay, so he wasn't going anywhere.

"Have a seat, Mom," Meg called. "I'll bring your wine right out and you can tell me all about what's going on."

Kyle turned to see Patti had given up on Floyd and was puttering around the living room picking up picture frames and putting them back down again. She snatched a little glass tiger by the neck, turning it upside down to admire the bottom. Her bulky charm bracelet hit the edge of a small elephant figurine, and it toppled from the edge of the table toward the ground.

"Oh!" she gasped as Kyle leapt forward and caught the figurine six inches from the floor. He set it down on the table as Patti wandered off. Glancing back toward the kitchen, he was rewarded by a thankful look from Meg.

She had a bottle of white wine in some sort of chilling sleeve, a white wine glass, and a bowl of something he recognized as her home-made cheese straws.

Sticking around didn't seem like such a hardship with those cheese straws to fortify him, so he turned back to the couch.

"Why don't we have a seat, Patti?" he suggested. He started to guide her toward the love seat, then realized that would put him on the couch beside Meg. Something about that didn't feel right. He should be the one seated as a bystander to whatever emergency mother and daughter needed to discuss.

"Right here," he said, settling Patti on the sofa before claiming a spot on the love seat. Bindi trotted over and parked herself at his feet, while Floyd ambled behind his new best friend. The cat paused long enough to sniff Patti's shoe, then growled and hopped up on his favorite paisley chair.

"So, Mom," Meg said as she set the tray on the table and seated herself beside her mother. "Talk to me. What's wrong? What's happening?"

"It's your father," Patti sniffed. "He's having an affair. *Again*."

Meg winced, and Kyle wished like hell he could put his arms around her. She didn't look terribly surprised, but she did look defeated.

"I'm so sorry," Meg said, placing a hand on Patti's knee. "How do you know?"

"I found text messages on his phone from the whore."

"Hell," Meg said. "You're sure she's not just a friend?"

"Do you send your friends photos of you naked with your ankles behind your head?"

Kyle choked on his wine, but Meg managed to keep a little more dignity.

"Not usually, no," Meg said.

"Then I'm guessing she's not a friend."

Meg swallowed a big slug of wine while Kyle tried to think of something helpful to say. "Did you—uh—confront Greg about this?"

Patti nodded and fiddled with a cheese straw. "He said, and I quote, 'Patti, I don't have time for this right now. I'm late for a meeting.'"

"Oh, shit," Meg said. "So now what?"

"Now I pack up all his things, set them on the front lawn, douse them with lighter fluid, and—"

"Not again, Mom. Remember what happened last time?"

"I learned my lesson from the fire department, dear. I went out and bought one of those portable outdoor fire pit things like the one we used to roast marshmallows on when you were little. Actually, it's in the back of my car right now, and I could use some help unloading it at the house. Kyle?"

"What?" He blinked, not sure if she was soliciting his help to move the fire pit, light clothes on fire, or help with s'mores. Either way, he suspected his answer should be no.

"Kyle has plans, Mom," Meg said, swooping to his rescue. "Besides, I'm sure he doesn't want to risk ending up with an arrest record."

"This is true," Kyle agreed. "Though those s'mores do sound tempting."

"Let me ask you something, Kyle." Patti turned and pointed a finger at him, and Kyle suddenly wished he'd made that escape. "Can you think of any reason for a grown man to look at his faithful, loving, loyal companion and think to himself, 'It's totally fine if I go screw someone else behind her back?'"

Kyle glanced at Meg, pretty sure he knew the right answer here, but not certain he should get in the middle of this. Meg gave him a small shrug, which he figured was permission to speak freely. "Definitely not," he said.

"And can you think of any situation in which it's acceptable for a man to have a girlfriend on the side while his wife waits at home keeping his dinner warm?"

Kyle gripped his wineglass a little tighter, thinking of that night. How had Matt justified his call to Annabelle, making arrangements to meet her in secret while Meg waited for him back home? What on earth had he been thinking that night?

You know exactly what he was thinking, his conscience told him. *And it's all your fault.*

Kyle took a slug of wine, barely tasting it as it burned down his throat.

"No," Kyle answered again. "I can't think of any acceptable reason." He didn't meet Meg's eyes, afraid of what he might see there.

Patti huffed and took a sip of her own wine. "That's what I thought. But Greg thinks he can just stick his pecker wherever he likes, and all he has to do to get back in my good graces is buy me another charm for my bracelet and all will be right with the world."

She held up her arm, the charms jangling as she moved. Kyle stared at it, not sure what he was supposed to say. "That's a lot of charms."

"Exactly." Patti shook her head. "So why do I put up with it?"

Meg shook her head sadly. "I have no idea. You should put an end to it, though. Once and for all, just get out."

Kyle looked at Meg, a little surprised by the bluntness. "Well, it's true," she said. "You've been putting up with it for years and I don't understand why. Don't get me wrong, I love Daddy, but why on earth do you keep letting him come back?"

"Oh, Meggy," she sniffed. "You just don't understand."

Kyle watched the heat flare in Meg's eyes. "I don't understand being cheated on by the man who's supposed to love me forever?"

Patti's eyes widened a little, and she seemed to consider her words. "You don't understand the sort of commitment it takes to say, 'I take you for better or worse, and right now we happen to be smack-dab in the middle of worse.'"

"You're right, I don't understand that," Meg said. "I don't understand sacrificing myself to a man who doesn't love and respect me enough to avoid screwing someone else."

Kyle felt himself stiffen. Meg's gaze shifted to him, and he realized she'd probably caught the gesture. "Sorry, Kyle. I don't mean to disparage your brother—"

"His *late* brother," Patti reminded her.

"Thanks, Mom," Meg muttered through gritted teeth. "You think I'd forgotten?"

"Of course not, dear. All I'm saying is that sometimes a little forgiveness goes a long way."

"Oh really?" Meg bolted up off the couch, her cheeks flaming now. "Where has forgiveness gotten you, Mom? Cheated on how many dozens of times? I'm sorry, but I wasn't willing to put up with that. Not then, not now, not ever."

"Meggy, honey—"

"Don't patronize me. I'm sorry for what you're going through with Dad, I really am. But if you want my honest opinion, you're better off without him."

"Meg!"

"Well, it's true." Her gaze swung to Kyle, and he had a sudden urge to apologize for his brother. *Again.* But he kept quiet, sensing Meg needed to rage without interruption.

"I have a lot of regrets in my relationship with your brother," she said. "But drawing the line over the affair wasn't one of them. He always knew that was a deal breaker for me."

"Understood," Kyle said softly, his mind swirling with his own regrets. He wished he could take her in his arms, but he knew now wasn't the time.

Meg's gaze swung back to her mother. "Mom, I'm so sorry for what you're going through. You don't deserve it."

"I know," Patti said, dabbing her eyes with a tissue.

"If you just want a hug, I can do that. But if you're ready to say you've had enough, I'll help you find a divorce lawyer and we can end this thing once and for all. Do you want to take that step?"

Patti looked at her daughter, her eyes watery and her mouth etched into a frown. She looked over at Kyle, and he wondered if he should offer words of encouragement or just keep his mouth shut.

Before he could say anything, Meg sat down beside her mother and put her arms around her. "You don't have to decide right now, Mom. But when you're ready to take charge of your life, I'm there for you. I hope you know that."

"Thank you, sweetie." Patti stroked Meg's back, and it was such a tender moment Kyle could overlook the snot she was smearing all over Meg's shoulder. "I'll give it some thought."

Kyle sat watching mother and daughter locked in an embrace, his heart aching for reasons that had nothing to do with their conversation.

◆　◆　◆

It was after midnight by the time Meg's mom finally left the house. Meg felt exhausted and emotionally drained, which she knew was nothing compared with how her mother must be feeling.

She watched her mom's car pull down the driveway, her taillights flickering in the darkness. Meg had tried to get her to stay the night, but Patti had refused. "I want to be there when your father comes home," she'd said. "Maybe we can talk this through."

So Meg watched as her mom's car vanished around the corner. If there was something else she could do to help, she didn't know what it was.

"You okay?"

Meg turned to see Kyle standing beside her in the entryway. He had his keys in his hand, and an uncertain look on his face. He stood close enough that only a thick sliver of light separated her body from his, but it felt like they were a million miles a part.

"I'm all right," she said. "You'd think I'd be used to this by now, huh? It's not like this is the first time it's happened."

"I can't imagine it's ever easy seeing your father hurt your mother that way."

"No. I suppose it isn't."

"My dad hasn't always been around, but at least when he is, he tries to make my mom happy."

"I always envied what your parents had," she admitted.

"It's not perfect, but it seems to work for them." He paused, keys still in his hand. "Do you want me to stay?"

Meg hesitated, not sure what he was asking. Was he offering moral support or something else? Which did she most want right now?

Both. Neither. Her heart felt trampled and bruised, and she wasn't in any condition to be making big decisions right now.

"I'll go," Kyle said at last, deciding for both of them. Even though it was what she knew was the smartest choice, Meg still felt a wave of disappointment flush through her.

"That's probably best," she said.

"I wish I could do something to help."

"You already did. Just having you here helped a lot. If nothing else, it's good for my mom to see not all guys are assholes."

He smiled and shifted his keys from one hand to the other. "I don't know about that."

"Have you ever cheated on someone?"

She felt startled by her own question, and Meg started to take it back. But Kyle was already shaking his head.

"No. I've been an asshole in plenty of other ways, but not that one."

"Good."

"You?"

Meg shook her head. "Not unless you count fourth grade when Derek Jones asked me to go with him and I didn't know where he wanted me to go, but I said yes and didn't know that meant I had a boyfriend until Tommy Simmons kissed me on the playground and the other kids called me a slut."

"Ouch."

Meg gave a halfhearted smile. "Can't say relationships got a whole lot easier from there."

"I don't know about that. Don't you sometimes miss the days of kiss tag and flipping up your skirt to let a boy know you like him?"

"Who says I don't still do that?"

Kyle smiled and looked down at his keys. He seemed to be weighing them in his palm, maybe weighing something else in his mind. When he looked up at her, there was something dark in his gray-green eyes.

"For what it's worth, Meg, my brother wasn't lying when he told you it only happened once."

She swallowed hard and held his gaze. "How do you know that?"

"I just do."

For some reason that seemed like enough of a reason to believe him. Still. "Once was enough to matter to me."

"I know. But I thought you should know he wasn't a serial cheater like your father. Not with you, anyway."

Meg nodded. For some reason she did find that comforting. Even when Matt had broken the news to her, her mind had been drifting to what else he might be hiding. How many other women had there been? And did it matter if there had been one or one hundred?

"Let me ask you something," Kyle said.

"Fire away," she replied, willing to discuss just about anything to keep him here with her just a little while longer.

"Do you think your mom will leave him?"

"Definitely not."

There was no hesitation in her voice, which seemed to surprise Kyle. "Really?"

"Not a chance." Meg shrugged. "I don't mean to be a pessimist, but she's been letting my dad run rickshaws over her for years."

"Roughshod."

"What?"

"Run roughshod over her. That's the expression."

"Whatever," Meg said, waving a dismissive hand, and it occurred to her that Kyle's gentle conversational corrections felt nothing at all like when Matt used to do it. "My point is that she's not going to stop the cycle. Not now, not ever. It's just the way things are with her."

"How many affairs has your father had?"

Meg snorted. "That we know about? At least a dozen. I'm sure it's more than that."

"Do you think it's some sort of weird turn-on for your mom?"

"I don't think so. I've considered that before—I mean, as much as I've been willing to think about what turns my mom on—but I don't think that's it."

"So what is it?"

She shrugged. "Low self-esteem? Force of habit? Refusal to back down from her marriage vows?"

"Love?" Kyle supplied, and Meg couldn't tell if it was a question or a statement.

"Maybe. But it's not any kind of love I'd want to be part of."

"But you are part of it. Like it or not, you're their daughter. You're a product of that."

"In more ways than one."

Kyle leaned against the door, studying her with an intensity that made Meg start to squirm. "If that hadn't been the story of your child-hood, do you think you might have forgiven Matt and gone through with the wedding?"

Meg hesitated a moment, then nodded. "Yes."

Kyle nodded, and something flickered in his eyes. "That's what I thought."

"That doesn't mean it would have been the right thing to do. But I wouldn't have known that at the time."

He looked at her a moment longer, then pushed away from the door, shifting his keys from one hand to the other. From her spot in front of the fireplace, Bindi poked her head up and looked around. Meg knew she should just let him call his dog and walk out the door and go home to his own home, his own bed, his own life.

But something made her reach out and touch his arm. "Kyle?"

"Yes?"

Meg hesitated, biting her lip. "Please stay."

He looked at her, his gray-green eyes unblinking. He didn't move toward her, and he didn't move away. "What are you asking?"

"I just—I don't want to be alone."

"I see." He hesitated. "Maybe Jess can stay with you."

She shook her head. "No, that's not it." God, he was going to make her spell it out. She took a shaky breath and met his eyes, her hand still on his arm. "I'm asking you to stay the night. We can keep all our clothes on and just sit on the sofa talking all night, or we can make mad, passionate love until we fall asleep exhausted. I just want you to stay."

Kyle nodded. "Which of those two options would you prefer?"

"The latter," she admitted softly. "But the former sounds nice, too."

Kyle stared down at her, his eyes dark in the dimness of her foyer. "Are you asking because you don't want to be alone, or because you want to be with me?"

"I want to be with you."

He reached for her, pulling her tight against his chest.

Meg tilted her head back and his lips found hers. They stood there in the entryway kissing until they were both breathless. She was the first to draw back. "Come on," she said, taking him by the hand. "This way."

She pulled him toward her bedroom with her legs feeling like jelly. Her heart was thudding hard in her ears, and she said a silent prayer there'd be no interruptions this time. No needy parents or unwanted phone calls or oven timers with a mind of their own. Just the two of them, doing this thing they'd agreed mere hours ago they absolutely shouldn't do.

What the hell was she thinking?

She wasn't thinking. She was *feeling*. And dammit, that felt good. Meg stopped in the doorway of her bedroom, turning to look at Kyle. He was staring at the bed.

"It's new," she said. "I got it last year at a clearance sale at Sleep Country. In case you're wondering if I ever—"

His kiss cut off the rest of her words, which was just as well. Knowing her, she would have kept babbling about the damn bed and the fact that she never slept in it with Matt or did anything else that probably crossed his mind.

Of course, there were the sheets—a wedding gift from a college friend who'd insisted she keep them even after the wedding didn't happen. The pillows, too, had a history, and Meg tried not to recall the argument she and Matt had gotten into over firmness and thread count and a million other stupid features that seemed worth fighting over at the time.

Had Kyle ever made love to Cara on that cot in his studio? She hadn't thought of that until just now, and the idea of it was jarring.

But as Kyle laid her back on the bed, Meg felt her mind let go of all those thoughts. She forgot about Matt and Cara. She forgot about lawsuits and book sales and families and adultery and everything else.

For the time being, she let herself dissolve in Kyle's arms.

CHAPTER FIFTEEN

Kyle woke early with the distinct feeling he was being watched.

He opened his eyes to see Meg sitting cross-legged on the bed beside him, a mug of tea in her hand and a silky blue robe hiding her breasts and everything else from his view.

"Morning," he mumbled, reaching for her.

"Good morning," she answered, smiling a little. "I already let Bindi out and fed her some leftover poached chicken breast. I hope that's okay."

He grinned and rolled to his side. "She's going to want to stay here forever."

Something about the word *forever* sounded too big for this bedroom, this situation, but Meg didn't seem to notice. "Do you want coffee?" she asked.

"Actually, I'll take some of that tea if you don't mind." He reached up and flipped the tag dangling over the rim of her mug. "Earl Grey sounds great."

"Since when are you a tea drinker?"

"Cara got me hooked on it. Started sending me all these articles about how it's healthier for me than coffee. I gave it a try, and it turns out I like it better."

"Here, you can have this one." She handed him the mug. "I haven't even taken a sip yet. I'll go make another."

Kyle laughed and sat up, letting her press the mug into his hands. "You really think I'd be worried about sharing a mug with you at this point considering all the places my mouth has been?"

Meg flushed pink and she scrambled off the bed and headed out the door. "I'll be right back."

She bustled out to the kitchen, while Kyle set the mug on the nightstand and moved into the bathroom to clean up a little. Splashing water on his face, he spotted her toothpaste in the little clay mug she'd used when she lived with Matt. He turned the cup around, admiring the star pattern on the front and wondering where she'd gotten it and how she and Matt had decided Meg got to keep it when they split.

He smeared some Aquafresh on his finger and used it to scrub away some of the morning breath. He heard Meg shuffling back into the bedroom, so he rinsed his mouth, pushed the door open, and watched her crawl back under the covers.

"I brought some milk and sugar, too," she said as she set the tray on the nightstand.

She looked so beautiful sitting there with her hair loose around her shoulders that for a moment he forgot she'd said anything.

"Milk. Sugar. Yes, thanks." He walked back into the bedroom and slipped between the covers with her, scooping up the mug. "So, this is new."

"I got it last week at Townshend's Teahouse down on—"

"I didn't mean the tea," he said, blowing on his mug. "I meant waking up in bed together."

Meg nodded and blew on her own mug. "Are we back to feeling awkward again?"

"A little bit."

She smiled and took a sip of tea. "So Cara left you with a tea habit. Is she also responsible for your switch to boxer briefs?"

He snorted into his tea, spilling some onto his bare leg. "Ow! How the hell did you know what kind of underwear I used to wear?"

"I remember you and Matt arguing about it once. He was making fun of you for wearing regular boxers, and said you were going to end up with your junk hanging down to your knees. You told him his tighty-whiteys were going to give him a low sperm count, and he told you that would save a bundle on birth control pills."

"I can't believe you remember that," he said.

Meg shrugged. "For the record, Matt didn't actually pay for those. The birth control pills, I mean. I always bought them myself."

"I'll make sure my mother omits that from the amount owed in the lawsuit then."

He'd meant for it to come off as a joke, but the tiny lines that formed between her eyebrows told him he'd missed the mark. "Sorry," he said. "I didn't mean to bring that up."

"It's okay. There's already enough awkwardness here. A little more won't make a huge difference." She looked at him over the rim of her mug. "My mom called about an hour ago."

"How is she?"

"Good. She said she thought about what I said, and she's decided she's ready to move on."

Kyle blinked. "You're kidding."

"Nope."

"She's really leaving your dad?"

"That's what she says." Meg shrugged and blew on her tea again. "I don't know, she could still change her mind, but this is the first time in thirty-five years she's even entertained the idea. I think that's progress."

"That's huge," he said. He put a hand on her knee under the covers as it occurred to him he shouldn't sound so jubilant. This was her father, after all.

"Are you okay with all that?" Kyle asked. "He might be a philandering jerk, but he's also your dad."

Meg nodded. "It's about time. My mom needs to reclaim her life and her pride and herself while there's still anything left."

"Good for her."

Kyle touched his lips to his mug, his mind already circling back to the previous conversation. "So what else is awkward for you right now?"

She shrugged. "You mean besides the lawsuit and the fact that I was engaged to your brother?"

"Besides that."

She took a deep breath. "Do you ever think about how weird it is in modern relationships how you find yourself looking around and thinking, 'that belonged to another guy.'"

Kyle frowned. "You mean thinking of you like a possession?"

"No, I mean actual possessions. Or habits. Like the tea or the boxer briefs. Those are things you got from another woman."

Kyle looked down at his underwear, dismayed to realize he was wearing a pair Cara had given him when they'd decided to celebrate Groundhog Day. *These will make your junk look hot,* she'd teased, reaching around to grab his ass the way she used to.

He didn't miss her. Not really. But sometimes he missed the ritual of being part of a couple.

"I hadn't thought about it," he admitted as he took a sip of tea.

"Sure you had. You can't tell me it didn't cross your mind last night when we walked back here to the bedroom. I saw you pause. You were wondering if I'd ever been with Matt in this bed, weren't you?"

Guilty as charged. "What are you, a mind reader now?"

"So it's true?"

He hesitated, then shrugged. "Yeah, mostly." Kyle turned his mug around, dunking the teabag in and out to give him something to do with his hands. "That wasn't the only thing on my mind at that moment, but I did consider it."

"I understand. I mean, that's why I said what I did. I was just thinking about Cara's vagina and—"

"Wait, what?"

"The sculpture in your gallery." Meg sipped her tea. "The one you told me was modeled after her hoo-ha?"

"Right, I get it. What about it?"

"That's part of what I'm talking about. Those little souvenirs of past lovers are pretty much always going to be there. Like I noticed the tie you wore to the funeral was the one you got for Christmas six or seven years ago from the girl you were dating back then. Aurelia or Olivia or something like that?"

"Olivia." Kyle laughed, taken aback by the memory. "I'd be impressed by your powers of recall, except that it's the only tie I've ever owned and you probably know that."

"I might've guessed. I remember that gift didn't go over too well."

Kyle shook his head, surprised to feel a niggle of annoyance after all this time. His mother had been thrilled by Olivia's not-so-subtle attempt to nudge Kyle toward a desk job, maybe something with a steady paycheck and an office that didn't have steel shavings on the floor. Kyle remembered holding that tie, torn between the need to thank his then-girlfriend for the present and his urge to wonder if she knew him at all.

The relationship had imploded within three months.

"There's a lot of history there," he said. "Relics from past romances. I guess unless you lose everything in a house fire, you're bound to have tangible souvenirs sitting around."

She nodded and took another sip of tea. "My history's a little more limited considering I started dating Matt at twenty-three and we were together almost ten years."

"Oh, I don't know. I noticed you're still using that trivet you got in Morocco when you went there with that old boyfriend."

"See?" She laughed and nudged his elbow. "You do notice stuff like that."

"Only because Matt always hated that trivet."

"Do you think that's why? The reminder that I'd gotten it with another guy?"

"Maybe."

Meg smiled and drained her mug, then set it aside on the nightstand. "So you won't blame me when I confess I noticed you've still got your keys on Melody's keychain."

"Melody!" Kyle laughed. "God, I'd almost forgotten her."

"You dated for almost a year."

"Yeah, but it was eight or nine years ago. How do you remember that?"

"Women remember things like that. I could probably name all the girlfriends you've had over the years in chronological order. Let's see, there was Jodi, Shonna, Melody, Karen, Olivia, Hailey, Cara . . . "

"Damn, I'm impressed."

Meg shrugged and shifted on the bed, tucking her legs up under her while Kyle thought about that keychain. Why did he still have it? Force of habit, or was it something else?

"She found that keychain in an antique store in Paris," he said. "It's the original key to an old chapel where she said she wanted to get married someday."

Meg laughed and nudged his knee with hers under the covers. "And did it occur to you that was a hint she might've wanted to marry *you*?"

"Yeah, it crossed my mind." Kyle put his hand on her bare thigh, a casual caress that felt like the most natural thing in the world. He scanned the room, looking for relics from Meg's past romances. He wasn't jealous, but he was curious.

His gaze landed on a small shelf in the corner, piled with paperback novels and magazines. "Isn't that Matt's bookshelf?"

"He built it, if that's what you mean. For our five-year dating anniversary." She drew her fingertips over his bare thigh, making him shiver. "Where'd your wallet come from?"

"My wallet?"

"I noticed it last night when you pulled it out to get a condom. Tooled leather, that intricate pattern around the edges—"

He grinned. "You don't think I picked it out for myself?"

"Did you?"

"No," he admitted a little sheepishly. "It was a gift from Kelly."

"Kelly?"

"We only dated for a couple months after Cara and I split, but I had a birthday right in the middle of that."

"Ah, so that's why I don't remember her." Meg smiled. "So you've got Melody's keychain, Olivia's tie, Kelly's wallet, and Cara's ladybits, underwear, and tea."

Kyle laughed and looked around the room, trying to identify something else he recognized as a tangible reminder of another relationship. It was true he'd only known her when she'd dated his brother, and that relationship had lasted nearly a decade.

The duration in and of itself was enough to give him twinges of discomfort. He may have collected souvenirs and yeah, a number of notches on his bedpost. But he hadn't collected the same sort of memories Meg had gathered with Matt. Christmas mornings and sick days and career changes and plans to build a life together. He pushed the thought from his mind, determined not to feel jealous of his brother.

Kyle was here now, and that counted for something.

He caught a movement out of the corner of his eye, and looked over to see Meg tugging her ear. He reached out and touched her wrist. "Busted!"

"What?" She dropped her hand. "No. I'd gotten so much better lately, I swear!"

"I noticed," he said, grinning. "So this must be a good one. Confession number one: I'll admit it would have bugged the shit out of me to know you'd been with Matt in this bed. Confession number two," he continued, hurrying so she wouldn't call a halt to the whole game. "Cara not only bought me this underwear, she told me she liked the way the blue piping outlined my junk."

"I did notice that," Meg said, tucking a curl behind her ear and blushing ever so slightly. "For what it's worth, I like the boxer briefs."

"Thank you. Confession number three, I've had to pinch myself at least a dozen times since I woke up because I can't believe I'm really, truly here in this bed with the girl I've fantasized about for the better part of a decade."

"Oh." Meg's eyes went wide, and she looked at him in stunned silence for a moment. Her hair was tousled and her cheeks looked beard-burned and she was more beautiful than she'd ever been in all the years he'd known her.

"That last one kinda slipped out," he admitted.

Meg smiled, but the dumbfounded look didn't leave her eyes. "So you haven't really fantasized about me for years?"

"Would it make me the worst brother on the planet to say I have?"

She seemed to hesitate a moment, then shook her head. "No. But I can't say the same about you."

"Okay," Kyle said, wishing that didn't sting.

"I don't think you'd want me to. Not really. As the brother of my ex-fiancé, wouldn't you feel kinda awful if I sat here and told you I used to fantasize about another man during the ten years I was with your brother?"

Not if the other man was me, Kyle thought, but he didn't say that. "I guess so."

Meg looked down at her hands. "I can't say it never crossed my mind. Do you remember that one Thanksgiving—"

"Yes," he said, probably a little too quickly, and she looked up again. "I know exactly which Thanksgiving you're talking about," he added.

"The doves," she said, nodding. "You do remember."

"Of course. It was the one time I thought maybe there was something between us. Something besides my unrequited crush on the girl who probably just saw me as the deadbeat younger brother."

"I never saw you as a deadbeat," she said softly. "And yeah, I felt it, too. Standing there in your parents' study with you being so sweet to me." She looked down again. "I always knew it couldn't happen, so I never let myself think about it, but that one time—"

She broke off there, and Kyle didn't say anything, willing her to finish the thought. But Meg just folded her hands in her lap and stared at them like they held the script for what she should say next. When she looked up, her expression was guarded.

"I wondered about it," she said at last. "That day, I mean. I thought about what it would have been like to be with you instead."

He nodded, feeling a small flutter of pride at that small admission. But hell, even that felt disloyal to Matt. Just being here now—in Meg's bed with her bare leg pressed against his—felt disloyal.

"So does that count as my confession?" she asked softly.

Kyle looked back at her. "Not unless it's what you were thinking when you tugged your ear."

Meg sighed. "Okay, but you have to promise you won't laugh."

"All right."

"And you won't be mad or offended."

Kyle raised an eyebrow, not sure whether to be intrigued or concerned. "You know I can't promise something like that."

"Fine. But you have to remember that you have a five-foot replica of your ex-girlfriend's vagina in your gallery."

He stared at her. "Um, okay."

Meg took another breath and stared straight ahead at the wall, her gaze not meeting his. "There's this website Jess found a few years ago," she said, talking fast the way she did when she was nervous. "It's this thing where you take a mold of a guy's, uh—pork sword."

"Pork sword?"

"Right. And you send it in and they make this sex toy out of it. So Jess found out about it and forwarded the link to Matt, and he surprised me with that as a Christmas gift."

"Wait, what? What are you saying?"

Her cheeks turned bright red, and she tugged at a loose thread on her quilt. "I'm saying I have a—um, an—uh—"

"Dildo?"

"Right. Modeled after your brother's—um—"

"Dick?" God, this was the weirdest game of Mad Libs ever.

"Right," Meg said, and tugged at the thread again.

"Holy shit." Kyle frowned. "I don't remember you unwrapping that under the tree in front of the family."

She looked up then, and he saw her eyes filled with equal parts embarrassment and amusement. "It was that Christmas you were living in Montana and didn't come home," she said. "And obviously Matt didn't have me open it in front of family."

"Right, of course," he said, thinking the reason he'd fled to Montana in the first place was the same reason he wasn't sure he wanted to hear the rest of the story.

"Right, so anyway, I still have it."

"What?" Kyle shot a look at her nightstand drawer. "You've got my brother's dick in a drawer?"

"Not there! I mean, I don't still use it or anything."

"Okay—"

"But I wasn't sure what to do with it after we broke up. I mean, it's not the sort of thing you just stuff into the kitchen trash can and wheel out to the curb."

"It's not?"

"So I stuck it in a shoebox and forgot all about it until a couple weeks ago when I tore my house apart looking for proof of what I'd paid to Matt so far, and then I thought I really can't just toss it in the trash at this point. Now that he's gone, that seems like a terrible thing to do."

"I can see that," Kyle said slowly, trying not to get hung up on the image of his brother creating a mold of his dick. Christ, how did that even work?

"The thing is," Meg said, "I'd like to get rid of it, but I don't know how. A trash can seems so disrespectful of the deceased, but it's not like I'm going to pack it up and take it down to Goodwill. So what does that leave me with?"

Kyle shook his head, not sure whether to feel horrified or amused or jealous or some mix of the three.

But he did know exactly what to do with Meg's problem.

"Come on," he said, setting his mug on the nightstand and turning back to her so he could squeeze her knee. "We're going to shower— *together*—and then I'm taking you out for breakfast."

"Okay," she said, looking wary. "Don't forget I have to finish the food for the bachelorette party and drop it off by noon."

"No problem," he said. "I'll help. Then after that, we're picking up your mother and going to my gallery. I have a plan for all of us."

◆　　◆　　◆

Meg put her hand on her mother's shoulder as they stood together in Kyle's studio, the heat from his forge warming their faces. They all wore protective goggles, but she could still feel her eyes watering.

It probably wasn't just the heat.

"You ready, Patti?" Kyle asked.

Meg watched him adjust the face shield he'd flipped on top of his head. He wore a heavy black apron over his clothes and thick gloves that made his hands look even larger as he held one palm out in front of him.

Meg's mom nodded and lifted her closed fist, then unclenched her fingers to drop the silver charm bracelet into Kyle's hand.

"There's even a new charm on it," Patti said, wiping her hand down the leg of her jeans like she'd touched something unclean. "The one he brought me last night to apologize."

"Because nothing says, 'Sorry I cheated' like a silver corn cob," Kyle muttered.

Patti gave a lopsided half-smile, and Meg squeezed her mother's shoulder. "You sure about this, Mom? You've had that bracelet forever."

"I know I have," she murmured. "That's why I'm sure."

Meg felt Kyle's gaze shift to her as his fingers closed around her mother's bracelet. "I'll let you handle yours on your own," he told her.

He picked up a large graphite crucible with one hand and dropped the bracelet into it. Then he held the vessel out to her. Meg reached into her purse and pulled out the purple velvet bag with a ribbon drawstring cinching the top closed. She started to tug the ribbon, but Kyle stopped her.

"You can go ahead and leave it in the bag."

"You sure? It'll burn okay like that?"

"Pretty sure. I've never melted latex in my forge, but I can say with relative certainty that the melting point for plastics isn't very high."

Meg nodded and stuffed the velvet bag and its contents into the crucible on top of her mother's bracelet. Kyle set it on the edge of his worktable, used his teeth to pry off one glove. Then he reached into his pocket and pulled out his keys. Meg watched as he unhooked the keychain at the silver ring at the center of the cluster.

"You don't have to do that, you know," Meg said. "It's an antique, and I know you like it a lot."

Kyle shook his head. "Not that much. Besides, it's important to the symbolism. The idea of letting things go, moving on, sending them up into smoke—"

"Melting a dildo in a steel forge," Patti supplied.

Meg sighed. "Thanks, Mom. I still can't believe I told you that."

"Well, what were you going to do? Pretend that's a bag of M&M'S? Besides, I think that's pretty nice symbolism. Burning the penis of the man who broke your heart when he stuck it in someone else?"

"Beautifully put," Kyle said.

Meg rolled her eyes at her mother. "A man who happens to be the departed brother of the man performing this ceremony for us right now. Show a little respect."

"Sorry," Patti said, looking up at Kyle. "Your brother had many fine qualities."

"It's okay," Kyle said. "My brother chose cremation for himself. This is a fitting way to dispose of the last memento of his physical being."

Meg nodded, glad he could look at it that way, or at least put up a good pretense of pretending he did. Honestly, Meg wasn't sure she would be so cavalier about handling a replica of Kyle's ex's genitals.

Then again, she had stuck her head in that calla lily sculpture. Frankly, she was relieved he hadn't chosen to torch that. He'd suggested it, but she'd pointed to the price tag and assured him his symbolic gesture would work just as well with an object that didn't cost more than her car.

"Okay," Kyle said, dropping the key into the crucible before pulling his glove on again. "I'm not a preacher or anything, but I feel like we ought to say a few words of remembrance."

Meg nodded and took her mother's hand. Patti squeezed her fingers, and the intensity of her mom's grip gave Meg an unexpected surge of strength.

Kyle cleared his throat. "Here's to memories of past loves, and the way they shape our future loves. We can't forget them, but we can build from them, learn from them, and then let them go when the time comes."

"Amen," Patti said, squeezing Meg's hand.

Meg stared at the velvet pouch, wondering why she hadn't gotten rid of it before now. Nostalgia? Habit? Guilt? Or maybe mere forgetfulness.

Kyle looked at her, and Meg cleared her throat, wondering if she should say something, too. "Here's to taking the best of what we learned from past relationships, and letting everything else go up in smoke."

"Agreed." Kyle picked up the crucible again and reached for a pair of wicked-looking tongs. He flipped down his face shield and looked at Meg. "You might want to take a few steps back."

Still gripping her mother's hand, Meg moved backward, stumbling a little over a discarded metal pipe. They stepped back until their spines pressed against the far wall. While Kyle stoked the flames in his forge, Meg turned to look at her mother.

"You okay?" she whispered.

Patti nodded and offered a faint smile. "Not yet. But I think I will be."

"I'm proud of you, Mom."

"Thank you, honey." Patti glanced at Kyle, who was still focused on the forge. She leaned closer to Meg, her voice so low Meg had to strain to hear her.

"I'm proud of you, too," Patti whispered. "I never told you that. After you left Matt? I told you I was sad for you and that I'd do anything I could to help. But I never told you I was proud. That you did the right thing."

Meg felt tears pricking the back of her eyes. "Thank you."

"It's not our fault, you know. When men cheat? It's taken me thirty-five years to realize that, but it's true."

Meg nodded, not sure she trusted herself to say anything. Or maybe she could manage one thing.

"I love you, Mom."

"I love you, too, baby."

Kyle turned then and smiled at her, and Meg felt her whole body go liquid and warm. The studio was cozy around her, and the smell of smoke and hot metal hovered thick and heavy. Floral wisps of her mom's perfume made a soft net over her, and Meg watched in fascination as Kyle picked up the crucible with the tongs.

"Ready?" he asked.

Meg looked at him, admiring the broadness of his shoulders, the muscles in his arms, the creative genius of a mind that filled this whole studio with art and her whole life with something she hadn't realized she was missing until this very moment.

"I'm ready," Meg said, and gripped her mother's hand.

CHAPTER SIXTEEN

Meg had been dreading this moment from the first time her agent suggested that finding proof of an agreement with Matt could be a solution to all their problems.

Okay, she'd been dreading it a lot longer than that. As she stood on the doorstep of the home she'd once shared with the man she loved, it occurred to her she hadn't been here since three weeks after the wedding that hadn't happened.

After Meg had pulled her runaway-bride move, Matt had refused to let her stop by the house to collect her belongings. She'd spent several weeks living out of the suitcase she'd packed for their honeymoon until Kyle finally called to say she could come get her things. Matt hadn't been there at the time, and the whole transaction had the aura of a bank heist. She'd scrambled furtively from one darkened room to the next, grabbing her possessions and wondering where Matt had gone.

She'd assumed he'd taken their tickets to Tahiti and invited Annabelle. She hadn't wanted to know. She'd just been concerned with gathering as much of her stuff as possible while Matt was out of the house. She hadn't wanted much, really. A few family heirlooms, her clothes and personal things. There had been no fight left in her at that point. She just wanted to get in and get out with as little conflict as possible.

But as she stood here now on the doorstep, it occurred to her she should have fought for more. She ran a hand over the small copper fountain she and Matt had found together at an antique store, its surface smooth and turquoise with patina. Should she have laid claim to it? Or had she been smart to cut her losses and go?

The door swung open, jarring her from her memory. Meg looked up to see Chloe staring at her with a blank expression. "It's you."

"It's me," Meg confirmed. "You said two o'clock worked?"

"You're five minutes early."

"I'm sorry." Meg glanced at her watch. Dammit, how did she always manage to do that? "I can come back if you want."

"It's fine." Chloe held the door open and Meg stepped through, thinking how weird it felt to have another woman granting her entrance to the home that used to be hers.

It hadn't really been hers, though. Not legally, anyway. Matt's name had been the only one on the loan, and it had just been easier to walk away and let him have it. After everything that had happened by then, it wasn't like she wanted to live there anyway.

Now she stood here in the entryway, hands folded in front of her so Chloe could see she wasn't armed and didn't plan to take anything that didn't belong to her. Or was that even a concern?

"Like I said, I don't know what you're going to find," Chloe said, pushing the door shut behind Meg. "We've already gone through all the file cabinets."

"I know." Meg swallowed, knowing she had to tread carefully here. "It's just that something might jump out at me that wouldn't necessarily catch your attention or mean anything significant to Sylvia or—"

"I'm not getting in the middle of this," Chloe interrupted, putting her hands up as though surrendering. "That lawsuit thing, you know that's not my doing, right?"

"I know." Meg swallowed. "And I appreciate you letting me look around."

"Yeah, well, I wasn't thrilled when Sylvia told me she'd filed that suit. I was engaged to him. I think I should have had some say in his estate, don't you think?"

Meg nodded, not sure it was her place to comment and not wanting to say anything that would make it worse.

But maybe she could make it a tiny bit better.

"I don't think Sylvia means any harm," Meg said softly. "She just sees relationships as 'less than' if there's no certificate attached. Just because you didn't sign your names on a piece of paper doesn't mean the relationship was any less valid. The history, the understandings you had together as a couple—those things existed, even if you didn't walk down the aisle and say those two words."

"I do," Chloe murmured, nodding. "I do get it."

Meg stood there silent for a moment, not sure if she should offer a hug or a smile or a snarky comment about her former-future-mother-in-law. None of those things felt right, so she just stood there with her hands clasped in front of her and Chloe watching her like she was still trying to figure out Meg's place in her life.

"I'm sorry," Meg said at last. "I'm sorry you didn't get to marry him. And I'm sorry for anything I might have done to make him less inclined to hurry down the aisle again."

Chloe dabbed the corner of her eye with a tissue she pulled from the pocket of her cashmere cardigan. "Actually, I think it was the opposite. I think he was more eager to go through with marrying me to prove he was capable of it. That he could commit to forever with someone, even after everything that happened with you."

"That makes sense."

Chloe shook her head and stuffed the tissue back in her pocket. "That was one thing I never understood about him," she said. "The constant need to measure himself against everyone else."

"Matt was always competitive," Meg agreed. She kept her voice soft, expecting at any moment that Chloe would remember they weren't girlfriends, that they didn't really owe each other explanations or confessions or even kindness.

But Chloe seemed to be in a talking mood. "It's like he had this idea that his parents set the bar so high for a happy relationship, and he wanted so badly to get that right in his own life."

"Wow," Meg said, not sure she would have made that same observation. Is that why Matt had been reluctant to marry her? The desire not to screw up something his parents had done so well? "I never thought about it like that."

Chloe shrugged. "I've had a lot of time to think these last few weeks. You're right, his competitive nature probably drove a lot of it. Not just with relationships, but with everything in his life."

"How do you mean?" Meg asked, not sure it was her place to pry, but intrigued by Chloe's line of thought.

"Take Kyle, for instance."

"Okay," Meg said, hoping nothing in her face gave away the flash of emotion that arced through her at the mention of his name.

If Chloe saw anything, she didn't let on. "It just always seemed like Matt had this brotherly competition with Kyle going on in his mind—who had the most career success, who had the nicer car, who had the most notches on his bedpost. And the thing is, I don't think Kyle even knew they were competing."

"He didn't," Meg said, too quickly, perhaps. Did she have any right to speak for him? But she knew with absolute certainty she was right. "Kyle's not the competitive type," she added.

"And then with you—" Chloe swallowed, seeming to consider her words for the first time. "I probably shouldn't tell you this, but Matt always kept tabs on you."

"Really?" There was a funny roaring in Meg's ears, and she felt herself twisting her fingers into tighter knots.

"He didn't stalk you or anything," Chloe said quickly, turning to straighten a framed photo on the wall. Her family, from the look of it. "It wasn't like that. But sometimes he'd be distant, so I'd check his internet browser to see if there was something suspicious going on. And I'd see that he'd been looking at your Facebook page."

"But we weren't even friends," Meg protested. "Facebook friends, I mean. Matt's whole family unfriended me right after the split."

"I know. But you must not have your profile privacy protected?"

"That's true."

"And you still had mutual friends in real life. Every now and then I'd hear him ask them about you. He wanted to know if you were seeing anyone, if you'd found someone else."

Meg bit her lip and studied Chloe's face, expecting to see anger or bitterness or jealousy, but it wasn't there. She thought about Kyle, wondering how hurt she'd be if she found him lurking on Cara's Facebook page or asking around about old girlfriends.

Then again, maybe everyone checked up on exes. God knows she'd done it at first, though she hadn't gone near Matt's Facebook page for over a year now. She hadn't even known about Chloe until a few weeks ago.

"That must have been awkward for you," Meg said, not sure what else to offer. "Having him show an interest in an ex."

"Not as awkward as you might think. I wasn't threatened by you, honestly."

"I—um, I'm glad?" Meg bit her lip, unsure of the correct responses to anything. This whole conversation was new territory for her, like visiting a foreign country populated only by women who'd loved the same man she had.

Chloe just shrugged. "I don't mean that in a snarky way. Just that I never got the sense he was checking up on you because he wanted you back. He was checking up on you because he wanted to be sure he was happier. That his life was going better than yours was. He wanted to know the choices he'd made had landed him in a better place than the ones you'd made had done for you."

"I didn't realize we were competing."

Chloe laughed. "You were always competing. Everything was always a competition for Matt, remember?"

"I guess so."

Meg's head was spinning, and she couldn't decide whether this whole conversation was enlightening or depressing. Either way, Chloe seemed oddly undisturbed by it.

"I think it would bother me more," Meg said slowly. "Knowing someone I loved was checking up on someone he used to be with. I don't think I could be as cavalier about it as you are."

Chloe shrugged. "That's the difference between us. I'd rather know about all the skeletons in the closet. I'd rather throw all the baggage on the bed and open it up to see what's inside so I know how to deal with it."

"That's very adult of you."

"I try." She turned away. "Come on. Speaking of going through baggage, I guess you'd better get started. File cabinet's in here."

She led Meg down the hall, headed toward the last room on the right. Meg knew it well. It had been their office, too, back when she lived here with Matt.

They'd bickered for months over the perfect paint color, finally ending up with a pale mint-green he'd chosen when she left town for a weekend wine tour with her mom. They'd jokingly dubbed it "the baby's room," their heads swimming with visions of rocking chairs and cribs and the possibility of starting a family someday. In the interim, it had remained an office and a guest room and a catchall for clutter and extra furniture and the hovering ghosts of all their dreams.

But the possibility of children had always been there, right up until the moment Meg had walked away.

She hadn't realized she was holding her breath until she rounded the corner and saw the color of the walls. "You painted," Meg said on an exhale. "The gray is really pretty with the yellow curtains." She turned to look at Chloe, whose eyes flickered with a touch of pride.

"Thank you," Chloe said. "He let me decorate it however I wanted. This was going to be our baby's room someday. I was going to start stenciling little giraffes around the border when—" She broke off there, her eyes clouding with tears.

Meg hesitated, then reached out and squeezed Chloe's hand.

"It would have been beautiful," she said, meaning it with every ounce of her being. "I can picture it in my head, and it's perfect."

◆　◆　◆

Two hours later, Meg sat cross-legged on the floor with an empty teacup and a distinct sense that she wasn't going to find anything useful here. As if on cue, Chloe strolled in wearing a crop top and yoga pants Meg suspected were chosen for actual yoga, unlike her own.

She looked down at her own stretchy pants with a tiny bleach spot on one knee. She'd donned them that morning because they were the closest thing to wearing pajamas. Her T-shirt seemed appropriate, too, with its large bubble letters that read, *Exercise? I thought you said extra fries.*

"Any luck?" Chloe asked.

Meg shook her head. "Not really. I appreciate you letting me go through it all, though."

"It's fine." Chloe performed a hamstring stretch that left Meg wondering if the other woman could put her ankles behind her head. Then she thought about her father's mistress, the one who'd sexted him those photos, and she couldn't decide whether she wanted to laugh or cry.

"I have to take off for my class in about thirty minutes, so maybe you could wrap things up?" Chloe said.

"Of course." Meg got to her feet with the empty teacup in one hand. "Thank you for letting me stay as long as I have."

"Sorry you didn't find anything to help."

"I guess I can't feel too disappointed since I didn't really know what I was looking for to start with." She shifted the teacup from one hand to the other, looking down at it for inspiration. "Can I ask you something?"

"Sure."

"Why are you being so open about this? About letting me come in here and sift through the file cabinet?"

"I have nothing to hide," Chloe said, pulling the other leg up for a stretch. "All of my stuff's in another room, so these are just Matt's files. I've already gone through it all, so I know there's nothing dark and scary or threatening to my relationship with him. If it could give you closure, why not?"

"Closure," Meg said. "I didn't really get that, but I appreciate it anyway."

Chloe nodded, studying her for a moment. "He really was doing well," she said abruptly. "These last few months? He was happy. I know he was."

"I believe you."

"He was eating right, seeing a counselor, getting his physical and mental health in order."

"I'm glad," she said. "I could never even get him to go in for a checkup."

"He left me this house," Chloe said, her voice breaking a little. "And a life insurance policy that covers the whole mortgage. I wasn't expecting that."

"Congratulations," Meg said, not sure what else to say.

"Thanks. Now I can pour everything I have into opening my kombucha company. He knew that's what I wanted more than anything, so he made it happen for me." Chloe's eyes filled with tears, and she looked up at the ceiling to hold them back. Putting both feet on the floor, she swiped her thumbs beneath her lower lashes. "Anyway, I guess that gave me the closure I needed. Knowing he was looking out for me?"

"I'm glad," Meg said, meaning it. "He must have really loved you a lot."

Chloe looked at her, seeming to assess whether Meg was being serious or patronizing. "Truly," Meg added. "I know there were a lot of us over the years—lovers and girlfriends and flings who had some place in Matt's life. But for what it's worth, I think he really loved you."

Chloe was blinking hard now, no longer pretending she wasn't stifling tears. "Because of the life insurance?"

"No," Meg said. "Because he let you paint the room gray. Because he cared about being healthy for you. Because he invested in your career. Because I've never seen him smile the way he's smiling in that photograph right there."

She pointed to the framed image on top of the bookcase, and Chloe's gaze followed the direction of her finger. She looked surprised for an instant, then thoughtful. "Kyle took that the day Matt and I announced to the family that we'd gotten engaged," Chloe said softly, turning back to Meg. "Sylvia just kept saying, 'Thank you for making him so happy,' and I swear I didn't stop smiling for a week."

"It's beautiful."

"Thank you." Chloe stared at her, seeming to decide something. "Before you go, why don't I have you take a look at one more thing."

◆　◆　◆

"What the hell is this?" Jess set aside the top to a cardboard bankers box and peered inside, a mystified look on her face. She lifted the box onto Meg's coffee table as Meg peered over her friend's shoulder.

"That would be the Halloween mask Matt made out of papier-mâché in 2008," Meg said. "And a bunch of notes from a photography seminar he went to in Dallas the year after we started dating. And those look like movie tickets from—" she grabbed the stubs, frowning down at them. "I have no idea who he would have seen *Pocahontas* with in 1995, but it must have been significant."

"Good Lord. How did I never know you were marrying such a pack rat?"

Meg shrugged and pried the lid off another box. "It's not like he advertised it. He was weirdly sentimental about stuff. He wasn't very organized about it, though, so he'd collect all these trinkets and tokens and then just shove them in boxes and forget about them."

"Where the hell did he keep all the boxes?"

"The garage, when we lived together," Meg said. "Chloe made him keep them in the attic. Apparently she needed the room to store all her bikes and workout gear."

"This is nuts."

"We've got three dozen of them to go through, and I'm guessing they're all like this."

"Good thing I made Bloody Marys."

"Amen." Meg took a sip of hers and set it down, then began pawing through her own box. There was a program from a play he must have seen a year or so after they'd split up. A pack of chewing gum with three pieces missing. A tiny blue piggy bank with a crack down one side, a relic from some other period Meg hadn't been privy to in his life.

She spotted a printout she'd given him from a page on the Humane Society website, and she pulled it out, skimming more closely. It was a cat she'd hoped desperately to adopt when they'd first moved into the house together, but Matt had insisted he was allergic to cats. She couldn't for the life of her think of why he might've kept these pages, creased and faded with age.

"There's nothing in here but junk," Jess muttered.

"I know," Meg said, setting the paper aside. "But look at it all anyway, just in case."

"Here's an electric bill from 1997."

"I'm sure he paid it at some point. He was always good about that. Just not at throwing things out."

She continued digging through the box, pushing aside broken pens, a bottle cap, a Tyvek race number he must have worn for a competition during the era he'd taken up triathlons.

Meg spotted a paperback of e. e. cummings poetry in the bottom of the box. Nostalgia washed over her, and she scooped it up, breathing in the familiar scent of the used bookstore she used to frequent before Matt bought her a Kindle for her birthday.

"I didn't fancy Matt as a fan of poetry," Jess mused.

"He wasn't. I gave it to him when we got engaged. Thought maybe we could find a poem together to have Kyle read at our wedding."

"Kyle," Jess said, smiling a little at the mention of his name, while Meg flipped through the book. "Did he agree to do it?"

"We never even asked him. Matt thought the poetry idea was stupid, so I dropped it."

"Funny he kept the book."

"Don't read too much into it," Meg said, dropping the book back into the box. "He also appears to have kept ticket stubs from the Joni Mitchell concert his mother dragged him to in college, and I know for a fact he hated Joni Mitchell."

"Can I see the book?"

"Sure." Meg picked it up again and handed it over. Tucking a curl behind one ear, she went back to sifting through the box. "Knock yourself out. I don't even remember which poem I bookmarked for him."

"Hmm," Jess said, turning a page as her eyes skimmed over the words. "'A politician is an arse upon'?"

Meg laughed and pushed her box aside, reaching for another. She pried the lid off and began to sort through more junk. "The word *arse* certainly would have been fitting at that wedding."

"How about 'sonnet entitled how to run the world'?"

"That does sound like one he might've picked," Meg mused. She picked up a hand puppet made from a brown paper bag, wondering whether Matt or someone else had glued on the yellow yarn hair and the pink felt cheeks. Why on earth had he kept this, and what had it meant to him? She set the puppet down and picked up a matchbook, turning it over in her palm. It was from the restaurant they'd gone to on their first date, and she wondered if he'd kept it all this time or if he'd gone there more recently with someone else.

Beside her, Jess turned a page in the book. "The poem you chose," Jess said softly. "Was it 'since feeling is first'?"

"Maybe," Meg said, setting the matchbook aside and reaching for an unopened envelope marked with the name of the local cable company. "Why? Is that page dog-eared?"

"No. That's not it."

Something in Jess's voice made Meg look up. Her friend had an odd expression, and she was holding something that looked like a stained cocktail napkin.

She looked up at Meg, then down at the napkin again. The book slid off her lap, but neither of them made a move to grab it as Jess held the napkin out to Meg.

"I think I found what you're looking for."

CHAPTER SEVENTEEN

"Look at this one! I think it's my favorite."

Kyle leaned closer to his mother, peering down at the photograph she marked with the pale pink tip of her fingernail. His heart twisted a little as he saw which image it was.

"That was our first day of Little League," he said, wondering why no one told him his ball cap was so crooked. Matt looked mischievous and adorable with his missing front tooth and a smattering of freckles across his nose, and Kyle noticed the way his brother's arm looped around his neck in a gesture that was half brotherly love, half strangulation attempt.

"You were so nervous," his mom said, sliding her fingertip over the faces in the photo as though committing them to memory. "Remember that? Matt played the year before, but this was your first time."

Kyle remembered. He put an arm around his mother, staring down at the photograph until the faces were burned into his brain. "He took me around so I could meet all the coaches. Then he introduced me to all the players. Said, 'This is my kid brother. Anyone messes with him, you answer to me.'"

His mom laughed, leaning back against Kyle's arm like a cat craving affection. He thought about Floyd the fickle feline and wondered how Meg was doing, but he pushed the thought from his mind for now. He should be focusing on his mom, on her need for support and love and the affection of her one remaining child.

Kyle needed to be a better son, dammit. He'd only stopped by today because his afternoon appointment got cancelled at the last minute and he was already in the neighborhood. It wouldn't kill him to do a better job making time for her, checking in to be sure she was coping okay. Hell, he should probably take her to lunch a few times a week or come to dinner on Saturdays the way he used to before he'd reached the point where seeing Matt and Meg together at family meals grew too unbearable.

He cupped his hand around his mom's shoulder, noticing how bony she felt.

"He was always looking out for you," she said. "Such a good big brother." She looked up at him, her smile fading as her eyes went watery. "I know you two didn't always get along well, but you know he loved you, right?"

Kyle nodded as his throat tightened. "I loved him, too."

She smiled, but the sadness in her eyes left Kyle feeling like someone was standing on his chest. "I'm glad to hear you say that."

Kyle swallowed hard, trying to force the lump back down into his gut. "I've been missing him every day," he admitted. "Which seems dumb since we used to go months without speaking. But something funny will happen and I'll think, 'I've gotta remember to tell Matt about that,' and then I'll remember I can't. Not ever."

"Oh, honey." His mom snuggled closer beneath his arm and turned a page in the album. Kyle thought about the last time he'd had the urge to tell his brother something. It was the other night when he'd been cutting up penis vegetables with Meg, and he'd come across a red pepper that looked like it had a scrotum. He'd laughed so hard he'd nearly stabbed himself in the hand, and he almost pulled out his phone to text Matt a picture of the phallic vegetable.

Then he'd felt like hell, not just because Matt was dead. If he were still alive, would Kyle have told him about Meg? About cooking with her and laughing with her and making love with her in the big bed she'd never shared with anyone else?

Kyle took a deep breath, pretty sure the answer was *hell, no.*

Which brought him right back to the fact that he was a pretty shitty brother, in addition to being a lousy son.

He let his gaze drop to the photo album again. So many memories there. His brother fighting with him over who could do cooler tricks on the shared scooter. The Halloween when they bickered about whether they were too old to trick-or-treat, then cut eyeholes in old bed sheets and ran around the neighborhood pretending to be ghosts. Prom night when Matt tried to get him to bet over who had the better chance of getting lucky.

The line between affection and rivalry was so blurred in his memory that he honestly wasn't sure where one stopped and the other started.

"I always loved this one," his mom said, smoothing her thumb over a shot of them giving the family dog a bath when they were both in middle school. Matt was smearing a handful of suds into Kyle's hair, while Kyle laughed and scrubbed Ginger's ears. "You might have fought like wild animals half the time, but you laughed together, too."

"We did," he said. "I wish we'd done it more. The laughing, I mean. Especially as we got older."

His mom closed the photo album and looked up at him with tears pooling in her eyes. "I just can't believe he's gone. I know it's been four weeks, but it still doesn't seem real."

She took a shaky breath and looked up at the ceiling like that might help her stave off the tears. "He'll never take another photo or send silly jokes to my email or give me grandbabies."

Kyle pulled her closer, putting both arms around her in an awkward, sideways hug. "I know," he said, wishing he could think of something more comforting to offer. "I know."

"Do you think—" she drew back, looking at him with an earnest expression before casting her eyes down at the closed photo album. "Never mind. I suppose now's not the time."

"What, Mom? Say it."

She looked up at him with a flicker of hope in her eyes. "I just wondered if you ever thought about settling down. Finding a nice girl, maybe having a child of your own."

The ache started deep in Kyle's chest and spread outward, radiating through his arms and legs. It took him a moment to catch his breath. "Sure," he said at last. "I've thought about it."

"I mean, I guess you'd want to be in a relationship first. That's important."

His subconscious poked him in the ribs. *Tell her. Tell her about Meg.*

But he couldn't say that. He didn't know where things stood with Meg, but he hadn't stopped thinking about her all week. They'd called and texted and flirted on the phone until two in the morning in the three days since they'd melted their relationship relics. Since then, she'd been busy with radio interviews and catering jobs, but they'd made loose plans to see each other Friday night.

He looked at his mom and wondered what she'd think if she knew. Would it break her heart? Lord knew the last thing his mother needed right now was more heartache.

Then again, she used to like Meg. Loved her like a daughter, she'd said, or at least she used to before Meg's disappearing act.

"I want you to be happy, baby," his mom was saying. "You've dated a lot of lovely girls over the years. I know I told you I thought Cara might've been the one—"

"She wasn't." He started to apologize for the gruffness of his reply, but his mom didn't seem fazed.

"I know that," she said. "And I know she wanted to get married and you didn't. So did Melody. So did—"

"Mom, I couldn't see myself spending the rest of my life with them."

"So you do see it with someone?"

"I—" he stopped himself, not sure what it meant that he was picturing Meg again. Meg smiling up at him with a veil in her hair and a bouquet of daisies clutched in her hand. Meg sleeping beside him, her curls spread across the pillow in a tangled web. Meg holding a baby—*his* baby—or cheering at a Little League game or hugging him at a high school graduation ceremony . . .

"I don't mean someone specific," his mom said. "But you think there's a woman out there that you could spend the rest of your life with?"

The hope in her voice was almost too much for him to bear. He thought about telling her then. About confessing everything, not just the last three weeks of growing closer to Meg, but *everything*. The years of pining silently for her, watching from afar, picturing himself in Matt's shoes, in Matt's life, in *her*—

"Mom, I—"

The doorbell chimed, and his mom stiffened under his arm. She glanced toward the door, then looked down at her watch. "She's early." Sylvia sighed. "She never could show up on time. Always five minutes early, never right on the hour."

Kyle felt all the blood drain from his face. He knew someone who fit that description. "Who's *she?*"

"Meg Delaney. She called this morning, said she had something she needed to show me. She's bringing her lawyer with her, so obviously I've got Albert joining me, but he can't make it until three-thirty."

His mom stood up and started for the door while Kyle sat frozen on the sofa. Part of him wanted to flee. Maybe he could make it out the back door and let his mother handle this alone. Meg had her lawyer, and his mom would have hers. Neither of them needed him here. A smart man would remove himself from the situation and let them work things out without him.

He stood and grabbed his keys, ready to make a run for it. But the instant his mom threw the door open, his chance of escape vanished. "Hello, Meg," Sylvia said crisply. "I assume this is your attorney?"

"Franklin Hatfield, pleasure to meet you."

Kyle stood up, his hands balling at his sides as though his subconscious expected a fistfight. The room tilted a little as he moved toward the door. He stepped up beside his mother, who turned and smiled up at him. The love in her eyes was so fierce that Kyle stepped closer, feeling oddly protective.

Then he looked back at Meg. Her eyes had gone wide, and she looked at him like he was the last person on earth she wanted to see.

"Kyle," she said, licking her lips. "I wasn't expecting you to be here."

"I didn't realize you were stopping by."

"Yes, well, we're all here now," his mom said, swinging the door wide. "I'll grab some refreshments and we can wait for Albert to arrive. Kyle? Would you mind showing them to the study?"

Kyle swallowed, his gaze flicking back to Meg's. He shouldn't be here. Maybe he could still make an escape. "Actually, Mom, I was just about to leave. Sounds like you've got some personal stuff to deal with, and you don't need me in the middle of it."

A look of intense relief washed over Meg's face, and he felt glad he'd been the one to put it there. Her lawyer nodded in agreement.

"Certainly some of the details we'll be discussing are of a rather—*intimate* nature. It's best if we confine the discussion to only the parties involved in the case."

The word *intimate* prickled the back of Kyle's brain, and he gripped his keys tighter in his palm. They felt different without the keychain, unfamiliar and less weighty.

"Kyle, sweetheart, I'd like you to stay." He turned toward his mother's voice and saw her standing at the entrance of the kitchen, her hands twisting in her skirt. She looked unusually small, and her face was pale from four weeks of crying. He wanted to wrap her up in his arms and make the hurt go away, to pay her back for all the times she'd kissed his skinned knees and tucked twenty-dollar bills into thinking-of-you cards when he was struggling to make it as an artist.

The look she gave him nearly split his heart in two. "Your father can't be here, and I'd like another member of the family on my side. Please?"

Kyle swallowed hard, then nodded. "Okay, Mom." He fought to keep his eyes off Meg, certain he didn't want to see disappointment on her face. He knew she didn't want him there any more than he wanted to be there, but he owed it to his mother.

He owed it to Matt.

"Okay," he said again, turning to lead the way down the hall. "I'll stay."

◆　◆　◆

The air in the study felt too thick to breathe. Meg gripped her water glass and looked at her attorney, struggling not to glance at Kyle. Staring at Franklin was safe, albeit nerve-wracking. Her attorney was terrifying, with steel-colored hair and a charcoal suit that looked like it cost more than she made in a year.

More than you used to make in a year, she reminded herself. *You're a bestselling author now. You won't be digging quarters out of the sofa to pay the phone bill.*

She couldn't bear to look at Kyle. If she saw his face, odds were good she'd leap from this stiff maple chair and hurl herself into his arms, yelling at everyone that they should just call this whole thing off.

But she couldn't do that. Coming here today, saying the things she was prepared to say—this was about standing up for herself. Not just as a professional, but as an artist, as a *woman.*

Beside her, Franklin yammered on about oral contracts and the statute of limitations, using words that went flying over her head. The Midlands' lawyer was yammering back, and she tried hard to focus on their words. Something about inseparable parts of a unitary whole? It would almost sound romantic if both men didn't look like they were on the brink of throwing their briefcases at each other. Or at her.

Meg dared a glance at Sylvia, who sat stiffly between her lawyer and Kyle, her hands folded in her lap. She didn't meet Meg's eyes. Neither did Kyle, who stared with rapt attention at the lawyers. Meg did the same, commanding herself to pay better attention. This was her life, for crying out loud.

"I know you're familiar with the details of Thomson v. Larson and the statutory definition of *joint work,*" said Meg's lawyer in a voice that reminded Meg of burning her tongue on boiled molasses. "As you'll recall from the outcome of Thomson's request for declaratory judgment establishing coauthorship of the Broadway musical *Rent* under the Copyright Act of 1976 . . ."

He droned on, and Meg took a swallow of water, then held the glass in her lap so she wouldn't have to set it down on the maple side table. She wished she had a coaster and thought about asking for one, but maybe it didn't matter at this point. Sylvia already hated her. A water ring on her furniture wouldn't change that.

Against her better judgment, she dared a glance at Kyle. His face was pale and drawn, and he looked as ill as she felt. She took another sip of water and set the glass down, willing her hands to stop shaking.

The Midland family's lawyer—Albert, was it?—was talking now, his words bearing a striking resemblance to the mysterious language Meg's lawyer seemed to speak. Something about intellectual property and derivative works?

He paused for breath, and Meg's attorney jumped in again. "In Childress v. Taylor, you'll recall it was established that the claimant bears the burden of establishing each of the putative coauthors made independently copyrightable contributions to the work, and fully intended to be coauthors. I think we can all agree that Mr. Midland made a choice not to have his name appear in the credits for this book, and further—"

"I agree to no such thing!" Sylvia interrupted. She pointed a finger at Meg, and Meg had to fight the urge to bite off the tip. "I know my baby, and he would have wanted credit for his work. That woman took it upon herself to cut him out of the deal because she was jealous of his success as an artist."

Meg shook her head, ready to argue, but Franklin put a hand out and signaled her to stop. Something told her the language of this conversation had shifted from "lawyer" to "human," so she bit her tongue and let Franklin do the talking.

"Look, we can go around in circles all day about copyright law and coauthorship, but that's not why we called this meeting today." He cleared his throat and looked at Albert. "I think we'd all like to avoid going to trial if we can, would you agree?"

The other lawyer folded his arms over his chest and didn't answer, his response neither an agreement nor a denial. Christ, is this what it would be like in a courtroom? Meg felt the walls closing in on her, and she wondered if Kyle had the same sensation of choking on his own thoughts.

Franklin continued, flipping the clasps on his briefcase as he spoke. "We brought with us today some irrefutable evidence that Mr. Midland did not wish to receive monetary compensation for his contribution to the book, and that he did not intend to be credited as a coauthor or contributor in this work."

"What?" Sylvia sputtered. "That's impossible."

"It's quite possible, I assure you. In fact, I believe you'll see he saw the whole project as a frivolity. A joke. A creative endeavor he didn't even pretend to take seriously."

Meg swallowed hard as her eyes began to burn. She ordered herself not to cry, but she honestly couldn't tell where the threat of tears was coming from. Anger? Sadness? Humiliation?

Maybe all of the above.

She saw Sylvia and Kyle and the other attorney straighten a little in their chairs, and she knew her lawyer's words had gotten to them. She knew what was about to happen, and part of her wanted to stop it. She could put her hand on Franklin's arm right now, tell him she'd changed her mind.

"Evidence?" The scoff was clear in Albert's voice as he looked from Franklin to Sylvia and back again. "Do you intend to present it to us, or just wave it around as a threat until we get to court?"

Meg's attorney sighed. "As I already explained, we're hoping to avoid going to trial. We believe what we've brought with us here today will allow us to settle this whole matter out of court. My client has made a generous lump-sum offer, which you'll see spelled out on the last page of the packet I handed you at the start of this meeting."

"We're not even going to discuss it until you show us what you have." Albert gestured at the briefcase, then folded his arms over his chest. "Your move, counselor."

"As you wish."

Meg watched as Franklin reached into his briefcase and pulled out a plastic baggie. No one said a word as he held it up, displaying the cocktail napkin for everyone to see. She dared another glance at Kyle, who squinted at the baggie from across the room, confusion evident on his face.

Sylvia scowled. Franklin stood up and crossed the room to stand in front of her, his imposing height towering above her in a way that almost made Meg feel sorry for her former-future-mother-in-law.

"Mrs. Midland," Franklin said, holding the baggie behind his back for a moment. "I'm very sorry for your loss."

"Thank you."

"I need to ask you—is this your son's handwriting?"

He brought the baggie in front of her face, and Sylvia reached up to clutch the edges, holding it steady. Meg couldn't see Sylvia's face, which was a relief.

But she heard the gasp.

When Franklin drew the bag back, Sylvia's cheeks had lost all their color. Her jaw was clenched and her eyes looked like granite.

"I can't say for certain," she said tightly, giving nothing away.

"But it does look like Matt's writing?"

Sylvia gave a curt nod. "I suppose it might."

Had she read all the words, or simply glanced at the handwriting? Meg wasn't sure yet, but Sylvia's stony expression told Meg she'd probably seen plenty.

Albert leaned forward, catching the edge of the baggie. His eyes skimmed the cocktail napkin, too, and Meg watched him digest the words. She'd committed them to memory already. She'd almost forgotten it existed at all until she'd held it in her hand the other night, its edges creased from two years folded inside that book of poetry.

Albert gave a snort of disgust, and her own lawyer drew the bag back and turned to look at Meg. A wave of shame washed through her, hot and sour. She closed her eyes, wishing she could be anyplace but here. She opened them again when Franklin's voice broke through her thoughts.

"Ms. Delaney, Mrs. Midland, I apologize in advance for the language I'm about to use, but we're all adults here."

Across the room, Meg saw Kyle stiffen. She stared at him, willing him to look at her, to meet her gaze one last time before he read those words. His eyes swung to hers, and Meg drew a sharp breath. His gray-green gaze was cold and expressionless, and Meg took a shaky breath.

"What does it say?" Kyle folded his arms over his chest and tore his gaze from Meg's. "Are you planning to read it aloud?"

Franklin gave her a questioning look. She nodded silent consent, then closed her eyes again. The room was still for a few beats. Then Franklin began to read.

"I, Matt Midland, agree to take photos for Meggipoo's smutty cookbook," he read. His voice went up on the word *smutty*, and Meg tried not to flinch. She could picture the words in her mind, the drunken blur of Matt's handwriting on a stained napkin, the memory of crumpling those words into a ball and throwing them at him. *You never take me seriously*, she'd shouted. *I'm a professional, too, dammit.*

Franklin kept reading. "In exchange, Ms. Delaney will provide a minimum of twenty-five sloppy BJs between now and June 26. Signed, Matt 'Big Bone' Midland."

The room was silent. Meg's eyes were still closed, and she entertained a brief fantasy that everyone had stood up and left the room. That none of this was really happening—the humiliation, the shame, the ridiculousness of this whole case coming down to blowjobs and a goddamn cocktail napkin.

But as the silence drew out, she forced herself to open her eyes again. Everyone was staring at her. Meg heard her own heartbeat hammering in her ears, and she looked down at her hands as she wiped her palms on her jeans.

Her attorney was the first to speak. "I think it's clear from this note that Mr. Midland was not inclined to take this project seriously. As you can see, the only compensation he requested was—"

"BJs?" Sylvia stared at Meg, then looked at Kyle. "I don't know what those letters mean. Is that what I think it is?"

Kyle stared at his mother like he'd never seen her before. He nodded once, then looked away, his expression conveying nothing more.

It was the Midland family lawyer who came to his rescue. "I believe that's slang terminology for fellatio," he said to Sylvia, the tips of his ears glowing tomato-red as she frowned back at him. He turned to Franklin and cleared his throat. "If we're to believe that note is authentic, it appears Mr. Midland was suggesting his photography skills could be purchased at a rate of twenty-five occurrences of oral stimulation, which is preposterous."

"Preposterous?" Meg's lawyer pounced, his eyes taking on a rabid gleam. "I can assure you the note is authentic, and furthermore, if you'll refer to the case of Jones v. Jones referenced in your packet—"

"You can't honestly think that would hold up in court?" Albert stood up, his eyes blazing like he wanted to take a swing at the other lawyer. "A cocktail napkin? A note that was most likely written by someone in a state of intoxication? An implication of *prostitution* and—"

"Even if you try to argue this isn't a legally binding contract, the fact remains that Mr. Midland, by penning this particular missive, was indicating a general irreverence for the project, and for my client. I don't think I need to remind you that—"

"Were the terms of the contract fulfilled?"

Kyle's words hit Meg like a punch in the abdomen. Everyone stopped talking at once. Meg looked at Kyle and felt a surge of ice wash through her veins. He wasn't avoiding her eyes now. He was staring at her, his gaze boring into her, drilling through her mind, her soul, her heart.

"I beg your pardon?" Franklin said, directing his attention to Kyle.

"I wasn't talking to you," Kyle said, his eyes never leaving Meg's. "I was speaking to Meg."

"I—um—what?" Meg stammered. She tucked her hands between her knees to make them stop shaking.

"Were the terms of the contract fulfilled?" Kyle repeated, his gaze still locked with hers.

"This is ridiculous," Sylvia sputtered. "It's obvious Matt wasn't in his right mind when he wrote that, and even if he were, that's hardly the sort of evidence that would hold up. Twenty-five sloppy BJs? For the love of God, what kind of—"

"Answer the question, Meg." Kyle's voice was hollow and felt like a stake driving into her chest. "Unless you want me to?"

The attorneys' gazes were swinging back and forth between the two of them, realization dawning as they seemed to grasp that there was more going on here than legal wrangling.

Beside Kyle, his mother sputtered. "This is asinine. I want everyone to stop this line of discussion immediately. It's disrespectful, crude, and entirely irrelevant to the case at hand."

Kyle tore his gaze from Meg's, and she felt the floor drop out from under her. This couldn't be happening. He couldn't really be throwing her under the bus like this.

"They're the ones who took it to this level," Kyle said, his voice eerily soft as he spoke to his mother. "If they're going to make the claim that this is a legitimate contract, and these are the terms Matt supposedly set out, then I think we're within our right to address whether the terms of the contract were fulfilled."

He looked back at Meg, and she could see something in his eyes that hadn't been there before. Remorse? Jealousy? Sadness? She couldn't identify it, but she could identify the feeling in the pit of her own stomach.

Betrayal.

Not the first time she'd looked into a pair of gray-green eyes and felt a sinking sense that her whole life was about to unravel.

Every pair of eyes in the room had shifted to her, and Meg wondered if it was possible to pass out from sheer humiliation. She looked up at her attorney, who for the first time ever, seemed at a genuine loss for words. He shook his head. "You don't have to answer that."

"You're right, she doesn't," Kyle said. "I'll do it for her."

CHAPTER EIGHTEEN

Kyle had never hated himself more than he had in that moment.

That's not true, his subconscious reminded him. *And right now you're making up for the one time you hated yourself more than this.*

He looked at Meg, wishing he could hit rewind on this entire conversation and do things differently. But if he had the option to rewind, there was a different moment in time he'd choose to erase. Would any of them be sitting here right now if it weren't for that?

"Meg," he said softly, not sure what he planned to say next. *I'm sorry? I had to do it? Don't hate me?*

But his brain flashed to an image of Matt in a hospital bed two years ago, his face drawn and pale and racked with guilt. Kyle could picture it in his head like it was yesterday, the doctors murmuring about depression and suicide risk while Matt gripped Kyle's arm with alarming force. "Swear to me you won't tell anyone," Matt had hissed. "Not a soul."

And Kyle hadn't. Not ever.

Now, Meg stared at him, her expression somewhere between shock and hurt. He watched her throat move as she swallowed, and he wanted to jump from his seat and tell her she didn't have to answer. That it was no one's business how many blowjobs she'd given his brother. That he'd give anything not to know.

But he did know. He knew because she'd told him in hushed tones on a cot in his studio. He knew because he remembered the feel of her bare breast under his palm while she told him her most intimate secrets.

"No." Meg's voice was so soft the word dropped like a feather in the center of the room.

Albert leaned down, still towering over her, probably enjoying this moment more than he'd enjoyed anything else in his career as an attorney. "I beg your pardon, dear?"

Meg looked at him, her eyes flashing with humiliation and betrayal. She looked back at her own attorney, who held up his hand again to urge her to stay silent. Part of Kyle hoped she might.

He watched her left hand start to lift, her fingers en route to her earlobe, and he knew she was planning to bite back the retort bubbling inside her. But as her gaze swung back to his, her hand dropped like a dead bird. She looked at it lying there on her lap, then back at him.

"No," she said again, her voice stronger this time. "While my fiancé and I didn't keep a tally sheet in our bedroom, I can say with almost absolute certainty that between the date he took those photos and the date of our wedding, I did not—" she broke off there, shaking her head and giving a brittle little laugh that made Kyle's chest ache. "I did not give him twenty-five 'sloppy BJs.'" She made air quotes around the words, her eyes pooling with tears of embarrassment and anger.

She swung her gaze to his and shook her head. "As a matter of fact, I probably didn't give him even a dozen 'sloppy BJs,' or even half-a-dozen tidy ones. And if you want to get technical, I could probably count on one hand the number of times he went down on me the entire time we were together. Is that what you want to hear? Is it?"

Odd how her voice could be a shout and a whisper all at the same time. Kyle had never heard her sound like that, had never seen such bitter fury in her eyes.

"Meg!" Kyle's mother bolted up, her fists clenching in fury. "I want you out of this house right now! You've made a mockery of these proceedings and my son's life. I have never despised anyone more in my life than I do right this second."

Meg reeled back as though slapped. Even from across the room, Kyle could see her eyes brimmed with unshed tears. It was a miracle of gravity they weren't spilling down her cheeks in earnest, but maybe it was sheer fury holding them back.

As she swung her gaze to him, he felt sure that was the case.

She pressed her lips together, and he wondered if she was holding words in, or honestly at a loss for what to say. When she stood up, she had to catch the back of her chair with one hand to keep from wobbling.

"I'll show myself out," she said, nodding at his mother with a look that split Kyle's heart in two.

She took the steps to the door on legs that looked like they might not hold her upright, but she held her head high, the tears still not falling. Her lawyer looked down at the baggie in his hand, seemingly at a loss for what to do with it.

He shoved it in his briefcase, then nodded to the others in turn. "Counselor. Mrs. Midland. Mr. Midland. We'll discuss this further at a later date." He cleared his throat. "I'm very sorry for your loss."

Kyle's mother shook her head as she sat back down beside him. She grabbed a tissue from the box on the desk next to her. She blew her nose, her eyes red and filled with anger and pain and a whole host of other emotions Kyle knew all too well. He put his arm around his mother, not sure what else to do.

"We'll see you in court," she snapped at Meg. "Or in *hell*!"

The lawyer nodded again, then turned to catch up with Meg. She hadn't made it out the door yet, and Kyle saw her hesitate on the threshold, her fingers clenched on the doorframe. He expected her to march out of the room without a backward glance, but instead she turned to look at him.

Kyle held his breath, waiting for her to unleash the fury he knew he deserved. He sat frozen in place, expecting her wrath, welcoming it.

Forgive me, his brain telegraphed, willing her to hear him. To understand why he'd done what he'd done.

But instead, Meg shook her head. She didn't say a word, but her eyes spoke the two words she'd said to his brother before walking out of that church two years ago. The parallel should have comforted him. Here he was, finally in his brother's shoes.

But the unspoken words felt like icy daggers through his heart.

Forgive me, he telegraphed again, willing her to hear him.

I can't, that look told him. *Not ever.*

Then she walked out the door.

♦　♦　♦

"I don't know whether to be freaked out or glad you're not crying," Jess said, handing her a box of tissues. "But here are some snot rags, just in case."

Meg shook her head and pushed the tissues away. "I'm done crying. I've done so much of it the last few weeks—hell, for the last *two years*—that I don't have any tears left."

She thought about Kyle confessing his inability to cry over his brother's death and his breakup with Cara. What made the difference between the tears falling or staying locked inside? She looked at Jess and shook her head. "I never thought he'd betray me like that. Kyle, I mean."

"Right. Betrayal from Matt wasn't such a surprise, was it?"

Meg didn't say anything, too numb to form words.

Jess sat down on the coffee table in front of her and put her hands on both of Meg's knees. "Do you want me to tell you I think he should fry in hell? Because I can do that, if that's what you need."

"What's the alternative?"

"Telling you something that might be a little harder to hear."

Meg swallowed. "Which is what?"

Jess squeezed Meg's knees, and the warmth in her eyes was almost enough to thaw the iceberg that had lodged itself in the center of her chest the moment Kyle had spoken in that meeting.

"You did sort of back him into a corner," Jess said. "I know it was a shitty thing for him to do, and he betrayed your confidence, but—"

"But what?" Meg swallowed down the lump in her throat as the tears started to well. "Pillow talk shouldn't be admissible in legal proceedings. End of story."

"Right. I know. But you were the one to bring up the sex thing. Not that I'm blaming you. God knows you did what your lawyer told you to do. What your agent suggested. And you know I have no kind feelings for Matt Midland, may he rest in peace."

Meg took a shaky breath. "I was looking out for myself. It's something I did so rarely when I was with Matt. I thought—"

"I know, honey, I was there. I watched that man back over you for years before you finally called it quits. Even before he cheated, he was running you down in small ways every single day."

"It wasn't all bad."

"It wasn't, I know."

"It was even pretty good, most of the time." Meg sniffed. "At least I thought it was."

Jess nodded, her hands still warm on Meg's knees. "When did you stop thinking that?"

Meg hesitated, knowing the answer before her brain formed the words. "When I was with Kyle," she said softly. "When I saw how different it could be."

Jess nodded and reached for Meg's hands. "I know. It's like spending your whole life wearing the wrong-sized bra and not realizing it. Then when you finally get the right size, you wonder how you never noticed before how uncomfortable you were."

"Yes," Meg said softly. "That's it exactly."

Jess let go of her hands and Meg leaned back against the couch cushions. She shoved hard at the memory of sitting with Kyle on this same sofa. Had it only been four weeks since this whole mess got started? It felt like mere days. It felt like a lifetime ago. She honestly couldn't tell anymore.

"Come on," Jess said, standing up. "Let's make dinner together. It'll take your mind off things."

"Things," Meg repeated. "Like the fact that I'm destined to lose the lawsuit that would have assured me the royalties I worked hard for? Like how much Sylvia Midland hates me? Like the fact that I just lost the man I thought I'd started to love?"

Jess nodded, glancing to the side. "Or the fact that he's standing on your doorstep right now?"

"What?"

Jess nodded to the front of the house, and Meg followed the direction of her gaze to her own front porch. Her gut twisted at the sight of him standing there. She couldn't see his face through the frosted glass, but she'd have known his shape anywhere. She'd studied it with her hands, with her mind, with her heart.

"I can get rid of him," Jess said. "Either send him away, or arrange for him to meet a gruesome, painful death."

"No," Meg said, standing up. Her legs weren't shaking anymore, so she headed for the front door. "I want to get this over with. I want to hear what he has to say for himself so I can tell him goodbye to his face."

Jess stayed seated on the coffee table, a look of worry crossing her features. "Okay," she said. "Do you want me to stay?"

Meg hesitated, not sure anymore what she wanted. "That's okay," she said. "Thanks, though."

"No problem. Some conversations are meant to be private."

"Tell me about it."

Jess snorted and stood up, crossing to the front door where Meg stood with her hand on the knob. "A word of advice?"

"Don't sleep with him? Not a problem. I'd sooner remove my own spleen with a spoon."

Jess smiled and shook her head. "Hear him out. You owe him that much. You owe it to yourself to get closure. You never had that with Matt, and it ate at you for two years."

"Yeah," Meg muttered, glancing at the door where Kyle stood waiting, not knocking, not ringing the bell, just standing there waiting for her. "Point taken."

"Goodnight, sweetie," Jess said, wrapping her arms around Meg's shoulders and squeezing her with enough force to let Meg know she was loved beyond measure. "You got this."

"Thanks, Jess."

"Call me later?"

Meg nodded and opened the door. Even though she knew he'd be standing there, her stomach still did a flip when she saw Kyle on her front step, the porch light making a halo around his head. He nodded at her, then at Jess. "Meg," he said, his voice low and soft. "Jess."

"I was just leaving." Jess moved around him with a glare that made it apparent she'd do grave harm to him if he did further damage. "I'm only a phone call away, though, Meg."

Meg nodded, watching her friend walk down the path to her car. She couldn't bring herself to make eye contact with Kyle. Not yet.

When she finally did, the remorse in his eyes was enough to make her legs shaky again. She cleared her throat and willed herself not to blink. "Why are you here?"

"There's something else I need to say."

His eyes glittered under the porch light, and Meg stared at him, wondering if she'd ever really known him at all. She gripped the door tighter, willing herself to keep breathing. "I think you've said enough for one day, don't you?"

"No. I don't. And I think you need to hear me out."

Rage flared in her, and Meg leveled him with a glare. "I don't think I need to do anything you say, Kyle. You betrayed me. You took something I told you in confidence and you threw it in my face and—"

"Confession number one," he said, his voice loud enough to send Floyd skittering off the paisley chair behind her.

Meg shook her head and folded her arms over her chest. "I'm not playing your stupid game anymore! This is my life we're talking about here. Besides that, I didn't touch my damn ear."

"Confession number one," he repeated like he hadn't even heard her. "I was there when Matt cheated on you."

That got her attention. Meg closed her mouth as her tongue went dry and her throat closed up. "What?"

"Not in the room," he said. "It wasn't like some sort of voyeuristic orgy or anything. But I was with him when he made up his mind to do it. When he decided he wanted to cheat."

"Decided," she repeated dumbly, rolling the meaning of the word like a pebble on her tongue.

"It was a conscious decision, not a heat-of-the-moment kind of thing. That might be different from what he told you, or maybe from what he told himself."

Meg swallowed hard, not sure whether that made it better or worse. Did she want to hear the rest of this?

Closure, her subconscious whispered as Kyle studied her face.

"Do you want me to continue?"

She nodded, even though she hadn't made up her mind yet. Then she stepped aside, granting him entrance to her home. She thought they might just stand there in the foyer, but he moved right through it. He paused at the entrance to the living room, and his eyes were dark when he turned back to her. "Is it okay if we talk in here?"

"That's fine."

He nodded, then moved around her sofa, pausing again. He took a few steps to the left, then folded himself into the stiff, paisley-print armchair Floyd had just vacated.

Clasping his hands in his lap, Kyle waited for Meg to sit. She dropped slowly onto the edge of the sofa, not so much a decision to be seated as a certainty her legs wouldn't hold her up much longer. She took a few deep breaths, steeling herself to hear what he had to say.

"We went golfing," he said. "It was maybe two weeks before the wedding, sort of a brotherly getaway. He probably told you that part?"

She nodded, not sure what golf had to do with Matt having an affair, but knowing the details seemed important to Kyle. She remembered Chloe's words the other day. Something about dragging all the skeletons out of the closet and sorting through the bones to see what scary things lurked there. Is that what Kyle was doing?

Meg ordered herself to listen, to let the words sift through her ears and into her consciousness so she could absorb and process them, whatever they may be.

"The golfing was Matt's idea, of course," he continued. "I always hated it, but I thought we should spend some time together. Anyway, it was an awkward day of having him goad me about my swing and my score and—well, it doesn't matter."

"It must matter," she said, tucking a curl behind her ear. "Either to him at that moment or to you right now. That's why you're telling me this, right?"

"Right."

She watched his Adam's apple bob as he swallowed and looked up at the top of the doorframe. "It was always a competition with Matt. He wanted to have the better golf game, the better career, the nicer car, the higher number of notches on his bedpost."

Meg felt herself flinch, not sure what any of this had to do with her. But she waited, and Kyle continued the story.

"After we got done golfing, we went to this bar. Matt's phone kept buzzing, like he was getting text messages. At first, I thought it might be you."

"It wasn't," she said softly. "I went out of my way to leave him alone that weekend. To give you some guy time."

"I know. I asked him who it was, and he wouldn't tell me at first."

"Annabelle." Hearing the name again—even in her own voice—sent a dull, icy spear through her heart.

Kyle almost looked relieved that she'd been the one to say it first. "Yes. Annabelle. I thought at first he was just trying to schedule an appointment. He gave me some bullshit about acupuncture helping his golf swing."

Meg rolled her eyes. "Yeah. I'm sure it loosened him right up."

"Right. I don't know when things turned flirtatious, but after we'd been sitting there maybe thirty minutes or so, I could see from the look on his face that something had shifted."

"He was drinking."

"Yes. A couple beers, but he wasn't wasted. He was still in control of his actions."

She nodded, letting the words wash over her. So far, none of this information was new. The details were a little different than the polished version Matt had delivered two years ago, but there was nothing earth-shattering in Kyle's version. Nothing to tell Meg she'd had it wrong all this time.

Still, hearing the story from Kyle's point of view was like poking Q-tips into wounds that hadn't quite healed.

"Do you remember I texted you that evening?" he asked.

Meg frowned, trying to recall the details. "No. I'm sorry, I don't. What did you say?"

"I sent some silly photo of us drinking beer on the golf course. Nothing memorable, but I asked how you spent your day."

She nodded, a twinge of memory flickering in her brain. "I think I remember that. I texted back that my mom caught my dad cheating again."

"That's right," Kyle said. "Nothing new, right? But you sounded upset."

"I was." Meg clenched her fists in her lap. "That time was pretty bad. Mom caught him in the act, heard him saying all kinds of sexy things to the other woman that he'd never said to her." She stopped herself, aware that she was rattling off details that probably didn't matter at the moment.

"Right." Kyle took a shaky breath. "It got me thinking."

There was a dark note in his voice that made Meg slide her hands between her knees and press them tight together. "About what?"

"You sounded bitter. And resigned. And so very, very angry at your dad."

"I was." *I still am.*

"And I thought about your childhood and your history with your dad's infidelity and I thought—" He stopped, taking a shaky breath. "I thought about what you'd do if Matt cheated on you."

Meg stared at him, trying to process the words. "And what conclusion did you reach?"

"I knew you'd leave him."

She nodded, not sure where he was going with this, but not liking the dull twinge in the pit of her stomach. Kyle took another breath, and she wondered if she should offer him something to drink. A glass of water or a beer?

But he spoke again, so she stayed rooted in place. "I started goading him," Kyle said. "First it was small stuff. Still bullshitting about golf swings and who had the better score. Then I told him about my date the night before. About this hot girl with killer legs and these big, beautiful t—" He cleared his throat. "Anyway, I told him about her, and about another girl the week before who gave me a hand job under the table at dinner and the one I met on Tindr who let me take her from behind in an elevator and—"

"I'm not sure I need to hear this." Her head was starting to pound, and she had a sour feeling in the pit of her stomach.

"You *do* need to hear it."

"You mean you need to say it," she snapped.

He nodded once, his jaw clenched in determination.

"All those women," Meg muttered. "Weren't you dating Cara then?" She was struggling to remember, struggling with the ugly mental pictures he was painting, and trying to make the whole thing fit within the timeline of her own life.

"No. This was during that month we split up because Cara wanted to reevaluate our relationship."

"And apparently you wanted to fuck everything that moved." She hated the seething judgment in her own voice, but Kyle just shook his head.

"That's just it. It wasn't true. None of it."

"What?"

"There was no girl with the killer legs. No girl who gave me a hand job under the table. No Tindr girl in the elevator."

"I don't understand."

"I was provoking Matt."

Meg stared at him, not sure she understood. She knew she should be asking questions, trying to make the puzzle pieces fit together, but they just tumbled around in the box, rattling against each other with a dull clack.

Kyle took a deep breath. "I told him how great it was to be single. To sample the fruit of a dozen different trees. I teased him about only having one woman for the rest of his life."

"Me." The word came out like a croak, her voice dry and crackly, but Meg stayed rooted in place, not willing to run for a glass of water.

"That's right." Kyle rubbed his hands over his eyes, closing them for a moment before opening them again to continue the story. "Anyway, things kind of took off from there. I could see he kept texting Annabelle. He got up at one point to use the restroom and he left his phone on the bar. I read some of the texts."

"What did they say?"

"I don't remember the exact words, but he was making plans to meet her that night. It was clear my jabs had the intended effect."

Meg gripped the edge of the sofa, determined not to let her eyes fill with tears. Determined to get some answers. "Your intended effect," she repeated, not sure she was following. "You *wanted* Matt to cheat on me?"

He nodded, avoiding her eyes. "Yes."

"To hurt me?"

"Absolutely not." His voice was sharp, which might have been sincerity or guilt. She couldn't tell anymore.

"But why—"

"I wanted him to cheat and I wanted him to tell you about it," Kyle said, meeting her eyes again. "I didn't mean for him to wait until the night before the wedding. That was a mistake. Hell, the whole goddamn thing was a mistake, but that part especially—" He shook his head. "Anyway, after it happened, I pushed him to tell you. I told him he needed to start the marriage with a clean slate. I told you deserved to know, that you'd appreciate his honesty and that you could start your life together with no secrets between you."

Meg shook her head, trying to understand. "Did you really believe that?"

"No."

"So why—"

"Because I wanted him to falter in your eyes. I wanted him to do the one thing I knew you'd never be able to forgive." His hands balled into fists on his lap, and he looked at her with an expression that held more self-hatred than she'd ever seen from anyone.

Meg swallowed, choking back the urge to feel empathy. "Because you hated him that much?"

Kyle shook his head. "No. Because I loved you that much. And because I didn't want him to have you."

The words felt like a kick to the gut. She stared at him, trying to make sense of it all. "So you manipulated your own brother—"

"Yes."

"And me."

"Yes."

Her brain replayed the conversation, hanging up on the part about love, but knowing the manipulation was the part she needed to focus on. "You changed the course of my whole life," she said. "Of Matt's life."

"I'm sorry, Meg. It was a selfish thing to do. If I could take it back, I'd do it in a heartbeat."

She stared at him, trying to imagine what that would look like. She'd be married to Matt now, maybe with a child. They'd be enjoying the riches of her cookbook success together.

No you wouldn't, her subconscious pointed out. *Matt would still be dead. And you would have spent two years trapped in a marriage that didn't make you happy.*

"But I wouldn't have known I wasn't happy."

"What?"

Meg hadn't meant to say the words aloud, but her head was spinning. She didn't know what to think. She didn't know what to feel. Something hollow and empty and aching had grabbed hold of her gut and wouldn't let go.

She started to stand up, but realized her legs wouldn't obey the command. She pressed her feet into the floor, struggling to feel the ground beneath them. "I think you should leave, Kyle."

He looked at her for a few beats. "If that's what you want."

"It is."

He nodded. "I'll show myself out."

She watched him stand up, wiping his hands on his jeans before turning to walk around the chair. His movements were slow, and he looked back at her like he wanted to say something else. But Meg just watched him, unmoving, unwilling to say anything else.

When he got to the door, he turned back and looked at her. "I never stopped loving you, Meg."

She swallowed hard, ordering herself not to cry. "Lying? Manipulation? Deceit?" She shook her head. "That's not what love looks like."

"I know that now."

So do I, Meg thought, wondering why she had to keep learning that lesson the hard way.

Kyle nodded, the haunted look in his eyes radiating from this far away. "Goodbye, Meg."

"Goodbye."

She managed to hold the tears back until the door clicked shut behind him.

CHAPTER NINETEEN

Two days later, Kyle stood barefoot in his dining room polishing a piece of copper. He'd been rubbing the same hunk of metal for an hour, sliding the cloth over the grainy surface until his hand had gone numb.

He should be working in his studio instead of his house. He'd already made a mess of steel shavings in his kitchen sink, the shiny flecks reminding him of the glitter in Meg's eyes.

But the studio held more memories of Meg. Of her touching his sculptures, confessing her secrets, making love with him on the cot . . .

The doorbell rang, and Kyle looked up from the warm wedge of copper. He set it on the table as his pulse began to gallop. Maybe it was her. Maybe she was ready to talk. Maybe he'd managed to conjure Meg with the force of his own memory.

As he started toward the door, he found himself chanting it in a silent mantra. *Please be Meg, please be Meg, please be—*

"Cara." His voice sounded flat as he held the door open and stared at the woman he'd once laughed with, cared about, lived with.

"Don't sound so excited," she deadpanned, offering him a wide smile to show she wasn't really offended.

"Sorry, I just wasn't expecting you. That's all." He ran a hand over his chin and realized he hadn't shaved for days. When was the last time he'd showered?

"I brought you something," Cara said, holding out a cardboard box.

Kyle looked down at it, staring into the clutter of his past life. Cara's arms bowed a little under the weight of it, so he reached out to take it from her.

"What is all this?" he asked.

"The stuff I told you about the other day. Just a bunch of knick-knacks you left behind at the house."

Kyle stared down at the contents of the box. He spotted a charger for a phone he'd lost years ago and a sweat-stained baseball cap he used to wear on camping trips. There was half a roll of wintergreen Life Savers she couldn't possibly have assumed he still wanted, but he thanked her anyway.

"I appreciate it," he managed. He looked back up at her. "Did you want to come in for a second?"

He hoped she'd say no, but she smiled like he'd offered her a box of kittens. "That would be great." She stepped around him, breezing into his home like she'd been here a dozen times before.

In truth, it had only been once, just a few weeks after their breakup. She'd stopped by to reclaim the muffin pan he'd forgotten was hers to start with, and they'd laughed about it and agreed to remain friends when all was said and done.

From her bed in front of the fireplace, Bindi raised her head. She looked at Cara for a few beats, then laid her head back down on her paws and closed her eyes.

Cara headed for the kitchen bar and pivoted to face him. She smiled again, and he noticed she wore a low-cut black dress he used to love on her. Her dark hair was held back with a blue and green silk scarf that matched her eyes. She looked fresh and polished and beautiful and not a single thing inside him stirred.

"I like the scarf," he said, for lack of anything better to say.

"Thank you. You gave it to me for my last birthday."

"I know."

"I thought I was getting an engagement ring."

"I know," he said again. "I'm sorry."

She shrugged and leaned back against the granite counter. "It seems silly now," she said. "Water under the bridge."

"Right." Kyle set the box on his dining room table. "Want something to drink? Wine or beer or water or something?"

"Beer would be great!" She sounded entirely too upbeat for a woman who used to hate beer, but Kyle rummaged in the fridge and found an amber ale he thought she might like. He poured it into a glass, trying to be a good host but mostly feeling like a curmudgeonly asshole who just wanted to be left alone.

He handed her the beer and eased himself onto a barstool beside her.

"You're not having one?" she asked, seeming to hesitate as she raised the glass to her lips.

"I'm good," he said. "Gotta work."

"Work," she said, taking a small sip of the beer as her eyes scanned his dining room. "How's that going?"

"Good. Sold a piece to a gallery in Wisconsin."

Cara smiled and reached out to trail a finger up his arm. "Not *my* piece, I hope? The calla lily?"

Kyle shook his head. "No. Not that one."

"Good. I want you to have something that makes you think of me."

"Why?"

The bluntness of his question seemed to startle them both, and Cara took a moment to answer. "Because," she said slowly. "Look, I'll just lay my cards out on the table here. I think we should give it another shot between us."

"What?"

"I've been thinking about you since I saw you out with your mom the other day, and I miss the way we were. Don't you?"

The word *no* was on the tip of his tongue, but that would be unnecessarily cruel. He didn't want to hurt her. He just didn't want to be with her. Especially not now, with his desire for Meg burning a hot hole through the center of his chest.

"You deserve better," he said at last.

"I think I deserve you." She gave him a small smile and set the beer down on the counter, her manicured fingers still clenched around the glass. "I think we belong together."

"No." Now that he'd said the word, there was no taking it back. Her smile vanished, but Kyle pressed on, knowing he needed to make himself clear. "I'm sorry, Cara, it's not you. It's me."

God, that sounded lame. Cara must have thought so, too, because her brow creased with those tiny little lines she used to call her devil horns.

"No, it isn't."

"What?"

"It's not you. It's also not me." She let go of the glass and folded her hands in her lap. "It's the same thing it always was, isn't it?"

"I don't know what you're talking about," he said, even though he had a pretty good idea.

Cara aimed her index finger toward the corner of the room. Kyle didn't have to look to know what she was pointing at. "It's her, isn't it? It's always been her?"

He turned anyway, even though he knew what she was looking at. He stared at the sculpture, at the delicate curves of copper, the burnished brown iron, the sloped steel angle that looked like a shoulder blade. The piece was clearly feminine, but it was abstract, not recognizable as any one person.

At least that's what Kyle used to think.

"I always knew it was her," Cara said softly, dropping her hand back in her lap. "All that time together, you loved someone else."

Kyle swallowed hard and closed his eyes. It seemed stupid to argue, but some stubborn, idiotic part of him did it anyway. "I don't know what you're talking about."

"Of course you do."

He opened his eyes to see her shaking her head a little sadly. He'd expected to see anger in her eyes, but it looked more like pity.

"Meg Delaney," she said. "Your brother's wife."

"They didn't get married."

"I know. I was there, remember?" He watched her head tilt as though angling to conjure the memory. Kyle remembered, too. The lavender scent of the unity candle behind him. The high giggles of the twin flower girls. The heated itch under his collar, the sensation of choking to death on his bow tie or his guilt or some combination of the two.

Beside him now, Cara spun the beer glass on the counter. "I watched your face that day," she said slowly. "When she turned and ran out of that church?"

"I don't—"

"I've never in my life seen you look at me that way." She gave a hollow little laugh. "I've never seen any man look at any woman that way. Like you wanted to chase her down that aisle."

He shook his head, wanting to argue, but knowing he didn't have a leg to stand on. She was right. All of it, every word she'd said.

"I'm sorry, Cara," he said at last. "I wish it could have been different."

"It's okay. I knew before I came here today how things would turn out." She gave a small shrug and picked up her beer, taking a tiny sip before setting the glass down again. "I had to give it a shot."

"I appreciate that," he said. "It takes guts. More guts than I ever had."

Cara smiled. "Does she know?"

Kyle looked at her. He thought about continuing to pretend ignorance, but what was the point?

"She knows," he said softly. "For all the good it does."

"Really?" Cara frowned. "She's not still hung up on Matt, is she?"

"Not like that, no." He cleared his throat. "It's—complicated."

"The best things usually are."

She studied him for a moment, and Kyle felt the same prickle of alarm he always used to feel when Cara looked at him for too long. Like she could see straight into his brain, into his heart, into his soul.

None of those things had ever belonged to her. Not really.

As the silence stretched out, Cara nodded toward the sculpture again. "You know I don't say this lightly when I tell you that's the most beautiful piece you've ever created."

"Thank you."

"My vajayjay and I can concede defeat." She reached out and touched his arm. "If she stirs that kind of passion in you, Kyle, you owe it to both of you not to give up so easily."

"I'm not the one giving up."

She shook her head, then dropped her hand from his arm and gave him a swat on the butt. "Then get off your ass and prove it."

◆　◆　◆

Meg sat in her attorney's office with a glass of tepid iced tea beside her and a pen clutched in her hand.

"Are you sure about this, Meg?" Franklin looked at her with a concerned expression. At least, that's what she registered with her peripheral vision.

Meg's focus was on the pen. She turned it over in her hand, looking at the sturdy, curved shaft and the elegant gold tip. "Do you know where I got this?"

There was no response from her attorney, so she glanced up to see him staring at her like she'd just stuffed bananas in her ears.

"The pen?" he asked. "No. I'm afraid I don't. Is it significant?"

Meg turned the pen over in her hands, marveling at the weight of it, at the exquisite beauty of something so basic and functional. "It's a Waterman. Sort of the Ferrari of pens."

"I see," Franklin said, clearly not seeing at all. "It's important to have a good pen."

"My former-future-mother-in-law gave it to me at my wedding shower."

"Okay," Franklin said slowly, folding his hands on the desk in front of him. "If you need more time to think about this—"

"She gave me a card with it," Meg said, looking up at him again. "It said the pen was so we'd always have something beautiful to use for signing important documents—our marriage license, maybe birth certificates for our babies someday." She set the pen down and looked at Franklin. "But do you know what she said to me as she was leaving the shower?"

"I have no idea."

Meg cleared her throat. "She said, 'You can use it for other things, too. Maybe someday you'll be famous and you can use it to sign autographs or something.'"

Franklin frowned and steepled his hands in front of him. "Meg, that seems like further evidence she considered the cookbook *your* project. If she gave it to you at your bridal shower—"

"No, that wasn't my point." She slid her palm over the pen, rolling it back and forth across the big cherry desk. "The point is that she believed in me. Matt might have seen the whole thing as a joke, but Sylvia didn't. Not totally, anyway." She stopped rolling the pen and clasped her hands on the desk while her attorney continued looking at her like she'd lost her marbles.

"It was never just about me and Matt," she said. "That whole relationship, all ten years of it—it wasn't just about the two of us. It was more about family. About how we supported each other through lousy stuff and picked up each other's slack and made up for each other's weaknesses with our own strengths. That's what I loved more than anything. It's also what I missed most these last two years."

Franklin nodded again. Meg could tell he was trying to look wise and supportive, but instead he looked pained. He didn't agree with anything in the documents she was ready to sign, but he'd prepared it just like she'd asked. He reached out and rested a hand on the corner of the paperwork, drawing her attention back to what she was here to do.

"What did your agent say about your plans to credit Matt's estate with such a high percentage?" he asked.

"She wasn't thrilled."

"You don't say." His voice was dry, but not condescending. She might be giving up a huge chunk of her royalties here, but she was still the one paying the attorney fees.

"There's no telling if Matt's family will retain Straight Shot Literary Agency to represent their portion of the deal," Meg admitted, "which means Nancy's only getting a portion of *my* proceeds, which means—"

"Your proceeds get a helluva lot smaller if you go through with this."

"Right." Meg picked up the pen again and looked down at the documents. She'd studied them all morning, and the night before, and the night before that. She didn't need more time to think about it. She knew what she had to do. What she *wanted* to do.

"You're signing it." Franklin's voice was flat as Meg scrawled her signature on the first line, then the next.

She nodded and flipped to the next page, not looking up at him. "It's the right thing to do. If I don't, this could eat at me for the rest of my life. I don't want to live with that regret."

"You don't think you could regret signing away such a huge chunk of money you're entitled to?"

"Maybe." Meg looked up at him, holding a finger on the page where she'd left off. "But I'd rather go through life regretting that I tried to do the right thing—even when it doesn't go like I hoped—than to spend my life wondering if I made the greedy choice. The choice that only considers myself, instead of other people whose lives I affected."

"I see."

Meg went back to scrawling her signature on the pages, flipping faster now. She knew the words by heart, even though some of them made her throat tight and achy. She scrawled her name again and again and again until she reached the end. When she finished, she took a deep breath and pushed the whole pile at Franklin. "May I have two copies, please?"

"So you can send one to your agent? I already have that covered."

"No." Meg reached into her purse and found the decorative blue and gold box she'd kept tucked in her desk for two years. She opened it up and put the pen inside. "There's someone else I'd like to give them to."

"The Midland family?" Franklin frowned. "It's best if you let the lawyers handle it from here, Meg."

She shook her head. "I need to do this myself."

◆　◆　◆

Meg walked out of the office and took a deep breath. She had an hour to spare before her lunch date with Jess and her mother. There was just enough time.

She made the drive to the Midland home in a daze, her brain barely registering the blur of orange and red and gold on the trees that lined the boulevard. The sky was a milky gray, and she cracked her car windows to breathe the scent of impending rain.

The look on Sylvia's face when she opened the door was one of stunned shock. In the instant before it could turn to fury, Meg thrust the blue and gold box at her.

"Here," Meg said, holding out the pen. "You gave this to me. Do you remember?"

Sylvia looked at it, leery, then nodded. "Yes." She didn't take the box, but she didn't push it away, either.

"I want you to have it back," Meg said. "And I want you to use it to sign these." She reached into her purse for the manila envelope containing the paperwork, forcing Sylvia to take the pen. Her former-future-mother-in-law watched her with a guarded expression, her mouth tight. When Meg pulled out the envelope, Sylvia frowned.

"Albert said you were making this offer. He didn't tell me all the details, but he said I'd be pleased."

"You won't be."

Sylvia blinked. "I beg your pardon?"

"Your son is dead." Meg shook her head, feeling the prick of tears at the back of her eyes. "Anything that happens from this point forward isn't going to change that. No amount of money, no amount of apology, no amount of regret over what anyone should or shouldn't have done."

Sylvia's eyes turned misty, and she gave a faint nod. "That's true."

"But this agreement. This is close to what you wanted. Maybe better. There's a stipulation in there that Chloe gets a small stipend. It's not much, but I wanted to make sure she got a piece of Matt's legacy. Something that was his and will now be hers."

"But why—"

"Because she was his family. Even if they didn't walk down the aisle together. That counts for something."

Sylvia nodded. "Like you."

"Yes."

"I understand that."

Meg swallowed, wondering if she should say something else. There was so much she could say—so much regret and anger and confusion she'd never given voice to.

But maybe voicing those things wasn't the way to find closure. Maybe shutting the hell up was the best form of peace she could offer.

"I loved having you in our family, Meg," Sylvia said at last. "For what it's worth, I don't hate you."

"I don't hate you, either."

"That sounds like a start."

It was an odd choice of words, considering they'd likely never see each other again after this. But it was a common phrase, something easier to say than acknowledging the end.

Meg turned to go.

"There's something you don't know about those weeks after you left," Sylvia said.

Meg turned around. She stood rooted in place, waiting to see if Sylvia would continue or wave her away with those taunting words hanging between them in the damp, chilly air.

When Sylvia spoke again, her voice was barely a whisper. "It all hit Matt very hard. The guilt, your leaving, the feeling that he'd disappointed everyone." She gripped the envelope tight in her fingers, her knuckles white as she creased the edge of it. "I know you were hurt, Meg, and you had every right to be. But the sadness that took Matt—he went to a very dark place."

Meg stared at her, trying to understand. "Depression, you mean?"

Sylvia gave a tight nod. "Yes."

"I see." Meg remembered Chloe's words about Matt getting his mental health in order. Is that what she'd meant? "He always showed little signs of it," Meg said softly. "Mood swings, anxiety, sleeping a lot. I used to suggest he see someone about it, but he refused."

"This was worse." Sylvia took a deep breath. "Much worse. It was terrifying. It took over completely after you left. He shut himself off from everyone except Kyle."

"I had no idea." A needle of guilt pierced her through the breastbone, and she ordered herself to keep breathing.

"No one knew," Sylvia said. "That's how Matt wanted it. He didn't think I knew."

"But how did you—"

"Mothers know these things." Sylvia pressed her lips together. "Just like I know Kyle is the reason your cookbook became a bestseller."

"What?"

"He never said a word to me about giving the book to that actress. Do you realize that?"

Meg blinked, trying to make sense of what Sylvia was saying. Kyle might have betrayed her in one way, but he'd held back that crucial piece of information. He'd known his mother would use it against her, and he hadn't said a word. Maybe it hadn't mattered, not in the grand scheme of the lawsuit.

But somehow, it mattered to Meg.

Sylvia cleared her throat, breaking the silence that hung heavy in the air between them. "I'll look these over with my attorney and get back to you," she said, holding up the envelope.

"Okay," she said softly, still reeling. She started to turn away again, pretty sure they'd said all there was to say.

"And Meg?"

She turned back to Sylvia, pulling her jacket tighter around her to guard against the crisp fall air. "Yes?"

"My son would have been lucky to have you."

Meg nodded as her stomach flipped over. She closed her eyes and pictured Kyle, the way his gray-green eyes crinkled at the corners when he laughed, the way he could never remember names or celebrity gossip but remembered exactly how to julienne a carrot when she'd only showed him once.

Then she pictured Matt, remembering him with a fondness that felt more like friendship than passion or true love or any of the things she thought she'd had with him so many years ago. She remembered the way he made her laugh, cajoling her from a premenstrual funk with goofy faces and raunchy jokes. She remembered his love of family, the way he took his mother to brunch the last Sunday of every month. She remembered the hurt in his eyes the instant before she turned and ran from that church.

They'd loved each other once. It wasn't the kind of deep, all-consuming love meant to last forever, but it was love just the same.

When she opened her eyes again, Sylvia was watching her.

"Thank you," Meg said. "Thank you for letting me love your son."

Then she turned to go.

◆　◆　◆

Meg arrived five minutes early for her lunch date with her mom and Jess. She took a few minutes to study the spotless decor, the creative menu, the cheerful patrons lined up at the door waiting to get a table at Portland's hottest new restaurant.

"Sorry I'm late," Jess said, sliding in beside Meg and dropping her giant purse on the floor beside her. She unfolded her napkin in her lap and looked around. "This place is nice. Very hip."

"One of Matt's ex-girlfriends owns it," Meg said. "Brittney Fox."

Jess frowned and picked up her water glass. "Was this a girlfriend he had before, after, or during your relationship?"

"Before. Or maybe after. I don't remember."

"Oh-kay," Jess said. "You sure you're doing all right?"

"Positive." Meg waved to her mother across the restaurant. Her mom spotted her and hustled over.

"Good Lord, parking is atrocious out there. Sorry I'm late, baby." Patti stooped and kissed her on the cheek before moving on and giving Jess a hug. "It's good to see you, girls."

"You, too, Patti," Jess said. "How are things?"

"Good. Better." Meg's mom smiled. "I had my lawyer draft divorce documents and I'm looking them over tomorrow. Things are moving fast."

"Wow." Jess looked at her. "I'm not sure whether to offer congratulations, or condolences."

"I'll take both," Patti said. "But thank you."

Both women picked up their menus and began to skim. Meg had already made up her mind to order the halibut cheeks with beurre blanc and a side of creamed fennel, but she studied her menu anyway, thinking about how much thought and care and planning had gone into it. She set the menu aside and folded her hands on the table.

She looked up to see her mom and Jess studying her. Her mother spoke first. "You're really doing okay, Meg?"

Meg nodded, and the other two women exchanged a glance. Jess set her menu down and reached for Meg's hand. "Have you heard from Kyle?"

"No." She shook her head and trailed a finger through the condensation on her water glass. "He called once the day after he told me everything, but since then—" She shrugged, looking down at her glass. "It's probably for the best. I spent two years having zero contact with him. I can just go back to the way things were."

"Bullshit."

Meg looked up, surprised to realize the word had come from her mother, not Jess. "I beg your pardon?"

"Honey, no offense, but you can never go back to the way things were before."

"What's that supposed to mean?"

"Just that I'd never seen you the way you were during those weeks you and Kyle were spending time together," her mother said. "You were all lit up inside."

"It's like the bra," Jess added. "Now that you know what a properly fitted bra is supposed to feel like, you can't go back to wearing something two cup sizes too small with pokey underwire and straps that dig into your shoulders."

"I can find another bra," Meg argued as a waiter walked past and gave her a startled glance. "There are plenty of them out there. Lacy bras and silk bras and bras with gel inserts and comfort straps and crazy colors."

Jess shook her head and glanced at Patti before turning back to Meg again. "Not one that cups your boobs exactly the right way."

Meg rolled her eyes, annoyed to be having this conversation with her best friend and her mother. She was spared from having more of it when the server came over. "Would you ladies like to hear about our chef's specials?"

"Please," Meg said, turning her attention to the eternal comfort of food.

"We have a caprese salad with fresh heritage tomatoes, buffalo mozzarella, and basil from our own garden. For entrees, there's an apple-brined pork chop with apricot compote and tahini roasted cauliflower on the side. You'll also want to make sure you save room for dessert. There's a key lime tart I think you'll really enjoy."

Meg nodded, wondering if it was a coincidence two of the three specials were variations of Matt's favorite dishes. Probably not. Somewhere back there in the kitchen, even Brittney Fox couldn't escape the relics of past love.

"I'd like the halibut," Meg said.

"The chef's salad for me," Patti said, handing over her menu.

"I'll try a small Caesar salad and the pork special," Jess said, looking at Meg. "We'll see how it compares to that one you always used to make."

Meg took a sip of her water as the waitress walked away. "So really, Mom, you're doing okay?"

"I'm fine, Meggy, but I don't want to talk about me. I want to talk about this thing with Kyle."

Meg rolled her eyes, feeling like a petulant tween. "There's nothing to talk about. Weren't you the one who stood there in his studio not two weeks ago and said there's a point where you have to put your foot down? Where forgiveness might be possible, but forgetting never could be?"

"I did say that," Patti said. "And there's no way you *should* forget. Neither of you."

"What's that supposed to mean?"

"That you've both learned so much from your past mistakes. You're works in progress, and it would be a shame to have you both come this far, only to throw in the towel and waste all those lessons learned on someone who's not really your soul mate."

"Soul mate," Meg muttered, picking at the bread basket. "I'm not sure I believe in the idea of soul mates."

"Believe or don't believe," Jess said, tearing off a thick hunk of sourdough and casting a look at Patti. "It doesn't really matter. We both watched you for ten years with Matt and for one month with Kyle, and there's no question which man made you happier."

"That's different," Meg said, not sure whether to feel intensely loved or intensely picked on. "Infatuation doesn't last. And I didn't know the whole story when I got involved with Kyle."

"Honey, you knew the things that mattered. You knew he loves his family. You knew he'll help you out in a pinch. You knew he's a man with flaws who's willing to own those flaws and learn from them."

"But above all," Jess said, "you knew he loves you like no one else ever has."

Meg shook her head and took a big pull of ice water. "Can we please talk about something else? Please?"

Jess gave her a pitying look, then turned to Patti. "So you're moving ahead with the divorce?"

"That's the plan." Patti looked at Meg. "Your father said you two had dinner last night?"

Meg nodded, wondering if she should feel worse about the breakup of her parents' marriage. She knew she ought to feel a certain level of sadness or nostalgia, but mostly she felt relief.

"I'll always love you, Daddy," she'd told him last night after dinner as she handed him a Tupperware container with two slices of her home-made blueberry pie. "But liking you hasn't always been easy."

"I know that, sweetheart. Liking myself is no picnic, either. Especially right now. Will you tell your mom—" He'd stopped, then shook his head. "Never mind. I owe her more than sentiments relayed through a third party."

"You do. But you can tell me anyway."

"Tell her she deserves better. And I hope she finds it."

Now, Meg reached across the table and squeezed her mother's hand. "You deserve the best, Mom."

Patti smiled and squeezed back. "So do you, baby. And it's not too late to get it."

◆　◆　◆

Kyle kicked a dirty sock under his couch and wondered if he should have done a better job tidying up before inviting a big-shot Hollywood producer to his home.

From across the room, Bindi scurried over and flopped on her belly beside the sofa. With a grunt, she stuck her nose underneath and pulled out the sock. She got to her feet and trotted over, depositing the sock in front of Kyle with an intense look of pride.

He grimaced and turned his attention back to Emmett Ashton. The man hadn't noticed a damn thing, and probably couldn't care less about an over-attentive canine or the cleanliness of Kyle's home.

Emmett reached out and stroked a hand over the metal sculpture, his expression more reverent than any Kyle had seen from someone admiring his work. It should have made him proud.

Instead, Kyle just felt empty.

"It's incredible," Emmett said, circling the piece from the other side. "Even better than it was in the photos. The grace, the beauty, the lines—"

"I know," Kyle said. He should probably be more humble, but he was long past that point now. He had a billionaire TV mogul standing here next to the thrift-store sofa he'd never gotten around to replacing. Humility was beside the point.

Spotting a dirty paper napkin on the end table, he leaned sideways and grabbed it. He tried to crumple it into a discreet ball, but Bindi trotted over, ready to fetch. Kyle shoved the ball in his pocket while the dog whined and pawed at his pants.

"I have to admit, I was surprised to get your message," Emmett said. "All that talk about how you'd never sell this piece?"

"I know," Kyle said. "I still won't. Not for money anyway."

Emmett nodded, looking at Kyle with practiced patience. He turned back to the sculpture, grazing a palm over the bare thigh, and Kyle had to tamp down the inexplicable flare of jealousy in his gut.

"You know I can't make any promises," Emmett said. "If she sucks in the screen test, there's nothing I can do about that."

"She won't," he said. "You saw the clips. The one of her on the *Today* show, and that interview with the local TV station?"

"Yes, but what you're talking about—" Emmett shook his head and dropped his hand from the sculpture. "It's different."

"So is she."

Emmett barked out a laugh. "She must really mean something to you."

"She does."

"You want a word of advice from a guy who's been married four times?"

Kyle opened his mouth to reply, not sure whether a guy who'd been married four times was the best or the worst person to dole out relationship tips. Seeming to read his thoughts, Emmett waved a hand in front of him.

"Look here, this is a nice gesture. What you're doing with this deal. But you've gotta talk to her about it. You can't go sneaking around behind a woman's back pulling the puppet strings and trying to make her life turn out the way you think it ought to. Even if you're well-intentioned, that shit will bite you in the ass."

The words hit him like a punch to the gut. Kyle just nodded, not trusting himself to speak.

"Manipulating the pieces of someone else's life?" Emmett shook his head. "No good can come from that."

"I know," Kyle said with a grimace. "Believe me, I know. But just this one last time. To make up for what I did the last time."

Emmett nodded and turned back to the sculpture. Kyle looked around his living room again, wishing he'd at least run a dust rag over the horizontal surfaces. A sketchpad lay sprawled on his coffee table, its pages marked with pencil. A totally normal thing to have in an artist's home, if not for the doodles of cat faces and cubes. This was clearly the work of a man whose inspiration had left the premises.

"What did you say the name was?"

"Meg," he said, then realized Emmett wasn't asking that at all. "Oh, the sculpture? I didn't."

"So what is it?"

"*Si Seulement.*"

"French?"

He nodded. "France is where she did her culinary training."

"She," Emmett repeated, not looking surprised. "And what does *si seulement* mean?"

"If only."

"I see." He touched the statue again. "Are you sure about this?"

"About the statue or the girl?"

"I meant the sculpture. If you're making this deal, it's pretty fucking obvious you're sure about the girl."

"I'm positive," he said. "More sure than I've ever been about anything."

"Even if it doesn't work out?"

Kyle nodded and shoved his hands in his pockets. "At least this time I know I'm doing it for the right reasons."

CHAPTER TWENTY

"We're back in the kitchen with Meg Delaney, author of the international bestseller, *The Food You Love: An Aphrodisiac Cookbook*. If you're just now joining us, Meg's been showing us how to make a chocolate soufflé that's guaranteed to make your toes curl in more ways than one."

Meg forced her exhausted jaw muscles into a shape she hoped resembled a smile. It was getting tough to tell. They'd been at this for hours now, though it felt like days. The producer kept trying different strategies, interacting with Meg like a talk-show host or cueing her like an offstage announcer the way she was doing now. None of it seemed to work.

Meg had never wanted anything as badly as she wanted this TV show, but she had a feeling she was blowing it.

The thought of wanting something—or maybe it was the notion of blowing something—conjured up images of Kyle, which just made Meg's gut feel like someone had kicked her with a steel-toed boot. Her smile was feeling more forced, so she ordered herself to do something useful.

"That's right, Kelly," Meg tried to chirp, though it was probably more of a croak. "I can guarantee this soufflé is going to have you licking your lips—or maybe someone else's." She gave a practiced wink at the camera—something the producers had suggested she try.

But she could tell from Kelly Conrad's face it probably looked more like she had a facial tic.

"Cut," the young producer said, giving Meg an encouraging, albeit exhausted smile. "I don't think the wink is working out."

"You mean I look like a rapist?"

Kelly grimaced. "More like an escaped mental patient."

"Sorry." Meg blew a curl out of her eye and tried to look upbeat, but she knew she probably just looked defeated.

"It's okay. How about we focus on some of the aphrodisiac stuff?"

"I can do that," Meg said, wishing for a tactful way to wipe her brow. Smearing sweat all over her arm probably wasn't the best way to demonstrate her poise and camera presence as a professional TV chef. Then again, neither was sweating like a porn star.

"Ready?" Kelly asked.

Meg nodded and took a deep breath.

"Aaaaand—*action!*"

Meg cleared her throat and pushed her cheeks into a smile again. "As I was saying earlier, chocolate is a great source of serotonin. That's a monoamine neurotransmitter that's biochemically derived from tryptophan and—Good Lord, shoot me now." Meg gripped her head in her hands and closed her eyes, conceding defeat. "Seriously, shoot me right now, right between the eyes with a marshmallow gun. I think I just put myself to sleep with that."

She opened her eyes again to see Kelly giving her a weak smile. The producer adjusted her headphones and patted Meg on the shoulder. "It's okay. Part of this screen test is about figuring out what works and what doesn't."

"Kinda like love," Meg muttered. "You've got to screw it up a whole bunch of times to get it right."

Kelly brightened a bit at that as a makeup artist came out and began to powder Meg's face with something that smelled like burned vanilla. "That's good! We need more of that! Inject a little more personality, a little more of your personal experiences into this, and I think we'll be on the right track."

Meg tried to grin back with equal enthusiasm, but she wasn't feeling it. She wasn't feeling much of anything these days, except for longing. And regret. And—

"And, action!"

Kelly gave Meg an encouraging smile, and Meg forced the corners of her mouth to head north again.

"So the secret to a perfect soufflé is to use eggs that aren't too fresh," Meg announced, not ready to give up quite yet. "I know that sounds counterintuitive, but egg whites thin as they age, which makes them easier to whip. All you ladies out there feeling concerned about your eggs aging if you're alone and in your thirties without a relationship in sight, you might want to take heart!"

Meg looked at Kelly. Kelly looked pained. She pulled off her headset and slid it around her neck. "How about we take a break for about fifteen minutes?"

Meg nodded, her cheeks hot and sweaty. God, she was ruining this. Her one chance at having her own cooking show, and she was totally, completely bombing.

"Sounds good," Meg said. "I just need a few minutes to regroup."

Kelly looked at her for a moment, probably thinking she needed a helluva lot more than a few minutes to salvage this lame attempt at television stardom. Then she smiled, patted Meg on the shoulder, and walked offstage.

Meg took a shaky breath and wiped her hands on her apron. The makeup artists and light crew all dispersed in opposite directions, probably to snicker about her behind her back. Even the cameraman vanished, leaving his equipment set up near the front of the stage. Meg couldn't blame them. If she didn't feel like crying, she'd probably laugh at herself, too.

A commotion near the door of the empty auditorium caught Meg's attention, and she squinted against the bright lights of the studio.

"I just need to talk to her," someone was saying. "It will only take a few minutes."

Kyle?

"Sir, you can't go in there. Sir! They're in the middle of taping."

Meg turned to see him rushing toward the stage. His hair was disheveled and his green plaid shirt looked like he'd used it to dust the dashboard of his truck. His eyes were wild and his jaw was unshaven and he was the best damn thing she'd ever seen in her life.

"Meg," he said, and she clutched the edge of the faux granite counter to keep from doing something dumb like reaching for him.

"Kyle."

Good. She'd gotten that syllable out. Now what?

Kyle ran his hands through his hair as he looked around. "The attendant out front said you were on a break. You've been avoiding my calls all week, and obviously I haven't been able to catch you at home."

"I've been staying with my mom," Meg said, wondering when he'd tried to visit. He hadn't left a note, but then again, she hadn't been home for days. Sleeping in the same bed she'd shared with Kyle for only one night had left her restless and wretched, so she'd packed up Floyd and went to stay with her mother for a little while.

"She needed company," Meg said. "My mom, I mean. My dad's been moving all his stuff out, so she needed moral support."

"Right," Kyle said. "I just need a minute to talk to you."

She glanced around, waiting for someone to argue. But everyone had vanished, even the security crew that had given him chase at first. It was just the two of them, for the first time since that night in her living room.

Meg swallowed, remembering his words in her ears. *I never stopped loving you, Meg.*

Even now?

"I just got off the phone with my mom," he said. "She said she got the first check from the publisher and she told me the amount. I can't even—" he raked his hands through his hair. "Did you have any idea how much money you'd agreed to give up?"

She nodded and gripped the edge of the soufflé bowl with both hands. "It was never about the money, Kyle."

"I know that. It was about respecting your career and you as an artist."

She nodded, taken aback by how quickly he understood. "That's right."

"But for me, it was about loyalty to family. To the brother I stabbed in the back. I know the split with Matt hurt you, too, but it was different for him."

"Your mother told me," Meg said softly. "About what Matt went through after the breakup. I landed on my feet, and Matt didn't."

His eyes went wide for an instant, and he didn't say anything. He nodded once, his face still frozen in a look of shock and dismay.

"It's okay," she said. "You don't have to tell me about it. I understand, though. About your loyalty to Matt. About why you felt like you owed it to him to have his back."

He gave another tight nod. "It was my fault."

Meg ran her finger around the edge of the bowl and shook her head. "Matt made his own choices, Kyle. You didn't force him to cheat. You weren't some great puppet master dictating his every move."

"I know that." He cleared his throat. "But I suppose I should tell you I might have pulled a few strings to get you this audition. While we're talking about manipulating people and situations and—well, I thought you should know that."

"I already did."

He blinked. "You knew?"

"Yes. The producer let it slip this morning when we were getting ready to start taping."

"And you're not mad?"

"Mad? Why would I be mad? You tried to make my dream come true."

"But I did it behind your back."

"Yes, but you did it with the best intentions."

Something that looked like relief passed over his face. He nodded and reached for her hands. "Even when I made the wrong choices, I always had the best intentions."

"I know." Meg bit her lip and glanced toward the edge of the stage. No one had reappeared, so either they were giving her some space, or they really were done with her.

"Look, Meg—I love you," he said. "I've always loved you. Even when it was the dumbest thing in the world for me to do. Even when I had no hope of having you love me back."

Meg felt tears pooling in her eyes, and she wondered how pissed the makeup crew would be if she melted off all their perfectly good cosmetics. "I love you, too," she murmured.

It was the first time she'd spoken the words aloud to him, and it seemed to take them both by surprise.

She swallowed, seizing the chance to say what she needed to say while he was still too dumbstruck to interrupt. "I don't have this long, drawn out story about a lifetime of loving you in secret. This is all new to me. Loving you, forgiving Matt, forgiving myself—I'm figuring it out as I go along."

"I like your story just the way it is. Knowing you loved Matt—that's how it should be. I'd feel awful if I thought you hadn't."

She swallowed hard, determined to force the words out before tears clogged her throat completely. "And maybe that's part of what gives me the capacity to love you now. To love you better than I could have if I'd fallen for you years ago."

Kyle smiled. "So where do we go from here?"

"Forward," she said. "Lugging all our baggage and our skeletons and all the things that make it possible for us to love each other better than we could have before."

"I like that plan." He squeezed her hands in his. "I promise to make you happy, Meg. Or at least to spend every damn day trying my best to do it."

"Okay," she breathed, conscious of the flutter just beneath her breastbone. "So here's to learning from past mistakes."

"And future mistakes."

"And mistakes we haven't even considered making yet."

He grinned. "I love you, Meg."

"I love you, too."

He kissed her then, softly at first, then with an urgency that left her swaying a little on her feet. He held her upright, steadying her, supporting her, kissing her silly. It seemed to go on for years maybe, for more than a decade. Maybe that's the way it had always been, even when she hadn't known it.

The sound of applause broke through her consciousness, and Meg turned to see the production crew standing in front of the stage, their headphones looped around their necks and goofy grins on their faces.

"That's perfect," Kelly said. "A little more passion like that and you'll have this baby nailed."

Meg laughed and pressed her hands to her face, trying to cool the flames. "How much of that did you hear?"

"You're still miked, honey," Kelly said. "We heard every word. We even got the heavy breathing."

"That might come in handy sometime," the soundman called, grinning at Meg from the edge of the stage.

She grimaced and turned back to Kyle, who squeezed her hands in response. "I'm okay with broadcasting it to the world," he said. "I love you with all my heart, Meg. Here's to fresh starts and second chances."

"Cheers to that," Kelly said, grinning from the side. "Go for it, Meg. We'll start the audition over if you like. Just show us more of that passion."

"Okay," Meg breathed, but she wasn't looking at the producer. She was looking at Kyle, whose gray-green eyes held a question she didn't need him to ask.

Or maybe she did.

"What do you say, Meg?" he asked. "Can you see yourself giving us a shot? Taking a stab at a real relationship?"

Meg nodded and looped her arms around his neck. "I can."

EPILOGUE

One year later

Kyle kicked his toe through the big pile of leaves, breathing in the scent of wood smoke and pumpkin pie spice clinging to the sleeves of his wool coat. Or maybe it was in Meg's hair. The cinnamon had kinda gotten everywhere.

Thanksgiving-morning kitchen counter sex was definitely worth scratching off the bucket list.

Meg's mitten-sheathed fingers were warm in his, and he squeezed her hand tight, then let their linked hands fall between them, swinging as they walked. He looked at his mother, who was smiling, albeit a little stiffly.

But it was still a smile. When had she started to do that again? It must've happened gradually, like a slow thaw. Kyle could still see sadness there, too—it would probably always be there—but warmth seemed to seep into her eyes more regularly now.

His mom caught him staring and reached out to touch the side of his face. "You have whipped cream on your cheek."

"Thanks," he said as she brushed it off.

His mom dropped her hand and glanced at Meg. Perhaps sensing the gaze, Meg looked back and gave her a shy smile. "How are you doing, Sylvia?"

"Fine." She seemed to realize her reply sounded terse, and she offered a sheepish half shrug. "Thank you, dear. I'm glad you could be with us."

Meg's smile widened. "I'm glad to be included. I always loved being part of your family holidays."

"It's nice to have you. And we're proud of how well your new cooking show is doing."

Such a simple exchange, but one Kyle knew meant a lot to both of them. Things were still a bit awkward, but they were trying. All of them were.

Kyle's dad put his arm around Sylvia. He didn't say anything, but the gesture spoke of a deep, easy affection between them. It was something Kyle had always admired.

On the other side of Meg, Patti walked hand in hand with a tall man with a gray beard and a gentle smile. Meg's mom had only been dating Gary a few weeks, but he'd seemed delighted when Patti had asked him to join their dual-family Thanksgiving celebration.

Patti caught Kyle staring at her, and gave a small wink. Right. She knew what was about to happen.

They were approaching the spot now. Kyle looked up at the overhead wire. It was bare now, but he remembered the shape of that dove. The lonely shadow teetering above while its mate lay cold on the ground below.

But Bindi pranced happily beside him, reminding him of new life, new beginnings, new paths to joy.

Kyle dug his hand into his pocket. His fingers closed around the metal circle, warm from being pressed against his leg. He felt his heart start to gallop as he stopped walking and let go of Meg's hand. She took another step, then turned, surprised either by the movement or by the sound of his voice.

"Meg Delaney." Her eyes flashed with astonishment, then joy as he dropped to one knee on the cold, dry asphalt.

"I love you," he said, reaching for her hand again. "The past year with you has been amazing, every single day, and I want to spend the rest of my life with you."

He caught the tip of her mitten in one hand and gave a tug, sliding it off as she gasped in wonder. He dropped the mitten on the ground and slid the band onto her finger—a perfect fit, beautifully snug. She looked down at it, and he watched her eyes as she recognized the layers of Damascus steel, the glimmer of the blue sapphire at the center.

"My grandmother's birthstone." Her eyes met his. "You remembered."

"I remember everything," he said. "Maybe not names and celebrity gossip, but I remember the things that matter. And I want to make a million more memories with you for the rest of our lives. What do you say, Meg?" Kyle grinned, pretty sure his heart was about to burst. "Will you marry me?"

"I will." She laughed as a tear slid down one cheek. "I'd be honored."

Kyle felt his mother step closer and place a hand on his back. He looked up to see she was touching Meg's shoulder, too. She moved her palm on his back in small circles the way she used to when he couldn't fall asleep as a young boy.

Then his mother turned and smiled at his fiancée. "Welcome to the family, Meg. Again."

ACKNOWLEDGMENTS

I'm grateful to Michelle Wolfson of Wolfson Literary Agency for selling this book before I even had a subject in mind, and then for not freaking out when I explained I'd like to write about death, grief, and infidelity, and that *maaaaaybe* we could keep that quiet so the editors wouldn't fret that I was writing the most depressing romantic comedy of all time.

Thank you to Chris Werner and Krista Stroever for ensuring I didn't write the most depressing romantic comedy of all time. I'd be lost without your guidance, expert suggestions, and careful massage (er, on the book, not me, though I'm open to considering massage as a bonus in future book contracts).

Thank you also to Anh Schleup, Jessica Poore, Kimberly Cowser, Marlene Kelly, Nicole Pomeroy, Hannah Buehler, Shasti O'Leary Soudant, Sharon Turner Mulvihill, and the rest of the Montlake team for doing such a bang-up job getting this book polished and into the hands of so many wonderful readers, and for making me feel like a well-loved member of the Montlake family.

I owe a huge debt of gratitude to my sister-out-law, Tamara Zagurski, for opening up your heart and your brain and letting me sort through all those lovely pieces. I might actually love you more than I love your brother (don't tell).

Many thanks to the grief counselors, psychologists, and legal experts whose knowledge helped shape this story's edges. I'm also grateful to Chef Bette Fraser of the Well Traveled Fork for your culinary wisdom, and to Meg West for lending me your name.

I can't thank my critique partners and beta readers enough for your super-fast turnarounds, brilliant insights, and endless patience. Big hugs to Cynthia Reese, Linda Grimes, Larie Borden, Bridget McGinn, and Minta Powelson.

Thank you to the Bend Book Bitches for being the best book club a girl could hope for after more than fifteen years together. We're aging like fine wine, or maybe it's just that we're drinking a lot of it.

Endless love and thanks to my family for all your support over the years, especially David and Dixie Fenske, Aaron "Russ" Fenske, and Carlie Fenske. Love you guys!

Big thanks to Cedar Zagurski for naming Kyle. I'm sorry to say that does not mean you get 50 percent of the royalties for your allowance, but you do get a big, sloppy, embarrassing hug, and the knowledge that I love the ever-loving heck out of you. Ditto that for you, Miss Violet. You're the best stepdaughter anyone could ask for, and I'm pretty darn lucky your hot dad didn't run away screaming when that crazy romance author started chasing him.

And of course, thank you to Craig Zagurski. Being married to a deadline-crazed, head-in-the-clouds (or under the bedsheets) romance author can't be easy, but you handle it with grace, patience, and a tireless support for my career. I love you, and there's no one else I'd rather share this crazy journey with, babe.

BOOK CLUB QUESTIONS

1. What differences do you note in how the characters handle grief? How does Kyle's grief look different from his mother's? From Meg's? Does unresolved anger make it harder or easier to mourn someone who dies?

2. What are Matt's redeeming qualities? What did Meg see in him, and why did she stay with him as long as she did?

3. Kyle's complicated relationship with his brother and mother add conflict to his budding romance with Meg. What's the role of family when it comes to making romantic choices? How much does family approval or disapproval matter? Does birth order make a difference when it comes to a sibling's ability to influence another's relationships?

4. Kyle knew infidelity would be a deal breaker for Meg, but her own mother was willing to tolerate it for many years. What made the difference? Under what circumstances (if any) is it okay to tolerate cheating or forgive the cheater?

5. We learn that Cara always sensed Kyle had feelings for Meg. Knowing what you do about Matt, do you think he noticed? Why or why not?

6. How do you think things would have played out if Kyle had kissed Meg that Thanksgiving in his parents' study? How would the circumstances of that connection have impacted their relationship in the future?

ABOUT THE AUTHOR

Tawna Fenske is a fourth-generation Oregonian who writes humorous fiction, risqué romance, and heartwarming love stories with a quirky twist. Her offbeat brand of romance has received multiple starred reviews from *Publishers Weekly*, which once noted, "There's something wonderfully relaxing about being immersed in a story filled with over-the-top characters in undeniably relatable situations. Heartache and humor go hand in hand."

Tawna lives in Bend, Oregon, with her husband, stepkids, and a menagerie of ill-behaved pets. She loves hiking, snowshoeing, stand-up paddleboarding, and inventing excuses to sip wine on her back porch. She can peel a banana with her toes and loses an average of twenty pairs of eyeglasses per year. To learn more about all Tawna's books, visit www.tawnafenske.com.